Raves for the previous Valdemar Anthologies

Feuds

All-New Tales of Valdemar

Edited by
Mercedes Lackey

DAW BOOKS
New York

Cover art by Jody A. Lee

Cover design by Adam Auerbach

DAW Book Collectors No. 1970

DAW Books
An imprint of Astra Publishing House
dawbooks.com
DAW Books and its logo are registered trademarks of Astra Publishing House

Printed in the United States of America

Library of Congress Cataloging-in-Publication Data is available upon request

ISBN 9780756419523 (trade paperback)
ISBN 9780756419530 (ebook)

First edition: November 2024
10 9 8 7 6 5 4 3 2 1

Contents

The Price of Anger
Brigid Collins

Lillia Heilin wasn't a reclusive girl, but she enjoyed her solitude from time to time. She especially liked to be alone when she practiced her Gift.

Liked? In truth, she often *needed* to be alone for that. Bard Callia, her mentor, was about the only person she felt comfortable enough with to let hover over her while she worked. Things might be different if Lillia could ever make significant progress in her training, rather than the dribs and drabs of strength she'd gained over the past few years. If she were able to consistently see the happenings of the past *without* projecting it to everyone in the vicinity, perhaps she'd be able to handle an audience.

Then again, maybe it wouldn't make any difference at all. People always found the promise of ghosts too alluring to leave her alone. Once someone learned she "saw" such spirits with her Pastsight, the requests to contact loved ones or call up malevolent spirits for a lark came all too quickly. No matter how often Lillia explained that the people she saw weren't true ghosts but simply imprints of the past, the idea lingered like a stubborn cobweb.

She had learned that lesson at a young age, thanks to her father—her real father, that was. When Lillia was a child, Gaspard Heilin had utilized his daughter's uncontrollable Gift by chaining her in the burned wreckage of an old cider press on his land and leaving her unable to keep from projecting the horrific images to the visitors at his "haunted orchard."

Then Papa Kimfer had come, him and her Uncle Simen, who

was better known as the Sovvan Bard. Together, they had taken her from her chains and brought her here, to Haven and the Bardic Collegium, where she was free to learn to control her Pastsight.

Even if it took absolutely forever.

Still, she was grateful. She was thirteen years old, lived in the Heralds' wing of the palace with her Papa Kimfer and her Mama Marli, could beg Marli's Companion Taren for a ride more often than not, could exercise in the Salle whenever she wished, and had access to not only Bard Callia for her lessons, but also the library.

Which was where she was now, seeking her solitude.

She breathed in the paper-and-ink-scented air. The place wasn't always empty, of course. Students from all the Collegia came here to study often enough. But today she had the shelves to herself. And no wonder, given the golden shafts of afternoon sunlight streaming in through the tall windows. The weather was lovely, one of the first fine days after the long chill of winter. Nobody wanted to be indoors on a day like this.

With growing anticipation, Lillia moved deeper into the stacks. A few days ago, she'd found an imprint of a young librarian shelving some books that, in Lillia's time, were quite old. She wanted to see if she could find him again and determine how old the imprint was. Already, her fingers were dipping into the pocket where the small notebook she used to document all the imprints she was studying around the Collegium rested.

She rounded a corner to step into the open study area and drew up sharp. She wasn't alone after all.

Though how she could have missed the noise of such a gathering of Bardic students, she couldn't fathom. Not at first, anyway. Then she noticed the flickering at the edges of her vision, the echoing quality of their voices, and the taste of something like cinnamon at the back of her throat: the tell-tale signs of her Pastsight activating.

She bit back a sigh. She hated stumbling upon an imprint like this. But she couldn't help finding something fascinating about each one she discovered. Resigned, she opened her notebook to a fresh page and put down the first broad descriptions of the scene.

Seven Bardic students arrayed in the library, she wrote. *All standing among the desks. Look quite perturbed with one another. Time: undetermined.*

The students were five boys and two girls, all a few years older than Lillia, and they were split into two clear groups. A scowl marred each face, and one of the girls had her arms crossed as she sat in stubborn defiance upon one of the study desks. The other girl stood nearly toe to toe with one of the boys from the other group. Those two looked as if they were about to leap upon one another like a pair of feral dogs. Even their teeth were bared.

"The lute is useless for someone like you, Helge," snarled the boy. *"So take your entourage and go bother someone else."*

The girl—*Helge,* Lillia noted—grimaced harder. *"How ridiculous can you be, Lyran? That lute wasn't meant to be squirreled away for some scribbler to plunk out notes on while getting his nasty, inky fingerprints all over it. It belongs on a stage, in the hands of a true performer. It belonged to a master, after all."*

The boy, *Lyran,* didn't back down. *"Master Garyen would have wanted me to have it. He often said the songs I write are sublime, especially when I have a good instrument to work on."*

"Ha! Master Garyen knew I was his most impressive student. Why else did he spend so long training my voice and my fingering? He always said the lute was the best instrument to pair with my singing. He meant for it to go to me."

The two students bristled. Lyran's hands twitched as if he wanted to choke Helge. Helge's feet shifted as if she was preparing to deliver a sharp kick to Lyran's shin.

The edges of Lillia's vision flickered more intensely, and she gritted her teeth to hold onto the imprint. If the two were about to physically fight one another, she didn't want to miss it. Not that she enjoyed watching altercations, but who knew how long it might take her to trigger this particular imprint again?

She squeezed her pencil so tightly her fingers went numb.

Helge had opened her mouth again, but her voice was too echoey to make out what she was saying. Lillia leaned forward, straining everything to hold on.

"Lillia! I knew I'd find you skulking about in here!"

Startled, Lillia jumped.

A boy her age stepped around the bookshelf behind her, his fringe of black hair sweeping over his eyes and his rust-colored uniform rumpled as always. He sported a large grin, which only grew when Lillia met his eye. Unlike the imprints she'd been watching, there was no question this boy was made of flesh and blood.

Kerrick. Of course. Was there nowhere she could go that he couldn't come to bother her?

With a grunt of exasperation, Lillia spun back to the imprint. Maybe if she ignored him, she could catch the end of the altercation. But the imprint flared one more time, then faded away right as Helge was pulling her arm back, fingers curling into a fist.

Lillia grimaced at her notes. She'd scribbled every detail she could, but still the page was only half filled. She'd have to come back later, once she'd rested, to examine the scene more closely. Already a headache was pounding behind her eyes.

Though that could as easily be caused by a certain nuisance as by her attempts to strain her Gift.

"I saw some of that as I came in," Kerrick said. "Who knew ghosts had fights?"

Wonderful. She'd been projecting again.

"There are plenty of stories of entire ghost armies engaging in never-ending battle, which a Bardic student like yourself ought to know by heart," Lillia said. She didn't bother correcting him about the ghostly status of the imprints; there was no point. "What do you want, Kerrick? I'm busy."

His smile went lopsided in that way he clearly thought was charming. "Why, I want the same thing as you. On beautiful spring days that have lesser minds milling about outdoors, great minds take the opportunity to poke around in dusty old places without any gawkers to bother them."

"If only it had worked," Lillia deadpanned.

"Come on, Lillia," Kerrick said, dropping the smile. "Why won't you let me see your ghosts with you? I could write something worth letting the Sovvan Bard hear for once." He brushed his hair out of his eyes with an irritable swipe, but the fringe of black swung right back into place. Lillia wondered if he'd ever been introduced to a pair of shears.

"Have you tried using your imagination?" she asked, closing her notebook with a snap and sliding it into her pocket. Her headache was getting worse, not helped by the musty library air. She shouldered past Kerrick and headed back toward the library entrance.

"Artists use reference material all the time," Kerrick said, trotting behind her.

"Well, then, maybe go look in a book. There's a few around."

As Lillia reached the open library door, Kerrick grabbed her wrist, pulling her back with a jolt.

"Hey!"

"Please, Lillia. Your ghosts have stories to tell."

Anger flared, and she wrenched her wrist away. She managed not to rub the spot where he'd held her, despite the lingering sensation of iron bands clamped against her skin.

"They're not ghosts, and they certainly aren't mine," she snapped. "But if you can't accept those truths, at least learn this one: Leave me alone!"

Then Lillia stormed off before she could burst into tears in front of him.

She went into the gardens, seeking a secluded spot where she could calm down. Though plenty of people milled about the grounds, she managed to avoid direct engagement. The brisk pace she walked at easily explained the heightened color in her cheeks and indicated that, wherever she was headed, she was in a hurry.

She steered clear of places where she'd documented imprints before. In such an emotional state, she was sure to project again. That would draw more than just Kerrick to gawp at her, and she couldn't be certain she wouldn't bite the next annoyance's head off.

But in the gardens, she found a place between the boughs of a rosebush and the trunk of a young oak tree. She curled herself into the space and breathed in the earthy scent of dirt and leaves. A few buds speckled the bush, not quite open yet. Their faint perfume laced the warm air.

Lillia pulled her knees up and cradled her wrist against her thighs. Fury at Kerrick thrummed through her, mingled with self-hatred. The memory of the old cider mill and the chains that had held her lingered in her mind.

She'd thought she'd be able to put all that behind her once she'd studied enough here at the Collegium. Clearly, she had more work to do. But sometimes it was so hard, and her progress so infinitesimally small, it felt like she might as well have stayed chained up.

No, she admonished herself. *No more self-pity.* It wasn't as if she were completely on her own, after all. She had her family and Bard Callia to lean on. She would master her Gift, and her memories. Even if it took the rest of her life.

Still, she pressed her forehead to her knees and let out a sigh before sniffing back the last of her tears.

Another sniff sounded behind her like an echo.

Stiffening, Lillia strained her ears. Someone else was in her little sanctuary, and she hadn't even noticed them coming in. Had they been here all along? Embarrassment prickled along her spine.

The sniff came again, from the other side of the oak. Cautiously, Lillia twisted to look.

A rust-colored sleeve poked out from beyond the trunk, and a wisp of brown hair curled down over a shoulder hunched in misery.

"Are you okay?" Lillia asked.

The girl on the other side gasped and turned her tear-streaked face toward Lillia. "Oh!"

"I didn't mean to startle you," Lillia said. "I didn't think anyone else was here. But it's a good place to have a bit of a cry, isn't it?" She gestured at her own puffy eyes in camaraderie.

The girl let out a shuddering sigh. She was younger than Lillia, but old enough to wear those Bardic student robes, though they did hang loosely about her huddled frame. "They said my song was rubbish, even though Teacher praised it."

"Your classmates?" Lillia asked. When the girl nodded tightly, Lillia smiled. "Other children can be such rats, can't they? If they're not picking on you, they're dogging your steps to bother you wherever you go."

"That's true enough." The girl swiped a hand over her eyes. "It helps to hear I'm not the only one who has trouble. Do you study here?" She glanced at Lillia's outfit—a pink tunic embroidered with floral patterns over a pair of comfortable trews—definitely not the uniform of any of the Collegia.

For a moment, regret burned through Lillia. "I've only one Gift, and not one of the ones needed to enroll in Bardic properly. I train my Gift with one of the Bards here. My mother's a Herald, and I think she has hopes I'll be Chosen one day, but . . ."

Though Lillia spent lots of time out by Companion's Field, none of the unattached Companions had shown more than passing interest in her. She tried not to let it bother her. She liked the freedom she had to structure her days as she wished. If she were Chosen or enrolled in a Collegium, she'd lose that.

Who knew when she'd have the time to crawl under a rosebush and have a good cry then?

"That's a shame," said the girl. "It would be nice to have a friend in my classes."

Lillia smiled. "I don't see why we can't be friends anyway. Would you like—"

"Lillia?"

Papa Kimfer's voice cut across the garden, interrupting her invitation to dinner before she could make it. Lillia twisted about to see him striding along the path toward her. Mama Marli was behind him. Both wore dark scowls, but not the kind that said Lillia was in trouble, just the ones that said they'd been fighting. Again.

Lillia sighed. Her parents were lifebonded, which meant they loved one another and couldn't stand to be apart, but it didn't mean they liked it. Lillia supposed it was to be expected when a Herald and a former bandit were thrust together. Still, she wished they could communicate without bickering.

Thinking of the imprint she'd discovered earlier, she wondered if there was ever a time when people weren't at each other's throats in some fashion. The thought made her feel bad about her snappish reaction to Kerrick. Not bad enough to invite him to look at the imprints, but a little.

"Lillia, time for dinner," Papa Kimfer said. Affection rang in his voice, and the scowl lifted some. It was nice to know that, despite their resentment of each other, both her parents loved her by choice.

Lillia nodded, then turned back to the girl to say goodbye. But the space behind the tree was empty. Not surprising, given two adults were approaching, and one was a Herald. But disappointment at the missed chance to make a friend tugged at her heart.

"All right, I'm coming." She gathered her notebook and crawled out from the rosebush carefully.

"Everything okay?" Mama Marli asked. She passed a concerned eye over Lillia's twig-and-dirt-strewn clothes and her probably still tear-streaked face. "I thought you were going to the library today. We looked there first."

Lillia brushed herself off. "I'm fine. Just couldn't stay inside on such a nice day. Let's go to dinner."

The Salle was never truly quiet, but Lillia always made a point to come when it was least crowded. Not only did she prefer to work her drills by herself, she was always aware of the danger her lack of control over her Pastsight posed. If an imprint should catch her up in the midst of a sparring match, it would be dangerous, even if she didn't project.

She worked through the exercises the weaponsmaster had

shown her at her last lesson, letting the clatter of practice weapons from the two Herald trainees sparring behind her serve as a drumbeat to follow. Her muscles burned, a pleasant distraction from her whirling frustration.

Her parents had started the morning with one disagreement, which had spiraled into snide comments and vague insults. By the time Lillia left for her morning meeting with Bard Callia, they were on the verge of shouting in one another's faces.

They weren't always so bad, she thought as she sank into a lunge. All the previous year they'd been able to be kind to one another, if not affectionate. She wondered what had happened to ruin that. There was nothing she could recall, no event that clearly set them at odds again.

Sometimes Lillia could control her Gift well enough to call up an imprint from a specific location or item. She'd done it once to help Papa Kimfer when a horrible nobleman was trying to frame him for theft. If only she could find the place where Papa Kimfer and Mama Marli had gone wrong. If she could see that moment, maybe she could fix it.

As if her wish had been heard, a tingle of cinnamon grew in the back of her mouth, and the edges of her vision flickered— sure signs of an imprint coming on.

"Oh, no," she said, wobbling as she tried to pull out of her lunge.

In the mirror, she saw two familiar figures—the Bardic students Helge and Lyran. They were sparring, but they held their wooden practice swords as if they meant to draw blood. Lyran sported a blackened eye, indicating Helge had indeed punched him in the library.

Frustration surged in Lillia. She didn't want to see more fighting today! But she couldn't wrench herself away from the imprint, and she quickly switched her attention to clamping down on it so she wouldn't project.

"Master Garyen would be disappointed in you," Helge hissed as she pressed the attack. *"Too many hours tucked away in your writing corner, too few working your muscles. A* performing *Bard must keep in shape."*

Lyran staggered backward and brought his sword up to block. *"A working Bard knows to choose his exercise carefully, lest he damage his fingers. But some exercises are worth the risk."*

He thrust through an opening in Helge's defense. Helge side-stepped barely in time to avoid getting a scratch along her cheek.

"My face!" she gasped. *"You* would *be so underhanded!"* She leaped forward, sword raised, a killing rage twisting her lips.

But an older, muscle-bound woman came hustling over with anger and an air of authority to back it up. The weaponsmaster of the time, Lillia supposed.

"I won't have such behavior in my Salle," the woman growled. *"If I see you . . ."*

The imprint was breaking up, the sound going too echoey to understand the rest of the weaponsmaster's lecture, the edges of Lillia's vision flickering so intensely she felt lightheaded.

She blinked, and realized she was kneeling on the floor. One of the Herald trainees squatted in front of her.

"I think she's okay," he called, then he looked her in the eye. "Trouble with your ghosts?"

Embarrassment flooded her. She didn't recognize this boy, but he knew who she was. Under his concern, she read a layer of curiosity.

Her head was pounding. "I'm fine," she said. "Must have pushed too hard."

"Well, get some rest, then."

Though the vision was already over, Lillia centered and grounded as she'd been taught. Only once she felt herself firmly anchored in the present moment did she stand and leave the Salle.

So much for her exercises.

By lunchtime, Lillia was calm again. She sat with a group of Healers' Collegium students, not taking part in their conversation, but listening with half an ear as she scanned the meal hall. Her second vision of the feuding Bardic students had reminded her of the girl she'd met. Was that girl still having trouble with her classmates? Lillia hoped she might spot her again. This time, she'd make sure to extend an offer of friendship.

She was so distracted by this train of thought that she didn't notice someone approaching until his tray slid into place across from hers.

"I heard you saw another ghost in the Salle this morning," Kerrick said, his gray eyes shining eagerly through his unruly fringe of black hair. "I don't suppose you'd share the tale?"

Irritation flared, but, remembering her earlier regret at having snapped at him, Lillia bit down on her reflexive response. Instead, she spoke in a measured tone. "I'd appreciate if you would listen to me when I say what I see aren't true ghosts. They aren't restless, or seeking to tell their stories."

"I wouldn't be so sure about that. Remember, I've seen some of your visions. They feel pretty ghostly to me. I wrote a song about that one from a few months ago—the girl climbing the tree to fetch an arrow, you remember?—and Bard Lorca said it was the most entertaining thing I'd written yet."

He had the cheek to grin as he stuffed a whole meat roll in his mouth.

Fury drove all peaceful intentions from Lillia's mind. A taste coated her throat, not the cinnamon that preceded one of her visions, but a smoky, sooty grit. Her ears roared with memories of children screaming and a wagon full of spectators rattling past, seeking amusement.

"Entertaining?" she said, her voice low and harsh. "You believe the things I see are real spirits, real people, but you think it's okay to turn their suffering into *entertainment*?"

The Healers' conversations stopped, and Lillia felt them staring at her. But she couldn't focus on their attention. Not when she was so angry.

Kerrick swallowed his food and scowled. "The arrow girl wasn't suffering. People like stories."

"People are insensitive vultures," Lillia said. "And the ones who exploit that fact are worse than the carrion they offer."

"Well, I don't see how it should matter, if they really aren't ghosts," Kerrick shot back.

Lillia drew in a swift breath. Then, with an abrupt motion, she stood and scooped up her tray. She barely managed to keep from stomping as she walked away and dumped the remains of her lunch.

She wasn't hungry anymore.

The library was a different place after dinner. It was empty in a calmer way than during a nice day, the scant candlelight flickering against the nighttime shadows, the air itself feeling sleepy, yet still studious.

Lillia had crept down here after her parents thought she was in bed. Her growing discontent with her lack of control led her to seek further practice. While she'd rather try for the librarian imprint she'd been looking for the other day, her encounter with the Bardic students today indicated she'd better focus on them. She didn't want to develop a sensitivity to them and start seeing them everywhere they'd had a shouting match.

But, once again, as she entered the open study area, she found she wasn't alone. She was pleasantly surprised to see her companion wasn't Kerrick, but the girl she'd met in the garden. She had a book open on the table, and was scratching a quill at a piece of paper much blotted with ink.

"Late-night study session?" Lillia asked.

The girl looked up, and a smile lit her face. "I'm working on a new song."

"I'd love to hear it when it's ready for listening," Lillia said. She came to the table and set her notebook down across from the girl, then took a seat. "I'm Lillia, by the way. What's your—"

"Oh!" said the girl, looking over Lillia's shoulder. Adoration spread over her face, and she stood so rapidly her chair nearly toppled. "Lyran! You came!"

Lyran?

With a strange, hollow feeling, Lillia watched as the girl she'd been speaking with rushed to embrace someone Lillia had only seen as an imprint. She noticed now the flickering of her vision, the taste of cinnamon. The girl's voice as she spoke to the older Bardic student echoed.

Those sensations hadn't been there a moment ago. Lillia knew that for certain.

What was happening?

"Of course I came," Lyran was saying. *"I can always make time for my little sister."* He scowled as he said it, though, and the girl pulled back.

"Why do you look so upset, Lyran?" she asked. "You're not really going to challenge my bullies to duels, are you? I heard about your fighting in the Salle today. You know Mother wouldn't like that."

A dark shadow crossed Lyran's face. *"The masters have decided to pass Master Garyen's lute to Helge."*

The girl gasped. "They can't! He so clearly meant you to have it, to write your beautiful songs with."

"It seems he didn't make it clear enough."

"But you could work with her, couldn't you? Your writing and Helge's performance would make a wonderful piece together, I think."

Lyran chuckled. *"Work with Helge? Now there's a recipe for disaster. Never you mind about that, Derra. I'll take care of making it right. Now, what's this you have over there? A new song, perhaps? Let's see it."*

The girl—*Derra*—came eagerly back to the table where Lillia still sat. Lillia leaned away as she approached, horror squeezing her throat. Seemingly unaware, Derra snatched up her ink-stained paper and smiled at Lillia. "See you later, I hope."

When she turned back to her brother, the imprint wavered, then collapsed, taking both siblings with it.

Lillia sat alone in the library. Her entire body felt cold, and her mind kept repeating one word.

Ghost.

Lillia spent a sleepless night jumping at every small noise. When the gray light of early dawn crept through her window, she abandoned the futile exercise and drew on yesterday's clothes. Then she slipped from her family's rooms and dashed off to find Bard Callia. Her mentor was always an early riser.

She'd be available to talk Lillia through this terrifying revelation.

Except when Lillia skidded to a halt outside Bard Callia's rooms and knocked upon the door, she received no answer. A grave kind of quiet hovered about the entryway, and Lillia certainly did not want to be thinking of graves of any kind now, but she couldn't stop her brain from going to such places. Exhaustion played a tug-of-war against her mounting fear.

She paced outside Bard Callia's door for what felt like candlemarks as the morning brightened, and still no sign of life stirred within. Bard Callia must have spent the night out.

But she must have left word of her whereabouts with someone in case of emergency. Lillia would classify her situation now as an emergency.

Desperate, she dashed off once again, heading for the Dean of Bardic's office. Surely, if anyone knew where her mentor was, it would be him? Surely he would tell her?

She was out of breath before she reached the corridor outside his office, her heart beating against her lungs. When she got there, she found she was not the dean's first visitor of the day. A boy sat in one of the chairs outside the closed office door, his black hair falling in his face as he hunched over a notebook on his lap, his rust-colored student's robes disheveled as if he'd slept in them.

Kerrick. Of course.

He looked up as she clamored into the hallway, and their eyes met. Anger flashed on his tired face, but it quickly became concern as he took in her own disheveled appearance.

"Lillia? Are you okay?"

"I—" she started, uncertain. "Kerrick, I don't know—I've seen—*oh!*"

The imprint slammed into her without warning. After a night of no sleep and hours of fretting, Lillia had nothing to pull on to keep from projecting.

Lyran and Helge stood between Lillia and Kerrick, both of them gripping the neck of a beautiful lute. She'd not yet seen them so animalistic in their rage at one another as they were now, grimacing and growling as they both tugged at the instrument.

"How dare you try and take what's mine?" Helge spat.

"It was never yours to begin with!" Lyran shouted. He was so red in the face his veins bulged.

"The dean herself declared it mine, you cur!" said Helge.

The two tussled some more, and the lute came dangerously close to clanging against the wall.

"Let go, you monster!"

"Not before you do, fiend!"

"Wait!" came another voice. Lillia trembled to hear it, but she was powerless to keep from seeing the girl—Derra— entering the hallway.

A chill ran down her spine as Derra spared her a glance before powering on to the two feuding Bards. "You'll damage the lute if you keep fighting like this," she said, standing between them as if she could force them to stop as the weapons- master had. "Can't you share it?"

"Share it?" Helge laughed. *"With* him? *My career couldn't bear the insult. Now get your filthy hands away from my lute. Bad enough having* one *scribbler touching it."*

She gave a wrenching twist, and her elbow knocked Derra aside. With a cry, Derra tumbled to the floor, putting a hand out to catch herself.

Lyran did not let go of the lute. He stepped closer to Helge, pressing his grimace nearly to hers. *"How* dare *you hit my sister?"*

On the floor behind him, Derra shook her head and blinked as if seeing stars.

"Get away from me!" Helge shouted. She gave him and the lute a great shove.

Lyran, clearly not expecting it, went off balance and stumbled backward.

Lillia's breath froze in her lungs, but somehow she couldn't keep from calling out, "Derra! Look out!"

Derra lifted eyes already sparkling with tears to Lillia's, her mouth open in a premature gasp of pain.

Then Lyran's foot came down on her hand.

Derra's piercing shriek as her bones broke rippled in the echo of the imprint, and Lillia fought the urge to cover her ears. Kerrick, too, winced in sympathy.

Lyran cast a horrified look at his sister, then whirled on Helge with renewed fury. *"Take your precious lute, then. But if my sister never writes again, I swear I'll destroy you. You'll never be able to feel secure in your career without looking over your shoulder for me. Even if I die, I'll haunt you, Helge!"*

The imprint wavered, the image fading as Lyran's final words echoed again and again.

I'll haunt you, Helge. I'll haunt you. Haunt you!

"Oh, no," Lillia moaned. She was falling, her legs giving out under her after the intensity of the imprint.

Kerrick caught her, and they both slid to the floor, right where poor Derra had had her hand crushed.

"I'm haunted," Lillia said, leaning against Kerrick's shoulder. "Derra's haunting me. You were right, Kerrick. She's a real ghost, and I don't know what to do!"

Tears spilled down her cheeks, but she did nothing to stop them.

Kerrick shook his head. His unruly fringe swayed limply across his intensely thoughtful expression. "You're not haunted. That girl's not a ghost. At least, she wasn't as of this morning when I left the house."

Lillia swiped a sleeve over her eyes and stared at him. "What?"

Now Kerrick looked apologetic. "She's my great-aunt Derra. I kissed her good morning not four candlemarks ago."

"Oh, yes. My brother and Bard Helge," said the old lady reclining on her bed. "They never did work together, despite the beautiful music they could have made. Alas, the price of anger is often the loss of something that could have been lovely. Though, given that she predeceased him, Lyran probably didn't go on to haunt her, if such things do happen."

Lillia and Kerrick sat beside her, Kerrick respectfully, Lillia incredulously.

"But how?" Lillia asked. "How did the imprint of you in the past speak with me? Do you *remember* me, Lady Derra?"

"Not at all," Lady Derra said with a smile. "I've a suspicion, though. The Healers were able to fix my hand back then, but these days I find it pains me to hold a pen. But though I have lost the ability to write physically, that doesn't mean I am unable to be creative still, and I have my Bardic Gift."

She waved a crabbed hand—the hand Lillia had watched get broken this morning—toward the writing desk across the bedchamber. A sheaf of papers lay upon its surface.

"My granddaughter takes dictation while I work on my memoirs. I like to use my Bardic Gift upon myself during our sessions. I find it helps rekindle the feelings of the past, and I do have rather strong feelings about the events surrounding that particular moment. Perhaps I managed to lend my past self a bit of spirit, shall we say?"

She gave a papery old-lady laugh.

Lillia clasped her hands in her lap. "Would you . . . like me to help you? You have a story to tell, and I could help you see it."

Kerrick lifted his eyebrows, but said nothing.

"I appreciate the offer, dear, but I've got my tale well in hand. But there are others who haven't the talent—or the time—to tell their own stories."

Then Lady Derra offered to ring for tea, but Lillia felt she'd been away for too long already. She hadn't asked permission before haring off to meet Kerrick's un-ghostly relative.

Kerrick kissed his great-aunt again, then walked with Lillia back to the Collegium.

"No ghosts after all," he sighed. "You were right all along. I suppose I really must find my inspiration elsewhere. Impressing the Sovvan Bard will have to take second fiddle to keeping my marks high enough to remain at the Collegium."

Ah. Lillia had wondered why he'd been waiting outside the dean's office.

"I think what I see could be . . . up to interpretation," she said. "There must be something that causes some events to leave an imprint where others do not. Is it a ghostly influence, or simply random chance? If I can figure that out, I might finally get control of my Gift."

Kerrick turned hopeful eyes on her, though his unfortunate hair persisted in getting in the way. "Are you saying you'll let me do an interpretation?"

"I'm saying I'm open to collaboration. Lady Derra was right. Fighting only leads us to lose opportunities. I already have a firm example of that in my parents, unfortunately. And these people's stories . . ." She paused as memories of the old cider mill flickered in her mind. "They need to be told properly, not just as a distracting bit of entertainment."

Kerrick nodded. "I hear that."

They were at the gate that would put them back on Collegium grounds. Lillia stopped and held out her hand to Kerrick. "Partners?"

"Partners." Kerrick grasped her hand firmly, enthusiasm clear in his wide smile. "When can we start?"

Instead of answering, Lillia gave a jaw-cracking yawn. A moment later, Kerrick yawned, too. Then they both laughed.

"Not until we've had a nap, at least!"

Consequences
Dylan Birtolo

The display of sheer brutality was enough to stop Rashan in his tracks as he stood near the village border. For a moment, he could scarcely remember to breathe. Behind him, Kylelle snorted and gave a shake that caused her saddle to creak and jingle. He reached out to her, communicating across the bond they shared.

:So much for a routine visit. Stay close.:

Rashan stepped forward, walking around the first of several bodies littering the main road. Their wounds were fresh enough that the blood had not dried, but there was no movement or breathing he could see. A few streaks of reddish mud at the road's edge led to firmly closed doors. If he strained to hear, he could make out stifled weeping. The coppery odor was thick enough on the air to block out all other scents.

:This was recent. The attackers might still be here.:

Kylelle lifted her head, pointing her ears forward and to the left. *:I can hear the sound of steel on steel,:* she replied. *:We must hurry.:*

Trusting his Companion's senses far more than his own, Rashan jumped onto her back and let her choose the path. His right hand drifted to his blade as he rode, but it remained in its scabbard for the moment. It was a fine line between foolishness and bravery, but if there was a chance that some of the citizens of Sunpeak could be saved, he couldn't tarry.

Sunpeak was a small town, barely large enough to be called

such. Located in the difficult terrain near the Ice Wall Mountains, the vast majority of people didn't even know of its existence. Judging by the number of bodies he saw as he rode past the buildings, at least a third of the village had to be dead or dying.

:Bandits?: He couldn't help voicing the question.

:That seems unlikely. Did you notice all the dead wore a similar style of clothing? I'd wager they're all villagers. Whoever caused this needed overwhelming forces.:

:That's concerning.:

:I'd classify that as an understatement. With hope, we might have some answers soon.:

Kylelle charged forward, and Rashan bent low, gripping tight with his legs. As they approached the building's corner, Kylelle leaned hard to the side, her hooves threatening to slip in the mud, but she held her balance. As they rounded the back corner, they almost charged over two fighters engaged in combat, a woman and a man.

Kylelle dug in her back hooves and reared up, kicking at the air with her front feet. As she did, Rashan loosened his grip and slid to the ground, landing on the balls of his feet at her side. Even before his boots stopped sliding in the dirt, his sword was out, the point leveled in the general direction of both fighters.

"Hold!" he shouted.

Their sudden arrival forced the two fighters back, separating them from each other by a couple of paces. Both were drenched in sweat despite the coolness of the building's shade. The man's hair was matted, a gash on the side of his head turning his otherwise light blond hair a deep crimson. The wound looked terrible, but head wounds always did, even when shallow. His clothing had multiple tears, the smooth edges on most of them a telltale indicator of their source. His chest visibly rose and fell as he gulped air.

The woman across from him looked no better. She had a deep cut across the top of her right arm that trailed blood down to her hand. Her grip shook enough to cause the blade to rattle as she held it. Her eyes glanced at Rashan and his Companion before settling back on the adversary before her. For a moment, her head drooped, but she snapped it back into place.

"Drop your weapons," Rashan said.

When they didn't immediately do as instructed, Kylelle stomped one of her front hooves, adding a note of authority that brooked no argument. Both fighters dropped their weapons. Rashan noticed both combatants dressed in the same style as the corpses, and remembered Kylelle's earlier observation.

"I am Herald Rashan, visiting Sunpeak as an official emissary and representative of Queen Selenay of Haven. What's happening here?"

He gestured with his blade for the other two to sit, and they did so. The man collapsed in the dirt, slumped over his own knees, while the woman fell with her back against the wall and slid down. Once they were both on the ground, Rashan put his blade away and Kylelle took a couple of steps back. She snorted once before lifting her head and flicking her ears to the wind, searching for any other sounds.

"They killed our swordmaster. We couldn't let that stand." Even though the man answered Rashan, he glared at the woman across from him, eyes narrowed as he spoke.

She spat at her opponent. "Your swordmaster should've never accepted a duel. Even in his prime, he wouldn't have stood a chance."

"Only because your school doesn't know anything about honor."

"Honor means nothing if you're lying dead on the battlefield." She paused just long enough for the hint of a smirk to touch the corners of her mouth. "Just ask your swordmaster."

The man growled and leaned forward, his hand moving toward his sword. A quick stomp from Kylelle snapped the fighter's attention back up to the Companion and her Herald. The man eased back with a sigh, and his chin struck his chest. The woman closed her eyes, but stopped attempting to hide her amusement.

"You're telling me you weren't attacked by outsiders? This was a fight among *your own people*?"

The answering silence spoke volumes.

"You killed each other, people you lived with for years, and for what?" Rashan's voice came out as a whisper, not believing the words even as he spoke them.

"To prove we're superior. We always have been." The woman looked up at Rashan, defiance in her eyes. When she met his gaze and saw the disappointment and confusion, she at least had the self-awareness to look away and squirm.

"A worm can never be superior to a lion," the man sniped.

"Enough!" Rashan shouted.

The two fighters cringed away from the Herald as much as their positions allowed them to. Rashan's fists clenched, and his arms trembled. So much meaningless destruction. He wanted to rage and shout, draw his blade and . . . do what? What could he possibly do with his rage beyond add to the tragedy?

:What we can do is see who is not beyond our assistance. We need to gather those we can and determine if there are enough people left to make this town viable. We might need to bring the survivors down from the mountains and find them new homes in safer and gentler lands. This much death will draw scavengers and worse.:

As usual, Kylelle was right. Rashan nodded.

"Come. We'll save who we can. Leave your weapons. You'll need all your strength to carry the wounded you left behind. Maybe then you'll question the cost of your supposed superiority."

Rashan doubted his words would spark any epiphanies, but he needed all the strength he could find.

:In all my lives, humankind's capacity for violence never ceases to astound me. I wish I could say differently, but there are far too many cases to the contrary.:

Rashan reached out and put a hand on Kylelle's neck as they walked beside each other. He rested it there, drawing comfort from their contact. *:Sometimes I wonder why we continue struggling for peace,:* he said.

:Because no matter how deep the wells of darkness, the bursts

of light outshine them. And besides, someone has to lead so others might follow.:

Rashan found his steps lighter, and he lifted his chin as he approached the terrible scene on the main thoroughfare. Once it came into focus, he stopped. Even knowing what he would find, the sight of it stunned him for a moment.

:I still don't know how it could come to this,: he said.

:Nor do I, but such questions are lost to time. Come, we have work to do.:

Fael stood at the circle's edge, watching the two fighters in the center move around each other, their wooden swords flowing back and forth through the air. Her lack of allegiance gave her a bit of space, as most of the town considered themselves students of one swordmaster or the other. They had segregated themselves to either side of Fael, as if she were oil separating two bodies of water.

:You have to wonder just how hard they're fighting to impress you. Or is it to win you as the trophy? Are you going to sit on the winner's shelf?: Ryse said in her mind, letting out a short whinny at his own joke.

:You're just jealous because it's taking away from your attention.: Fael made the statement in jest, but she knew how much Ryse enjoyed being lauded. Several children sat nearby and looked up at him with wide-eyed fascination.

:I can't help it if I'm the more regal looking of the two of us. Not to mention, have you seen even a horse here? Sure, people they see every day, but a Companion, now that's something special.:

Fael conceded the point. Sunpeak was small, and likely didn't get much in the way of visitors. Still, King Theran wanted to make sure that Heralds went to all corners of Valdemar to check on those who didn't have easy access to Haven and weren't on the major trade routes.

When she had arrived, each of the two rival sword schools wanted to be responsible for hosting her. While she had insisted it was not necessary, they refused to accept her protests. But the question of which school would serve the honored guest had led to the current duel.

So, in a way, she was the trophy.

Watching them fight, the differences in their styles would be clear even to an untrained observer. Gorrin held his sword in front of him whenever he wasn't attacking or defending, and his strikes favored large, powerful swings. His movements were the definition of precision, controlled by arms that looked to be sculpted from stone.

In contrast, Ahrid relied on constant movement, staying light on his feet and never remaining in one place for longer than a breath. His weapon whipped out and back so fast it was hard to believe it was made of wood and not something more supple. It reminded Fael of a skilled whip dancer performing their art.

While Ahrid had managed to land a few hits, none had been hard enough to hamper Gorrin's movement. The larger man relied much more on offense than defense, accepting blows if it gave him a greater chance of connecting with one of his massive swings.

His moment came as Ahrid's foot slid in the dirt and he stumbled. Seizing on the opportunity, Gorrin rushed forward, committing his entire body weight behind a horizontal blow. Fael winced; even though the weapons were wooden, that much force behind the blow could break bones.

But Ahrid leaped forward, his slip appearing to be a ruse. He dashed toward Gorrin, getting within the larger man's reach. Ahrid swung down at an angle as he passed, striking Gorrin's front ankle, the one bearing all of his weight. The crack of the wood on bone was audible before the larger man crumpled with a shout of pain.

Ahrid spun around and lifted his weapon, bringing it down on Gorrin's side. He brought it down a second time before Gorrin's students rushed forward, enraged. Ahrid's students responded in kind, the entire area about to become a battlefield. Before it got to that point, Ahrid dropped his sparring blade and lifted his hands, backing away to show he was no longer threatening the rival swordmaster. Gorrin's students surrounded their master, glaring at their rivals as Ahrid approached Fael.

"As it turns out, our school will have the honor of hosting you, Herald. Not that it should be a surprise." He was smiling wide, but his panting and the sweat streaks on his face betrayed how hard he had been pressed.

"While I appreciate the gesture, I still insist it wasn't necessary. I don't want you injuring each other, especially on my account." Fael pointedly looked to where Gorrin needed assistance to walk off the field.

"Perhaps I was a bit . . ." Ahrid paused as he searched for an appropriate word.

:Excessively aggressive,: Ryse said, accentuating the thought with a brief snort.

"Enthusiastic," Ahrid eventually supplied. "But it will give them something to think about when they try to claim their school is superior. Every now and then, they could use that reminder."

The crowd started to disperse, with most people going back to their daily activities. A handful of students continued to escort Gorrin to his training grounds, with more than one shooting the occasional glare in Ahrid's direction. Fael and Ryse joined Ahrid as he led them to the opposite end of Sunpeak.

"How often do you fight each other?" Fael asked.

"Not too often. We have small tournaments at the changing of the seasons. It's a way to keep our skills sharp and add a bit of much-needed celebration to our difficult lives."

:I'm sure he'll remind you just how difficult their lives are when it comes to the topic of Haven providing some sort of assistance,: Ryse said.

Fael agreed, but listened as Ahrid continued, "Real duels are rare. In fact, that is only the second duel I've had since I became the school's new swordmaster."

"Just make sure it doesn't grow out of hand," Fael said.

"How could it? We are far too careful for that."

* * *

Herald Corin strode down the packed dirt that served as the village's only road. The entire community was scarcely more than a few buildings, and most of them looked temporary in nature. Several people crowded themselves into the shelters at night. It would be a while before the people had enough homes to house them all comfortably.

But the settlers had chosen the ground for their village well. It was in a natural valley in the mountains, sheltered on three sides. They weren't high enough to be above the tree line, so they had ample access to resources. Plus, Corin and Tallidar had been able to get up here without any difficulty, even if the trail was long and not marked. A normal horse could make the journey with a competent rider.

Besides his Companion, two women accompanied Corin, to form a group of four. Elltir and Bryn pointed out various sites as they walked, indicating the plans they had for their village. The rest of the people here followed the two women, entrusting them to lead their village to safety and some semblance of comfort.

"You realize that this far from Haven, there is little Queen Elspeth can do to support you," Corin said as they came to a stop at the end of the cleared section.

"We're aware," Elltir said. "She's got her hands full making peace with any who will listen. We're not asking for much."

Bryn nodded her agreement. "These folks here, they just want to get away from the squabbles and the wars. They want a chance to carve out a little section for their own lives, and we aim to give it to them. So, you see, we picked this place on purpose, wanting to be far enough away to not got pulled into border disputes or the like."

Tallidar sent warmth and compassion to Corin through their bond, adding images of what this place might look like, given enough time. The meaning was clear, and Corin agreed.

"You picked a wonderful spot. What will this village be called?"

In response, Elltir pointed over Corin's shoulder. He looked to where the sun was dipping below the ridge of the mountains. Most of it was obscured behind a single peak, giving the snow-capped structure a glow like metal left in a forge.

"Sunpeak."

"It's a good name, and a fitting one."

Bryn turned to walk back toward the center of the village, leading the others as she spoke.

"The snow melt gives us plenty of water year-round, with a small lake where it pools. As you can see, we won't be hurting for resources. Growing crops might be a bit of a challenge, but we'll make it work. Sunpeak might not ever become a city, but with some time and some effort, it will become an actual town one day."

As they described it, Corin could almost see their plans manifesting in the air before him. He shared the mental images with Tallidar, wanting him to experience the vision. It had a simplicity and a calmness to it. Especially after the recent years of war, he couldn't fault these people for wanting to get away. In fact, a part of him envied them for the life they would carve for themselves.

Not that he had any illusions of joining them. His sense of duty was far too strong for that. Queen Elspeth had her own grand plans, ones that would take a lot of work and all of her Heralds. He wanted to see those plans come to fruition as well and help her build the peace she envisioned.

"I'm not sure when we will be able to spare someone to come check on you, but I'll make sure the Heralds know about what you are doing here."

"That's all we ask," Elltir said.

"What about predators or bandits? These lands are far from safe. While you two are formidable swordmasters, two of you can't defend the entire village."

Bryn drew her sword and carved a line in the dirt. She positioned herself on the opposite side from Elltir.

"We have a plan for that," she said. "We're going to need

new recruits, and we're going to need to train them hard. So we're going to create a friendly rivalry of sorts to get the people riled up and motivate to train with either Elltir or myself."

"Plus, having regular opponents to challenge who aren't from the same school will keep skills sharp," Elltir added.

"So you're going to pretend to be rivals to keep people motivated and create training opportunities?"

Both women nodded.

"What's the worst that can happen?" Bryn asked.

A Bad Business
Jeanne Adams

*Events in this story take place immediately after the events of
Skif's story,* Take a Thief.

Herald Beryl watched as Weaponsmaster Alberich and his
trainee, Skif, trotted toward the palace. Having seen the aftermath of the warehouse fight, her respect for Alberich re-
doubled.

Nearby, Talamir, the Queen's Own Herald, coaxed three
grubby, terrified girls to eat. They'd been wrapped in blankets
and given warm bread with cheese.

"Well, young Beryl." Herald Investigator Ryvial clapped her
on the shoulder. "They've left it in our hands. Let's be at it."

Together, they turned back to the innocuous warehouse
where Trades Guildmaster Vatean had perpetrated terrible
crimes. "This is a bad business. It's going to be a right mess to
untangle," Ryvial said. The interior was bright now, with large
lanterns to illuminate the evidence.

Guildmaster Vatean's body lay on a stretcher. The hired
thugs Alberich had dispatched had already been carried outside. A fellow Herald Investigator was going through Vatean's
pockets. She patted along the hem of his rich waistcoat, then
turned up the edge and fiddled with the fabric.

"Got a key here, boss."

Ryvial moved closer to examine the key on the woman's
palm.

"Interesting . . . Strong box? Trunk, perhaps?"

"Who's watching Vatean's home and business?" Beryl asked.
Ryvial would have seen to that right away.

"Two of ours on his business, Guard Barkman on the residence." Ryvial's drawl turned to amusement. "And guards on the houses of both his mistresses."

"Two, sir?" Beryl didn't quite throttle her surprise.

:Busy, busy man,: Beryl's Companion, Giselle, interjected, laughter ringing in her tone.

"Indeed. One a noted court beauty." Ryvial glanced at Beryl. "That would be Vivette Coleur. Her husband, Lord Emberson, is three times her age."

Beryl coughed to mask an inappropriate laugh, as Giselle's snicker rang in her mind. "Uh, I see."

"I'm sure you do." Ryvial grinned. "The second lady is equally beautiful, but more elusive, according to Herald Theon, our man in court. Alisan Reminy is from Menmellith. She's in trade as well. Gems. She's wealthy enough to mix with the nobles, and popular for her innovative fashion."

Fashion and nobles. Two things Beryl knew little about. As the daughter of a blacksmith, she knew good iron and steel, trade, and the economics of hard goods, not frills. She loved never having to consider fashion. For years now, she'd had her trainee Grays, then her recently earned Whites, to wear.

"May I bring Herald Esta in on the investigation, sir?" Beryl was sure her fashionable friend could help.

Ryvial looked pained. "No. This whole adventure . . ." His vague gesture encompassed the building and the body on the floor. "Must remain cloaked, until we ferret out who's involved in Vatean's child-trafficking. Officially, Vatean and his guards were set upon, and died defending themselves in a completely different part of Haven."

"Really, sir?" Beryl immediately saw the benefit. Another locale would distract the curious from activity at Londer Galko's warehouse. The Investigative Heralds could then watch the building. Meanwhile, they could observe Vatean's widow, see who came to offer condolences, who tried to take over Vatean's business, and who gloated over his sudden death. "Is the widow involved?"

Beryl didn't ask if the widow was capable of abetting such

heinous business. As an Investigator, she'd already seen the dark side of crime.

"Doubtful," Ryvial answered. "Lissa Coros, Vatean's wife, is minor nobility. She's distantly related to Queen Selenay and focuses on charitable works."

"Any children, sir?" Beryl hated to think of Vatean having children of his own.

Apparently Ryvial had had the same thought. "No, thankfully. Small blessings. Herald Theon will fill us in tomorrow. Court and the Trade Guilds are his area of expertise."

Beryl had seen Theon earlier, helping the weaponsmaster. Shortly thereafter, Theon and his Companion had galloped for the palace.

"Next steps?" Ryvial asked.

"As part of our investigation, we'll offer Lissa Coros our help, on the Crown's behalf," Beryl said, thinking it through. "Insuring no one cheats her of her due, right, sir?" They had done that on other investigations during Beryl's training. It helped any widowed partner, male or female, who might not be savvy to their spouse's business. It frequently had the side benefit of uncovering the culprit of whatever crime had been committed as well.

"Exactly." Ryvial poked at the growing pile of items pulled from Vatean's clothes. "This is nasty." He pointed to a vial filled with little crystal chunks.

"Pony, I'd wager," the searcher muttered, her anger apparent.

"Dangerous. Remind me why, Beryl." Ryvial never missed a teaching moment.

"Pony's a drug from OutKingdom. It's a rare and infernally expensive sleep agent, akin to poppy, but less predictable. In some cases, the tiniest dose sends the patient into a coma-like state, often with lethal results."

"Very good. We can guess Vatean's uses for such a tool." Ryvial grunted and pointed to another item. "What do you make of that?"

A small, stoppered bottle of ink. "A special ink? Something for coded messages?"

"Likely, else why carry it?" Ryvial hefted a ring of Vatean's keys. "We'll put Hans on the ink when he's feeling better. These are probably normal keys, unlike the one from the waistcoat."

"That's the lot, sir," the searcher stated, rocking back on her heels.

"Very good, Mace. Thank you." Ryvial motioned to two guardsmen. "Stage the death near Traitor's Gate, far enough from the Whore's Guild that their guards wouldn't have heard the shouts. Then have one of our people raise the alarm."

"Very good, sir." The men headed out with Vatean's body.

Ryvial looked at the blood-soaked floors when they were gone. "Only Martag can set this right." He sighed. "He's going to charge us double."

Beryl hated court. She wasn't a pretty woman, and the courtiers reminded her of that with their glances and whispered asides. Beryl was strong, she was smart, but pretty? No, she'd never be accused of that.

:You're beautiful to me.: Giselle's staunch, unconditional support warmed her. It was all she needed. It had been everything to Beryl since the day, seven years prior, when Giselle had trotted into the family blacksmith shop and knocked Beryl into the horse trough.

:Did not. I merely nudged you. You did the falling all on your own.:

"Right," Beryl murmured, smiling at the memory. She'd emerged, dripping and shocked to meet those glorious blue eyes. Chosen. Always and forever.

:And now we're Herald Investigators. Though this isn't much of an investigation, if you ask me.:

Beryl hid her smile and resisted the urge to tug at the collar of her fine court clothes. Along with her somewhat plain looks, she had inherited her blacksmith father's broad shoulders. She always had to go up a size to get a shirt to fit properly in the shoulders. Thankfully, her best friend, Herald Esta, had taken in both shirt and tunic at the sides, or Beryl would have felt like she was wearing a tent.

"You need real court clothes. You're only going to have more and more occasions like this," Esta had commented. She was likely right. Esta knew Beryl couldn't talk about why she needed formal Whites so quickly. Esta had simply made it happen. "Take some of my girth to fill this out, won't you? Please?"

They'd laughed, and Beryl had hurried to court with a lighter heart. She and her fellow Investigators were part of the Herald rotation for an evening event celebrating a trade deal Vatean had been a part of. Some memorial words were planned, so Beryl and the others would watch for reactions. She was also there to referee, as it appeared that Vatean's widow, Lissa, had instigated a feud.

"All right, people, get to your places," Ryvial instructed. He strode out of the small parlor. This room was always open and stocked with water for anyone who needed a break from the crush of people at large events. Heralds Campion and Duram followed Ryvial at short intervals. Beryl waited out her interval.

Before she could leave, however, a cloaked figure slid through the door. A glinting knife had Beryl bracing to fight.

"I'll be quick. You'll have help here any minute through your Companion," came at a whisper. The voice shook, but the knife was steady. "Don't search for me. I'm bound back to Menmellith."

"Alisan?" Beryl made the logical leap. There were only so many women they were actively searching for.

"I didn't know about the children." Alisan's whisper turned to a snarl. "I'd have killed Vatean myself if I'd known." She tossed a sheaf of papers and a ring of keys to the floor. "That's what I have on Vatean. The keys fit rooms in Partridge Eave, two doors down from his warehouse. I met with him, trying to find a leak in trade secrets coming from Menmellith." Alisan pushed back her hood, revealing her drawn, determined face. "I'm a spy, Herald, but I don't traffic in children's lives."

With that, she snatched the room's key from where it hung along the doorframe. Knife still brandished, she backed out. Beryl got to the door in time to hear it lock.

"Dammit!" she cursed. By the time Campion and Ryvial rescued her, thanks to Giselle, Alisan was long gone.

The ballroom warmed as people filed in. Beryl watched for her targets, turning Alisan's words over in her mind. Ryvial had collected the notes and pouch from Beryl, and taken them to the Investigator's offices, leaving Beryl and the others to monitor the event.

:Are you wandering again?: Beryl asked Giselle. Her Companion hated waiting in stables. She preferred to ghost around Haven, poking into things while her Herald was otherwise occupied.

:Of course. Ryvial never spotted me when I trailed him back to headquarters. A little fun for me. Unlike your assignment.:

:Don't jinx it.:

Lissa-watch, as they'd dubbed it, was no sinecure. Vatean's widow hadn't known of his infidelities, and was embarrassed, angry, and grieving in equal measure. From that stew of emotional pain, Lissa had decided the mistresses must pay. She'd instigated a thread of vicious gossip about both women. Alisan had stayed out of it, but Vivette had reportedly retaliated with several ill-mannered tricks aimed at Lissa. As the Lissa/Vivette feud heated up, the court gleefully chose sides.

In public, Vivette weepingly declared her innocence, and devotion to her spouse. Her husband, Lord Emberson, called on Selenay to intervene. Half the court believed Vivette wrongly accused.

Others joined Lissa's side of the feud.

Since Alisan Reminy was reputed to also be the mistress of yet another Trades Guildmaster, people chalked her disappearance up to embarrassment. Many in court celebrated Vatean's cunning, laughing over his cuckolding his business associates right under their noses.

With Alisan's reappearance, and her revelations to Beryl, however, it seemed she truly was off the chessboard.

The room filled, and the evening event thrummed with anticipation, since both Vivette and Lissa were attending. The court had gleefully fed the feud. In an otherwise humdrum season, their battle was a rare spice. When the Investigator's very public, two-week search of Vatean's house and business premises had revealed the mistresses, Lissa had vowed revenge. Things had gotten nasty behind the scenes, but so far, they'd been contained in public.

Unfortunately, while the search had sparked the feud, it had yielded no other fruit. They'd turned up ledger upon ledger of records, confiscated racks of keys and reams of letters and a few bottles of the odd ink Vatean carried. While Investigator Hans puzzled over the ink, Beryl had gone cross-eyed with reading letter after letter with no apparent connection to anything but actual trade.

So far, the letters, ledgers, and keys— —neatly labeled in a precise hand— —were a dead end.

:When we find Vatean's hidden records, they'll be just as precise, I'll wager,: Giselle commented.

:We can hope.: Beryl nodded to a passing page. She considered Giselle's comment and wondered if they'd ever find justice for this nasty business. As she watched the mingling people, one repeating detail from the numerous letters nagged at her. Three buildings in different parts of town were mentioned in most of the missives.

The wildly varied premises around Haven were as empty and echoing as Londer Galko's warehouse. But the names kept cropping up. Beryl mentally repeated the street names, hoping to jog an idea.

:Let it rest.: Giselle's practical advice was edged with irritation. *:You're making me want to jog you. With my hoof.:*

:Ouch.: Beryl's laughter faded. Lissa had arrived with her entourage and the atmosphere in the room changed. *:Uh-oh.:*

Lissa's fiery, hair-obsessed rival, Vivette, was already present and having a grand time. Lord Emberson wasn't in attendance— a surprise since he generally kept an eagle eye on his young wife. How Vivette had managed a raging affair with Vatean was a mystery.

Vivette's circle of friends and confidants whispered and

tittered as Lissa marched in. Lissa was obviously searching for Queen Selenay, ignoring the other women.

:Let's hope it stays that way.: Giselle had no more uttered the words than an angry curse blued the air.

"Bitch!" Lissa's declaration silenced every other conversation. "How dare you! That's *my* necklace!"

"Oh, horsecrap." Beryl hustled to grab Lissa. Herald Campion went for Vivette. "My lady——" Beryl began, but her outstretched hand met thin air.

"Give it back!" Lissa leaped on Vivette, hands scrabbling for the necklace. Vivette shrieked and fought her off. The cater-wauling, cursing mass of skirts and fury scattered people like ninepins.

"Stop this at once," Herald Campion shouted, tugging at Vivette's arm, only to get a feminine fist to the nose for his trouble. People formed a ring to watch, point, and cheer.

:They're taking bets,: Giselle drily informed her Chosen.

"Dammit." Beryl waded in. She'd been expressly instructed to prevent a scene. She had the strength necessary to wrench the two women apart, but it took two courtiers and a bleeding Herald Campion to keep them that way.

When Queen Selenay arrived, she frowned in fury at the two weeping women. "Who started—" she began. "Never mind. It doesn't matter. Lissa, you're overwrought. Lady Vivette, are you harmed?"

"N-n-no," the flushed beauty stuttered. "A little, maybe. I'm bleeding." She held up her arms, displaying angry, red scratches. She then promptly fainted into Beryl's arms.

"Oh, for haven's sake. Lissa, come with me," Selenay ordered, corralling her weeping relative. Selenay met Beryl's gaze. "You've got Vivette?"

"Yes, Majesty."

"Good. Thank you." Selenay hustled a copiously weeping Lissa away, leaving Beryl with her hands full of semi-conscious fluff. Beryl was strong enough to carry Vivette, but she didn't think it would look good. However problematic, the aftermath of the brief battle gave her a chance to get Vivette alone. Lord

Emberson had hovered throughout their initial visit to Emberson Manor.

:You can finally ask all the pointy questions you want without offending Emberson,: Giselle remarked, then grunted. *:What was Lissa thinking?:*

:She wasn't,: Beryl shot back. *:That's the problem.:*

"Here now, let's get my lady up, and into a quiet place." Herald Campion's rescue was timely. Beryl ignored the renewed tittering as Campion, his bleeding nose stanched for now, carried the much-rumpled Vivette into a side chamber. Vivette's companions, denied entry, resorted to being catty.

". . . she's a big one, isn't she?"

". . . as horsey a face as her Companion . . ."

Campion shot Beryl a worried glance. She deliberately rolled her eyes and smiled, despite the courtiers' verbal jabs. "Don't worry about it," she reassured him.

Giselle flooded her with love, allowing Beryl to shrug away the sting. She had love and purpose. That defied any spiteful comments.

Campion frowned.

"Really, I'm okay. Go get cleaned up," Beryl told him. "I've got this."

When he'd gone, Beryl applied the smelling salts she'd found in a nearby table. "Lady Vivette?"

"Ooh! That's horrible!" Vivette jerked back from the small pot. "Why would you do that?"

"You fainted." Beryl couldn't decide if the faint had been real or staged.

"Me? Faint? I don't think so!" The woman patted herself——breast, waist, hip, hair——before refocusing on Beryl. "My goodness. You shouldn't wear white. It looks terrible on you."

"I'm a Herald, milady." Beryl explained. Somehow Vivette's blunt critique didn't sting.

"So?" Vivette looked blank.

"We always wear white, milady."

"That's just wrong." Distracted, Vivette once again patted the same places in the same sequence.

Giselle snorted in Beryl's mind. :*I'm not sure she gets it.*:

"Do you remember me, milady?"

"You came to the manor?" Vivette looked vague.

"Yes. Do you want a healer for the scratches, milady? Or would you rather I had your coach brought round?"

"My coach? Why would I want my coach? I haven't had any dances." Vivette frowned. "Have I?"

"No." It went on that way as Beryl tended the shallow scratches, with Vivette continuing to periodically pat the same places. Beryl wondered what was hidden there. When she asked about Lissa's attack, Beryl finally got a real response.

Eyes narrowed, teeth bared, Vivette shoved herself up from the settee, and angrily strode around the room. "How dare she accuse me? How dare she attack me!?" She pivoted back to Beryl, clutching the offending necklace. "It's my necklace. You need to lock her up! She's a nasty woman, Vatean said so."

"She's Guildmaster Vatean's wife and heir."

"Poor Vatty!" Vivette clasped her hands at her substantial bust. "Poor man!"

:*Vatty?*: Giselle interjected, snorting her laughter.

"Guildmaster Vatean told you he disliked his wife?"

A sly look whipped across Vivette's delicate features. "Of course not. Why would he confide in me? I've just danced with him from time to time." She waved a hand as if to say she danced with many men, and Vatean was only one. "I love to dance. Darling Emberson encourages it. I'm too energetic if I'm cooped up at home," she confessed.

"Then how do you know Vatean and Lissa weren't a love match?" Beryl decided blunt questions were the only way to get through.

"Them?" Vivette laughed. Her pacing had brought her to the room's mirror. "Oh, no! Look at my hair! She's ruined it, that wretched bitch." Fuming and muttering, she picked yellow gems and glittering gold birds from her coiffure. "I just hate her."

Beryl watched, fascinated, as the seemingly hapless woman briskly unwound the complicated style, then retwisted it into a new, intricate configuration. Vivette set the pins and baubles to perfect effect in her rich brown hair. "There. That's better."

"Vatean lists you in his documents, and has jewelry in your name," Beryl prodded.

Vivette gasped, clutching her hands to her bosom. "Really? He did? That sweet man!" Then her face fell. "Do I get them, though? With him dead?"

Beryl couldn't believe the track the conversation was taking, so she temporized. "I don't know, I'll see what I can do."

"Oh, that would be wonderful. He was always so generous."

"Why was he generous?"

Another sly look, there and gone so fast Beryl wondered if she'd imagined it. "He and Emberson did so much business together. *So* much." Vivette patted her hair, then adjusted one of the baubles. "He paid Emberson in jewels." Now she jingled the numerous bracelets she wore and patted the lovely necklace. "I benefitted."

:So much business?: Giselle echoed the remark. *:Theon reports, through Cassius, that nothing in the records indicates Emberson and Vatean did more than cursory business. Only big, group deals, like the one this evening's event celebrates.:*

Beryl loved that she and Giselle Mindspoke so clearly. *:And paying in jewelry isn't suspicious at all.:*

:No, not at all. I'll let Ryvial know to check Lord Emberson's finances.:

"What kind of business?" Beryl asked, as she brushed off the back of Vivette's gown. Lissa hadn't torn the highly fashionable silks, but the dust of the floors showed.

"Oh, you know. Business-business." Apparently, that answered everything, for Vivette. "Can I go back to the dancing now?"

"Of course."

"Thank you." Vivette paused at the door. Turning back, with an earnest look, she added, "You have really lovely hair. You should do more with it. But you really, really shouldn't wear white." On that note, she swept out of the room. Beryl heard the sudden conversational pause in the ballroom beyond, then the rise of feminine comment as Vivette's friends rushed to console her.

Beryl glanced at the mirror as she tidied up.

:She's right, you're better in colors. Too bad about the Herald Whites.: Giselle paused her teasing, then added contritely, *:Sorry I jinxed the night.:*

Beryl managed a laugh. *:It was brewing anyway.:*

"And that was it," Beryl finished recounting the evening's events to Ryvial the next morning.

They had Alisan's papers spread before them. Meetings with Vatean dated back two years, and were noted with what information was planted, results, and new tactics. There were pages missing, and scant notes on another trader, Guildmaster Harbing. Those were a mere scrawl from Alisan, questioning Harbing's skills.

It read: *What does Harbing do all day?*

The notes on Vatean indicated frustration. Alisan knew Vatean was involved in the trade leak from Menmellith but couldn't find proof.

"We need to talk to her." Ryvial fingered the keys from Alisan's pouch.

"Yes. Did you know she was a spy?"

Ryvial shrugged. "Suspected more than knew, if you get me."

Before Beryl could comment, there was a knock at the door. "Heralds, you'n's better come. They's found that woman you'n's lookin' for."

Beryl's dread grew on the ride to Partridge Eave. Herald Theon was already there. "We'd set up a watch rotation on the warehouse, and the new set of rooms you learned of," he explained, waving toward the original properties. "When the alarm came from down the street, we responded. They said a woman was dead." In this quiet area of working people, murder stood out. "We locked down the scene and sent for you."

:Whaddya bet—: Beryl began.

:No bet,: Giselle said. *:Especially if you're wagering that it's Alisan.:*

:That would be the bet,: Beryl commented with grim surety. She smelled bloody death as they walked up the stairs.

"Throat's cut. From behind." Ryvial made notes in his book. When the guard removed the body, he and Beryl searched the room. It was tidy, and Alisan's bags were packed.

"Dammit, she shouldn't be dead." Beryl hated it. She should've been able to do something—though she didn't know what—to prevent it.

"Stop thinking that way." Ryvial pointed at Beryl. "Alisan was what she was, and did what she did. No one true way, remember?"

Embarrassed that she'd been read so easily, Beryl nodded. "Right."

"Good. Look there." Ryvial pointed to two packs by the door. "She was running."

"Maybe." Beryl noted the full trunks, each locked and marked. "But those are travel tags." A stack of neatly folded clothes lay next to a final, open trunk.

"Right." Ryvial crouched to finger the travel tags. "Porter's markers, for a caravan. She'd planned her exit, but not in haste. Until something spooked her." He stood, tugging a strip of leather from his pocket. He ran his thinking strap, as he called it, through his fingers. "She was worried enough to find you. Confess her status." He shot Beryl a sharp glance. "Did you believe her? About the kids?"

Beryl nodded. She'd learned from Ryvial and the others how to judge character and sift truth from lies. "Yes. She was appalled. She said she'd have gutted him for it herself if she'd known." She frowned. "How'd she know we were looking at him for the kids?"

Ryvial cursed. "Someone's talked." He stepped to the door. "Theon!"

He pivoted back to Beryl. "You didn't tell Esta? Anyone else?"

"Not a word, sir." She checked with Giselle. *:Did you say anything?:*

Her Companion's answer was an indignant snort.

When Theon poked his head in the door, Ryvial explained. "We've got a leak. The dead spy knew we were looking at Vatean for the children."

Theon cursed more colorfully. "What do we do?"

"Keep working the problem. Now that we know Vatean used other rooms along Partridge Eave, we check for rooms around Ticker's Gate and Tallow Lane. That key has to fit somewhere."

"Right." Théon dashed off.

To Beryl, Ryvial said, "Our window's closing. They're cleaning up loose ends. Vatean's fifth hired guard, the one who ran from Alberich, was found floating in the Terilee yesterday." He sighed and rubbed his eyes. "Now Alisan today. We're going to have to protect Lissa and Vivette."

"How?" Beryl hoped someone else had that duty.

"Safe house. Both of them." Ryvial winced. "As soon as possible. One or both of them will be next."

"Because Vivette, at least, is a loose end."

"And these devils snip loose ends."

:This is soooo boring.: Giselle's mock whine made Beryl laugh.

:You wouldn't be bored if you were up here listening to them shout at one another through the walls.: Beryl winced at a particularly graphic accusation from Lissa. *:They're yelling insults about gown quality at this point.:*

:Really?: Giselle's curiosity rang through the question. *:Tell me all the juicy bits!:*

:There's a great deal of discussion about the size of their jewels . . . :

Giselle's mental snicker had Beryl's lips curving in response.

:It's usually the men who're bragging along that line.: Giselle sent an image of two men waggling their hips and pointing. Beryl laughed out loud, which yielded a pause from the feuding women.

Theon called out, then thumped up the stairs to relieve her from her watching post. "Any trouble?"

"No, but be prepared to plug your ears. They've been shouting for hours."

A startled Theon asked, "About what?"

"Oh, about how much Vatean loved Lissa. How much Emberson loves Vivette. How they're both so sad. Much weeping. Renewed insults. Last bit's been about how big their jewels are."

Theon snickered, much as Giselle had. "Where are the maids?"

Both women had insisted they couldn't possibly stay the night away from home without their maids. For a wonder, Lissa was taking the enforced night away from home much better than Vivette, who'd pouted.

"Lissa's maid is with her mistress. Vivette's rather formidable maid is in the kitchen, making tea." Beryl grinned at him. "She growled at me that she wasn't *our* maid, so no tea for us."

Theon shook his head in mock sadness. "Naught but water and crust for us poor Heralds. At least, till our relief comes on."

"Exactly."

Glad to leave the ladies' verbal sparring behind, Beryl trotted downstairs to the parlor. The safe house was in a quiet, well-to-do section of Haven. The property was deeded to Selenay's great aunt, Lady Hesselbatt, who never came to court. It was most often used as a haven for the Queen's Handmaidens, women secretly working in various households for the crown. It was a safe, out-of-the-way spot to rest, and to either change their names and looks, or, when necessary, hide.

:Are you really going back to those irritating letters?: Giselle asked. *:Haven't you ridden that horse to the end of the trail?:*

:I don't think so. Not yet.:

Something about the consistent repetition of the property names gnawed at her. When Beryl had confessed that to Ryvial, he'd handed her five new stacks of Vatean's correspondence from the Partridge Eave rooms to read. Beryl hoped it would prove fruitful.

:More like sleep-inducing,: Giselle decided, making snoring noises.

:Hush, horse,: Beryl said with a laugh. *:I know there's something there.:*

:Yeah, yeah, yeah. I'm going back to my wandering.:

:Stay safe.:

Hours later, Beryl had begun to think Giselle had the right of it. Partridge Eave, Ticker's Gate, and Tallow Lane featured in most of the correspondence, as did other properties, but she still didn't get their significance.

"No visible connection," Beryl muttered as she stood to stretch. She'd be grateful to turn over the watch. She picked up the last letter, turning it into the light. *Wait a minute . . .*

:Are you nearly ready?: Giselle interrupted her discovery.

:Yes,: she responded absently. *:And I'm starving. Vivette's maid relented and made Theon tea, at least,:* Beryl told Giselle, still scanning the document.

:Not you?:

:She offered, but I'm all tea-d out.: Beryl had switched to water. She tilted the letter again. There! Some of the letters in the document . . . glinted. There was another!

"Partridge Gate . . . then a line," Beryl traced down with her finger. "Glint-y letter."

She grabbed a pen and a fresh scrap of palimpsest. "F. Next glint-y letter is O. U. R. Four. Four what? Four F." She traced further, excitement bubbling. "Four females? Two M. Two males?" She scanned further down. The letter was to Guildmaster Harbing. "Holy havens. It can't be that simple, can it?"

:What is it? You're excited. Tell, tell!:

:I have to check it with Theon!: As Beryl hurried out, paper in hand, she realized it was past time for their relief to have arrived.

She ran to the stairs. "Theon?"

No answer. *:Giselle!:*

:Getting help!:

Beryl found Theon slumped on the chair in the hall, an empty tea mug at his feet. Lissa's maid lay on the floor in her open room, but both Lissa and Vivette, along with Vivette's scowling maid, were gone. In Vivette's room, the window was wide open.

:Giselle!?:

:Marcus and Carter are out cold. Their Companions have been drugged. Ryvial, Talamir, and the others are on their way.:

Beryl castigated herself for their plight. How could she not have noticed the time? Why hadn't she checked in sooner?

"Dammit, Theon," she said, tapping his cheeks as tears stung her eyes. "Wake up!"

When Theon moaned and his eyelids fluttered, she nearly cheered. "Wha . . . ?"

"Oh, gods, Theon, I'm so sorry." Beryl wept with relief.

:Help's at the door. They have a healer.: The locks rattled open, and footsteps pounded up the stairs. She moved aside.

"Vatean used Pony," she said, wringing her hands. "Check for that."

"There are healers on Marcus, Carter, and their Companions," Ryvial reassured. "Quit blaming yourself and talk to me," he ordered, as another healer tended to Lissa's maid. "What happened?"

She rattled off the sequence of events.

"Wait, you figured it out?" He grabbed her arm, tugged her downstairs. "That may tell us where they've taken the women."

Relief coursed through her, along with a sliver of hope. She tried to quash it, but it persisted. Maybe, just maybe, she could salvage this disaster. Why hadn't she checked on Theon sooner?

:Stop that,: Giselle chided, her Mindvoice both stern and loving. *:Focus.:*

"Hold it sideways." Beryl demonstrated with one document. "See the glint? Certain letters are traced over with a different ink."

"That explains the ink," Ryvial muttered, turning his document on an angle. "F.I.V.E.F.?"

"Five females. At least I think that's what it is. First there's a property name, Ticker's Gate. Then a number and either F or M. Then an M, an H, an R . . ." Things clicked into place. "Menmellith, Hardorn, Rethwellan?"

"Yes. Others, farther south. Yes. Well done." Ryvial shuffled through the papers. "We have watchers on Partridge Eave, Ticker's Gate, and Tallow Lane. We'd already know if they'd taken the women there. Look for other property names."

They tilted and read. "Five Gables Street, that's the Londer Galko warehouse. That's covered." He picked up another.

"Dovecote Alley?" Beryl read. "Where is that?"

"Near Exile's Gate," Ryvial snapped, leaping up. "That'll be it. It's easy to get a body to the Terilee from there. Let's go."

Ryvial's Turian and Beryl's Giselle barely waited for them to vault into the saddle before taking off for Exile's Gate.

"Giselle has ghosted around there," Beryl shouted over the chiming hoofbeats. "She remembers the building on Dovecote Alley. She says it's never occupied, but always in better repair than the rest of the street."

"Tell the others."

Heralds weren't welcome around Exile's Gate. At this late hour, the considerable activity faded away before them as they galloped in. Beryl hated their loud arrival, but if Lissa or Vivette was still alive, they were running out of time. This was not the time for subtlety.

"Break it down," Ryvial demanded as they reached the address. His Companion, Turian, pivoted and kicked the door off its hinges. "Thanks."

Sliding out of the saddle, he drew steel, as did Beryl. "We're not Alberich. Our only job here is to delay, delay, delay until help arrives."

"Got it." They crept in. The building was dark, save for flickering firelight in a lower room.

"Down there," Ryvial hissed. "Step quick. They'll have heard the door."

Jumping down the uneven steps, they landed in a wide, dank room. Lissa and Vivette were there, gagged, hogtied, and tossed into a shallow punt. The rickety boat lay near an open hatch that disappeared into nothingness. Vivette's sturdy maid was tying up the cover.

The ersatz maid rushed them, daggers drawn. Ryvial danced back and Beryl struck out. The woman dodged and whistled loudly. Heavy footsteps pounded on the upper floor. Beryl braced for multiple attackers, but there was a scream from the front of the property.

:*Got one!:* Giselle exalted, then, :*But there's more coming!:*

A thuggish man plowed into the room. When he came toward her, Beryl's heart stuttered, but Alberich's stern tutelage held. She pivoted away from his rush, sidestepped, and brought the hilt of her sword down on the man's head as he stumbled by her. The blow wasn't fatal, but it dropped him next to the open hatch. For just a moment, as he struggled to rise, he was off balance. Beryl kicked out, catching him on the hip. He tumbled into the hole. For a moment his fingers scrabbled for purchase. He didn't find any.

His body disappeared into the darkness without him ever uttering a sound. There was a distant splash below.

Before Beryl could process that unnerving detail, a woman rushed in. "Heralds?" she snarled, before leaping on Ryvial's back.

That distraction allowed Vivette's maid to slice at the rope holding Vivette and Lissa's boat steady on the slanting edge of the hole. Beryl flung herself forward, grasping the rope's end as it separated from the main line. Straining against the weight, Beryl prayed her strength and body weight would counter the drag.

It was a vain hope. Beryl was strong, but not stronger than gravity. She struggled for purchase, but slid inexorably toward the hatch.

Then, miraculously, there was a firm grip on her tunic. :*I've got you!:*

:*Giselle!:*

:*Hold on!:* There was a mental grunt as Giselle kicked at the woman on Ryvial's back. Beryl heard the crack of bone but didn't dare look. A scream, then warm blood sprayed over Beryl's exposed forearms as Ryvial dispatched Vivette's maid.

"Hold on, Beryl. Hold on!" Ryvial threw himself down next to her, gripping the rope as well. "We just have to hold on."

Shouts sounded behind them. "Gods, I hope that's our backup."

"Me too."

"Close call," Ryvial noted, as a healer wrapped a wound on his neck. Two other wounds were already bandaged.

"Too close," Beryl agreed. The healer slathering ointment on Beryl's rope-burned palms grunted her agreement.

"Theon, Carter, and Marcus are recovering, as are their Companions," Talimar reported. "We've arrested Emberson and Harbing. Vivette's maid was Emberson's accomplice, not Vivette. Vivette didn't know about anything but the jewels."

Ryvial held up Vatean's key. "Investigator Mace says there's a massive chest in the parlor, full to the brim with ledgers."

Beryl grinned. "Check Vivette's dress," she added, thinking of Vivette's patting pattern. "Even unwitting, I think she's a mule."

:Unwitting is right,: came Giselle's tired riposte. A healer tended the brave Companion, who'd scraped both flanks coming through the doors to rescue Beryl.

"Highly likely," Ryvial added.

After a few minutes of contemplative silence, Talimar spoke again. "Look there." He nodded toward Lissa and Vivette, who wept in one another's arms. "I guess that's a good end to a bad business."

He rose, smiling at both Ryvial and Beryl. "Well done, Heralds. Well done."

A Tale of Two Cooks
Charlotte E. English

Dawn broke on the most important day of the Haven social season, and the pig was late.

Chef Tregan, second to arrive in Mr. Rainard's spacious, well-appointed kitchen, turned puce with horror at the discovery. Several choice expletives fell from his lips; then, "What," he said, with deadly calm, "am I supposed to serve to *her actual royal highness* with no pig?"

Lila, first to arrive, and impeccable in her cook's blacks, stood smartly chopping onions at the great stone-topped table. "I'm sure it'll get here soon, sir," she said, unperturbed, if you didn't count an internal sinking sensation as perturbation.

"It was supposed to be here *last night*," snarled the chef, clutching at his perfectly starched hat. "It was supposed to be here *yesterday*."

He had a tendency to panic, Chef Tregan. Lila observed the effects with a dispassionate eye, her knife flashing without pause. A perfectly futile response to a crisis, of course, but you couldn't reason with artists. "I'll find out what's become of it, shall I?" she suggested, when the panic showed no signs of abating.

Chef Tregan cast himself into the unsympathetic arms of a heavy oaken chair, perpetually poised to the left of the great hearth. His supervising spot, ordinarily; he'd sit enthroned like a king before his court, firing criticisms like arrows into the assembled ranks of his troops.

He also sulked in it, occasionally. "It's no use," he informed

Lila as kitchen maids and scullery lads slipped into the vast room, casting anxious sidelong glances at their tormented overseer. "It's a disaster." He added, in a bitter aside, "Hemmet never has to deal with such ill luck, does she? Oh, no. Everything goes perfectly for the great Chef *Hemmet*."

He would work his way out of his fit of self-pity, but not immediately. Until he did, the kitchen was the worst place in Mr. Rainard's grand Haven mansion to be.

And he wasn't wrong to be distressed, not really. An entire, well-fatted, premium pig was neither cheaply nor easily procured in the heart of Haven, and without it the long-planned feast stood in grave peril. No pig meant no sausages, no cormarye, no Tregan's specialty spiced pork pies. It meant they were one spit-roast short, and the calves' feet would have to stretch to all the jellies, which they wouldn't.

Lila quietly set down her knife. "Somebody get him some coffee," she instructed, and took herself out of the line of fire. Fortunately—or unfortunately, depending—she had a shrewd notion as to what had become of the missing pig.

Opposite the stone-built, luxuriously apportioned dwelling in which Lila worked stood another house taller still. If Taff Rainard's possessed all the advantages of newness and fashion, Lady Morgan's bore the unmistakable elegance of very old money. Within, the handsome old house ran with the smoothness of long habit, her ladyship's staff and retainers inherited from her aristocratic parents-in-law along with her title.

Not that Lila could just walk in. She'd tried that once, quietly slipping in at the servants' entrance at the rear, perfectly unsuspicious that she would be recognized, questioned, challenged, evicted. *Spy,* they'd called her, come skulking in to learn how things were *properly* done. She'd rarely attempted it since. But today, with her red hair stuffed under a nondescript hat and a shapeless old coat shrouding her figure, perhaps she could get away with it.

The wide street was near deserted at this hour, only a stray dog slinking past Lila on its way to beg scraps from the kitchen.

She trod softly over the smooth cobblestones as she trotted across the road and around to the servants' yard behind the house.

There was more activity there, much more; Lady Morgan had probably hauled all her staff out of their beds at three in the morning. Personally. Lila didn't know whose idea it had originally been to hold a dinner on this of all days; but whether the idea had originated with Lady Morgan or Taff Rainard, the result was as inevitable as the tides. Two houses, two hosts, two talented chefs, and two sumptuous society dinners. One victor.

Lila only wanted peace, but there wouldn't be much of that to be had today. Certainly not with Chef Tregan's pig missing.

She walked into Lady Morgan's house with the cool assurance of a person who belonged there. Terse orders emanated from the kitchens as she passed, Chef Hemmet's distinctive drawl snapping rapid commands to her underlings. Lila had no need to infiltrate that hallowed space; she knew what the menu would be, had known for weeks. Much as she might have resented being labeled a spy herself, these houses bristled with suspicion for good reason.

Besides, Ernald wasn't likely to be in the kitchen at this hour. She found him in his usual place: ensconced in his steward's office, hunched over his narrow oak desk, door open in invitation. "Enter," he said distractedly as she approached, his plum-dark eyes fixed upon a sheaf of lists before him. He was superbly neat as always, his black hair smoothed back, the black coat of his livery impeccable.

Lila didn't waste any time. "Morning, Ernald," she said affably. "Where's the pig?"

He still didn't look up. "How should I know?" he said, in a tone of bland disinterest.

Lila merely waited, arms folded, blocking the doorway.

Finally he glanced up at her, brows crimped with annoyance. "Are you going to stand there all day?"

"I would prefer not to. I've a dinner to cook for, if you hadn't heard."

For a moment, she saw in his handsome features the same

weary irritation she felt herself. It was the source of their friendship, if friends they could be called: a shared, long-suffering irritation with their employers' absurd contest. "Look, I had nothing to do with that," he told her at last.

"I don't suppose you did," she said, with perfect honesty. "But someone did—probably Hemmet, if I had to guess—and Tregan's having a crisis. I'd like the pig back, please."

"Lila. I can't help you—"

She sighed. *"Really?"*

"—because I don't know where it is. They didn't tell me."

Lila studied him. Steward of the house, meticulous at his duties, and not know what the servants had done with an entire *pig*? "And why didn't they tell you, Ernald?"

"I expect they realized I would tell *you*."

Well, so much for her secret fraternization with the enemy. "I'm not likely to find half of it turning on a spit over the kitchen fire, I suppose?"

He actually laughed a little. "If my lady wanted anything so common as *pork* served at her royal banquet, she would have directed me to buy one."

"What's common about—" began Lila, and stopped herself. He was only echoing Lady Morgan's opinions; there was no use arguing with him about them.

He answered her anyway. "Nothing, but it's no auroch, is it?"

"Or swan, I suppose," muttered Lila on her way out. "Peacock, why not?"

She briefly considered searching the house for the missing pig, but abandoned the idea. She didn't have time to go skulking, and there was too high a chance she'd be caught and thrown out anyway.

No, it was time for a much more direct course of action.

Tregan objected to the commandeering of his entire staff, at least at first.

Lila overrode him. "Do you want the pig back or not?"

"Yes, but how exactly—"

"No time for arguments!" Lila barked. "We're going. Bring everyone."

They made for an intimidating cavalcade, a grim line of black-clad servants advancing across the road in near silence, boots thudding in lockstep. Nobody tried to stop them as they advanced into Chef Hemmet's sacred domain; nobody could have.

The great lady of the kitchen had condescended to knead dough with her own hands, such was the importance of perfection today. Splendidly enormous and with the regal bearing of a queen, she stood in the place of honor at a vast, marble-topped table, fixing her arch-rival Tregan with a stare worthy of a basilisk.

"Is that new?" said Tregan, nodding at the costly table.

"I suppose you're still using wood," sniffed Hemmet. She would be a handsome woman if it weren't for the expression of sheer loathing twisting her broad, smooth features. "Oak? Deal? Hopeless for pastry."

"This'll stain," countered Tregan, rapping his knuckles against the cold marble. "A year, maybe two, and it'll look like—"

"What are you doing?" snapped Hemmet, whirling in sudden horror.

"Helping ourselves," answered Lila, liberating a large jar of preserved lemons from a shelf. She added another of pickled cherries to her haul—they'd be superb for the Pelagir garden salad—and moved on to snatch bowls full of chopped and salted vegetables standing ready upon a sideboard. Around her, Tregan and the rest of his staff were similarly employed, efficiently stripping Hemmet's kitchen of every comestible in reach.

"This is theft!" bawled the stout chef, grabbing a box of sugar crystals off a cringing kitchen maid.

"Yes," Lila agreed. "Yes, it is." She handed off her acquisitions to Kitty from the scullery, and went swiftly on, elbowing aside any of Hemmet's folk who were so unwise as to try to stop her.

"I'll have you all arrested!" shouted Hemmet, as red as her famous pickled cherries, breathless with rage. "Drop it! Drop it now! Percy, call the watch!"

Chef Tregan had closed the kitchen door, and placed himself in front of it. He wasn't a large man, but he was strong; with his feet planted wide, his arms folded, and an air of immovable resolve, he made a formidable enough barrier.

"Call the Watch," he invited her. "Go ahead. And I'll be filing a report about a certain missing pig, which I am sure nobody would be likely to find upon these premises. Would they?"

There was a heavy silence, broken by Hemmet. "Any fool can see I'm doing you a favor, Lars. Pork, indeed! For the cream of Haven society!"

"Flashy ingredients don't make for a better dish, Nance," he retorted. "Only skill can do that. My pig, please."

"Fine," growled Hemmet. "Percy, escort *Mr.* Tregan and two of his staff down to the cellar, please. And then escort them and their *pork* out again."

Ten minutes later, Lila emerged into the free air of the street with Tregan and George at her elbow and a remarkably heavy carcass slung between them. The mood, once back in their own kitchen, was jubilant, but Lila couldn't shake a gnawing sense of doubt. Had they cleverly outwitted Nance Hemmet and her staff, or had it all been just a little bit too easy?

"Do you think," she said to the chef in an undertone, "we maybe shouldn't use it?"

Tregan, engaged in butchery, stared at her in horror. "What? We just got it back?"

Lila, uncharacteristically uncertain, hesitated. "I know, but . . ."

Tregan didn't wait for her to finish her sentence, already shaking his head. "I don't know what you're worried about now, but it's too late. We don't have time, Lila. If we could've just replaced the pork dishes with something else, we would've done that to begin with, hm?"

There was no answering that: he was absolutely right. And

what did she have to set against his all-too-reasonable argument? Nothing but a vague sense of unease, and a notion that
the meat hadn't felt quite right under her hands. But it looked
fine, smelled fine, in all likelihood *was* fine. So, then.

Lila went back to her tasks and tried to put the matter out of
her mind.

And when that didn't work, she took the first opportunity of
penning a note to her cousin. Having given it to a kitchen boy
with strict instructions to deliver it within the hour, she felt a
little better.

Afternoon was winding down into evening before Clea remembered about the dinner.

It had been all she could think about when she'd woken that
morning, too early after a night of fitful, broken sleep. She had
a headful of fading nightmares and a sinking sensation of impending doom, easily attributable to the looming specter of
Taff Rainard's latest extravaganza. The man was a liability, a
social climber with a network of carefully cultivated connections across all strata of Haven society. Too powerful to be ignored, he was not to be too much encouraged, either.

That meant the princess wasn't going anywhere near his
"Royal Gala," held in her honor or not.

It also meant somebody else needed to show up in her place.
Someone with enough prestige to pacify the man when his
guest of honor failed to appear. Someone capable and steady,
with the skills to manage the situation should it turn difficult.

Clea, King's Own, and with over twenty years of experience
as a Herald behind her, fit the bill perfectly. Worse luck for her.

She'd gone out with Daly, her Companion, around the middle of the morning, clattering into the city with a view to enjoying *something* about her day—only to get bogged down
mediating a dispute between two tavern-keeps. Not really her
job, but she'd been the Herald on the spot, and the matter had
somehow taken hours to resolve.

"A quiet night in our rooms for both of us, hm?" she said to
Daly when, at last, they'd toiled wearily back up the hill to the

palace. "And a *bath*." She slapped him gently on the rump, speeding him on his way to food and rest, dreaming of both herself. Her youth had deserted her some years ago, leaving a lot of inexplicable aches in its place; she wanted to *lie down*.

Daly snorted, and lipped at her sleeve. *:If only.:*

"What do you mean if—oh, no." The gala. Taff Rainard. Clea's heart plummeted into her boots.

:You may have time for the bath, though.: Daly snorted again, rather explosively, and added, *:Hopefully.:*

"Point taken." Clea trudged back to her rooms at what she hoped would pass for a smart pace, entertaining wistful day-dreams of a smooth and easy dinner event, and an early night after all.

The folded note slipped under her door swiftly put paid to that idea.

Trouble, the note read in a familiar scrawl. *Don't eat anything with pork in it, right? Just in case! —Lila.*

In case? In case of *what*?

Clea worked her way through three minutes of deep breathing, and hustled to bathe and change. If she hurried, she *might* have time to track her cousin down prior to the gala's opening, and find out what exactly she meant by *trouble*.

And what it could possibly have to do with pork.

The great Taff Rainard could almost have been mistaken for a king, such was the extent of his sumptuary. Painted and coiffed, draped in velvets, perfumed, even—what a mess. Clea kept her distaste from showing in her face only through an effort of will, smiling blandly as she offered herself in substitution for the princess.

He wasn't pleased. He had a pinched face, formed for petulance, but what she saw in it as he clasped her hands in greeting more nearly resembled rage: a vicious flash of it, there and gone behind an insincere smile of his own. His glance flicked away from her, out of the grand front door standing open onto the street: beyond it, guests in dazzling finery were arriving in a steady stream of dignitaries, some of them entering Rainard's house, and some his neighbor's opposite. Lady Morgan.

Clea reclaimed his attention with a pointed cough. "Herald Faye shall be representing her highness at Lady Morgan's festivities, I believe."

She watched him work it out. Faye was well respected, but she wasn't the King's Own. He brightened. "Ah! And you are stuck with me, Lady Clea. I trust my poor entertainments will prove sufficient consolation." He shook back a stray blond ringlet, lavishly oiled, and smirked.

All too willing to suppose some particular compliment was intended to him by her presence in his house, rather than his rival's, which suited her purposes well enough; she let it pass. Actually, they took it in turns to humor the troublesome two, but it was just as well that he hadn't noticed.

"I am sure I'll be delighted," she said, a blatant lie, and permitted herself a small sigh. Gods, but she hated politicking. "Particularly if it might be possible to—oh, forgive me, I shouldn't presume . . ."

"Not at all, dear lady," he said grandly. "It is of course my pleasure to fulfill any wish of His Majesty's Own."

Clea's smile was making her face hurt; she needed to get away from him. "Oh, it's a silly thing, but—I amuse myself with a little cooking, when I am not on duty, and I'd be so interested to see how your excellent staff prepares for such a banquet."

An odd request, by any measure. She hoped he would attribute it to a sort of aristocratic eccentricity, rather than the natural product of her common upbringing. She certainly wouldn't be so foolish as to admit she was a close relative of one of his kitchen employees; not just now, anyway. If there was trouble brewing, she needed him on her side.

"Ah . . . by all means, Lady Clea, by all means!" he said, with a little laugh. "My chef is not to be disturbed at present—delicate procedures, I'm sure you understand—but I shall put his second at your disposal." He bowed beamingly, and a grand gesture brought a black-suited young man to his side. "Escort our guest of honor to the kitchens," he instructed, already turning away, toward other, less peculiar guests.

Clea, eager to get herself out of the train of finery and falsehoods, followed her guide away from the crush and the chatter with a sense of profound relief.

The clamor of raised voices, clattering pans, and running feet in the kitchens rivaled the tumult upstairs. At least this was the racket of honest labor; Clea felt rather more at home there, even if it was as hot as a furnace. She scanned the crowd of black-clad workers until she spotted a familiar wisp of flame-red hair peeking out from under a dark cap.

"Lil!" she roared.

Lila came over at once. "Thank goodness you're here," she said, pushing a sweat-soaked curl out of her eyes.

"Why? What's happened?"

Lila took her elbow, and walked her back out into the relative quiet of the corridor beyond. "There's been an incident," she said gravely, and then proceeded to relate a tangled tale of pranks, petty theft, and pork dishes. Clea heard it with a growing sense of incredulity.

"I have no proof that anything's wrong," she concluded. "And I might be wrong—hope I am—but Tregan wouldn't listen and I thought—"

"Have you told Rainard?" Clea interrupted.

Lila just stared at her. "Have you *met* Rainard?"

Excellent point. Clea sighed. "There isn't much I can do without more information, and it's very late in the day—"

"It might be contaminated," Lila said.

"The meat?"

"Yes."

"You think these people would commit *murder* to win this absurd contest?"

"No," said Lila firmly, to Clea's relief. "Not on purpose. But can you imagine the social drubbing Rainard would get if half the guests at his Royal Gala took sick after? Tregan would lose his job, which would please Lady Morgan's chef. Unfortunately, the rest of us would, too. And it might not take much of a misjudgment to put any guests in fragile health in serious danger."

Clea felt the beginnings of a severe headache blossom at her temples. "Tell me at least that your lot haven't counter-sabotaged Lady Morgan's party."

"Of course we haven't. That I would never permit."

She'd said "I" rather than "we," Clea noted, which implied that Chef Tregan might have had other ideas. "You were all in that house, though, weren't you? This morning? Could you know for certain that nobody slipped a few herbs into a soup pot on the way out?"

Lila opened her mouth to deny it, but couldn't. She swore instead. "I'll ask," she said. "On pain of a summary firing if anybody lies."

"Don't bother," Clea replied, steeling herself for a scene. "I think the situation's already gone beyond that."

"What are you going to do?" Lila's round face had lost its customary smile, pinched instead with worry.

"I'm going to make myself very unpopular," Clea said. "Send Tregan up. Tell him he's wanted by the King's Own."

Clea left him to stew while she marched over the road and collared an anxious-looking lad in the livery of Lady Morgan's household. She sent him to fetch Faye, trusting that her forbidding countenance—she really was rather severely annoyed—would have him running at top speed. She waited outside, feet planted in the middle of the street between the two houses, arms folded, radiating resolve.

The other Herald arrived promptly, elegant in her dress Whites, though she looked almost as tired as Clea felt. "Problem?" she said quickly, taking in Clea's combative stance.

"We need to shut these parties down," Clea said.

Faye's dark eyes widened. "Is there a threat?"

"Sort of," Clea replied. "Health hazard. Can you get Chef Hemmet to come up here? Then start getting the guests out. Send them home. Dinner's canceled."

Faye didn't waste time asking questions, mercifully. She vanished back into Lady Morgan's house, and within a few short minutes Clea found herself with an outraged chef on either side of her, and a fine headache throbbing behind her eyes. "We appear to have some things to discuss," she informed them.

"Not now, we don't," snapped Hemmet. "I've an important dinner to finish."

"I have the most important dinner of the season to finish," countered Tregan. "You'll excuse *me*, if you please."

"You don't," said Clea. "Dinner's off. There's a health hazard, or hadn't you heard? Contaminated food."

"Errant nonsense," blustered Hemmet, transferring her glare from Tregan to Clea herself. "My kitchen is kept impeccably clean—"

"That's ridiculous!" said Tregan at the same time. "Nothing is more important to a great chef than keeping *his* tools and environment in—"

Clea interrupted. "You," she said, pointing a finger at Hemmet, "extracted a certain pig from the storerooms of Mr. Rainard's house early this morning."

Hemmet abruptly shut her mouth. "A harmless prank," she tried. "They got it back, didn't they? No harm done."

"Not yet, no thanks to you. You didn't quite return it in its original state, did you? You added something. An emetic? A poison?"

"Poison!" gasped Hemmet. "I would never—" But a guilty flush stained her cheeks, and Clea didn't miss the sideways glance she directed at Tregan.

"And you—" Clea barked at Tregan, when he seemed minded to interject, "—did much the same to some of her dishes when you were in *that* kitchen this morning."

"You have no proof I did any such thing," retorted Tregan hotly.

"I don't," Clea admitted. "But I also have no proof that you didn't, so I have no choice but to shut both these events down and send all guests back to their homes. I imagine you will both find yourselves in search of new employment after today—and since it is by fortune only that her highness isn't here tonight, and thus has not been put at risk, you may be grateful that you aren't in far greater trouble."

That silenced them at last, though from the twin glares of pure, murderous rage they were directing at each other, Clea judged that they had yet to fully absorb her message.

"Don't blame each other," she told them. "You are both responsible for this debacle." Together with Lady Morgan and Taff Rainard, probably, but they were a thornier problem to handle. She'd leave them to someone else, someone with the delicate touch necessary for convoluted politics.

She paused, for it struck her that their mutual loathing really had written itself across both faces in similar ways. Hemmet was by far the larger of the two, her features cushioned under layers of fat, but still, the resemblance . . .

"While we're here," said Clea through a sinking feeling. "Perhaps I can be of assistance in mediating your dispute?"

Clea's name was now mud with at least half of Haven's nobility, but that was all right. At least they weren't sick. At least nobody was dead.

It was past three in the morning, and she badly needed sleep. But she needed another kind of rest more—repose of the spirit, say—and for that, she wanted Daly. With a curry comb in hand and the familiar scents of her Companion's glossy hide around her, she was rapidly calming.

"They're siblings, can you believe it?" she told him, leaning against his reassuringly sturdy flank. "Half-siblings, that is."

:All too easily,: Daly opined. :There's a sad story there, I think.:

"Yes," sighed Clea.

She and Faye had split the two chefs up after a while, and spoken to them separately; there was no getting sense out of them while they were still raging at one another. There had emerged a disjointed tale of an unhappy marriage, one parent favoring the boy, the other the girl. Of an endless contest no one could win; of a brother and sister pitted against one another, goaded to ever greater attempts to prevail, at any cost. Abominable. She'd felt pity for them both, despite her disgust at their recklessness.

"Still," she said. "What is pitiable in a child is harder to excuse in an adult. And these two would have endangered a great many people."

:I don't suppose you got them to make up, did you?: asked Daly.

"Of course not," Clea sighed. "I don't think they could hear each other at all. All they could see was the favorite of the parent who hated them. The best I could do was get them to agree to stay away from each other in the future, though I think we may have to keep an eye on that."

Daly lipped at her sleeve in his usual gesture of approval. *:Sometimes that's all you can do,:* he told her. *:Not all wounds can be healed, no matter how much you want to.:*

And that was the one thing Clea struggled with as a Herald. Undeterred by peril, she could even tolerate the politicking, however much she disliked it. But the sense of helpless failure when she couldn't *fix* something—that stung. She'd remember the unhappy siblings for some time to come.

:Time to sleep,: Daly nudged her. *:Get a cake, too. You'll feel better in the morning.:*

"A cake for me and none for you?" Clea smiled. "Surely not."

:One cake for you,: Daly said firmly. *:Two for me.:*

Clea laughed. "Coming up," she said, and went off in search of yet another kitchen.

A Bite and a Pint
Louisa Swann

The Companion exploded into a run, hooves not quite thundering through the soft sand covering the beach. Petril clutched at the pommel, desperate not to fall. He swallowed hard, trying to force his heart down out of his throat.

:*I've told you over and over—I won't let you fall. Relax and listen to the beat of my hooves. Rhythmic, yes? Graceful as a dancer, someone once said. I flow over the earth like an early morning breeze . . . wish I could remember who told me that. I'd love to give that man a bracelet*—Watch yourself! *I said "listen to my hoofbeats" not join my hooves on the ground!*:

"I'm try . . . ing!" The words jounced breathlessly from his mouth, joining the wind in his ears, the slap of his bottom against leather, Rina's heavy breathing, and . . . whining? Was that *him*? *Whining*?

:*Tell me about your village.*:

"I . . . already . . . did . . ." Somehow, he managed to get the words out through gritted teeth. Experience had taught him that opening his mouth while Rina was moving faster than a walk almost always led to biting his tongue.

:*Practice your Mindspeech,*: she ordered. :*Then you don't have to open your mouth.*:

Petril growled deep in his chest. Mindspeaking had come naturally to him—until Rina had shown up, insisting he shield himself from the emotions that kept hammering at him. Somewhere between shielding and Mindspeaking, his mental tongue got tangled worse than a fishing net in a storm.

:And that's why you need to practice. Trust me. One day you'll wake up and both shielding and Mindspeech will come naturally. Now, tell me about your village.:

:On . . . th' . . . shores . . . of . . . Lake Evendim—:

He groaned as Rina jumped a small pile of driftwood, and he slapped down on her back with a loud *smack!*—

Followed by an emotional thunderstorm. *Anger, confusion, dismay, outrage, fear* . . . Petril's head started to throb.

:Shields, youngling.: Rina slowed to a walk. *:You can't let a bit of jouncing break down your shields.:* Judging by the bell-like ringing coming from the Companion's hooves, the sand had given way to jagged gray stone.

Pain and confusion warred in his head—

:That's because you keep trying to force the shielding just as you force your Mindspeech. Relax, and be at ease. Building a proper shield is like trying to get a butterfly to land on your hand. If you try to force the butterfly to land, all you'll do is squash it. Stop squashing your shielding and your Mindspeaking. Relax, put all the pieces in place, and let it happen.:

Petril's answer was interrupted by an angry shout.

"Ye almost killed me, ye stupid fishwife!"

:That doesn't sound like a warm welcome.:

Startled, Petril glanced around. He'd been so focused on the pain in his head, he hadn't noticed they'd arrived at the village.

The familiar sight sliced through him, leaving a burning trail through his heart.

Home.

The village longhouses—one for each of the families—radiated off a central firepit like spokes on a cartwheel that had been cut in half. Oakwood smoke wafted from the pit, its familiar scent drifting through the air. He was surprised to see the fishing boats pulled up on the shore when most of the men would normally be out fishing.

Instead, everyone seemed to be gathered around the firepit—not feeding the fire, chopping vegetables, mixing dough, and otherwise preparing the evening meal—but waving their fists and *arguing.*

"'Tweren't me what done it! Don't have ta kill no one ta prove me sweets is better'n that swill ye call ale."

That voice was as familiar to him as his own. Petril stretched tall in the saddle, striving to see over the knot of villagers. Looked like everyone—nigh on fifty fisherfolk—had gathered for whatever was going on.

"Yer *sweets*'d gag a nanny goat raised on nettles—"

In the dusk, it was difficult to tell one villager from another. He knew the two women by the fire, women who looked about to pull each other's hair out. One of them was his mum.

"Guess news o' this 'ere feud done gone all the way ta Haven." A man taller than most of the others shouldered his way through the milling villagers. He jerked his chin in Petril's general direction. "How about it, Herald. Ye 'ere on official business or wha'?"

Feud? Herald? Petril glanced over his shoulder.

:*They mean you, youngling.*: Rina snorted, tossing her head up and down.

"Tha' ain't no 'erald," another man said. It took a moment for Petril to recognize Old Man Woodson. "Tha's Willow's boy, gone nigh a year now. Whatcha doin' on tha' fancy 'orse, boy?"

"Petril? Is that you, son?"

A hand waved at him from the sea of faces. Petril's heart hop-skipped like a startled bunny. No mistaking the "thunder rumbling off in the distance" sound of his da's voice. Petril's throat tightened as he realized how much he'd missed his da—missed his whole family, in fact.

"Da!" He lifted his hand to return the wave as a raven swooped out of a nearby oak.

Something warm and gooey and oh-so-stinky plopped on his head, trickling through his hair and down the back of his neck. With a loud croak, the raven sailed over the villagers' heads and vanished between longhouses.

"Erk!" Petril swiped at his hair. His hand encountered a blob he didn't want to identify. A heartbeat later, his nose confirmed what his hand and mind already knew—he'd been bombed by that blasted raven.

The raven swooped back in his direction, abruptly changing course and diving at the woman his mum had been arguing with.

"Get tha' thing off me!" The woman confronting his mum waved wildly at the air. "First ye try ta poison me, then yer raven attacks!"

Her last words ended in a shriek.

Petril used his sleeve to scrub the goo from his head . . . not a good idea, considering he had only two tunics—the one he wore, and a spare in his saddlebag.

:You stink like a raven roost.:

"Shame on ya, Gilly girl," said his mum. "Ye know better'n tha'."

Gilly? Who was *Gilly*?

:I believe she was talking to the bird who just used your head as a privy.:

"Whatya doin' on tha 'orse?"

Petril looked down, not surprised to find his little sister had wormed her way through the mass of villagers. "Rina's not a 'orse," he replied. "This 'ere's a Companion. *My* Companion."

"Come on, then. Ye ain't no Herald," Tinnie said. She wrinkled her long nose the way only Tinnie's nose could wrinkle. Other than being taller and skinnier, his little sister looked the same as she had when he'd left a year ago. Dark, short-cropped hair that stood on end, falling victim to whatever his baby sister's newest "adventure" might be. "And if'n ye ain't no Herald, tha' there's no Companion. It be a 'orse."

:Don't kick 'er,: Petril warned. *:She don't know any better.:*

:I don't kick children.:

"Yer right, I'm not a Herald." Petril grinned at his sister. "Not yet, anyway. After I finish training, ye'll be telling a different story. But Rina be a Companion, no question about it." He started to slide off Rina, thought about how foolish he'd likely look, half-falling to the ground—and stayed in the saddle.

"Tha' ain't the same 'orse ye left 'ere on, son. Whatya been up ta? Come on, Lizzie, give me some space." Da carefully moved a young woman aside, then grinned up at Petril.

"I'm guessin' tha's a story best told after supper—" Mum said, shoving her way through the milling bodies until she stood beside his da. Petril was startled to see some of the villagers—maybe half—glaring at her as she passed.

She planted both hands on her hips. "Don't ye let these no-account idiots fill yer head wit lies, now."

:Three sides to every story—:

:Yers, mine, and the fly on the wall.:

:So you were *paying attention.:*

Petril studied the villagers, surprised to see so many strangers. "Wha's going on, Mum?"

"Yer mum tried to poison Brewsmistress Hannah, is wha'," someone said.

"Ain't wha' happened and ye know it!"

The villagers started talking over each other, turning an otherwise peaceful evening into a maelstrom of noise and emotion.

Petril closed his eyes and reinforced his shields, struggling to remain calm and in control.

:Good.:

:There anything I can do? Besides sending for an actual *Herald?:* Petril wasn't sure he could Mindcall that far. He'd never tested his gift over any substantial distance.

:While you can't sit in judgement, you can learn the facts. Figure out what exactly is going on. I've a feeling there's more to this feud than we're seeing . . . or hearing.:

:They won't listen ta me. Ta them, I'm just a boy.:

:Give it a try. I'll help where I can.:

He raised his voice, directing it as best he could over the grumbling crowd. "Listen. Most o' ye know me. Petril, son of Okenbar and Willow. I went away 'bout a year ago, escortin' a stolen 'orse and 'er babe back to Haven, then ta Kata'shin'a'in where they belonged. Bunch o' stuff happened while I was there. Including this Companion 'ere—Rina—Choosing me. No, I ain't no Herald, not yet. I'm headed fer trainin' once we leave 'ere. But I always been good at puzzles and riddles, so Rina says we kin check out the facts. Pass 'em on to a full-blown 'erald if'n need be."

"Don't need no boy stepping in." Petril didn't recognize the man speaking. "Wha' we need is—"

"Shut yer mouth, Robby Nicks," the woman who'd just been attacked by the raven said. She'd followed Mum through the crowd. "This is 'tween Willow 'n' me."

"And the entire village!" someone yelled.

"Companion or not, this is Willow's boy," the woman continued. "How can we be certain he won't take his mum's side?"

With a start, Petril realized the woman speaking was Miz Hannah, wife of the local brewer. She was stockier than the last time he'd seen her, and gray streaks lined her dark hair.

:A brewer? In a village this small?:

:The smaller the village, the more need for brew—that's what Brewmistress Hannah used ta say. Not sure why she and Mum're at each other's throats. They always got along, though they weren't close.:

"I wouldn't be passin' no judgements," Petril said, raising his voice again. "Jus' findin' out wha' the world's goin' on." *Easy peasy, bluegill breezy.*

Rina snorted, the movement jangling her bridle. *:Suggest we start after the evening meal. My belly's about to meet my backbone. You know how I get when my blood sugar is low.:*

:How kin I not know? Ye won't let up bout yer empty belly till it's filled.:

:Sounds like a youngling I know—:

"I did nothing ta your weak-minded ale—" Mum's voice rose above the general roar of the villagers.

"Ye poisoned it, ye miserable fishwife! Poisoned it good. Looks 'n smells like a barrel o' rotten plum juice. No one'll drink it now."

"I did *not* need ta poison yer already poisonous brew in order ta prove me sweets be th' best."

"Why don't we all go eat supper and meet back around th' fire—" Petril started.

Miz Hannah dashed a mug of ale in his mum's face. "Ye drink yer own poison, then, Miz Baker of Rotten Goods. But ye ain't won th' day. I'll go brew another batch, taking me time, right and proper. One that ain't tainted. Then we'll see who's goods is th' best."

The woman spun on her heel and stalked off toward the far longhouse.

Mum glared after her, using the hem of her apron to dry her face. A dusting of flour highlighted one cheekbone.

"While ye been off doing who knows what, yer two oldest brothers found themselves wives," Da said as though Mum hadn't just been doused in ale.

"Twins, actually," Mum said, sounding just as unconcerned. "They live in th' next village over." She pulled a scarf from her apron. Instead of using it to dry herself a bit more, she handed the scarf to Petril and nodded at the goo staining his sleeve.

Heat flooded his face as he accepted the scarf and scrubbed at the sleeve, trying not to gag at the stench. He focused on the sound of waves not too far in the distance.

Whether the villagers decided to take Petril's advice or their bellies reminded them supper was long past due, fisherfolk shuffled off in different directions, families heading back to their longhouses, lighting torches along the way. A few travelers gathered close around the firepit.

Two brothers married, Petril mused. And he hadn't even known. "The Heralds were supposed ta tell ye I had ta go ta Katashin'a'in—"

Da nodded. "Message came sayin' ye was 'on a mission,' whatever tha's supposed ta mean. Got the point, though. Ye weren't comin' home. Ye ken yer brothers aren't the waitin' type. Figured ya'd find out when ye got home. And so ye did."

:Two down and five ta go,: he told Rina. *:Leaves five brothers scattered around the village somewhere.:* "Where they be hiding, then?" he asked. "Bennie and Jem and the rest o' the lot?"

He urged Rina a bit closer to the village well, where he not only managed to dismount onto the stone wall without falling *into* the well, but to look somewhat competent while feeling like he was in freefall. His hands clung to the stirrup leathers, refusing to let go until he'd reassured himself both feet were firmly planted on the stones. Then he loosened his grip and stepped down to the ground.

Rina busied herself munching grass.

He wanted to ask why the brothers weren't all nearby, protecting their mum, but decided that might be taking things too far—

"I'll take care o' yer 'orse." Tinnie snatched the reins from his hand before he could stop her.

"Ye don't stop callin' Rina a 'orse, she's gonna stomp ye right good." He extricated the reins from his sister's hand—not without a bit of difficulty. "Rina 'ere's a *Companion*."

"Don't see it," Trinnie said, standing with her fists planted on her hips in a manner eerily reminiscent of their mum. She cocked her head to one side, studying Rina. "If'n this be a Companion, tha' means ye was Chosen. No 'orse—magic or otherwise—would choose a scrawny bluegill like ye."

:Perhaps I'll amend my "don't kick children" rule.:

:She's jus' messin' wit ye. Part o' who she be.:

"Come along, Trinnie." Mum held out her hand. "Let yer brother take care o' his . . . friend . . . while we finish setting supper. Petril, do whatever needs doing ta make Rina comfortable, then join us."

Petril nodded. All he really needed to do was get Rina's saddle off along with her bridle and harness. There was plenty of grass around the well to fill her belly.

He used the well once again, this time as leverage to pull off the saddle. Saddling and unsaddling the Companion had been the hardest chore to accomplish during their journey from Ka-ta'shin'a'in.

"I need ta grow at least six hands ta be able ta care fer ye proper," he told Rina with a grunt.

:All in good time, Chosen. All in good time.:

"We got a bit o' time before the supper bell," Da said.

Petril glanced over his shoulder, surprised to find his da standing near the well. "Kin we talk while I finish gettin' Rina settled for the night?"

His da nodded, grabbing two stools from the base of a nearby water oak.

:Ye'll be good here, right?: he asked Rina. *:I could insist ye come inta the longhouse—:*

:I will not *spend the night listening to more humans snore!:*

Petril grinned as he stacked the saddle and gear in a neat pile near the oak, then slipped a soft brush from his saddlebags and started grooming Rina's silky hide, making rhythmic circles that had her purring contentedly as he worked.

:I do not purr. I hum.:

:Sounds like purrin' ta me.:

"Appears tha' things're going smooth as a fine day's sailing for ya, son," Da said. He'd stuffed his tanglewood pipe with sweetgrass and lit it, sending curls of sweet smoke drifting around the tree.

More than a handful of stools sat around the firepit, a common sight during the warm summer months. Most of the stools were occupied by folks Petril didn't know—men and a few women. They ate and talked quietly among themselves, casting a look or two his way now and again.

"I been holdin' me own," Petril agreed. He nodded at the folks around the fire. "This feud thing bringing in strangers, then?"

He climbed on the well wall, waited for Rina to move closer, then went to work on her back.

His da drew on his pipe and blew a few smoke rings before answering. "Yer mum and Brewmistress Hannah—"

"Brewmistress?"

"Brewmaster missed a line when 'e was out fishin' last spring. Took a tumble inta the lake. Never found 'is body. So Miz Hannah took over. Ye might say tha's when the trouble started."

"Miz Hannah—"

"*Brewmistress* Hannah," his da corrected.

"Brewmistress Hannah and Mum never did get on very well." As much as he loved his mum, Petril had been on the receiving end of a tongue lashing or two.

"The brewmistress don't much care for your mum's *assertiveness*."

"Stubbornness is more like it." The words were out of Petril's mouth before he had a chance to think about what he was saying. But his da only chuckled.

:*Someone seems interested in my saddle.*: Rina sounded more amused than irritated. Petril glanced at the saddle at the base of the tree, but didn't see anything out of place.

"Tha' too. Anyway, they got this thing goin'," Da continued. "Yer mum claims her sweets are far and away better 'n the Brewmistress's best brew. O' course, the Brewmistress won't stand for it. Thing is—she's not really *brewin'*, like her husband used ta do. More like distillin', takin' ordinary Evendim grapes and makin' 'em inta something special. Craftin's wha' she calls it. Craftin' her own special smokewine. An' yer mum's doing more'n baking honeybread. She's makin' sweets that'll melt in yer mouth. Every other fortnight, they bring out their best and force the villagers to try it. Half the village is partial to yer mum's sweets. Half prefers the wine."

:*Little creature is persistent,*: Rina noted.

Petril squinted at the saddle again and thought he might have seen movement. *Just smoke,* he decided, finishing Rina's back with a long stroke. He leaned close, inhaling her fresh scent.

"Somewhere along the line, their somewha' friendly competition turned inta an honest-ta-bluegill feud, complete with schemin' and prankin' and all sorts o' shenanigans. Never anythin' like this, though. Nothin' serious. Back and forth, like a sturgeon bone saw. Villagers don't hesitate ta jump in."

"Wha's yer opinion?" Petril asked, finishing Rina's grooming with a sturdy round of slapping with cupped hands. Rina groaned, leaning into his hands. :*Yer a mite bigger than I am. Keep pushing like that, and I'll end up like a squished ant underneath yer magnificent being.*: His Companion grunted, but the pressure eased enough for him to finish his chore.

"Ye know I'm partial ta yer mum's honeybread, and her new sweets be somethin' special. Gotta admit the new wine is pretty good, too. *Evendim Fine*. Tha's what the brewmistress calls it. Clear as spring pitch, and guaranteed ta knock a man outta his boat."

:Looks like your saddlebag has the creature's attention.:

Petril squinted at the saddle with the bags piled beside it. Was that a little . . . hand?

He closed his eyes and opened them, staring hard at the place he'd seen—or thought he'd seen—a tiny, black hand.

Nothing.

"Ye look ta be near done there." His da tapped out his pipe and gestured to the second stool. "Rest yer feet and tell me a bit about this Heraldin' business."

Petril didn't have the heart to tell his da he'd been resting his feet all day. He gave Rina a final pat, tucked the brush back into his saddlebag, and perched on the stool beside his da. "Not much business t' it yet. Rina's teachin' me a bit about shieldin' myself—mental stuff Heralds do. Most o' my teachin'll come when we get back ta Haven."

He kicked at the grass by his feet, then pulled a blade and chewed on it. "Can't seem ta get the hang o' ridin', though. Rina says I'm too distracted. I need to 'listen' to her feet, whatever tha' means." He blew out a breath. "I've tried, Da. Really tried, but it ain't workin'. *I* ain't workin'. What good's a Herald who can't ride his own Companion?"

For once, Rina remained quiet, her presence in his mind warm, but not intrusive.

"Ye know the water be me home," his da finally said. "Lived 'ere my entire life. Only made a few trips ta the Outside. I know boats like I know the color o' yer mum's eyes."

Petril nodded.

"Ye also know we get a lot o' travelers through here, lookin' fer cleaning stones and such," Da continued. "Shin'a'in as well as folks from other places. I remember one story. About learnin' to ride—no specifics, mind ye. Jus' general stuff. Fascinatin'."

Petril waited for his da to go on but the man seemed content to let the silence draw out. "Wha'd she say? About riding?"

"Wha?" Da looked like he'd been lost in a dream. "Not

much. Jus' tha' they start ridin' almost as soon as they ken walk. Bareback, ye see. Easier ta feel the horse tha' way."

:If you have anything of value in your saddlebags, you might want to secure it a bit better.:

:Wha' ye on about? Are ye hearin' wha' me da's sayin'?:

"Ye mean they ride without a saddle?" Petril gaped at his da. He couldn't imagine not having something to grab hold of.

"No saddle or blanket or anything," Da went on. "Way I understand it—they don't even use reins. Don't know how they manage to guide their horses, but . . ."

Again his voice trailed off, but this time Petril didn't interrupt the silence.

:Ye ever hear such a thing, Rina?:

:Of course. That creature seems to have found something he likes in your saddlebag . . . Yep. He's got your tunic.:

:Wha'?:

Irritated, Petril glanced at the saddle . . .

And saw his spare tunic—his only spare tunic—inching toward the fire. One side of the tunic dragged flat in the grass that gave way to sand around the pit. The other side was oddly shaped, like someone had stuffed a long tube into the tunic and halfway down one sleeve. The tube bunched and rolled, bunched and rolled, and somehow made progress.

"Wait!" Petril leapt to his feet, sending the stool over backward.

"Wha's wrong, son?"

Petril pointed at the tunic now halfway to the fire, bunching and rolling, bunching and rolling. "Tha's my tunic!"

Rina sighed, a dramatic sound that let him know what a suffering soul she was. *:Told you to pay attention. In answer to your other questions—bareback is one way of learning to ride. Supposed to be easier for a human to feel how a horse—or a Companion—moves.:*

"Appears ye might've brough a boggle wit ye," Da teased.

"Not funny." Petril jogged toward the tunic, reached down and grabbed at the hem . . . just as the tunic jerked away.

:I told you someone was interested in your things.:

Frustrated, Petril grabbed at the tunic again, only to have it move out of reach.

:*Did ye actually see wha' tha'* "interested thing" *is?:*

:*Not really. Just a little hand. Looked a lot like yours, come to think of it. In fact, I was wondering if you're missing a little brother—:*

He lunged at the tunic worming its way toward the fire and finally got a fistful of fabric. "Gotcha!"

He lifted the hem, expecting to see . . . he wasn't quite sure what he expected to see underneath. The tunic let out a sharp squeal.

Then it growled—sort of like a disgruntled cat . . . but not.

He still couldn't see the creature—whatever it was. Somehow it'd wriggled its way *inside* his tunic, not underneath it. He caught a scent of musk and fresh water, then the fabric heaved and twisted.

And attacked.

Growing up, Petril had imagined deaths of every kind—all properly averted, being that he was a pretend hero and all. But he'd never imagined Death by Tunic.

"Come on, then!" He skipped out of the way, doubled the end of the tunic over the heaving, hissing hump, and finally managed to roll the whole mess into a ball. He lifted the ball and held the surprisingly light bundle tight in his arms, wondering what to do.

Felt like he'd caught a small fisher cat—a small, extremely *angry* fisher cat.

The struggle intensified, punctuated by jabs with sharp teeth.

"Cut tha' out, now! No one's gonna hurt ya."

The bundle bit him. Sank its long fangs into his left forearm for what seemed an eternity.

Yep—Death by Tunic.

Da tucked his pipe away and rose to his feet. "Stay calm, son—"

Calm? How was he supposed to stay calm with a biting tunic attached to his arm?

The tunic let go just as Petril dropped the bundle and jumped back, blood spreading down his sleeve, managing to join the bird splatter near his cuff.

:Certainly didn't expect that.*:* Rina pointed her chin at the creature humping its way past the firepit, bedraggled tunic trailing behind as it wove between stools. Folks scattered left and right, doing their best to stay out of the angry creature's way.

Petril blinked, staring in confusion. "Was tha' a . . . *otter*?"

What was an otter doing in the village? And why was it making off with his tunic?

"Petril, meet Chomper, Brewmistress Hannah's 'pet.' Tha' creature's more trouble than yer baby sister, though it be hard ta say wha's worse—Chomper, or yer mum's bird."

Bird? The raven?

Petril hugged his bleeding arm close. "Didn't have ta bite me. I weren't hurting it none." He took a hesitant step toward the otter, who'd stopped on the far side of the firepit. It stood on its hind legs and peered around, as if trying to decide where to go.

"Come on, now. Tha's me only good tunic!"

The otter glared at him and growled, hand-like paws scrabbling at the fabric still clinging to its fur.

A scream split the air, more a scream of rage than a scream of pain. Petril glanced around, looking for the source as Chomper shook the tunic free and took off at a run, his long back rising and falling, fur glistening in the firelight.

"Tha' be yer mum." Da headed toward the longhouse, his long legs making short work of the distance. "Best see wha's got her net in a tangle afore someone gets hurt."

Petril grabbed the tunic and shook off the dirt, groaning at a new tear. He hurried after his da, arriving at the longhouse in time to see his mum leaving. He took a step backward as she stomped past, a determined look on her narrow face, the anger in her eyes reflecting the fire from the pit even at a distance.

Da moved in front of her. "Why don't ye tell me wha's happened?"

Mum shifted to the left, then to the right, but Da wouldn't let her pass.

"Tha' . . . *fishwife*," she snarled, then shouted, "Brewmistress Hannah! Ye git yerself out here! We're gonna settle this thing like true fishers!"

Villagers stepped from various longhouses, some heading toward Mum, nodding their heads in agreement. Others headed toward the brewmistress, who stalked from her longhouse, shoving up her sleeves.

Da rolled his eyes. "Now, Willow. Let's not go—"

"She done ruined my starter dough!" Mum screamed in his face. "Ye know how long it takes ta get a good starter. Has ta be nurtured and—"

"*Ye* tried ta poison me!" The brewmistress shook her fist. "Come on, then. No weapons. Jus' teeth and claws."

Da held up a hand, holding the brewmistress back. He slipped an arm around Mum's shoulders and turned, walking her over to Petril. Two of Petril's older brothers stepped outside the longhouse, followed by Tinnie. The expressions on their faces mimicked Mum's.

"Tha' old fishwife should be chopped up and thrown to th' sturgeons," Tinnie said, stomping her foot. "She made a right mess o' th' place."

Whatever had been done to that starter dough must have been bad.

"Not th' first time Mum's starter's been trashed," Petril said as Bennie, the oldest of the remaining five brothers, stepped up beside him. "She used ta always be whippin' up a new starter batch. And we'd always find a way ta wreck it. Even fed some ta th' fingerlings one year, remember? Ya'd think this be th' only starter in the world, way she's goin' on about it now."

Ben stood taller than Da now, though he was thicker through the shoulders and neck. "Ever since this neighborly 'competition' turned inta a full-out feud, Mum's been keepin' th' sweet dough starter hidden away, not lettin' anyone else touch it, not family, not anyone. She brung it out after noon taday, intendin' ta section off a bit 'fore hidin' it away again. Tha's when Miz Hannah—*Brewmistress* Hannah—started soundin' like a sturgeon caught in a net, goin' on and on about being poisoned."

He looked down at Petril.

"Then you show up outta nowhere like a ghost on tha' glowing white *Companion*." Jem, the next oldest son, slapped a hand on Petril's shoulder. Though not as tall as Da or Ben, he still peered down at Petril, his thin face mirroring the concerned looks on Ben's face. Both brothers had faces that could have been carved from the rock cliffs, craggy and strong.

:And a bit scruffy,: Rina added.

:My brothers are not *scruffy.:* Petril studied his brothers a moment. *:Maybe just a bit.:* he conceded.

Two more brothers—Virgal and Snare—stalked up, their faces mirroring their brothers'.

"Someone been inside," Snare said. "Could be more'n one." His voice was rougher than the other siblings, even though he was only sixteen. He'd gotten his nickname—and his voice— when he got caught in a fish snare and almost didn't make it out. "Kitchen's been tossed. Bowls and pans on the floor, flour over everything."

"Half Mum's starter dough's missin', an' the rest . . ." Virgal shook his head. "Look like th' village kids had a play day."

The sweet scent of honey and spice drifted out of the longhouse.

"Gather th' others," Da told the four brothers. "We'll meet at th' firepit. Time ta get this mess straightened out." He looked at Petril. "Ye might not be a Herald yet, but that Companion o' yours could help ye serve as witness, right?"

:Most definitely,: Rina said.

Petril nodded. "Tha' should work. Jus' as long as ye don't ask me ta pass judgment or any such thing."

It took less time than Petril expected for the villagers to gather around the firepit. They milled about as they took their seats, their murmuring voices rising above the waves lapping on the shore. The stink of dead fish drifted in on the night breeze before being chased back by the smoky fire.

Petril led Rina to the stool next to his da's, then settled awkwardly, feeling more like a fish out of water than when he'd been working at the stables in Haven.

:*This will be good practice.*: Rina gently nosed his shoulder. :*Open your shields just enough to let the barest hint of emotions through. There's likely to be a plethora of outrage and anger, but see if you can sense anyone who might be feeling guilty, or any other emotion that might be out of place. Don't let it over-whelm you, though. As with all things, you're seeking a bal-ance.*:

:*Plethora?*:

:*A fancy way of saying "an abundance."*:

:*Why didn't ye jus' say so?*:

Da raised his hand and the villagers quieted down. Da had always been a strong voice in the village, but watching him in this leadership position made Petril feel like an outsider. He'd scarcely been gone a year, and already things felt so . . . *different.*

He let down his shields just enough to let the strongest emo-tions leak through. Determination tinged with righteous indig-nation seemed the strongest.

For the time being.

"No use draggin' this thing out," Da said. "Brewmistress, say yer piece. Then Willow'll say hers. Petril and his Companion—" Da paused, "—are serving as witness. No judgment. Not to-night. Let's see if'n we can get this thing figured out. If'n it appears there been wrong-doing, we'll call for a full Herald ta come sit, official like."

"How do we know he'll tell it like it be?"

Petril recognized the speaker as one of the brewmistress's daughters. As stocky as her mum and almost as tall, Ailee was near the same age as Snare. Her righteous indignation flared so hot he raised his shields just enough to tamp down what prom-ised to become a raging fire.

"Part o' bein' a Herald," he said, keeping his voice calm. "Companions don't go fer lying an' such."

"Ain't much ta say," Brewmistress Hannah conceded. "Wil-low there tainted my wine, simple as that."

"Did ye see it?" Petril asked. He'd been a part of a similar discussion in the past, he realized. When Lord Fancy Pants had tried to weasel out of the part he'd played kidnapping the Shin'a'in mare and her babe.

"See wha'?" The brewmistress looked genuinely puzzled. "Ever'one knows she done it. Who else?"

"Jus' like ever'one knows you messed wit' her starter dough?" Petril studied the other villagers. He lowered his shields, tried to sense beyond the indignation.

There. Somewhere past the mass of villagers.

Curiosity.

And was that—

:I feel it too. Someone's planning for trouble,: Rina agreed.

"Yer th' one bashed up me kitchen." Petril's mum stood, fists planted on her hips, glaring at Brewmistress Hannah. "Or ye sent yer kiddos ta do th' deed."

"No more'n ye deserve!" yelled a voice that might have been the brewmistress's son.

"No one deserves havin' their home busted apart!" roared Ben.

Just like that, Petril's first attempt at reconciliation dissolved into chaos as villagers attempted to outshout each other. His da held up a hand, but his voice was drowned out by the other voices.

Petril raised his shields, struggling to keep control of the cacophony threatened to break through. He tamped down the anger, distrust, and outrage, focusing on the sense of mischief that seemed to keep growing—

:Duck!:

Rina's warning came a sliver before a snake flew past his head . . .

And smashed into Brewmistress Hannah's head with a resounding *thud*!

The brewmistress staggered back, staring as the snake disappeared into a tree. "Tha's part o' me distiller!"

Petril had no idea what a distiller was, but what he'd thought was a snake looked to be a curly glass tube of some sort.

Hanging from a tree.

Not hanging, he realized.

Clutched in the claws of a shiny black raven.

A raven oozing with mischief.

"Gilly girl," Mum said, shaking her head at the bird. "Ye know yer not supposed to fool with th' villagers' things. Bring tha' down 'ere right now!"

The raven stared at her, black eyes gleaming in the light from a nearby torch. The bird—Gilly?—lifted the tube in its—her?—claw and studied it carefully, turning her head one way, then the other.

Then Gilly dropped the tube, shaking her foot as though ridding her claws of debris.

"No!" The brewmistress lunged forward, snatching the tube in midair . . .

And landed flat on her bum, tube clenched triumphantly in her hand.

Gilly plunged from the branch, spreading her wings, swooping over the brewmistress's head . . .

Splat!

:That bird's been practicing,: Rina noted. *:Right on target, or so I assume.:*

By the way the brewmistress was spluttering, Petril decided his little "greeting" had been but a drip in Gilly-girl's bucket.

"Ye should get rid o' that blasted bird!" one of the other villagers shouted. "Always stealin' and dumpin'—"

"Dumped a load right in me soup ta other night. Been cookin' over th' firepit all day. Jus' about ready to call fer supper when, *splat!* There goes supper."

A suspicion tickled at the back of Petril's mind. Slippery as a lake eel, he couldn't quite put a finger on what was niggling at him.

"Where ye cookin' up yer wine?" he asked the brewmistress as her daughter helped her to her feet. Both wrinkled their noses at the stink covering the woman's tunic.

"On th' shadow side o' me home."

"She got th' side o' the longhouse all set for brewin' and dis-tillin'," her daughter said with unmistakable pride. "Goes in th' cave ta age, then back home for bottlin'—"

Someone shouted at the edge of the crowd. Villagers scattered one way, then the other, opening a path that led from a nearby longhouse.

His family's longhouse.

Gilly swooped into the torchlight like a winged shadow, gliding along the path opened by the villagers. Petril heard a familiar growl before a furry figure humped into view, hurrying between the villagers, raven darting down at him as he ran.

"Chomper?"

Gilly dove. Chomper hissed, though the hiss was muffled by something in the otter's mouth.

"Tha's *my starter dough*!" Mum charged after the otter. "Come back 'ere, ye little thief!"

"Looks like there be more'n one thief in th' village." Petril caught his da's eye. Da's eyes twinkled.

:I agree, Chosen. I believe the villagers aren't the only ones caught up in this feud.:

He had a pretty good idea what he would see in Mum's kitchen. Needed to tie one more knot before the fishnet called a "feud" was repaired.

"Mind if'n I look at yer still?" He asked the brewmistress.

The woman scowled at him, still scrubbing at the goo on her tunic.

"Show him," she said to her daughter. "I'll be there once I get changed."

The villagers gathered around, curious as Ailee led the way. The brewmistress had a nice setup, Petril had to admit. Tools and equipment—none of which looked familiar—set up neatly on a table bench that ran from one end of the longhouse to the other.

At the end of the bench stood a barrel that stank of fermented grapes.

As they watched, Chomper the otter—smear of Mum's

starter dough on its nose—scrambled up on the bench and dove into the barrel.

Looking like a child with a sweet, the otter turned on its back, both paw-hands filled with fermented grapes.

And burped.

Just then Gilly-girl swooped in, settling on a pot halfway down the table.

Chomper dragged himself out of the barrel, chittering and grunting at the raven as though telling it to go away. The otter wove his way down the bench, staggering slightly to one side, then the other.

Gilly croaked. With what looked like a well-practiced move, the raven nudged the lid from the pot, dropped its tail feathers in, and pooped.

"See!" Ailee said. "Yer mum sent that bird ta poison th' whole batch."

"Just like yer mum sent Chomper to destroy Mum's starter dough?" Petril raised an eyebrow. "Let's get back to th' fire. It's pretty clear wha's been happenin'."

Discussions lasted long into the night. Aside from a bit of bickering now and then, the villagers were mostly in agreement. Appropriate steps would be taken to protect both wine-making and sweet-baking endeavors.

:Didn't end th' feud.: Petril couldn't help feeling he had somehow failed. He sat on Rina's back, feeling the warmth of the Companion through his leggings, no saddle between them.

:Not exactly. But look.: Rina lifted her nose. On the far side of the firepit, Brewmistress Hannah perched on a stool next to . . . his mum!

Firelight flickered across Mum's tired face as she handed something to the brewmistress . . . who passed a small flask to his mum.

Mum took a sip from the flask.

Brewmistress Hannah popped a small ball in her mouth.

After a moment, both women nodded, grins tugging at their lips.

Rina bobbed her head. *:While the competition might go on, I do believe the actual feud is over. Shall we go for a moonlight run?:*

:Wha' about th' saddle?:

:You've been in that saddle for more than a fortnight. You know how to ride. Take a lesson from the Shin'a'in. Just relax and let it flow.:

Petril clutched Rina's mane as the Companion calmly walked down to the lake. Tiny waves lapped at the shore, but otherwise, the water was still. Moonlight reflected off the mirror-like surface.

:Listen to the water,: Rina said, her voice soothing his mind.

Petril felt his muscles relax, the stress from the village feud slipping away . . .

A breeze kissed his cheek. With a start, Petril realized Rina was cantering, moving beneath him like a rocking chair.

And he wasn't flopping around like a just-landed fish.

Off to his right, water splashed. He glanced at the lake in time to see a huge, rounded back rise above the water, then plunge back down, then another and another.

"Wave-wise." Petril's chest swelled with an emotion he'd only experienced once before—when Rina Chose him. He let go with one hand and waved at the creatures playing in the water as he and Rina raced through the sand.

Joy and freedom. Freedom and joy . . .

His emotions wove with the those of the Wave-wise—and his Companion.

:I'm riding. Truly riding!: He let himself move, let himself *feel.*

:I'm home.: Petril realized. *:I'm finally home.:*

:That you are, Chosen. That you are.:

Dueling Minstrels
Jennifer Brozek and Marie Bilodeau

Aimar Noteleaf stepped into the Rustic Mug with a smile on his face that disappeared as soon as he saw Ozan Newsong setting up on the small stage in the corner of the rural tavern. "No, no, no, you tone-deaf squawker! Tonight is *my* night! We agreed days ago, when you begged to take my spot during the full moon festival."

Ozan pushed his long dark hair from his face, paused, considered the other minstrel's words, then shook his head. "No. Not true. You already took my spot during the height of the trade season. We agreed then." He went back to setting up his lute, foot drum, and flute while Aimar sputtered his outrage.

"Absolutely not! That was payment for when you took my place during Helfrich and Kara's wedding, and you know it!" Aimar lifted his chin, his fair face flushed to the roots of his sandy blond hair, and stalked over to the stage. "Tonight is *my* night. You aren't the only one with debts to pay." He put his own lute case and fiddle case on the stage, shifting Ozan's drum out of the way, despite there being enough room on the stage for all the instruments.

Eyes narrowing, Ozan shifted his drum back to the position it was in, shifting the other cases toward the edge of the stage. "Do not touch another man's instrument. You know that."

"My left ear! I have every right." Aimar stepped onto the stage and into Ozan's personal space. "Especially when you're in the wrong. *I'm* playing here tonight. Not you."

"Tone-deaf ear, you mean!"

Both young men glared at each other, clenching their fists. Moments before one of them did something he would regret, a querulous voice from the back of the room demanded, "Get a room already! Gods' balls, you two argue worse than Duncle and Fadin!"

They turned to see old man Gunther, his hands wrapped around a half-full tankard, peering at them through his one good eye. "Yeah, I'm talking to the two o' you, ya fishwives! Every single time this happens, you harp and shriek at each other until, eventually, one of you gives in. I wouldn't want to be young and ridiculous like you two again even if it meant getting my eye back!"

Both minstrels shot him a dirty look and turned their backs on him. Gunther scowled, then yelled, "Linde!"

As soon as he yelled for the owner of the tavern, both minstrels rushed forward with pleading hands and shushing fingers to keep Gunther from summoning the one person with absolute authority in the Rustic Mug.

Glaring at them with his single gimlet eye, Gunther yelled, "They're at it again, and my head won't take it no more!"

Linde Siedel walked out of the back kitchen, wiping her hands on her apron. With iron-gray hair and a steel gaze that could stop a man's bellyaching with a glance, she already did not look happy. Her distracted air disappeared as she saw the two minstrels. Something tired and disgusted ran over her face before she asked, "Is there a problem?"

Ozan shook his head. "No, ma'am. No problem. Just setting up for tonight."

Aimar raised a finger. "Actually, there is a problem. Tonight's my night. We agreed to it ages ago—"

"No. It's my night. You owe me." Ozan kept his voice light and unconcerned.

Gunther snorted. "Sure. Be polite now." He waved his mug at the young minstrels, but didn't spill a drop of ale. "Squallin' like cats in heat, they were."

Linde's eyes narrowed as she put her hands on her hips. "What did I tell you boys about fighting in my tavern?"

Both Ozan and Aimar shook their heads.

"We weren't fighting."

"It was a small disagreement."

"It's supposed to be my night," they finished together, then looked at each other with mingled surprise and irritation.

She shook her head. "I'm done with this. Either you both play tonight or neither of you plays." She turned away and headed back toward the kitchen.

"But . . ." Ozan began.

"With him . . . ?" Aimar asked.

Both shut their mouths as Linde whirled back around, her cheeks glowing the hectic red of fury. "You heard me. Both of you play tonight. Together. In sweet-ass harmony . . . or neither of you ever plays here again."

Aimar fought his instincts—his *overwhelming* instincts—not to kick Ozan's drum off the stage. The tiny stage, made infinitely smaller by the two minstrels occupying it with their horde of instruments. He was certain Ozan took up more than his fair share, too, and would have complained if not for Linde's steely glance.

The crowd had grown in the last hour, the air thick with mead and laughter. Quitting time for workers on both Duncle's and Fadin's farms. By tacit agreement, the farmhands and other workers from the rival farms sat on opposite sides of the tavern. Everyone else was in the middle of the room as a sort of neutral no-man's-land. Gunther, grumpy as ever, helped serve the waiting patrons.

"I'll go first, since you're so slow setting up." Ozan whirled his lute around like a sword.

Aimar hoped it would go flying into the crowd and break, but alas, Ozan managed to grip it and strum a deep chord, to the crowd's enjoyment.

Cheers echoed as he launched into an old folk song about

the historic winter crossing leading to the founding of Valdemar. His tones shot up with hope, then dipped down with dread, the crowd merrily joining him as he droned on and on, the drama of this annoyingly crowd-pleasing song.

Then little Jorn's eyes stayed shut,
Sleeping in his mother's arms,
The sleep of death, the sleep of dust,
A mother's tears, a mother's warmth . . .

There was no historical accuracy whatsoever to this, a pure construct to play up the crowd. It was also boring as hell, and Aimar would have none of it. He swept up his fiddle and picked his moment—an easy thing to do with such a tired ballad.

A historically questionable one, no less.

Just as they reached the land that would become Valdemar, Aimar matched Ozan's cord and stole the song away from him with a practiced pull of his fiddle, and launched into a crowd-pleasing love song.

It's not the history
That's the story
It's not the romance
That's the dance
It's you!
Only you!
Alwaaayysss you!

The audience blinked, torn out of the drama of what felt like, in Ozan's unskilled hands, an interminable winter. For a second, Aimar feared he'd miscalculated, but a ripple ran through the crowd and they cheered. Couples clasped hands. A few even sang along.

Those from Fadin's farm who had been enjoying Ozan's melody seemed irritated by the change in tune and song. Several glared at the lovers and sank into their seats, intent on not falling for the lure of the music.

The crowd grew as more people entered, coaxed in by the song. Gunther took drink orders, and the place brimmed with energy and romance. Perhaps too much romance, as two lovers toppled off their seats in a loving embrace, to roll under their table.

Not one to be outdone by a romance-twaddling minstrel, Ozan huffed and, with a flourish of long dark hair, hit his foot drum to lead the crowd back into a war.

They came in the night,
To broker in might!
Down came the wall,
A cry in the hall!

The crowd blinked again, but it wasn't long before they'd gone from loving tune to a bloody battlefield. As Ozan's voice deepened and his drum slammed in time with it, the crowd grew more rowdy, banging on the table. The two lovers re-emerged, half-dressed, banging their table instead of each other.

Those from Duncle's farm pounded the tables a little too hard in their irritation at the change in tune, not to mention at the pleasure of those from the other side of the room. Dark looks and gestures flicked across the room from one side to the other.

The banging summoned Linde from the back, stormy eyes looking at Ozan, too wrapped up in his song to notice the fiery, terrifying threat in them.

Just as the hordes were pushed back with more drums, Aimar stepped forward, interrupting the war song with his lute, stringing along notes to shuffle them into an improvised song seeking to end the aggressive tune.

There in the ruins by the gate,
She found her love battered and dead, she knew,
She held him tight and called his name,
Until he shook and rattling breath he drew . . .

Not his best work, but the crowd lapped it up, swaying gently. Before Ozan could rile them up again, Linde's surprisingly thunderous voice boomed out the tail end of Aimar's quickly fizzling ballad. "Get your refills now, before the minstrels take us on our next song adventure!"

"That's a cue for a break if I've ever heard one," grumbled Aimar as he stopped strumming his lute.

"Anything to end that tired drivel you call a song," replied Ozan.

"Better than—"

"You two." Linde suddenly appeared before the stage, hands on hips. The two minstrels jumped back in perfect unison. "I need these people buying drinks, not destroying the place—" a glare at Ozan, "—nor making out on the tables. Or under them." Aimar straightened in turn as she sliced him with her eyes.

"It would be better if I could just do my full set," Ozan grumbled, swishing his dark hair dramatically aside, hitting Aimar in the face.

"Your whole set would see everyone asleep!" Aimar huffed after batting the hair away.

"I don't care what you do," Linde said. "But *share* the stage. And get 'em to buy drinks, or you're *both* out." She turned without another word and headed back to the kitchen.

Ozan focused on his instruments, but Aimar sighed. "We need to figure out a set that works for both of us," he offered, trying to broker a truce.

"With you," Ozan barely looked up from his instruments, "my pale-haired, paler comparison? I don't think so."

"Your hair tastes like oils of shame," Aimar said. Before Ozan could figure out what exactly he'd been called—something Aimar wasn't sure he could even explain—Aimar crossed the small stage and struck the foot drum, the dramatic percussion calling everyone to attention.

"Don't touch *my* drum," Ozan growled.

Aimar pointed up dramatically, accentuating the motion with another strike of Ozan's drum, calling the audience to attention. Before the lyrics of a gentle ballad slipped from Aimar's lips, Ozan crossed the stage and hip-checked him away, the dark-haired minstrel striking the foot pedal of the drum in one flawless movement as he launched into his own ballad, leaving Aimar to stumble and miraculously not fall off the stage.

Harken now, lend your ears to me,
A wondrous tale I will tell to thee.

The song of Valdemar, always a favorite. A ripple of excitement shifted the now thick crowd. Those at the bar turned to look at the minstrel and enjoy the music, drinks forgotten.

Linde's eyes trailed up slowly toward the stage, and Aimar swallowed hard. Her instructions had been clear: they needed to get the patrons to drink barrels of ale. And Aimar knew a drinking song. A great one. So great that he'd just created it at this very moment and interrupted Ozan with . . .

The first drink for sorrow,
The second for love,
The third for tomorrow
The fourth for oblivion!

By the third, mostly similar verse, hoots and hollers filled the entire space, making the crowded bar feel even more full. A pleased Linde nodded at him, and Aimar smiled as he kept strumming, strumming for his next lyric, which seemed to evade him . . .

Sensing his hesitation, Ozan played his flute loudly over the lute to change the very rhythm, the very *heart* of the song. Aimar steamed as the minstrel switched seamlessly to his lute, then he fumed even more as lyrics tumbled from Ozan's lips.

Following the song of a crazed buffoon,
Singing so bad he cracked the moon.

All Aimar could do was stare gape-mouthed at Ozan, the minstrel's annoyingly perfect hair glistening with lustrous darkness. Aimar viciously grabbed his fiddle and bow.

Nothing drowned out an annoying minstrel like a fiddler out for revenge.

He zinged and zanged so intently that two strings snapped, but that didn't stop him, nor even slow him down. In fact, he fiddled harder as Ozan began hitting his drum with abandon, trying to overtake the high-pitched notes.

The audience blinked wildly at the minstrels before turning glares upon their rivals. Yes, they were mere wheat farmers, the best in the land, but now they were enemies. There could only be one best. General shouts and jeers intermingled within the frenzied music. Ozan managed to be heard over the ruckus.

I heard them say you were boorish,
Turns out you were mostly just sluggish.

He looked directly at Aimar as he spoke, eyes lit with victory.

Aimar bellowed over even the drums, weaving words to the same tune, unaware every lyric from both minstrels raised the tension in the room even higher.

It's not that I was sluggish,
It's that you weren't interesting enough to speak to!

The second line was way too long and he stumbled on it, but it didn't matter, because Ozan was now fuming.

And so was the audience as both minstrels continued weaving songs and instruments and insults, banging and bashing and crashing.

Ozan opened his mouth with a rebuttal, but a mug smashing on the wall beside him stilled his tongue. Neither minstrel was unaccustomed to the occasional drunken revelry that could accompany show nights, but then another mug flew. Then a table was flipped with a cry of outrage and the breaking of crockery.

Ozan stopped the drums, and Aimar held up his arms, only to have a chair strike his gut, hard. He doubled over, and Ozan caught him before he fell. Aimar twisted the two of them out of the way of a flying man. Several more things were hurled in their direction—the last of which was a knife that stuck in the wall.

Ozan pulled Aimar off the stage, both young men huddling behind instruments and an upended table as the entire bar devolved into pandemonium. All around them shouts of anger and pain filled the air.

"What happened?" Aimar asked.

"I don't know. They've gone crazy." Ozan winced as a man with a bloodied nose fell next to them.

A serving tray landed next to Aimar. He grabbed it and held it like a shield over both him and Ozan. "What are we gonna do?"

Ozan shook his head, eyes wide.

The sound of the door crashing open was almost lost in the din of the bar gone mad. Then, a soprano voice cut through the noise. It scooped from low to very high in an impossibly loud tone, making everyone stop and cover their ears. Behind it, an angry horse bellowed a challenge and everyone stopped moving.

Silence reigned.

Ozan and Aimar peeked out from behind the table to see Herald Riora standing in the open doorway of the Rustic Mug with her fists on her hips, looking very displeased (and much like Linde at that moment). Behind her stood her Companion, Soren.

Riora raised her chin and her voice. "I think it's time everyone went home." Then she pointed at the two minstrels hiding behind the table. "Except for you two." When no one moved, she raised a hand and glanced at her fingernails. "*Now.* Please and thank you." She stepped out of the doorway to allow the patrons of the tavern to leave.

By ones and twos, the farm workers from Duncle's and Fadin's farms pulled themselves together, gathered what they could of their things and their dignity, and left without arguing with the Herald.

After the last patron walked out and those remaining—Riora, Linde, Gunther, Aimar, and Ozan—put the Rustic Mug back together as well as they could, Linde had a quiet conversation with Riora while Ozan and Aimar watched. The two minstrels were uncharacteristically but understandably subdued.

Aimar muttered, not for the first time, "I don't know what happened."

Ozan agreed, "It's not like we did anything."

This time, they said it within earshot of Gunther, who turned on them. "You two are stupider than cows eatin' green corn. Of course you did it. You made it happen. I saw it."

Both Ozan and Aimar stared at him with wide eyes.

"Did not," Ozan said.

"No, we didn't," Aimar said at the same time.

Gunther grunted. "Figures. First time in your lives you agree with each other and you're both wrong."

Riora's voice preceded her to the table. "I'm afraid Gunther is correct. You two, both of you, caused the bar fight that—" she gestured at the remains of tables and chairs and broken crockery, "—did all this. I could feel the power of your Talent from outside the tavern. You've both put Linde in quite the bind."

"No good deed," Gunther mumbled, then wandered away at a stern glance from the Herald.

Ozan and Aimar looked at each other. For once, neither one of them wanted to take the lead. Aimar nodded to Ozan and sighed. "We didn't mean to. We're sorry."

"Sorry isn't gonna mend furniture or pay for new mugs." Riora crossed her arms. "Linde and I have had a conversation about this and about you two. We've come up with a plan. I would like you two headstrong boys to listen until I'm done."

Both minstrels bristled at being called "boys," but when a Herald with silver in her hair calls you that, even two fools are not foolish enough to disrespect her.

She held up a finger. "First, both of you must work for Linde to pay off your considerable debt—or figure out some other way to pay for the repairs in full. *Both* of you are on the hook for the debt until it is paid off. That means one of you can't pay off your half and go on your merry way. *Both* of you must work until both of you clear your debt. As I understand the two of you have been fighting for ages, this will be difficult, but I believe in your ability to see things through to the end."

From the back of the room, Gunther asked, "Are you tryin' to help Linde, or punish her?"

Linde rolled her eyes, but continued to work behind the bar.

Riora ignored him and held up a second finger. "Two, both of you young minstrels have Bardic Talent. I have no idea how either of you got as old as you are without understanding that, but I know it when I hear it, as I have Bardic Talent as well."

A third, slender finger shot up. "Three, once your debt with Linde is paid off, you should contact me. I know people in the Bardic Collegium, and can help you get into it. You are not required to, but I really think you should. Talent such as yours needs to be honed and controlled. Not wasted on petty feuds."

Ozan and Aimar looked at each other, dumbfounded. Aimar asked, "Bardic Talent? We do?"

Riora nodded.

Ozan asked, "And we could go to the Bardic Collegium? In Haven? Become actual Bards?"

Riora nodded again. "You will need to apply. But I can help make that happen."

Ozan frowned, glancing at Aimar, "But neither of us can pay for it . . ."

The Herald smiled and shrugged. "That's what patrons are for. Again, I can help you with that. Good Bards are worth the patronage—and that's what I see before me: the potential for a couple of minstrels to become excellent Bards."

From the bar, Linde asked, "What about the people from Duncle's farm and Fadin's farm? They fight because Duncle and Fadin fight. This wasn't the first one—it was the worst I've seen—but it won't be the last one."

The Herald shook her head. "One feud at a time, my good

lady. Those families have been bickering since before I was a child. I don't think a single conversation is going to fix it."

"I bet you your drums I come up with a song that'll make them fall in love with each other." Aimar grinned at Ozan, already working up lyrics in his increasingly energized mind. The pain of the chair hitting his midsection was mostly forgotten, though it begged for attention with each excited breath.

"I should have let the crowd tear you to pieces like your lyrics tear harmony to shreds," Ozan muttered.

A reply almost slipped from Aimar's lips, his arguments with Ozan akin to a familiar ballad, but even he couldn't fail to notice the stinging gaze of the Herald.

His cheeks reddened, as did Ozan's, both young men feeling properly scolded.

"Should I just stop them from singing?" Linde asked from the bar, sounding curiously disappointed at the suggestion.

Riora sighed. "No, but perhaps don't let them share the stage. At least, not until they've learned to work together toward a common goal."

Aimar bit back his reply, and Ozan stared at the floor.

"Paying off their debt to me oughta do that," Linde said, then vanished into the back.

"I hope to see you both in the halls of the Bardic Collegium before too long." Riora nodded to the pair of awestruck minstrels.

Both young men awkwardly lowered their heads in a half-bow, half-nod, but the Herald failed to see it, as she'd turned to go.

"The Bardic Collegium," Ozan turned to Aimar and whispered once she'd exited. "We could go to the Bardic Collegium!"

Aimar grinned. "I bet I'll do better than you."

Ozan's attempt at looking insulted failed, though he still managed to push an insult through grinning lips. "Better at failing, sure."

The two young men continued cleaning the place with more

gusto than effectiveness, hurling minor insults at each other while dreaming of what they might one day become.

In the back, Gunther watched, shaking his head, wondering if the Herald had any idea what she'd invited to Haven. He figured she did, which just made him shake his head even more.

A Scold of Jays
Elisabeth Waters

This story is dedicated to Rodan, a bluejay so skillful with his claws that he could turn the boom box on—and the volume all the way up—repeatedly, early in the morning, while the humans were trying to sleep. Misty's wildlife rehabilitation license added so much interest to our lives.

Four years ago

"Are you sure he's going to live?" Rupert asked the Healer, trying to sound anxious and hopeful instead of angry and disappointed.

"Your brother is not going to die," the woman in Greens replied reassuringly. "Both legs are properly splinted, his dislocated shoulder is back into place, and we'll know more about the head injury when he regains consciousness."

"Will he make a full recovery?" their father demanded.

"I expect he will limp, especially when overtired, for the rest of his life," the healer said, "and it's too soon to know about any injury to the brain, but his skull wasn't broken, so the prognosis is good."

"But he's going to be a cripple and, for all you know, a drooling idiot," Lord Crane snarled.

"I don't believe it will be anywhere near that bad," the Healer said firmly. "Of course, having a supportive family will be important."

He's finally run out of luck, then, because there's no way this family can be called supportive. I still can't believe he survived that trap. I wanted to kill him, *not just his horse.*

Without a backward glance, Rupert followed his fuming father from the sickroom and into his study, closing the door behind him.

Lord Crane looked Rupert over from head to toe, noting artfully tousled blond hair, chiseled features, and rich clothing.

"You don't have your brother's knowledge of the estate, but you can learn. You're healthy and good-looking, at least. I'll train you as my heir, and when Keven recovers enough to be moved, we'll send him to some quiet temple where he can live out his life in decent obscurity. I'll tell anyone who asks that he died."

Three years ago

"Rupert!" Lord Crane stormed into their townhouse in Haven. "You won't believe what just happened at the Council meeting!"

While the proceedings of the King's Council were largely a matter of indifference to Rupert, his father's temper was something else. "What happened?"

"That girl you were supposed to marry—what's her name?"

"Lena. Lady Magdalena Lindholm."

"She's married to *Keven*—apparently the Prior at that temple performed the ceremony—and the King actually thanked me for releasing Keven from my family so he could join hers and reestablish it. I didn't want to reestablish her family; I wanted to *absorb* it!"

"I assure you that I am every bit as dismayed as you are." Rupert was, but he knew better than to throw a tantrum in his father's presence.

"What happened to the idea of your going to her room and compromising her so she would have to marry you?"

"I went there last week. She wasn't there, although her bed was still warm. She vanished from Court that night, and I assure you I searched for her daily."

One year ago

"Lord Crane." His father's steward, now Rupert's, bowed to him. "My condolences on your loss."

"Thank you," Rupert said. He could do empty civilities as well as anyone at court. "Now, how much money do I have?"

The steward looked unhappy. "There has been no upkeep on the estate in the last year—" he did not add *"since you took over its management,"*—"so it will need some investment before it starts making a profit again."

"That's money I'd *have* to spend," Rupert said impatiently. "I'm asking about money I can use as I see fit."

"Unfortunately, during your late father's illness, the expenses of this household and your personal expenditure both increased considerably. I'm afraid you will need to economize."

"You can't tell me what to do with my own money!"

"Of course not, Lord Crane. What you do with your money is your decision. What I am saying is that you need a new source of income if you wish to keep spending at your current level."

"Get out!" Rupert shouted. The steward bowed and hastily left the room. Greta, Rupert's dog, got up from the hearth rug and started across the room. He kicked her, and she hit the wall with a yelp and a satisfying thump.

Rupert stormed out, telling the butler to send Greta to the Temple of Thenoth, Lord of the Beasts, to live with the rest of the useless cripples, and to have his horse brought around. He knew just where to find a new source of income.

Mistress Efanya was a wealthy widow. She wasn't highborn, unfortunately, but her late husband had been a member of the King's Council, and she had a son, Sven-August, who was of marriageable age. Rupert married her, moved himself and his sister Sara into her house, rented out the Crane townhouse for the highest price he could get, and started planning advantageous—for him—marriages for both Sven-August and Sara.

Unfortunately, Sven-August's reaction to his mother's marriage was to elope with Stina, whose family had no money. The new Lady Crane was almost as livid as her lord. Then, just when Lord Crane was seeking the king's consent for Lady's Sara's marriage to a wealthy man disposed to be generous to his brother-in-law, *she* ran away. She was recovered the next day, but the king had involved Lady Lindholm, who had the Gift of Animal Mindspeech, in the search, and she told the king how young her husband's sister actually was. Not only did the king refuse his consent to the marriage, he said that he would not approve *any* marriage for a twelve-year-old—and, on top of that, he gave the wardship of Lady Sara to Keven and Lena Lindholm.

Rupert was furious—but if it had occurred to him to think of anyone other than himself, he might have realized that Keven, Sara, Lena, Sven-August, and Stina were just as angry at him, especially after some of his additional money-making efforts.

"No!" Sven-August's cry of anguish was quickly followed by his entrance into the parlor when Lena and Keven were sitting. "She can't do that, can she?" he implored them.

"I'm sorry, but I'm afraid she can." The man Sven-August had been meeting with followed him. "Given your legal status as a child, everything you have actually belongs to your parents."

"I'm *not* legally a child!"

"Sven-August," Lena interrupted, "what are we talking about, and are introductions in order?"

"My mother sold Jasper!"

"Out of *our* stables?" Keven asked. "I think we definitely need an explanation if someone removed a horse from our property."

"Introductions?" Lena prompted.

"Sorry," Sven-August said without sounding particularly sorry. "Lord and Lady Lindholm, may I present Master Petrus? He's my mother's lawyer."

"Master Petrus." Lena nodded politely to him. "Sven-August has not legally been a child since his marriage three months ago. Lord Lindholm and I were witnesses to the ceremony, which was performed by the Prior of the Temple of Thenoth and, moreover, has the King's approval."

"I'm sorry, my lady," the lawyer said miserably, "but since her recent marriage, Lady Efanya has been economizing—"

"We are acquainted with Lord Crane," Lena said grimly. "We know what they've been doing—or more likely what *he's* been doing."

"I think we should get Jasper back first, and then we can argue about the legality of the sale," Keven said practically. "To whom was he sold?"

"The horse market down by the fairgrounds. Same place Lord Crane sent his sister's horse; he said her husband would buy her a new one."

"Did he happen to mention that his sister is only twelve?" Keven asked with deceptive mildness.

"We'll leave you gentlemen to discuss the legalities," Lena said. "Sven-August, find Stina and meet me in the stables. Wear your novice habits. You're going to escort me while I go shopping for a horse."

The arrival of a richly dressed noblewoman with two attendants produced the owner of the horse market almost instantly. As Sven-August lifted Lena carefully off her horse and set her on her feet, the man eyed the habits he and Stina both wore.

"Good morning, my lady," he said. "I'm Nils, the owner here. How may I serve you?"

"I'm looking to buy a few horses," Lena said. "What do you have to show me?"

"Shall I bring a few likely prospects out, or—" he looked at her clothes, "—would you like to come into the barn to see what we have? I promise you, we keep the barn clean; you won't be wading through muck."

"The barn, then." Lena inclined her head graciously.

"Begging your pardon, my lady, but would your helpers be from the Temple of Thenoth?"

"Yes," Lena smiled at him. "Have you had dealings with the temple?"

"Aye. They've been helpful to me a time or two, and the Lord of the Beasts is a god I can worship." He looked hopefully at Sven-August. "Do ye have Animal Mindspeech?"

Sven-August grinned at him. "We don't, but Lady Lindholm does."

"Really?" Nils looked hopefully at her. "If you can talk to

one of the horses I got recently, I'll give you a good deal on whatever you want to buy."

"Lead the way," Lena said. "What seems to be wrong with the horse?"

"If she were a human, I'd say she was pining to death. Hardly eats anything, takes no interest in her surroundings, mostly just stands there with her head down."

He gestured to a stall, and Lena looked and quickly pulled the door open. "So the lying down on her side is new?"

"Thenoth help us!"

"Perhaps he has," Lena said. She knelt in the straw next to the horse's head. "Where did you get her?"

"From Lord Crane," Nils said. "He's sold me quite a few horses over the years—in fact, I'm expecting one today."

"I'd like to see that one when it gets here," Lena said. "In the meantime, let me see what I can do here. What's her name?"

"Brownie."

She reached out to the horse. *:Hello,:* she thought. *:Can you tell me what's wrong?:*

:I miss my human,: the mare replied miserably.

:Tell me about your human.:

:They call her Sara, and we lived in the country with other horses and humans. Her sire gave me to her when she was so small she had to be lifted into my saddle, and I was careful with her. Always! She loved me. She wouldn't have sent me here. But she had two brothers. One was nice, but something bad happened and he and his horse never came back to the stables. Then the other one brought us to the city, where the stable was much smaller and she wasn't allowed to spend much time with me. And then the not-nice brother brought me here, and I knew something really bad happened. Maybe my human is dead, and if she is, I don't want to be alive.:

:What does your human look like?: Lena asked.

The image looked odd to human eyes, but Lena had seen Sara through dogs' eyes. She passed the image back, adding the scent she had gotten when the dogs had searched for Sara at midwinter. *:Is this her?:*

:Yes.:

Lena added an image of Lord Ruven from his dog Greta's viewpoint, followed by an image of Greta. *:Do you know them?:*

The reply was instant. *:Bad human. Good dog.:*

Lena totally agreed. *:We'll find your human,:* she assured the horse.

A sudden commotion pulled Nils away: the clatter of hooves in a pattern that indicated a horse was out of control, men shouting . . . and a horse's mind screaming incoherently.

"Jasper!" Sven-August said, and started for the courtyard.

"No," Lena said firmly. "Stay here with Brownie. See if you can get her back on her feet, and let me see what the situation is before we add you to it."

It was Jasper, all right. Lena wondered how they had managed to get him out of her stables without anyone noticing, until she saw a young man who not only looked quite a bit like Sven-August, but was also wearing one of his habits.

She dove through the pile of bodies and put a hand on Jasper's neck. *:Stop, Jasper,:* she thought firmly to him. *:We'll fix this.:*

Jasper dropped to all four feet and leaned his head against her.

"You certainly do have a gift," Nils said in amazement.

"Yes, and it's a good thing I'm here. First, somebody please grab that fake novice. I have a few questions for him."

"Whaddaya mean, 'fake'?" the man said indignantly.

"One, I don't know you, and I've lived most of my life at the Temple of Thenoth. Two, that's not a novice robe from the temple; it's one of the extra ones I made when several of us were living up at the palace, which means you have stolen my property."

"Hey, lady, it was just a job. He—" he pointed to a man standing off to one side, "—took me to this stable, told me to take the longest robe on a line of pegs and put it on, and then lead the horse. I'm good with horses, honest. I don't know what got into this one."

"Oh, I'd say Jasper woke up and realized he was surrounded

by strangers. And, by the way, that was my stable you snuck into."

He smirked at her. "Maybe you should hire guards."

Lena reached out with her mind, and a few minutes later every crow in the neighborhood had arrived. They circled around him and darted at his face until he dropped to the floor and buried his face in his knees. The crows settled in a circle around him, staring intently.

"I don't need to hire humans with dubious morals," she said calmly.

"We didn't steal the horse," the other man said, handing a sheaf of papers to Nils. "It's not yours, and you're lying if you say it is."

"No, Jasper does not belong to me, but I don't think much of your sneaking him out of my stable in the dark. If this were an honest transaction, why would you do that?"

"My boss didn't want his child to kick up a fuss."

"Lord Crane?"

"So you admit that he owns the horse, and he can do what he likes with it."

"No, I do not admit that. Lord Crane has no children. The so-called child is a legal adult, and the horse was given to him by his late father, so it can easily be argued that Lord Crane does not have a right to the horse."

"Lawyer's talk," the man scoffed. "You planning to go to court over it?"

"My husband was discussing the matter with Lady Crane's lawyer when I left, and I will support whatever he decides to do. In the meantime," she turned to Nils, "what's a fair price for a horse that someone who is 'good with horses' can't handle?"

"He's not that bad," the man protested.

"Fine," Lena said. "We're surrounded by people who deal with horses for a living. I'll turn him loose." *:Don't hurt the humans beyond bruises,:* she told Jasper before stepping away.

Jasper leaped from the floor like a trained warhorse, all four feet lashing out. Three people went flying; Nils had backed off when Lena did. Jasper reared and screamed whenever anyone approached him, and nobody looked enthusiastic about trying to subdue him.

"He can't keep this up forever," Lord Crane's man said. "He'll tire eventually."

"I'm sure I can get a great price for a horse with a temper like this," Nils said sarcastically. "Possibly even a bit more than the knacker would pay." He named a figure that had the man gasping in horror.

"Lord Crane won't like that."

"Given the temperament of the horse and the questionable status of the sale, he should be glad to get that much," Nils pointed out. "Of course, you can take the horse back to him and ask him what he wants you to do."

The man sighed. "He'd probably kill it, and then have to pay to have it hauled off."

"Do the paperwork as if Lord Crane owned the horse," Lena murmured to Nils. "If I buy the horse, I don't want any complaints. I'll take Brownie as well, assuming I can get her back on her feet."

Nils nodded and went to deal with the paperwork while Jasper stood in the middle of the courtyard looking aggressive. Everyone gave him a wide berth.

Lena thanked the crows, who felt this had been great fun, and sent them outside. She looked down at the man still huddled on the floor. "You can get up now," she said, "and I hope you're wearing something under that robe, because I want it back." As he peeled it off and dropped it at her feet, she added, "I strongly suggest you never again wear the robes of a temple you don't belong to." The man took off without saying a word.

After Lord Crane's agent left with his paperwork and less money than he had hoped for, Lena bought two horses: Jasper, to be the sole property of Sven-August; and Brownie, in trust for Lady Sara Crane.

"Thank you for all your help, Master Nils," she said. "We'll be back, because we still need more horses, but I think these two are enough for today."

"I'm glad to see them go to a good home, Lady," he said, grinning as Jasper walked over and shoved Lena's shoulder.

"Jasper's tack is probably still in my stable." Lena shook her head. "What idiots. Shall we see how Brownie is doing?"

Jasper followed them back to Brownie's stall, but deserted Lena for Sven-August as soon as he saw him.

"I'll give you the paperwork when we get home," Lena said, "but Jasper is yours now." She handed him the novice robe. "I believe this is yours as well." She turned to see that Brownie was at least standing. "We'll have to go at a pace Brownie can manage, so it will take a while to get home, but I'd say this was a morning well spent."

This year

Rupert had put Sara, Sven-August, and their horses out of his mind, now that they were no more use to him. At least his wife was useful. She loved to entertain, and with Midwinter coming up, she would be sure to put on impressive parties, which would enhance their reputations and enable Lord Rupert Crane to make useful contacts.

Rupert's contemplation of a brighter future was cut short by a racket in the garden, followed by his wife's screams.

"Birds!" she shrieked, as she ran into the room and slammed the door behind her.

"Is that what is making all that noise in the garden?" Rupert asked incredulously. It sounded as if someone were being murdered out there. Actually, several someones. "We need to get rid of them. Our first Midwinter party is tonight!"

Efanya sighed. "I'll send an urgent request to the Temple of Thenoth. Fortunately, I've been generous to them in the past, and they should be willing to fix this."

Rupert, being more inclined to action, grabbed a broom on his way to the garden via the kitchen, and stepped outside, yelling "Shoo!" while waving the broom around. He managed to hit a couple of birds before the whole flock turned on him, and he hastily retreated to the kitchen coughing, his shoulders covered with feathers, and dabbing at bloody scratches.

A loving wife might have been concerned—especially about his gasping for breath—but after a year of marriage all Lady Crane did was to go in search of suitable writing supplies.

Apparently, the Temple of Thenoth did remember Lady Efanya fondly, for a novice arrived well before mid-morning. He looked about nineteen, tall and gangly, and introduced himself as Arvid.

"The Prior didn't feel he could come himself?" Lady Efanya asked, sounding displeased.

Arvid produced a bow that would not have shamed any of the highborn in Haven. "He sent me, Lady, because I have Animal Mindspeech and he does not. He felt my skills would be more apt to the job."

"Well, see what you can do," Lady Efanya said. "It is vital that they be gone and the mess cleaned up before this evening. I'm giving a party, and this is most emphatically *not* the ambiance I wish to display to my guests."

"Of course not," Arvid said promptly. "I'll go talk to them." He bowed again before heading for the garden.

"Well," Efanya said with a sigh, "at least he has nice manners."

"He should," Rupert wheezed. He had paid some attention to the Temple of Thenoth since Keven resurfaced there, and he knew who the novice was. "He's highborn. Lord Arvid Melander, the family's only son and heir. He's fostered at the temple so that his Gift can be properly trained." He added, "He probably knows Sven-August—and the rest of that pack. I wonder if they're friends."

"I don't care if they're bitter enemies, as long as he gets those wretched birds out of my garden before tonight's party!" Nobody could say that Lady Efanya did not have definite priorities.

After removing the birds from the garden, mostly by moving the pile of nuts he found there further down the hill and encouraging the birds to follow him, Arvid trudged back up to the house occupied by what Lord Rupert had called "the rest of that pack." He doubted that such a large quantity of nuts had landed in Lady Efanya's garden by accident—especially not on a day when most of the highborn in Haven knew she was giving a party.

After greeting Lord and Lady Lindholm properly, he added, "Really, Lena, you would have been justly served if I had brought that scold of jays here, instead of relocating them elsewhere!"

Lena looked at him blankly. "What scold of jays?"

"It wasn't you, then?"

"What wasn't me?"

"The person who snuck in and dumped a pile of nuts to attract jays to Lady Crane's garden. You did know she was giving a party tonight, didn't you?"

"I probably heard of it," Lena said, "but I guarantee you that Keven and I were not invited. Lord Crane hates us both." She paused. "Did you say that she woke up to a scold of jays in her garden?" She giggled. "Oh dear, that must have been so upsetting for her. She hates birds."

Arvid grinned. "Judging from the marks on Lord Crane's face and arms, he tried to chase them away with a broom— that's what they said in the kitchen, anyway."

"He tried to chase jays away from a pile of nuts. With a broom." Lena shook her head. "He's lucky they didn't peck out his eyes."

"I'd say that his hair will be in this year's nests, and they definitely drew blood." Arvid shook his head. "At least *she* has sense enough to send to the temple for help."

Lena sighed. "She could have asked me. I would have moved them for her. I mean, really, isn't being married to Lord Repulsive punishment enough?"

Arvid shrugged. "I don't know him, and I don't think I want to."

"You don't," Lena and Keven said in unison.

"But if you didn't do this," Arvid wondered aloud, "who

did? How many of us in Haven even *have* Animal Mind-speech?"

"You, me, and Tansy, and I don't think her Companion would have allowed this," Lena replied. "But we would not have needed nuts to lure the birds there. We could simply have asked them." She looked down at the dog sitting on her feet. "Orson, would you please get Sven-August, Stina, and Sara?"

As the dog trotted purposefully from the room, Keven sighed. "Do you really think—"

"Sven-August grew up in that house, Stina lived next door, and Sara spent time in the garden when she was living there. Any of them could have done this."

"I would like to think," Keven sighed, "that my sister, at least, would know better—and I hope she can't sneak out of this house unnoticed."

"She's probably pretty angry at the brother who sent away her governess, sold her horse—who almost died before we got her back—and tried to—"

"Sell her to an old man," Keven finished grimly. "If she did have a part in this, I will try to be understanding. But—" He broke off as his sister and their two most-trusted employees entered the room.

"So," Lena said. "Anybody want to explain the scold of jays in Lady Crane's garden?"

"All I did was mention the gossip about her fantastic party tonight," Stina said.

"I bought the bag of nuts out of my own allowance," Lady Sara said proudly.

"But that's all they did," Sven-August said. "I'm the one who snuck in, dumped the nuts, and imitated the bird calls to make sure the jays found the food."

"Why would you do that to your mother?" Keven asked. "Don't you know how important her entertainments are to her?"

"That's exactly why I did it. I couldn't possibly make her feel the pain I felt when she sold Jasper—and I do sincerely appreciate your buying him back for me, especially because that's how we found Brownie in time to save her life—but I figured I could make her at least a little bit unhappy."

"I wanted them to be sorry for what they did to Brownie," Sara added. "They aren't nice people."

"True," said several voices in unison.

"Well, her party is back on schedule," Lena said. She indicated their visitor. "Stina and Sven-August know Arvid, but I'm not sure Sara has met him."

"Lord Arvid Melander, my sister, Lady Sara Crane," Keven said.

"How much time did fixing this problem take?" Lena asked Arvid.

Arvid chewed his lip in thought. "I would reckon it at about six hours."

"Very well," Lena said. "Keven, do you think that having each of them volunteer six extra hours of labor to the temple would be reasonable restitution?"

"If the Prior agrees," Keven said. "I have no problem with it."

"I hope you don't expect us to make restitution to my mother," Sven-August said.

"I most sincerely hope that neither your mother nor her husband ever figures out that you did this," Lena said firmly.

"She seems to think it's an unfortunate accident," Arvid said. "If her party tonight is a success, she and Lord Crane may forget all about it. I really hope so."

"I'll ride back to the temple with you and explain everything to the Prior," Lena said. "With any luck, he'll agree that keeping this quiet and letting it be forgotten would be best for everyone."

She looked around the room. "Let's not have a repeat of this. We all know Lord Crane, Lady Crane, or both of them. Whatever our various grievances against them, we all survived, got away from them, and got your beloved horses back. Leave them alone from now on. They are probably each others' worst punishment anyway."

*   *   *

Unfortunately, Lena's attempt to avoid the Cranes didn't even last the rest of the day. She had taken Sara to one of the Mid-winter afternoon parties for young children, and they were leaving it when there was a sudden eruption of female screams mixed with the cries of jays. What Lena picked up from the birds had her sending Sara for a Healer while she ran toward Lady Crane's house.

Usually the housekeeper was reluctant to let Lena in, but now she grabbed her arm, shoved her in the direction of the garden, and cried, "Do something!"

Most of the people in the garden were backed up against the house, as far as possible from both Lord Crane and the birds. Lord Crane lay flat on his back near the pond, strug-gling to breathe, while Lady Crane knelt at his side and held his hand.

Lena knelt next to them. "I've sent for a Healer," she said softly, keeping her voice calm, "and I'll see to the birds."

Lady Crane nodded, still clinging to her husband's hand. His breathing had gotten worse in the few seconds Lena had been with them. She was afraid that very soon even a Healer wouldn't be able to help him, but she didn't want to say so. She moved to the other side of the pond and called the birds to her.

:What's wrong?: she asked them. The birds returned a clear picture of Lord Crane shouting and waving his arms around, hitting one of the birds so that it slammed into the fence and dropped to the ground. The angry birds had then swarmed Lord Crane until he fell to the ground. Lady Crane had shielded him with her body, which Lena thought was likely the bravest thing she had ever done.

Lena sighed, picked her way through the plants near the fence, and very carefully picked up the injured bird. Fortu-nately, it wasn't bleeding, but . . . .*:I'm pretty sure this is a broken wing,:* she said. *:Do you know where the Temple of Thenoth is? The priests there can set it and care for him until it heals.:*

The birds agreed to that, and they also agreed to leave Lady

Crane's garden. Soon the only bird there was the one Lena was gently holding in her cupped hands. When she turned around, she noticed there were also fewer guests.

Just then Sara arrived with the Healer. While the Healer knelt opposite Lady Crane to look at her patient, Sara ran across the garden and clung to Lena. "He's not breathing," she whispered.

"I know," Lena whispered back. "Do you know how to handle an injured bird?"

Sara nodded. "Sven-August taught me."

"Good," Lena said. "Take this bird inside—carefully, his wing is broken—and ask the housekeeper to find a box you can use to use to transport him. He needs to be taken to Brother Thomas at the temple. Ask Stina to help you, and tell Sven-August he's needed here."

Sara nodded, carefully transferred the bird to her own hands, and quickly disappeared into the house.

Lena knelt next to Lady Crane and gently patted her hand. She was surprised to have it clutched desperately. "I don't know what to do," Lady Crane said, tears still dripping down her cheeks.

Lena glanced at the Healer, mouthed *"Shock?"* and got a slight nod.

"Actually, you *do* know what to do," she assured her. "This is your house, and you've been having parties here for years. You just have to do the usual cleanup. After that, you have Keven and me, your lawyer, and Sven-August."

Lady Crane sobbed, "He'll never forgive me for Jasper."

"Apologize," Lena said firmly. "He'll forgive you if you do. We all know what Lord Crane was like."

"I didn't know before I married him how much he hated all of you. I'm sorry. It's hard when you have a husband who doesn't listen to you and only cares about what he wants." She frowned and turned to the Healer. "Why did he die?"

"Allergic reaction," the Healer said. "His throat swelled up, and he couldn't breathe. Apparently, he didn't know he was sensitive to birds when he tried to chase them out of the garden."

"For the second time today," Lena added.

"Really?" the Healer asked.

Lena shrugged one shoulder. "Look at his face. Not all of the scratches are fresh. Some are from when he took a broom to a scold of jays this morning."

"That would account for it," the Healer sighed. "It's unfortunate, but it's a natural death. It's not something that needs to be investigated. You can bury him whenever you wish."

Lady Crane shuddered. "It's just so sudden. I've never even thought about where to bury him!"

"I'd suggest next to his father," Lena said. "He's definitely his father's son."

"Do I even own that land? Am I still Lady Crane?"

"Yes, you're still Lady Crane; being widowed doesn't take away the title. As for the land, we'd need to see your marriage settlements and his will. The land probably belongs to either you or Sara. The title will pass to her, but even if she owns the land now, she should allow her brother to be buried with his family."

"Does she even know how to deal with the estate? She's only a child."

"That's why the King has me and Keven fostering her. He's familiar with the estate, and I grew up as the last member of my family, so I've been through the process of reestablishing a family."

The kitchen door opened, and Sven-August came out and joined them. "Mother, I'm so sorry."

"I'm sorry, too," Lady Crane said. "I didn't agree with him about selling Jasper, but he wasn't good at listening to anyone who disagreed with him."

"He really wasn't," Sven-August agreed, which Lena thought was a considerable understatement, especially given Rupert's "courtship" of her.

"If he hadn't tried to commit wholesale avicide twice in one day," she pointed out, "he wouldn't be sick, much less dead.

Arvid and I both know he attacked the birds. Everyone at the Temple of Thenoth knows that he kicked his favorite dog so hard he broke her ribs. Then there was the stunt with your horses. Maybe Thenoth finally decided he'd harmed enough animals. You don't necessarily have to worship a god to have him take an interest in your actions."

Future-Proof
J. L. Gribble

Every direction Cam turned, the layout of the dim corridors never shifted. His footsteps echoed on the scuffed flagstone, and bolted doors broke the plain stretches of dingy plastered walls to either side. No matter how hard he tugged, none ever opened at his touch.

After so many visits, he could walk them in his sleep. Therein lay the problem. He only traveled these halls in his sleep, almost every night. If the anxiety from the endless circling didn't wake him early, the inevitable shriek from next door served as an equally unpleasant alarm.

"I need my other pair of green slippers!"

With a groan, Cam dragged his pillow over his head. Usually, the walls muffled the woman's strident tones, but last night, he'd opened his balcony window to catch the breeze. Since the residents of the neighboring suite had had a similar idea, the morning's tirade reached him loud and clear.

Closing his eyes thrust him back to the empty halls, imprinted on the insides of his eyelids after months of vivid dreams. For the first few weeks, he had imagined the recurring visions might be Farsight or Foresight. Seventeen might be past the typical age, but stories existed of Heralds answering their Companion's call at every age. His advanced rhetoric class included a Herald trainee approaching forty.

As the years passed, though, no Companion approached. With the bang of a gavel, Cam abandoned his dream of being Chosen when the judge sentenced his older brother to prison.

"Not those! Those are sage!"

Most noble families would have fled Haven for their country estates to lick their wounds after such a disgrace. His parents, Lord and Lady Aylmere, on the other hand, launched an immediate campaign to repair the family's reputation, even moving the family into this small palace suite to maximize their time and connections. As much as Cam didn't want to withdraw from his courses at the Collegium as one of the unaffiliated students, being part of the insular community in the heart of Haven meant he no longer shed the weight of the suspicious stares and whispers by escaping to the family home farther into the city. After Silas's conviction in the wake of undeniable evidence, their sidelong glances and louder mutters almost seemed inescapable.

"I don't want silly excuses about your head! You need to make yourself useful!"

Cam tossed aside his pillow and lurched out of bed, intending to slam the door closed. He dared not engage with Lady Phran. No need to add to the tensions between their families.

A hitching sob stayed his hand. He stepped onto the tiny balcony before second-guessing himself, despite having no notion how to console a servant suffering Lady Phran's wrath. He blamed sleep deprivation.

The hunched-over figure, arms outstretched and braced on the railing of the adjoining balcony, was no servant. His head jerked up when he caught Cam's presence.

Cheery chirps from birds searching for their breakfast in the garden below contrasted with the tense silence as the young man straightened slowly, pulling his shoulders back. A different sort of awkwardness suffused Cam. He'd intended to express concern for a servant's distress, but Cam had nothing to say to Duri Phran.

Lady Phran shouted another demand. Cam caught Duri's minute flinch, familiar with the action himself. Without a word, Cam turned on his heel and retreated to his bedroom, firmly shutting the door behind him.

Turns out I'm truly no better than the rest of my petty, vindictive family.

* * *

Like every morning since his brother's arrest, Cam entered the Collegium wing with mask firmly in place. Chin up, shoulders back, eyes clear. Silas had gone out of his way to set the Aylmere brothers apart during his short time at the Collegium. In the time since, Cam had never attempted to bridge the gap with his fellow students, even the other noble Blues. He might not have enemies among them, but he also had no allies.

This morning, though, instead of sitting in a classroom, Cam slouched against the wall near the rear door of the packed auditorium at Bardic. The rain had forced everyone inside. The size of the gathering meant clusters of students stood near Cam, but none near enough to invite his inclusion.

"If I may have your attention, please?" Bard Kaplan's lyrical call cut through the excited chatter. "Welcome to the annual Collegium Academics Challenge!"

A brief cheer rose from the students, teachers, and assorted interested guests, which Bard Kaplan silenced with a sharp slice of one hand. Scholar Radu joined her. "Thank you, Bard Kaplan."

Cam half-listened to Scholar Radu's standard opening introduction, already familiar with the premise of the event. The competition absorbed each corner of the Collegium for a week in late spring. A secret group of teachers set the convoluted quest of challenges meant to put all students on equal footing, no matter the color of their uniform. After initially placing twenty-third the year he'd joined the Blues, Cam had steadily climbed the ranks at the event. Winners received nothing more than bragging rights, but this year, he would settle for nothing less than the top three.

"I'm sure you have all heard a certain recent rumor," Scholar Radu said, prompting a wave of whispers. "You'll either be delighted or disappointed to discover the rumor is true. This morning, along with receiving your first randomly selected clue, you will also learn the name of your randomly assigned partner."

Cam's heart sank. Even after Bard Kaplan restored order from the ensuing outburst, blood roared in his ears. Two Bards

carried baskets of old-fashioned scrolls to the table next to
Scholar Radu, who withdrew a list from his pocket. As he
called names, Cam spared little attention to the resulting cries
of excitement and dismay.

An older Herald trainee calmly accepted the scroll from the
nervous young apprentice Healer he'd been paired with. Two
older Bardic students traded jokes as they collected their scroll,
while two girls in blue and pale green shared squeals of glee
when their names rang out. The random element appeared to
be true, at least. Objectively, the wrinkle to the competition
intrigued Cam. Faced with reality, however, he foresaw abject
failure.

"Camryn Aylmere and Duri Phran!"

The auditorium crashed to abrupt silence. Although no one
truly knew Cam, *everyone* knew combining the Aylmere and
Phran names invited nothing but trouble, even before Silas had
destroyed any hope of reconciliation between the noble families.

A fragile layer of ice supported Cam's place in the Blues, and
his broken sleep stretched his already thin temper. As Duri
crossed the silent room to accept their scroll, Cam slipped out
the door without looking back.

Expulsion might have been kinder.

Halfway down the hallway, Cam's pride dragged him to a halt.
He lingered outside a vacant practice room and studied the
well-worn floor until a pair of expensive boots stopped in his
field of view.

He looked up to find thick black brows pinched together under Duri's shaggy fringe, though in pain rather than disgust.
Cam swallowed the natural urge of any decent person to ask
after his health. After all, he wasn't a decent person, and Duri
was a Phran.

"So, are we doing this?" Cam gestured to the scroll Duri
clutched. His tight grip already caused wrinkles to spread
through the paper, which might mar any clues hidden in the
texture of the parchment. Cam hoped they hadn't already lost
the game before they began.

"Why not?" Duri's question carried no enthusiasm, but he tilted his head to the practice room in silent invitation.

Despite the tension between them being thick enough to cut with a knife, they managed to unfurl the scroll and hold it open together against a music stand. Careful block letters formed a short line of unreadable text. A delicate tracing of scrollwork surrounded the random string of letters, with the remainder of the pale cream parchment left blank. Unbidden, a trickle of energy danced under Cam's skin. Pouring himself into his studies served as his chief mode for avoiding his family, and mysteries never failed to entice him. Even sharing the moment with Duri Phran didn't fully diminish his excitement.

He jabbed a finger at the looping design. "That design's carved into the doors of the old palace library. Books are—"

"Still kept there, despite the larger library built a few decades ago, yes," Duri said. "Let's get over there before anyone else."

Cam carefully re-rolled the scroll and cradled it with gentle hands. Duri followed in silence as Cam led them along an indirect route rather than risk exposing the scroll to the rain.

On their arrival at the old library, his inches on Duri meant Cam used the lantern from the hall to light those in the windowless room. The space did not invite a person to linger. Dusty shelves lined the walls, and a mismatched collection of hard-backed chairs surrounded a single reading table.

In silent agreement, once enough lamps illuminated the space, they split up to search the shelves. Cam lost himself in scanning titles stamped into the spines of leather- and cloth-bound tomes, some so faded as to be almost indecipherable. The first candlemark flashed by, but the second dragged as Cam's eyes burned with strain.

Duri's frustrated huff drew Cam away from a dim corner to the center of the library. A light coating of dust gave Duri's uniform a disheveled appearance. Cam assumed his fared no better. "What's wrong?"

"We're in the wrong place."

Cam pointed to the open doors. "The design matches."

"Perhaps the original artist carved more than one set."

"The library is the obvious answer."

"Or it's a misdirection, and we're wasting our time. No one else is here."

Cam scoffed. "No one starts with the same clue. Maybe you didn't know that? I don't remember your name among the rankings the last few years."

Duri heaved an aggrieved sigh and sagged against the rickety table, which rocked on uneven legs. "Aylmere, I can't—"

"Wait!" Cam had initially dismissed the haphazard trio of books left atop the table, but when Duri jostled the ancient furniture, the top book shifted to reveal a thin pamphlet. He arranged the texts into a single row. "Look here."

No common theme linked the treatise on human rights, selection of Valdemar's legal statutes, weighty tome on property and inheritance taxes, and pamphlet of amateur philosophical musings, other than the potential for boredom. However, dropping the articles from each title meant the first two letters in the remaining words spelled out the code from their scroll.

Duri offered no congratulations at the discovery. For a moment, he didn't move at all. Cam spared a sliver of fear that his reluctant partner might be the one to walk out. Finally, Duri sank into one of the chairs, rubbing his forehead with the pads of his fingers.

"Okay, genius," he said, voice tight. "What next?"

Cam settled into the seat across from him. "We read."

Not missing a beat, Duri shot back, "Do you even know how?"

The terrible insult sounded more out of habit than anything else. Still riding the adrenaline rush of success, Cam simply laughed.

One corner of Duri's lips twitched as he tugged the pamphlet closer and flipped it open.

Cam preferred the loneliness of eating alone to the stress of formal dining with the court. Although he dared not refuse when Lady Aylmere demanded his presence for supper, he begrudged every candlemark the meal stole from time better spent in the old library. As the second day of the competition drew to a close, he'd left Duri behind at the reading table, steadily turning pages. When he did not join the overdressed Lady Phran at her table, Cam feared Duri would uncover their next clue without him.

The weather had cleared, allowing the Aylmeres to cross the garden directly to the wing housing their rooms. Two Bardic students, their russet robes almost black in the garden path's lamplight, rushed past. They gave his parents respective nods and a wide berth, but the young woman who shared Cam's mythography class halted when she spotted him.

"Oh!" she said, taking in his formal dinner suit. "You've already found the key?"

Cam froze, mind racing. His parents paused, and under their piercing, expectant gaze, he assumed his blandest court smile for Lindy. "Of course."

Lindy gasped. "Well done, you! You and Duri must be making good progress together."

Lifting his chin, Cam donned the haughty attitude that kept everyone at a distance like a comfortable coat. "Enough progress to spare time for dinner with my parents."

"We've got catching up to do," Lindy's companion said, tugging at her sleeve. "Let's go!"

As they darted away, Cam faced his parents. Lord Aylmere cocked an eyebrow, obviously catching Cam's subterfuge; however, when he braced for disdain, his father only said, "Well played."

"Thank you, Father." Cam dipped his chin in gratitude, but also to cover his whiplash at the unexpected approval.

"Best not to allow word to reach the Phran boy that you've moved on without him," Lord Aylmere continued. "I'm sure you'll go far again this year without him holding you back."

Cam repeated his thanks. His parents dismissed the topic as closed, already returning to their previous conversation regarding the rudeness of someone at another table during the fish course. His mind whirled on the way to their suite, where he hastily changed out of his finery and then raced to the old library.

When Cam burst into the room, Duri lifted his gaze from one of the books and blinked owlishly. "You're back."

Ignoring the redness of Duri's eyes, obvious even in the low light, Cam planted both palms atop the table and loomed over the slighter boy. "Where's the *key*?"

"What key?" Duri asked, chair legs scraping the floor as he eased away.

"The key. The next clue. The one we should have found by now in these stupid books." Cam snatched the book away, scattering scraps littered with scrawled numbers. He grabbed one and tossed it at Duri. "The one you must be hiding from me, since you've clearly found something."

Duri gaped at him. "Are you accusing me of sabotaging us?"

"Considering my father just congratulated me for the same thing, when I had no idea what key Lindy meant? Absolutely. My parents may sink low, but I'm sure your mother would sink lower."

"That's insane." Duri jerked to his feet, clutching the edge of the table when he almost stumbled.

"The Phrans couldn't stop at making my brother take the fall for your crimes? You have to make sure I don't succeed, even if it means failing yourself?" Cam meant the words to sting, but each cut his tongue like a shard of glass.

Anger narrowed Duri's eyes, which at least hid their painful redness. "My family had nothing to do with your brother's arrest or trial. Though I'm sure your father had a hand in Silas implicating my uncle!"

"Then what are these?" Cam flicked at another scrap of paper.

Instead of answering, Duri swayed on his feet. Cam rushed around the table, ready to catch his elbow, but Duri's violent flinch at his approach almost sent them both to the floor. Finally, Cam managed to get Duri seated before he fainted dead away.

"Sorry." Duri directed his apology to the table's surface. "I thought you might hit me."

Cam bristled at the accusation, but backed away to give Duri space. "I may not be a nice person, but that's a line I won't cross."

"I know." Duri gave a half-shrug. "Your brother would have, though."

Collapsing into one of the other seats, Cam buried his face in his hands. He'd always suspected, but never confirmed, that his brother's heavy hand found other victims during his short stint at the Collegium. Did Duri want Cam to apologize on behalf of his brother in exchange for the key?

If so, where did the apologies end? The cut and fabric of their uniforms proclaimed them as more than simply two students. Despite escaping formal charges, Duri's uncle had left Haven in the wake of the recent scandal. Did the Phran heir demand a recompense of honor from the new Aylmere heir?

He'd never desired the position of Aylmere heir, and he despised the idea of assuming responsibility for a single one of his older brother's choices. When he lifted his head, he spoke to neither his classmate nor the next Lord Phran, but instead to the shadow of a wounded young boy who lingered in Duri's guarded gaze. "I'm sorry I didn't protect you from my beastly brother. I would have if I'd known."

Duri collected his strange notes into a neat pile. "Thank you."

Relief washed through Cam. Rather than examine how much he may have revealed with his shot in the dark, he acknowledged, "You're not hiding anything from me."

"No," Duri said. "When I ran over to the Collegium for a quick supper, a friend showed me what her pair found in Companion's Field. A combined cartography and land navigation exercise leads to an actual key."

"We're either incredibly far behind . . ." Cam glanced around the dim library.

"I can't even tell whether we're playing the same game." With a dry chuckle, Duri added, "I hate to ruin your chances this year, but I'm not exactly at my best. Headaches have plagued me for months. My mother's constant complaints about her new neighbors aren't helping." The quirk of his lips invited Cam to share in the joke.

"She should commiserate with my mother." Cam reached across the table, but stopped short of touching Duri's hand. "How do you feel now?"

"Better, since I ate. Nothing I can't handle."

Cam trusted Duri to know his limits. So long as the younger man found the energy to press on, he'd work alongside him. However, as he drew a book to hand, Cam wondered whether they would ever discover what they worked toward.

After a late night of no progress, they abandoned the disparate collection of texts and returned their attention to the original scroll. Cam's pride at his idea to use curved glass, borrowed from an Artificer, under bright sunshine to examine the parchment in the most minute detail was short-lived. The effort sent Duri straight into the painful embrace of a massive headache. He revealed the true scope of his agony when he made only a token protest at Cam's insistence he rest for the remainder of the day.

Unwilling to lose more time than necessary, Cam retreated to the old library and dove into the books. When he finally sought his bed much later, he might as well not have bothered. After a handful of candlemarks wandering endless corridors, he woke from his disturbed sleep even more exhausted than if he'd had no sleep at all.

Their takeover of the library hadn't gone unnoticed, as indicated by the replenishment of lamp oil, and Cam blessed whichever servant had delivered the tray of hot chava awaiting his arrival. By the time Duri stumbled in, he'd already downed two servings. He studied Duri over the rim of his cup when the younger boy dropped heavily into his seat. "Feeling better?"

Duri waggled one hand. "Yesterday was the worst it's ever been. I couldn't even hear the—" He flushed and busied himself with pouring chava.

Unfortunately for Duri, the attempted dismissal piqued Cam's curiosity. "Hear what?"

Groaning, Duri shot him a pleading look. "Please, drop it. You'll think I'm crazy."

"No crazier than the mess we're already in." Cam refreshed his cup, but he feared no amount of the blackest chava would solve the puzzle.

"The numbers." Duri shoved the stack of his notes toward Cam. "They come and go. I'm not sure whether they're a result of the pain or the other way around."

Cam set aside his cup and examined Duri's angled print. "Random? Or repeating?" The pattern emerged under his study even as he asked the question, and he ripped one of the smaller scraps further to isolate the combination.

Mid-sip, Duri gestured helplessly. Something about the numbers tugged at the edge of Cam's mind. Perhaps some sort of substitution cipher? He flipped one of the other papers to a blank side, but abandoned the attempt when no obvious solution coalesced. "Interesting."

"That's a polite way to say crazy," Duri said.

Two days ago, Duri never would have admitted any of this to Cam. Of course, four days ago, Cam would have laughed at anyone who suggested he and Duri spend any time together, much less work toward a common goal. Wouldn't be fair to allow Duri to claim all the craziness between them.

"I'll trade you," Cam said. "Your numbers in exchange for the recurring dreams that haven't allowed me a decent night's sleep in months."

"I'll pass on nightmares, thanks." Duri wrinkled his nose in distaste.

"Not nightmares, exactly. I'm walking the same empty hallways lined with doors over and over again." Cam selected a blank page of notepaper and sketched the general shape of the corridors. He'd done it often enough before—failed attempts to exorcise the dreams—that even freehand, the scale of his map matched his endless night wandering. He presented the completed layout with a sarcastic flourish.

Duri's laughter at Cam's attempted humor caught in his throat as he studied the paper. "Is this a joke?" he asked, tracing the map with a trembling finger.

"No more than your numbers, I'm assuming." He didn't

think Duri was a good enough actor to have faked his obvious pain the day before. "Why?"

Suspicion drained from Duri's face, replaced by confusion. "This is my house. I mean . . ." he said, shaking himself slightly, "where I grew up outside Haven. The original estate was already falling apart with age, and a fire destroyed most of it when I was eleven. Then Uncle moved my mother and me to the palace."

"Why am I dreaming about a place that no longer exists?"

"You're not." Duri returned the map. "This shows the cellar storage and workrooms. Our servants used to let me have the run of the place. Those might be relatively intact, though I'm sure anything left above it at this point is a deathtrap."

The drawing reshaped itself in Cam's mind with the new context. "Even if it does exist, I promise you I've never been here."

Slowly, as if testing each word for truth, Duri said, "I never imagined otherwise."

"So, what have we learned this morning?" Cam asked. "Somehow, the first person I share my dream with is one of the few who can verify its existence. And if I'm not going crazy, I doubt you are, which implies your numbers also mean . . . something." He hated his inability to solve Duri's puzzle as easily as Duri had presented the answer to his.

Duri glared at the scroll at the other end of the reading table. "I think we've learned we might not be playing the same game as everyone else."

"Maybe . . ." Cam said, following the paths of the map with a finger, "we're not playing a game at all."

He and Duri reconvened at the palace stables after changing into riding gear, wearing not a scrap of blue between them, and requested their mounts. Their guise of young noblemen out for a spring ride fooled no one. They left behind a trickle of whispers at the stables, sure to become a wave of loud speculation as the gossip passed through palace and Collegium.

Cam anticipated a silent ride, a return to their status quo

outside the bubble of the old library, but he forced himself to ask Duri for more information about his childhood home. Duri's description provided more than enough detail to prepare Cam for what to expect—land rented to the surrounding property owners and a tumbledown collection of burned and unmaintained buildings from the original estate tucked away in a wooded expanse.

To his surprise, the conversation broke the ice enough for Duri to share stories of playing in the cellar seen in Cam's dreams, which prompted Cam to share childhood stories of his own. They connected more than once over common moments as noble sons more inclined toward academics than the traditional social pursuits of their class.

After they departed the main road, Duri led them through crop fields and into the cool shade of woods. When they reemerged into the bright sun, the ruins stood in stark contrast to the bursting life of spring around them.

From his quiet shock, Duri also didn't expect the team of horses attached to an unmarked carriage. An unseen driver had hitched them to a new post at the less damaged wing of the house.

They halted their mounts. "I take it you weren't expecting guests?" Cam asked.

"I don't even recognize the carriage." Duri dismounted and tied his gelding to the remains of a garden fence, Cam following suit. No one appeared during their cautious approach to the carriage. A closer inspection revealed no further clues about the owner.

Cam stifled a cry of surprise at nearby yelling. The strings of curses, strong enough to peel paint, carried the unmistakable notes of anger and terror. Duri's wide-eyed alarm resolved into determination at the next shout, a panicked plea of *"Don't touch her!"*

Before Cam could stop him, Duri sprinted around the corner of the ruins.

Muttering a curse of his own, Cam hurled after him, catching up right as Duri clambered down stone steps cut into the earth. An open door, its newness as out of place as the un-manned carriage, stood open at the bottom. Ignoring Cam's hissed demand to wait, Duri disappeared into the darkness.

Cam had braced himself for anything, but nothing prepared him for his dreams come to life—except for the sounds and smells now assaulting him from all sides. Feminine cries rose above the stench of too many unwashed bodies in an enclosed space.

"Let me go!"

Duri's harsh demand broke Cam from his shock. Not far from the entrance where Cam collected his bearings, Duri ripped himself from an older man's grip and darted to Cam's side. Without hesitation, Cam stepped between Duri and the stranger storming toward them, though he gasped when the nearest lamp, one of the few lit high on the walls, illuminated his face.

"Don't you dare lay a hand on either of us, Uncle." A thread of fear wavered in Duri's demand, but he didn't cower behind Cam. Instead, he wisely used Cam's larger frame to block Lord Phran's approach.

The man's presence here made no sense, since court rumor placed him halfway across Valdemar. Even more shocking, another familiar man strode around the far corner, calling, "Yes, please refrain from manhandling my son, Markus." Lord Aylmere halted next to Duri's uncle, his disdainful sneer as sharp as the blade at his hip.

"Father?" Not the most eloquent opening, but pounding against the far side of a nearby locked door distracted Cam from saying more.

Without missing a beat, his father slammed the side of his fist against the door. "Silence!" To Lord Phran, he asked, "This one's slated for transport soon, right?"

"Yes, and not a moment too soon."

"Transport? To where?" Duri asked.

The lords exchanged a glance laden with unspoken conversation. Their ease with each other confused Cam further, but also helped him find his voice. "What's happening here,

Father?" he demanded. The men hated each other. His brother had tried to ruin Lord Phran's life, so why did they look up to their necks together in whatever horror surrounded them? Who kept people locked in the cellar of a supposedly abandoned estate?

With a put-upon sigh, Lord Aylmere explained, "We assist people without the necessary means to relocate to other parts of Valdemar, and find employment for them."

Duri scoffed. "Out of the goodness of your heart, right?"

"This is a business, not a charity. We host them here until we find them work, handle their travel, and cover their room and board whenever they arrive. There's also the interest accrued during this process, which can add a certain amount of time—"

"Silas was involved, wasn't he?" Cam's single glimpse of one of his brother's victims haunted his rare dreams that didn't feature endless dark halls. Glancing at those same halls surrounding him, nausea crept up his chest.

Lord Phran rolled his eyes. "You were right. This son is cleverer. We should have used him first."

"Your brother's recruitment techniques became too . . . enthusiastic," Lord Aylmere explained.

A gasp caught in Cam's throat, but Duri beat him to the horrified question. "These women aren't here willingly?"

"Certainly, they are." Lord Phran's dark chuckle indicated otherwise. "A few just required more convincing that they could do better than the slums of Haven."

"No wonder you've let everyone think our families can't stand each other," Duri said. "What better cover, misdirecting attention from all the laws you're breaking together."

Their cooperation ended now. Like a bolt of lightning, his mention of lawbreaking finally gave context to Duri's mysterious numbers. Cam whirled toward him. "Ninety-one. Six. Twelve. Eighty-two. Forty-seven."

"What about it?" Duri asked, startled.

"Chapter ninety-one, section six, of Valdemar public law declares any person found guilty of transporting a sentient being against their will faces up to twenty years imprisonment." Cam spoke faster the more certain he became of the connection, almost tripping over his words. "Title twelve, part eighty-two, of the most recent revisions to the tax code state any privately owned building used for short-term tenancy must have a valid, unexpired certificate of safe occupancy as determined by a Master Artificer."

Putting the same pieces together, Duri finished, "And page forty-seven of the human rights treatise included the decree eliminating any form of slavery in Valdemar. I remembered the ink had smeared on the number."

Trust another Scholar to have an exceptional memory for insignificant detail. He turned to his father, but Lord Aylmere made a dismissive gesture. "Your concerns are noted."

"We can't let you do this." Cam crossed his arms.

"You misunderstand me, boy," Lord Aylmere replied, smirking. "There's no 'let' about it. If you reveal anything to any authorities, I imagine you'll be hard-pressed to explain to them why so many travel documents list your name. Or where a significant proportion of the funds in your private account originated."

Lord Phran added, "Same with you, nephew. How else do you think your mother's kept herself in jewels and gowns these past few years?"

"You would be left with nothing if you exposed us." Lord Aylmere smiled as if he'd struck the winning blow.

Cam shared his own glance with Duri. Though neither exchanged a word, Cam found reading Duri's perfect agreement effortless. It seemed they remained in this together. He hoped he mirrored the strength and determination shining from the other boy at what they faced.

As one, they turned to the noblemen. "We're smart enough to know what you're doing is wrong," Duri said.

Lifting his chin, defiant of his father's machinations, Cam said, "I'm sure we're also smart enough to support ourselves without you."

"If you leave now, you'll be no son of mine."

"Then you're the one who misunderstood me." Cam

straightened to his full height, realizing for the first time he stood taller than the man who'd always loomed so large. "We won't let you do this. I would rather be anybody but an Aylmere if this is how far the name has fallen."

Without waiting for a response, he spun on his heel and marched to the stairs leading aboveground, Duri at his side. They needed to return to Haven as fast as possible. He hoped they sounded the alarm in time to save those left behind, trapped in his nightmare.

Cam emerged into the sunlight and drowned in an endless ocean of blue.

Pride and acceptance and joy encompassed him like every hug and word of affection he'd never received from his parents . . . but better, because all he had to do to earn this unconditional love was be himself. Be true to himself, and true to his instincts, and true to those in need.

No longer encumbered by the weight of the Aylmere name, he rose to the surface a brand-new man.

He opened his eyes as if waking from a deep and restful sleep. The old Cam would have fled, embarrassed to find himself clutching the neck of a horse, but this Cam never wanted to let go of Denae.

His Companion.

:I'll turn you into a cuddler yet.:

Cam laughed around happy tears. "We'll see." He forced himself to put an inch between them, enough to see the ruins of the Phran estate swarming with blue uniforms. Not of students, but in the color and fit of the Guard.

Beyond Denae's broad back, Duri's embrace with another Companion came as no surprise, but didn't explain how Cam already knew her name, Devia.

:We're twins,: a second Mindvoice sounded, which did come as a surprise. *:Oh, sorry. We always figured separate conversations with our eventual Heralds would be too much bother.:*

:Unless you'd prefer it?: Denae asked.

"Pretty sure you already know the answer," Duri said, using

his sleeve to wipe the wetness from his face. "I'm just glad your voice doesn't hurt anymore . . . and that I'm hearing something other than numbers."

The remaining clues tumbled together into a completed puzzle. "My dreams," Cam said, glancing between Denae to Duri and his Devia and back again. "Duri's memories?"

Duri interrupted Cam's line of questioning. "Why now, though? The dreams and numbers started months ago. Why give us this final test and mask it as part of the academic contest? Did solving it make us worthy of being your Chosen?"

The twin Companions eyed each other for a beat. Finally, Devia responded, *:You've both always been worthy of being our Chosen, but before, you both clung too hard to the belief you were worth no more than your family names.:*

:You may have found refuge in your intellects,: Denae continued, *:but your senses of self remained too tightly bound to those names. You had to learn your true worth before you'd accept being Chosen without them.:*

Cam shifted until he stood beside Duri, both of them sheltered by their Companions from the surrounding chaos. "Chosen despite them, maybe."

"Heralds don't keep their noble ranks anyway." Duri sank against Devia's flank, his eyes practically rolling in pleasure. "We'll be nothing more than Herald trainees. I can move into the Collegium dormitory, away from my mother."

:Don't get too used to it.: Denae's equine smirk echoed in her mental voice. *:With all the classes you two have already passed with flying colors? You'll be Heralds Duri and Camryn soon enough.:*

A Single Row of Vines
Brenda Cooper

Herald Witman folded the corner of the waxed leather sheet and held it up in one hand, a broom handle in the other. "This can be used to collect rain, or even particularly dense fog, into a cooking pot when necessary." He plucked a length of thin rope from his desktop and set about attaching a corner of the folded sheet to the broom handle. "Imagine this broom handle is one of two or three trees growing a few feet apart. Several knots will work for this . . ."

Marjom smothered a smile. Even though he'd been a field Herald and not a fighter like her, she loved Witman's stories, and knew their value. Hopefully the students would take his lessons on how to survive to heart.

Despite her growing attraction to her teaching partner, Marjom needed to spend extra attention on their students today. They sprawled around the too-empty room in wooden chairs with individual wooden desks in front of them. A group of eight had left for the front yesterday. Marjom missed them already; the absent students made the classroom feel big and empty, and reminded her of the escalating war with Ancar.

After decades at the border, she had been deemed too old to fight, was pulled back from the work she loved and assigned to teach these kids. They were clearly too young to fight. Chosen or not. But they might have to go, and must be ready.

Today, the job of preparing them felt hard. Most of the eight remaining students focused on Witman, at least appearing to take notes and occasionally offering an idea or asking a question. But two of them were fully focused on each other. Amica sat in the back right corner, her arms folded tight over her midsection. She was tall, dark, and so far the strong, silent type. Marjom couldn't remember ever seeing her smile. But she had seen her glare. At Freya.

Freya hunched as far from Amica as she could get without leaving the room. Thus, close to Marjom. Shorter than Amica by a third, slender to the point of skinny, and blond as afternoon sunlight. From time to time, Freya glared back at Amica, the challenge in her gaze bitter and withering. Neither girl seemed afraid of the other, at least not outwardly. She'd never seen them sit beside each other or share a kind word. Or a word of any kind, for that matter.

Teens were often jealous or snarky. Even those training to lead Valdemar had the same bursts of too-much-everything as any other teen. Maybe even more so, given that these trainees, in particular, were living inside a ball of pressure with the war so close. But Marjom had never seen two trainees actually *detest* each other. Unless the war started going better, these two would be called up, and division could create disaster.

Witman displayed his completed rain trap and wound his story to a close. "Always carry rope. Class dismissed. See you tomorrow."

Freya bolted for the door, and lunch. Amica slowly unwound her tightly clenched arms and began to gather her notes and gloves. Marjom walked over and stood between her and the door. "Amica?"

The girl's dark eyes looked metallic and dull. "Yes, Herald Marjom?"

"Is everything all right?"

A disingenuous smile barely touched Amica's full lips. "Of course. Why do you ask?"

"Between you and Freya?"

Amica threw her braid over her shoulder and straightened. She stood nearly a foot taller than Marjom, who was not herself particularly short. Her jaw tightened around the remainder of her smile.

Marjom pursed her lips and waited. She was a full Herald and Amica a trainee; there was no way Amica could or would step around her. Nevertheless, the girl stared longingly at the door before she met Marjom's eyes.

"Amica?" Marjom repeated patiently.

Amica took three long, tense breaths. Then three soft words—with edges—escaped her. "She's a liar." The words hung in the air for a moment, and then Amica added, "She comes from a family of liars and cheats. That's why we can't bear to hear from them. They lie." Amica shouldered past Marjom and out the door.

Marjom stiffened, but let the breach of protocol go. This once.

Witman looked over from where he was stuffing his satchel with papers. Marjom asked, "So you noticed it, too? Our little feud?"

He returned her smile, but gazed after Amica with a worried frown. "It's even more obvious now that the others have gone. I hope those two don't get assigned to be each other's sparring partners."

"That would be rather awful, wouldn't it? Amica told me Freya comes from . . ." How exactly had she put that? ". . . a family of liars and cheats."

"They're from different estates. Up near the Winefold region. I rode Circuit up there for ten years." His expression soured. "Before they were born."

Marjom held the door for him, since his hands were full of props from the class. "So, do you understand it?"

"The Winefold is full of good people. Farmers. Vintners. But they keep to themselves and spin tales about how good their wines are. I had to break up fights a few times."

She hoped he would say more on the walk back to Heritage Hall, but he only spoke of the cool wind and murmured about inconclusive news from the front.

The next morning, Freya and Amica sat in the same places. Lumps of light and dark resentment. Marjom spent the latter part of class demonstrating how to travel quietly. Neither Amica nor Freya offered a single useful question or idea.

Before she dismissed the class, she asked both girls to stay after. A cook's apprentice slipped in the door with a tray holding a large loaf of bread, chunks of cheese, and some of the season's first grapes.

"Come here," Marjom said, dragging a few desks together. Freya and Amica stood not quite in the farthest corners from each other, looking as if their boots had been nailed to the floor.

"Sit," Witman said in a tone that startled Marjom. She'd never heard him give a command before. "We are going to share lunch."

The girls sat on opposite corners, pushing their chairs back so far they could barely reach the desks. Marjom sat with Freya on her right and Amica on her left, and doled out lunch for herself. Witman did the same. Neither of the girls moved to take a plate.

"You need to eat," Marjom said.

Amica spoke firmly. "It would violate an oath were I to break bread with anyone from the Glassard family."

Freya sat in stony silence, glaring at her plate as if it were at fault.

Witman cleared his throat. "Your oath to Haven is the most binding of all. You took that when you accepted Malinora as your Companion."

Amica leaned back in her chair, putting another few inches between herself and Freya. "That can't invalidate oaths to my family."

"It might," Marjom said. "What if Freya gets harmed on the battlefield and you are with her? What will you do?"

Silence.

Marjom thoroughly enjoyed a bite of cheese and bread before she turned to Freya, who had still not spoken a word. "And you? Are there oaths other than to your Companion and to Valdemar? Promises?"

Freya's attention focused so entirely on the tips of her boots that her eyes looked crossed. She spoke so softly, Marjom could barely hear her. "I am not allowed to speak to Amica or any of her family. I could be disavowed by my own if I utter a word in her presence."

"Valdemar will disavow you if you harm each other," Witman told her. "You might go find a Bard and ask for some songs about Tylendel."

Freya drew in a sharp breath; doubtless she'd heard the rather apocryphal stories about what happened when a Herald's anger drove them to harm others. Amica didn't react, but then again, strong and silent . . .

Amica's face looked like stone, Freya's like fire. Finally, Amica spoke. "We have been wronged, and there have been deaths. I will not harm Freya if she does not break her oaths."

Amica stood and looked poised to flee. She added, "You cannot force me to work with someone from a family who killed one of our own."

Marjom flinched at the girl's words. That bad? She stood, unwilling to let Amica march past her a second time in as many days.

"If you don't bend, you may break," Witman growled.

Freya stepped back, mute, her eyes full of something Marjom couldn't read. Perhaps fear or perhaps defiance. Or both.

Witman stood, looking down at the untouched half of the platter. "Take your lunch with you, or you'll be hungry before your sparring session."

Amica grabbed a slice of bread and a single chunk of cheese and rushed out of the room.

At least they'd learned something. "Freya?" Marjom asked. "Would you eat with us?"

Freya scooted closer to the table. She silently took a few grapes and a bit of cheese, and began breaking the cheese into crumbs. She mumbled, "I need to fight for Valdemar. It may save my life."

Marjom's hand stopped halfway to her mouth and she nearly dropped her grape. "It could also kill you. While I wasn't able to join this war, I've fought many border skirmishes, and lost best friends. What could be more dangerous than that?"

Freya glanced at Witman. "You know."

He stiffened. "You couldn't have been born yet."

Freya's eyes widened. "But you know what happened, and so you must know that it is all a lie." Her voice sharpened and gained timbre. "Dominic was *not* murdered by my uncle. But Amica's uncle murdered mine. If we were boys, one of us would be dead already."

Marjom drew in a sharp breath. "I don't understand."

Freya pointed at Witman. "He does. He can tell you all about it." She offered Marjom a pained smile. "Can I go?"

Marjom was about to ask a follow-up question when Witman interrupted her train of thought. "Yes. But think hard. If a fellow citizen of Valdemar is more worry to you than Ancar is, you cannot go to the front."

Freya scooped up the rest of the grapes and stalked out the door—at least if anyone so slight that her Grays threatened to trip her could be said to stalk.

Marjom sat back in her chair. She had never heard such fervor in Witman's voice. She asked softly, "Do you have a story to tell me?"

He paused. Shifted. Looked uncomfortable. Then he spoke very quietly, his voice drawn tight with pain. "Once upon a time, a long time ago, I caught a boy poisoning a row of a rival family's vines."

"Oh! That's terrible." She paused a moment. "That's how this started. A single row of vines?"

He stood and began gathering the crumbs and napkins onto the tray. Then he picked up his satchel, and she hers, and they stepped out into the afternoon sunshine. "I don't know the whole story," he said finally. "Only the beginning."

"I'd like to hear that."

"Can we sit down? Even the beginning isn't a short story, and I want to tell it in the sunshine."

They walked half a block before she found a wooden bench and led him to it. After sitting, Witman stared at the tiny little patch of late spring grass in front of his boots. He took a deep breath.

She took his hand to give him encouragement. "When did it start?"

"Almost forty years ago. You know how that seems impossible? That you can remember something that happened that long ago?"

"I do." And she did. It was about forty years ago when she won her first fight. With mere bandits, and nothing compared to what she'd faced since, but at the time, it had frightened her to her very bones.

Witman stared up at the sky, clearly lost in memory. "The Winefold area is beautiful, with rich soil and rolling hills. Vineyards everywhere, and old barns, and small, friendly taverns near every one of the larger farms for tasting. Have you been there?"

"No."

"The town of Winefold has a very fine stone inn I'd love to take you to someday. But this occurred beyond the town's boundaries, in the hills, so I was the highest authority." He stopped and glanced at her, as if making sure she followed him.

She nodded.

"It was my first solo Circuit. I'd been out three times with a mentor, and done well, and the Winefold was known to be peaceful."

She tried to bring him back to the main story. "So, poisoning vines?"

"If this boy's behavior had been allowed—destroying vines that took a generation to grow—then the two fighting families might have destroyed each other, and also a valuable crop. It takes time to nurture a good vineyard. The boy was too young to really understand that."

"What happened?" she whispered.

"Well, he told his story, in tears the whole time. He had salted a whole line of about twenty-five mature vines. Apparently, over and over. Mature vines don't die easily. The family he'd wronged—Amica's, I guess—blamed him and his brother. Maybe the brother was the real culprit. But Dominic did the deed, going in the night and digging around the roots and putting in handfuls of salt. He got caught the fifth time, but by then the vines were so ill they had to be pulled out. Apparently, they were some kind of precious grape that took years to establish. Everyone yelled at everyone else."

He stretched his legs, stood, sat back down. "I felt very uncomfortable. I was young, and I had no idea people could be so emotional about plants, even if they needed them to make a living."

She could imagine. Witman himself seldom raised his voice. He wasn't a tall or imposing man, but rather a bit short. Kind and thoughtful, his strength in brain more than brawn. She thought back to his commands to the girls today. Had he already suspected these same families were involved?

He continued. "In the end, the only one I really liked was Dominic. Our culprit. A sweet kid, and he seemed to be sorry. At least for the pain he'd caused the vines. I don't know if he felt sorry for wronging the humans, but he apologized for killing living things that hadn't done him any harm. It made me admire him a little, despite his crime. But the families? They had enough bluster and killing anger to frighten me."

"What did you do?"

"I assigned him to a year of fosterage on a different farm, far from Winefold. I'd ridden through it the month before, and knew the family would be grateful. They had fewer young hands to help than they needed, and Dominic's family was large, and him the youngest. It seemed like an answer to benefit everyone." He let out a long sigh, hesitated. When he spoke again his voice was soft and slightly broken. "I was . . . going to take him with me and hand-deliver him. Make sure it all worked out."

"It made sense to move him away from the fight," she agreed. "How old was he?"

"Eleven."

"Oh, my. A baby. I agree; *someone* urged him on. And he needed a fresh start. How did it work out?"

"His father found him hanging from a tree the next day."

She gasped.

"There was a suicide note, but the father insisted it wasn't in the dead boy's hand."

Marjom fell silent for a while, and then whispered, "That's so . . . sad." The word felt small, inadequate.

"I cried," Witman admitted.

She had never seen him cry. Had learned, herself, how not to cry. Mostly. But he had been young, and to the young, pain is immeasurable. "I'm sorry," she whispered.

Witman's jaw tightened. "The dead boy looked like Amica. Tall for his age. Dark hair. A little belligerent, but then, I didn't meet him until he'd been caught and accused. There was ample evidence. Two witnesses, including someone who was the boy's friend. But killing himself seemed a bit extreme for the crime."

Forty years ago. Marjom did the math. "Would Dominic have been Amica's uncle?"

"Maybe." He let out a long sigh. "It was the generation before these girls, so probably yes. Or maybe great-uncle. Babies come early on farms. Forty years is long enough for the details of a death to have turned to legend, and for feelings to harden. If I can manage the Mindspeech for it today, I'll ask Juniper. Companions' memories . . ."

She laughed softly, slightly bitterly. "If your hunch is correct, I wonder why Companions would have chosen two younglings from opposing sides of a longstanding family feud? I can't imagine they didn't know what they were doing."

He stood again, offered her his hand. "We should go put our things away."

She had horrid knees, and his Mindspeech failed as often as it worked. Two old Heralds . . .

She used the walk to Heritage Hall to think. *Why are the Companions putting up with this?*

Hannra had often corrected Marjom's stupid choices. She reached out to her Companion. *:Hannra, are you aware of the family feud between Malinora's Amica and Vinni's Freya?:*

:*We are.*:

We. An interesting choice of pronouns. :*Do you have any suggestions?*:

:*This is best solved between humans.*:

:*But Malinora and Vinni won't help? Why did they choose feuding children?*:

:*Do you trust us?*:

:*Of course.*:

:*Then work the problem.*:

Hmmmm. Not what she had expected.

They arrived at Heritage Hall. Marjom held the door for Witman, and he stopped for a moment, looking as if he might lean in for a kiss. Kisses had become almost routine between them. But he hesitated, then touched her cheek. "Meet me back here in an hour?"

"Sure."

She watched him walk down the hallway toward his room. He seemed a bit hunched. Or maybe she imagined it. She sighed and went to her own room to clean up.

She usually napped a bit after teaching, but she felt too keyed up. They didn't have more than a few weeks to resolve this feud, not if she read the situation right. By then, there could be a new class, and they would have sixteen students again, and no time to focus. In spite of their hatred for each other, Freya and Amica were both good students. They could end up with their Whites within a few months, and then be gone. But they simply couldn't leave for the front in this state.

An hour later, she found Witman staring out one the windows that overlooked the pea patch–style garden that some of the residents loved. When she came up and rested her hand in the small of his back, he startled.

She smiled at him. "Lost in thought?"

"I have a few ideas," he said.

"Me, too!" She smiled again. "You go first."

"Well, I should go to Companions' field and try my chat with Juniper. You can go by the Collegium and talk to them."

"I was thinking I should go there. Ask if we can we separate the girls. And if the Companions know about deaths near Winefold in the last forty years?"

"Be careful," he teased. "If they ever let us out of this damned retirement home, I'm going to ask for you to ride Circuit with me."

"I love you, too," she riposted.

He stopped. For a moment, the humor left his face as he searched hers. "Do you mean that?"

She hadn't said those words to anyone but Hannra for decades. She hadn't been sure she was ready to say them, hadn't meant to let them slip forth now. But she couldn't very well lie to Witman, could she? Her voice dropped to a near-whisper. "I do. We work well together." That wasn't exactly romantic. She swallowed. "It feels good to work with you."

Now he gave her the kiss he'd skipped when they came in, and her body shivered at the touch of his lips. She hadn't expected to ever again feel so warm, so . . . young.

She stepped back, her cheeks heating. "I'll go now. Meet you back for dinner?"

His smile seemed to lift him, make him taller and maybe a bit stronger. He leaned in to whisper, "I love you, too."

She fled, her steps light and heart racing.

:*About time,*: Hannra told her.

:*Busybody.*:

:*Always.*:

Surely she was too old for a relationship. But Witman had been growing on her every day. She woke up looking forward to seeing him. There had been other attractive Heralds, of course, but riding the border made every relationship seem fleeting, and way too many friendships had ended in death. But she didn't have to fear that so much here behind the fighting lines and safe inside the walls of Haven.

She did, however, have to focus on the two trainees who wouldn't even talk to each other. She picked up her pace.

* * *

After dinner, Witman pulled her away from the kitchen cleanup. "Join me for some wine on the patio?"

Her chest opened a bit, and she smiled at him. "Of course. As soon as I finish."

She found him on a wooden bench near the rose garden. A small tray held a bottle of red wine, two glasses he'd poured half-full, and a small plate of sweets. Before they took the first sips, she raised her glass, intending to say, "To love," but he spoke first. "To stopping our feud."

Well, he had their priorities right. She approved. "Were you able to talk with Juniper?" she asked.

He laughed ruefully. "I took a few tries, but yes. Juniper confirmed Dominic was Amica's great-uncle, and the boy who *might* have killed Dominic—*if* he didn't kill himself—is also dead. He was Freya's great-uncle. Juniper said the feud is bad enough it might have come to Selenay's attention if there weren't so very many other things going on in the Kingdom right now."

"But you don't know if anyone else has died?"

"Juniper will try to find out. But he won't give me any direct advice."

She laughed. "Nor could I get any from Hannra. I tried."

Witman shook his head. "There's no telling what they'll help with and what they leave to us." He took a long drink of his wine. "What did you find out?"

She stretched her left knee out, rubbed at the tight muscles right above. "That I walked too far today."

He smiled softly. "I'm sure you did."

"No one thinks separating them is acceptable. So we don't get out of it that easily."

He shrugged. "It was worth a try."

"Well, we can't saddle future Heralds with the need to keep these two apart."

"Is your knee going to be okay?"

"After some sleep."

He changed the subject. "Did the Collegium have any records of other events near Winefold?"

She raised her glass. "This wine probably didn't come from there. The two houses have had to defend each other *from* each other. No more vines were destroyed, but each group has lost some harvest and had trouble hiring help. I found a wine steward who works over at the palace, curating the highborn wine cellar. He confirmed the story, named the wines, and then looked quite hopeful. I imagine *he* wants us to fix it."

Marjom finished her perfectly adequate wine. "Amica can't eat with Freya, and Freya can't talk with Amica. Maybe Amica can talk to Freya while Freya eats?"

He belted out a laugh and reached for the bottle. "Can I pour you some more?"

She covered the glass with her hand. "I need to sleep well tonight. I need an idea."

He smiled, poured himself a tiny bit more wine, and raised his glass to her. "Can we force them to work together?"

She leaned back and looked up at the dusky sky, searching for the first faint stars. "Can we trick them into it?"

"Like what? Blindfold them and have them each trust the other to lead them around?"

"That could result in accidental death," she replied dryly. "But maybe."

He held his hand out to her, and she took it, let him help her stand. She stood and stretched her legs, swaying a bit to loosen them, hating it that these days she had to prepare a little in order to walk normally. He took the wine glasses to the kitchen and she followed.

She hesitated a moment at the place in the corridor where they went two different ways every night. Had the words they'd said yesterday meant something would change tonight? Was she ready for it to?

He leaned down to kiss her, pulled her closer than usual, and kissed her longer than usual. But perhaps he wasn't sure if they were ready either; he hesitated for just a moment, then whispered good night and headed, by himself, toward his room.

*   *   *

It took two days to complete a plan. On the third day, she and Witman arrived early in the classroom. They created two circles of five desks each and stood in the front while the students filed in. Freya and Amica, as usual, went to their corners.

Marjom started. "We're going to do a three-day team-building exercise. We're lucky enough to have a small class. It's a great time to demonstrate how useful it is for Heralds who ride, work, or fight together to know each other well. We will share exercises to deepen your understanding of yourselves and your fellow trainees. Day one will be in the classroom. Day two will be in the field, with all of us. Day three will be a scavenger hunt. The winning team will get a set of new custom-made boots. And you may not know how valuable that is in the field!"

Most of the students looked excited. Amica and Freya scowled more deeply. Exactly as expected. "We'll start with two groups of four." That way she and Witman could each sit with a group and watch behavior. "We'll begin with Freya, Mick, Lisha, and Paol in group one, and the others in group two." She smiled at the relief in Freya's face and the stony look on Amica's. "Gather up!"

As soon as the students joined the circle, Marjom began a discussion. "Tell us about your first day in Haven." As she expected, the stories of confusion, pride, and longing were similar enough to build bonds among the four students. Freya contributed with the others.

After the first hour, they switched the groups up and put Freya and Amica together. The question, "Did you know how to ride before you were Chosen?" started the round.

Amica offered slightly more than Marjom had hoped for. "Yes, I had my own pony. Her name was Princess. A pinto. She was old, but I loved her, and I missed her a little after Malinora Chose me."

The most words I've ever heard her say. Marjom smiled approval.

Freya's answer was a nod. After a brief pause while they

waited for more, Daryl asked her if she'd had her own horse. Freya nodded again. Another short pause, and Rachel picked up the thread with her own tale, and Freya's behavior was ignored.

So it went. No outright fight or anger, but Freya would not speak. Each student was supposed to have a question. When it came to her turn, Freya looked at Marjom directly, careful to keep her eyes off Amica. "What is your goal?"

Marjom answered the unspoken end of Freya's question directly. "Heralds who cannot team with others may not be allowed to graduate. I am not the person who decides, but as some of your teachers in this final year of your work, Witman and I will be asked for our thoughts. I would like to offer a good opinion of all of you." Then, for complete avoidance of doubt, she added, "I want all of you to earn your Whites."

Freya's eyes grew wide. She sat back in her chair and refused to say another word. Rather than sunlight, today she looked like angry flame. Marjom hadn't expected it to go much better, although the fact that usually silent Amica had talked a little heartened her.

The next day, Witman led the class in field games.

Freya managed to throw the baton close to Amica in the relay, but it missed. *Better,* Marjom supposed, *than hitting her in the head.* The three-legged race was a disaster. Freya and Amica managed to complete it, but came in dead last even though they were both athletic. Witman, bravely, decided to try the blindfold exercise. Both girls led the other over harsh terrain. Freya fell once and Amica twice, even though she was far stronger. The other teams kept each other in good shape and looked pleased, while these two glared daggers at each other.

Witman gave the students a break and pulled Marjom aside to converse. "At least they haven't stabbed each other."

Marjom nodded. "Maybe you should deliver the same warning I did about failure. See if we can force them into understanding the stakes, and finding their own breakthrough."

Witman stared at the resting students for a while. "I don't like it."

"I know. You like honey. But this might be the moment for a stick."

The next events didn't pair the two, so they went well. Freya won a foot race and Amica and Lisha won a kettle-throw. Witman dismissed the class except for Freya and Amica. Freya looked winded and windblown, and quite unhappy to be detained. Amica stood like cold stone.

Witman used his command voice. "Today was a disgrace. We will keep you two together until you figure out how to work together, or we will recommend that the Collegium fail you both."

He glanced at each girl in turn. Amica's expression remained unchanged, although her eyes appeared slightly damp. Freya stared at her feet.

Marjom backed him up. "Do you understand?"

Amica folded her arms over her chest. "Yes."

Freya, still unwilling to speak in front of Amica, broke into tears.

Marjom kept the smile off her face. Even though the class had done a lot of hard, difficult work, neither of these girls had ever broken down in front of them. It could be progress.

Witman pressed Freya. "Do you understand that if you fail to earn your Whites, you could be repudiated?"

Freya nodded and swiped at her face.

"And you could die of that, and your Companions as well?"

Freya cried harder, and Amica, if possible, stiffened even more.

"Dismissed," Witman said. "We'll see you tomorrow."

As the girls walked away, Marjom commented, "Perhaps they'll speak with their Companions about this."

Hannra popped into her head. :*That will happen.*:

:*About time.*:

:*We would not have let them fail. But they needed to hear from humans. Their fear of each other runs deep.*:

:Fear?:
:Of course.:
:Thank you.: Then Marjom added, *:I love you.:*
:I know.:
Marjom laughed. *:Ass!:*
:I love you, too!:
:I know.:

Fortified, Marjom turned toward Witman, to find him pointing. She followed his finger to see Freya pelting across the field toward them. The girl pulled up just in front of them, eyes still red. "I need to talk to you."

"You were just talking to us," Witman pointed out.

"Alone."

"Go ahead," Marjom encouraged. She wanted to fold Freya in her arms. But she stood neutrally, waiting.

"I . . . I can't fail," the girl sobbed. "If I fail, Amica will kill me. Unless Dominic killed himself. Which no one knows, maybe Julian killed Dominic—and Rulf killed Julian. Then nobody died until the next generation, when both the youngest died. That was Deirdre killing Sam, and someone—we don't know who—killing Deirdre. We think no one said who did it because she was the first girl that died. But both Amica and I are the youngest, and she'll kill me if I'm not protected by Haven."

Too many names and deaths for Marjom to hold in her head all at once. "How do you know she'll kill you?"

"That's the only way she can retain her honor!" Freya's voice rose in despair. "Don't you see?"

Witman asked, "Does anyone in your family talk to anyone in hers?"

"I . . ." Freya swiped at a fresh batch of tears with a shaking hand. "I don't know."

Marjom asked, "Surely your mother doesn't want you to kill Amica?"

"No. She made me swear. When I was five. That I wouldn't. But there's nothing to stop her from killing me."

Unbelievable. "Her mother wants her to kill you? Even if that means another of your siblings might kill her?"

"She had three older sisters and two brothers. No one needs her. So . . . maybe?"

And that might explain Amica's cold demeanor. If she wasn't wanted, and she was being encouraged to do something dangerous and wrong, she might feel the need to stay shut tight against the world. Freya lit up talking with anyone but Amica, but Amica brightened for no one.

"I can't solve this for you. Neither can your mother, or even your Companion. But you can." She paused, let that sink in. "Tomorrow, we're sending the two of you on a scavenger hunt in Haven. You'll have to go together, and you'll have to work together, and you'll need to have certain shopkeepers or grooms sign off on tasks for you. You will have to talk to her to accomplish this. One of you must start the healing, and it might as well be you."

Freya stood still for three breaths. "I don't think I can."

"Didn't you just say that if you can't, she will kill you?"

Freya nodded, drooping with misery.

"Vinni wouldn't have Chosen you if you could not do this. Trust me. Go on. Go get lunch. In the morning, after you leave class and where no one who knows you can hear, but where there are other people to keep you safe, say something to her."

"Like what?"

"What have you ever said to her?"

Freya spoke in a small, miserable voice. "Nothing. Not a word. I was told never to."

"Then start with something simple," Marjom suggested. "Ask her a question. Hell, just ask her how she is. Try that."

"I can't."

"You can," Marjom said. "You must be strong enough for this, or you would not be here."

The girl fled across the field.

The next day, Marjom and Witman sent the students out in pairs, waiting in the classroom. An hour passed. Two. The classroom felt huge, and cold.

Lisha and Paol were the first ones in. They presented their

completed and signed-off card, looking quite proud of themselves. Witman rewarded them with a dismissal so they could
have an hour off before lunch to do whatever they wanted.
Mick and Daryl came next, also successful. Then Rachel and
Sarah, just barely making it in on time. After the two of them
left for lunch, a little miffed that they hadn't been first, but mercifully unaware that they hadn't even come close, Marjom and
Witman stared at each other.

The entire lunch period passed.

Then laughter poured through the empty and open door.
Freya's laughter. Amica stepped through first, handing them
the girls' completed card. Freya followed and smiled triumphantly at Marjom. "We did it."

"Was it hard?"

"Yes," Freya said. "But Amica found two of the things we
needed."

Amica's face broke into a smile. "Do we win the boots?"

Marjom shook her head. "No. But you got something better.
Don't you agree?"

The two looked at each other. While they didn't smile, they
also didn't glare. "Yes," Freya said. "We both hate the feud."

"That's a start, then, isn't it?"

They said "yes" in unison and walked out together. Not
touching or saying anything more to each other in the moment.
But it would be enough.

That night, after a good communal dinner and a private glass
of wine, Marjom and Witman walked down the corridor together. At the corner where they usually parted, Witman
tugged a little on her arm. In a quiet and hopeful voice, he
asked her, "Come with me?"

Marjom warmed. Another thing to celebrate. Without hesitation, she told him, "Yes."

He led her down the hall, and she felt younger than she had
in years. In spite of her sore knees.

Most True
Kristin Schwengel

It's hard to hold a duel
  When just one stands on the field.
  Hard to claim a victory
  With no one there to yield.

Nieko hefted the basket of vegetables, then hooked it over one hip for the walk back to her parents' cottage at the outer edge of town. She hid her smile from old Corrie, who was undoubtedly concealing a smile of her own at having gotten one over on the "youngling who'd been all the way from Covey to Haven and back." It always felt good to slip back into the familiar rhythms of life in the mountain town, and if a few coins more than what they both knew was fair helped smooth her way on her brief visits home, she was willing to pay.

As she neared the main gate out to the Trade Road, she heard the squeaking of cart wheels and the chatter of drovers. The words she could make out were Valdemaran, so it wasn't Traders, but more folks than Traders made their living on the roads. Nieko eyed the sun. Her mum wouldn't expect her back to the cottage for a half-mark or more, so she had time to watch and see who or what had come in.

She wasn't the only one, either. A handful of curious townsfolk had gathered on the outskirts of the large square, from young children looking to run errands for a few copper coins to older folks listening for the latest news from, well, wherever the travelers had been.

The caravan included several mounted guards and an assortment of carts and wagons, a couple of which were decorated enough to rival any of those belonging to the Traders. As these pulled to a halt by the town's largest inn and began to disgorge their occupants, she saw a swirl of skirts in a familiar rust-colored fabric. She glanced down at her green and brown garb; here at home she usually dispensed with her Bardic uniform, as she did not consider herself "on duty" and representing Bards. She shifted to get a clearer view of the wearer's profile, when the rust-clad woman turned—she bit back a groan.

Giulia. Of course if any of her fellow Journeymen would find their way to her hometown, it would be Giulia.

Nieko stepped to the side of the square, resetting the basket and turning toward her parents', hoping her scarf hid enough of her flame-red hair.

"Nieko? Nieko Brendan?" No one's voice carried like that of a trained Bard when they chose to use it, and Nieko swallowed another groan, eyeing with reproach the locks of hair that had already fallen out of her scarf to frame her face. No such luck, that she could avoid Giulia's sharp-eyed notice. She never had been able to, not from her first days at Bardic.

She turned again, waiting as Giulia stormed her way. No other word suited the action; Giulia's skirts were a tempest as she moved, her dark brown hair rippling in her wake. "Nieko! I thought that was your hair. What are *you* doing here?"

"I live here, Giulia," Nieko replied, resisting the urge to match Giulia's excessive drama with a heavy sigh of her own. They had entered the Collegium just months apart, and it seemed Giulia had resented her mere existence ever since.

"Really?"

Nieko chose not to respond to the skepticism in Giulia's tone, shifting the basket of produce once more, calling attention to her mundane errand and out-of-uniform attire.

Only then did Giulia actually look at her. "I knew you lived somewhere in the south, but I didn't realize you were actually from the Comb. How could your music not be filled with these mountains?" She gestured to the range of peaks around Covey.

"I write about people, not landscapes," Nieko replied. *Although maybe a little bit of atmosphere would help me with whatever's missing in my masterwork*, she thought with a hidden sigh of frustration. As usual, Giulia missed the hint of censure, that her own work lacked a broad appeal to her audience.

Reluctant to get into another unwinnable argument about how to compose, Nieko shifted her basket yet again. "My mum's expecting me; I'm sure I'll see you later. Covey isn't *that* large, after all."

Giulia blinked at her shortness, then waved a hand in the direction of the peaks. "You might not; I'm planning to experience all that these mountains have to offer. Sunsets, sunrises, even storms if they come!"

"Just have a care, Giulia," Nieko replied, realizing even as she said the words they were falling on deaf ears. Giulia had set her sights squarely on the path up the mountain, and it was certain nothing Nieko could say would change her mind.

A sword is only proven
  When it meets another blade.
  We never know the sun's heat
  From standing in the shade.

Nieko glowered at the note-filled scraps of paper in front of her. She'd never struggled so with any composition before. Of course, she hadn't expected a masterwork to come easily, but neither had she thought every phrase, nearly every note, would be such a slog. At least, it had been once she'd finished the first melodic line in a fluid blaze of inspiration.

Pushing the discarded ideas to the side, she pulled out the one page of music she had made into a fair copy. Elegant, tuneful, clear, and eminently *singable*, this theme had everything she was looking for. As Master Bard Kerith was fond of saying, a masterwork just *felt* different, and that was the feeling she got from looking at the notes, without even playing or singing them, but only hearing them in her mind's ear. It just needed something *more*, and she wasn't sure what that something was. A second theme, of course, but in all her fits and starts she had yet to produce anything that worked with this one.

She wasn't even sure what words to fit to the music yet. Her composition style had always been to find the music first, and get the feel of what she wanted the piece to say, then write the text to match. She needed to finish that second theme, to hear the whole and feel it in her heart and let it resonate so she could hear what it was trying to say.

At long last, she groaned and shuffled all the pages together, tucking them into her traveling writing desk before locking it and shoving it under her bed, behind her spare shoes. Maybe inspiration would well up to her while she slept.

"I sound like Giulia now, looking for some grand source of outside inspiration." The thought of her year-mate made her frown again, looking out at the late afternoon sun. She wasn't sure why she suddenly felt so responsible for the other young woman; maybe because Giulia was a stranger to Covey, and didn't understand the rhythms of the mountain.

Shaking out her skirts, she left the cottage and headed toward the town square and the inn, hoping to see Giulia's rust-colored garb among the old gaffers, gossiping away the warm spring afternoon.

Nieko had circled the main squares of the town twice without seeing or hearing a trace of Giulia, when one of the young lads who served as a message runner and general errand-boy came up to her.

"Yer mam sent me t' find you and say she'd be late back from Mistress Doney's, and that yer da was down with Trenza and the lambing ewes."

Nieko nodded. "Thank you, Jonny." No telling how late her father would be if there were problems with any of the sheep. Up in the mountains, any Healer would treat both human and animal patients.

Before the lad could turn and run off to find another task, she gestured at the mountain rise behind the town. "I know it's been sunny and dry these couple days since I've arrived, but what are the conditions of the trails?" Jonny's mother Clerra was often out foraging, and she was known for her intuition about the state of the mountain.

"Th' rock's likely t' turn, me mam said yesterday." The errand-runner tugged his too-small cap down toward his ears. The nearly shapeless wool immediately returned to its insecure perch atop his thick blond hair. "Too much rain earlier, she said."

Nieko sighed. "And knowing Giulia, she's gone up the mountain path." Her year-mate had always been drawn to the wilder side of nature, always looking for a great inspiration outside of herself.

Making her decision at last, she handed a copper to the lad. "Tell my mum I've gone up the mountain path to find Giulia. If anything happens—" She paused, trying not to think of the myriad possibilities. "She'll know what to do."

Turning, she tightened the folds of her shawl around her shoulders and headed down the Trade Road, toward where the smaller track that led up the steep slopes split off. It wasn't long until sunset, and the slopes would get dark quickly.

I will stand against you
  Most true of all your foes.
  No matter what the subject
  Your words I will oppose.

It was only after Nieko had passed the rough line where the tall trees turned into scrubby brush that she could see the rust-colored blob that was Giulia moving ahead of her, picking her way along the faint trail further up the mountainside, the low sun casting long shadows behind her. Fortunately, she stopped often to gaze around and admire the view, so Nieko was able to catch up with her before too long.

"Giulia, you probably shouldn't go any further up. It's been too rainy, and the ground is unstable." Nieko glanced up at the heavy rock outcroppings looming above them, then down at the stones beneath their feet. This far up the slope, there wasn't much of a path at all, just a less uneven section of dirt and rocks that wound still further ahead of them. "I know you want to see the sunset from here, but going back in the dark is too danger-ous. And it gets very dark very fast up here."

The other girl scowled at her from a few steps ahead. "So practical, Nieko. Don't you feel the charge here? The energy? I can smell inspiration, it's in the very air!" She swept her hand out in a dramatic stage gesture, and the rock wobbled under-neath her shifting weight.

Before Giulia lost her balance completely, Nieko closed the distance between them and, grabbing her flailing arm, tugged her back to a flatter section. The rock Giulia had been standing on continued to move, first turning against its unsupported neighbors, then sliding down toward the steeper slope.

Giulia stood and stared, watching in fascination as one slip-ping rock became three, a dozen, and more. Nieko pulled again, but the other girl resisted, mesmerized by the sliding stones in front of her, even as the noise of the shifting rocks grew.

Then, the ground beneath them began to quiver, and the shaking at last broke Giulia's rapt attention. Finally, she turned and followed a pace or two behind Nieko, trying to get back to stable ground.

A creaking, grinding noise came from the slope above them, and Nieko looked up to see one of the large boulders teetering on its edge. When it began to tumble, she had only a moment's warning as a torrent of rock and mud and gravel cascaded to-ward them. In that moment, knowing pulling would take too long, she leaned over and pushed Giulia with all her strength, hoping she could fling her to the other side of the boulder's path. Then the rock crashed down between them, the force of the surrounding slide carrying her with it, until a blazing pain at the side of her head was followed by blackness.

A sword is only proven
   When it meets another blade.
   The grinding of the whetstone
   Sharpens what was made.

* * *

"Nieko? Nieko, are you here? Are you all right?"

The faint voice seemed to come from a distance, drowned out by searing pain in Nieko's arm and an answering throb in her skull. She took sharp, shallow breaths in the technique her father had taught her years ago, trying to build a wall in her mind to close off her awareness of the pain, even while she turned to look at her injury. Her right arm was pulled away from her side, pinned between two boulders, and she closed her eyes against a sudden queasiness.

"Nieko, can you hear me?" Genuine fear filled the subdued words.

"Giulia?" Using her voice triggered a coughing spasm, and each movement of her chest spiked the pain until she was gasping more than breathing.

"I'm stuck, and my foot is hurt," came the reply, the pitch of Giulia's voice immediately more confident.

Nieko finally brought her breath back into her control, finally managed to get the pain walled off in a small corner of her mind. It sounded as though Giulia had ended up a little further down the slope. With the way her own body was caught among the gravel and rocks, she couldn't lift her head enough to see over the slide between them.

"Is your foot trapped?" If she had hurt less, she might have laughed that one of them would be pinned by the arm, one by the leg.

"No, it's my gown." Some rustling, the sounds of stones shifting, and a shriek.

"Don't try to pull free," Nieko warned. "It might start another rockslide." She eyed the size of the rocks beside her, trying to ignore her hand pinched between them. Far too large for her to have a chance of moving. She took a few more careful, calming breaths and turned her head away. "My family knows where we are, but now that it's nearly full dark, I don't think they'll come out to look for us until dawn. Too risky when you can't see properly."

She brought her free hand to the side of her head, feeling a tender lump. Fortunately she didn't feel anything sticky, and her fingers came away covered in dirt, so whatever she'd hit hadn't broken the skin. Head wounds always bled so much, and she had nothing but her filthy skirt within reach to blot it.

There was a long silence. "There won't be wolves, will there? Or bears?" Giulia's voice was tiny.

Nieko almost snorted. For all that she was drawn to the wild, Giulia was a city girl, born and raised in Haven. "Not this time of year. There will be bugs, though. And it'll be cold."

Another silence. "Nieko, are you all right?"

"My arm is trapped." She deliberately did not elaborate.

"So we're both stuck here until morning?"

"Yes."

"What should we do?"

Another moment Nieko could have found amusing. "Talk? Sing? I won't be able to sleep like this." *And with a head wound that knocked me out for a while, I probably shouldn't sleep, anyway.*

"What should we talk about?"

"Well, you know now that I'm from Covey, and that my father is the Healer here. My mother loves to sing, but isn't Gifted. I've no siblings, so I grew up with herbs and music. What about you? I only know that you're from Haven." Nieko shifted her hips, resettling her weight and pushing a few of the pebbles to the side so that she reclined a little straighter against the rock, her arm at a less awkward angle to her body. It wasn't exactly comfortable, but it was better.

A sigh from the other side of the rockfall, and Nieko heard some of the same sounds she had just made in changing her own position. "I'm the youngest of four, and the only girl. So I grew up following my older brothers and getting into trouble with them."

"What's it like, having siblings?" It wasn't the sort of question she'd ever felt she could ask her peers in Covey. She wasn't even sure they'd have understood what she was asking.

"Being the youngest, I was the tag-along, the unwanted extra the older ones had to watch out for."

"Wouldn't you have been cosseted, as the only girl?" She knew plenty who fit that description, no matter whether they were youngest or oldest or somewhere in the middle of the family.

"By my parents, yes, I admit they spoiled me a bit." Giulia paused. "More than a bit, if I'm honest. But to my brothers, I wasn't big enough, or fast enough, or strong enough to keep up with whatever games or tasks they set to, and so they saw me as spoiling all their fun. It wasn't until I discovered my Gift that I had something only I was good at."

Nieko pursed her lips, pondering. Small wonder Giulia had resented her, then, if she had finally come into her own, only to meet another girl a little younger than her and with a greater Gift.

"That's probably why I wanted so much to dislike you," Giulia continued, as though Nieko had spoken her thoughts aloud. "I was so happy to be at Bardic at such a young age, and then you were there, too, with a stronger Gift and even the color hair that I'd always wanted for myself."

"You *wanted* red hair? I'm only remembered as 'the red-headed one' wherever I go."

"But it's so dramatic!" Giulia protested.

This time, Nieko did snort with laughter. Only Giulia would say such a thing, and Nieko's chuckle brought an answering giggle from the opposite side of the rockslide.

"So, which is your favorite instructor at Bardic?" This time Giulia picked up the lead for their sporadic conversation, a tenuous peace in the darkness.

It was hard to track how long the silences became in the still watches of the night, interrupted only by the buzzing of the biting insects that liked the darkness. Perhaps a candlemark, perhaps only a half had passed since one of their periods of talking before Nieko felt the pain in her arm throbbing to life.

"Would you sing for me, Giulia? Please? I . . . need my spirits lifted." It was as close as she could come to admitting how much she was struggling.

"But your Gift is stronger than mine. Wouldn't it be easier for you?" The bitterness still present in Giulia's voice, despite her earlier words, struck Nieko like a blow.

"You know as well as anybody that it doesn't work that way. Healers can Heal themselves, if need be, but Bards can't influence themselves."

"But you always seem so happy when you sing, I thought it was just because my Gift is weak . . ." Giulia's voice trailed off, then the silence was broken by the gentle lilt of a familiar tune, a country lullaby.

As Giulia's voice strengthened through the first verse, Nieko felt the soothing touch of the other girl's Gift calming her mind, helping her strengthen the barrier between herself and the pain in her arm. By the third verse, she could hum the harmony, and the last two verses they both sang, Nieko's own Gift returning to Giulia what she had received.

It was barely after dawn when Nieko heard voices coming up the mountain path. They must have left town as soon as the pre-dawn twilight had filtered through to be up here this early.

"Here!" she called, her voice raspy from the night.

"Nieko! We're coming!" Her father's voice, and she nearly wept.

"We see the slide, but where are you?" A less familiar voice.

"I'm on the path side, Giulia on the far side." She craned her head around, her stiff neck protesting the twisting movement, to look up to where the path would have been. "Twenty or thirty paces below the path."

As she looked, she saw one of the innkeeper's sons lean over the edge of the path.

"I see you!" Tanner shouted, then took a small, testing step onto the rockfall above her. A rain of pebbles skittered around her, and he pulled his foot back.

"See if you can get to Giulia first," she called up. "It's just her skirts that are trapped and pinning her down, so it'll be easier to get her out."

The head leaning forward bobbed back out of view, and for

a long time there was just the sound of murmured conversation above them, then more rattling of rock above and on the other side of the slide.

"My foot is hurt, but I don't think too badly." Giulia's voice, in reply to a question that Nieko hadn't been able to make out.

Nieko listened to the rumble of voices, the sounds of a few stones shifting, and then the voices retreating as the others moved back up to the path.

"We've got Giulia out by cutting her skirts so's not to dislodge the bigger rocks, and Tepper is helping her back to town. Your Da won't leave without you, of course, but we're going to try to backtrack and come to you from the side. The rockslide on your side is less stable, and we don't want to make it worse." Tanner's voice, back up at the path where they had started.

Another long silence, as exhaustion dragged at Nieko's mental barrier against the pain. Without Giulia's presence, she suddenly felt very alone, even though she knew her father and the others were coming to help her.

"Nini, we're almost there, we can see the rockslide again . . ." Her father's voice trailed off, and she turned to see the three men carefully approaching through the scraggly trees, just above where she lay pinned. Even from this distance, in the early light she could see the shock on their faces as they realized how badly trapped she was. They worked down the slope in silence, her father in the front, scattering small stones around her in his haste to reach her.

Wordless, he held his hand over her shoulder, and she felt the touch of his Gift sinking into her, blocking the pain more thoroughly than her breath and Giulia's song had been able to. She sighed in relief, sagging into his supportive embrace while the two others examined the rockfall around her.

"I think we can move this one," Tanner said at last, touching one of the rocks that pinned Nieko's arm. "Not all the way off her, or it'll start another slide, but I think enough that . . ." He left the rest of the sentence unspoken.

"I'll hold Nieko and pull her out when the rock shifts," her father said, altering his position so that he was behind her, his arms coming under hers and clasping his hands tightly over her breastbone, anchoring her against him, his legs bracing on the ground below her. She closed her eyes, trying to let her body be loose and unresisting while she prepared her mind for what was to come.

"All right, then," Tanner said, "I'll get the lever in here, and Jamie on the other side . . ." Shuffling and more sliding rock. "And one . . . two . . . THREE!"

The two men pushed, and her father pulled, and the flood of pain as sense returned to her crushed limb overwhelmed the barrier her father had put in her mind and made her scream, until a blissful blackness took her.

The battle hones the fighter
  When he faces each new foe.
  And so we hone each other
  By sparring as we go.

Nieko woke in her own bed, in her parents' cottage, pain throbbing through her right arm. Her father leaned over her, checking her eyes, then immediately held a cup to her lips. She swallowed the bitter drink obediently, closing her eyes and waiting for the strong herbs to take effect. When the pulsing had faded to an ache, she opened her eyes and glanced down at her arm, tightly wrapped and splinted.

She looked up at her father, now in his Healer's Greens, and at the tears in his eyes.

"I'm sorry, Nini. It had been too crushed for too long," he said softly. "I could only save the thumb and most of the first finger, and they'll never be the same."

"But she's the best gittern player in the Collegium!" Giulia's outburst from the other side of the room was Nieko's first hint that the other girl was there, and she turned to look at her.

"And now you are," she replied, her voice soft, before turning back to her father, ignoring the stunned expression on Giulia's face.

"I knew it was likely," she said to her father, absolving him of his nonexistent failure.

"You knew? All that night we talked, and you didn't say anything? This was *your hand*! You knew you'd lose it, and you didn't say *anything*?"

"Better my hand than your head!" Nieko snapped, and Giulia reddened, silenced for the moment.

Before she could continue the argument, though, the healing draught took its full effect, and Nieko slipped back into dreamless sleep.

She woke to music, halting notes of an unfamiliar tune with long pauses, broken by the occasional scratch of a quill on paper or a hummed interval.

"Giulia?" Her voice was raspy, her throat dry. She managed to crack one eye to see the other girl stand from the stool against the wall, picking up a mug from the side table before approaching the bed.

Nieko worked herself up into a sitting position, then reached out with her left hand to steady the mug Giulia held to her lips before she drank. She recognized some of the herbs; no longer the heavy sleep-inducing ones, the flavor was bright and crisp, refreshing her mind as well as her tongue. Apparently, her father had decided she had done as much sleep-healing as she needed.

When the mug was empty, Giulia vanished down the hall, replaced at Nieko's side by her father, who placed his hand on her injured arm and closed his eyes, his Gift evaluating her healing progress.

"The bones have set as well as they will," he murmured, before opening his eyes and meeting Nieko's gaze. "How does it feel?"

"Weak and achy, but not the burning throb anymore."

"I want to keep it splinted and protected for a few days more, then you can start to relearn to use it."

"How long has it been?"

"Today's the third day since we brought you down; I didn't want to keep you dosed for longer than that." He paused, glancing down the hall through the open door, his voice dropping to nearly a whisper. "Giulia has barely left you, only sleeping when I insisted, for the sake of her sprained ankle. I think she bears her guilt heavily."

Nieko closed her eyes. She could read her father's thoughts in his voice, that Giulia's guilt was no more than she deserved for her foolishness. She was surprised at herself, in fact, that she carried no anger toward the other girl.

"I'm going to unwrap your hand for a while; I've Healed the skin, but I want you to start stretching it a little, just to get things moving." Nieko felt the unwrapping of the bandages, but kept her eyes shut until her father was finished.

A moment of silence stretched between them. "Do you want me to stay?"

Nieko shook her head, waiting until she heard the door latch click shut before she ever-so-slowly opened her eyes, and even more slowly turned her head to look at the hand that rested on the patched quilt covering her legs.

She sucked in her breath. Angry red scars webbed across the front and back, crisscrossing at the blunted ends where her last three fingers had been. Her forefinger now ended at the second joint, and the thumb bent inward toward it. Everything was swollen. She flexed and extended her wrist, and the range of motion seemed normal if a little stiff, so she didn't think any of the fine bones there had been shattered beyond repair.

Tentatively, she tried to open her palm, spreading her thumb out and extending her forefinger back. The muscles protested the movement after days of bandaging, and she felt the skin resisting. She reversed the motion, closing as though she could make a fist. The ropy scars puckered and pulled, but she kept alternating, flexing and extending as much as possible until her hand fatigued. It would take time before she would have the strength to pick up or hold anything.

She wondered how much she'd ever be able to do. A gittern would be impossible, she knew that, and she'd probably have to learn to write left-handed, but she should be able to manage tasks that required less precision. Nieko sighed and let her hand rest in her lap, waiting for her father to return to splint it again.

A sword is only proven
  When it meets another blade.
  A test against another
  To not leave skills to fade.

Nieko sat on the low bench in her father's herb garden, savoring the sun on her face after days in her bedroom. A swish of skirts caught her ear, and she turned to see Giulia approaching.

"You're up early this morning," Nieko said.

"So are you! I hadn't expected to see you out and about."

"Once I was no longer sleep-healing, I started to get stir-crazy from being cooped up. And I figured the warmth of the sun would be good to help my hand stretch."

Only then did Giulia look down, realizing that Nieko's hand was no longer splinted and bandaged. She gasped. "It looks awful!"

Nieko smiled wryly. "Thank you. It doesn't feel that wonderful, either."

Giulia gasped again, this time in obvious mortification. "I'm sorry, I didn't mean to be rude! I don't know what I was expecting . . ."

"It's . . . well, it's all right. It's still puffy and red, but it will get better, and I'll be able to use it a little more. Valdemar is full of people who get on just fine with worse injuries than this."

"How long are you planning to stay here, then?"

Nieko shrugged. "A little while longer, until I get used to using this—" She waved her mangled hand in the air between them. "Then I'll get back to being a true journeyman to finish my masterwork. There's no time limit for composition, and there's plenty of opportunities even for a one-handed journeyman if I never do it."

"But you must! You're too good a musician to *not* be a Master Bard!" Giulia's voice rang with genuine shock at Nieko's resigned words. "Even if you can't play the gittern anymore. If you want to learn to play a harp one-handed, I'm sure you can; and there must be other options if you don't. Surely there have been other Bards who lost a hand somewhere along the way."

Nieko held back a sigh. It seemed that Giulia had taken all the energy she once had poured into hating her and had transmuted it into some sort of hero worship, out of some combination of guilt or remorse or gratitude.

"How about you—how long do you plan to stay in Covey?" She raised one eyebrow. "You could head to Lake Evendim and try to find the source of those rumors of strange creatures there for inspiration for your masterwork. Unless you still want to see a sunset from the very top of the mountain instead of halfway down it."

Giulia shuddered, then her expression became uncharacteristically shy.

"I actually thought to stay here until you leave, to travel on with you and play to accompany you until you either learn the harp or figure out something else."

Giulia's offer might have come from a well-meaning place, but it grated on Nieko's nerves. "I want neither your pity, nor your charity, nor your guilt, nor your worship," she snapped. She closed her eyes, hoping Giulia would take herself and her *enthusiasm* away.

A long silence, then, in a small voice, "Will you take my friendship?"

Nieko slowly opened her eyes, meeting Giulia's. In the other girl's dark eyes she read only honesty. She thought back to the long hours of conversation and song the night they had spent on the mountain.

She gave a small half-smile. "Yes. That I will take." And almost laughed at Giulia's dramatic sigh of relief as she settled onto the bench by Nieko's side, tucking her feet beneath her and pulling a handful of sheets of paper from the bag she carried.

"Then, maybe, as a *friend*, you would listen to the start of my masterwork? I like what I have, but it seems to be, well, missing something."

Nieko nodded. "I would be happy to, and I even promise not to steal your best lines."

"Well, I don't have any actual words yet, just the melody and the sense of what I want to convey."

Nieko nodded again, surprised at the similarity to her own method. "I also like to compose the music first, and fit the words after."

Giulia pulled her gittern from her back—Nieko hadn't even noticed she'd had the strap slung over her shoulder—and strummed a chord, then started to sing a wordless line, melody unfurling until she reached a point where the notes faltered and she looked up from the scribbled sheet, frowning.

"You see? It starts out fine, but then it just feels, well, empty somehow."

Nieko almost gaped, her mind's ear fitting her own unsatisfactory composition against Giulia's.

"Sing it again," she said, and this time, at the moment when Giulia's voice faded, she sang her own refrain. Giulia's eyes widened, and she picked back up with her tune, their two voices handing off melody and counter-melody, lilting variations back and forth, testing and developing new lines against each other's.

When the last harmonic echo had faded into the stillness, for even the birds had gone silent while they sang, they stared at each other, until Giulia finally spoke, her voice hushed in awe.

"I don't know what the Collegium will do with a masterwork that's a duet. Has anyone even done that before?"

Nieko smiled. "They'll figure something out."

I will stand beside you
  Most true of all you know.
  For two in team are stronger
  Than each who pulls alone.

Detours and Double-Crosses
Angela Penrose

A welcome breeze wafted through the sweltering air, rippling through the endless rows of feathery greenery on the right of the hard-packed dirt road where two horses ambled along. Bard trainee Bruny turned her sweaty face into the breeze, facing the left side of the road, where the sandy-loam soil the color of oak bark had already been harvested bare. The scent of broken ground was familiar to Bruny, who'd worked plenty of hours in her family's vegetable garden, back in the Tolm Valley.

That was some years ago, though, and the living dirt smell was that rare in Haven, even within the bounds of the Collegium, which had plenty of outside within its walls, although most was set garden by the palace and pasture for the Companions.

Sometimes it was good to get out and smell the turned dirt.

Bard Harrond was riding next to Bruny, a couple of arm's lengths away, and looking out over the same harvested fields, no doubt for the same reason. He was a handsome man of about forty years, a baritone with a range from middle bass to low tenor. He didn't have the Bardic Gift, which Bruny did, but on its own his voice could keep an inn or tavern silent or laughing or stomping for hours. His main instrument was the cittern, but he had three more instruments in his sizable pack—a shawm, a tambourine, and two pairs of castanets. He was a master of all of them, or so it sounded to Bruny, who'd never seen castanets before, nor ever heard anyone do what Harrond could do with a tambourine.

Bruny considered herself the most fortunate trainee in all the Collegium to have been assigned Bard Harrond as her mentor for her journeyman rounds.

"We'll want to smarten up before we pass the river," he said, pointing to a line of trees in the distance. He ran a hand through his dusty hair to the tie holding it back, then scowled down at his grimy palm.

"Prepare for our entrance?" asked Bruny.

"Exactly." Harrond grinned at her and patted the bundle tied just behind his horse's saddle, between the hanging saddlebags.

Bruny had one just like it, where her rust-colored tunic was carefully folded away from the dust. It was her summerweight tunic, linen rather than the heavy wool of winter, but she still wasn't looking forward to putting it on in the heat.

Harrond glanced at her and gave her a wry smile. "It's all a performance, from first entrance to final exit . . ."

". . . And we play our roles with no fussing," said Bruny, completing the lesson. She knew the folk wanted their Bards to be happy and gallant and at their ease at festival time—most times, to say true—and that it was all part of the show. The Tolm never got so hot, though, and moving farther and farther southward in the summertime, Bruny was finding it that hard to pretend to be unbothered.

They paused in the grove of trees by the river—willows, appropriately enough, since the village they were heading for, the largest in the region, was called Willow Grove—leaving the light flow of folk heading into the village. Many of the farmers crossing the low bridge into town were pushing hand barrows loaded with carrots from the fields they'd passed on the way in.

The river provided Bruny water to wash with, and the drooping willows gave enough privacy that after a wash and comb, she changed her shirt as well as put on her tunic. She re-buckled her belt, sliding her dagger's sheath so it was out of the way and comfortable, dusted off her hat, and packed up her dirty things.

When she ducked out from under the willow, Bruny found Bard Harrond ready and remounted, sitting straight in the saddle with his shoulders back, his rapier polished, his scarlets immaculate, and his clean-brushed hair waving about his shoulders in perfect order, as though some magic animated it. Or maybe the magic was in his hat, a wide-brimmed, low-crowned thing, scarlet to match his uniform, with a fine black plume stuck in its black leather band.

Bruny, whose own brimmed hat was rust-brown to match her trainee uniform, and served to keep the sun from frying her brains well enough, but did nothing else she'd ever noted, re-mounted her own horse, and they clopped over the bridge.

"Welcome to Willow Grove," said Harrond with a grand gesture of one arm, "where they grow the best carrots in all the kingdom, and throw the finest carrot festival to be found in all the world."

The half dozen farmers within earshot let out a cheer at that, waving and tipping hats at the compliment.

The farmers were dusty from the road, but they wore their good clothes, clearly—Bruny saw no patches nor mends, and a bit of embroidery trimmed most of the armholes and wound around some of the grommets where the fitted, hip-length vest of the region laced on. It was an odd style, one she'd not seen before—rather than lacing down the front, as most such garments did, or even down the back, as one saw here and there, these laced down the sides, from the bottom of the armholes to the hem. It was an attractive style, emphasizing a curving figure on a woman or a trim waist on a man. The vests were laced with colorful ribbons, which couldn't be an everyday habit, ribbons costing more than plain cord. It must be for the festival.

The path from the bridge led straight through the village to the market square, where booths and awnings and covered bins were already set up.

Not everything on display was a carrot, of course. Cabbages, strawberries, summer melons, and beans of all sorts were tucked here and there around the mounds (and mounds and mounds) of carrots, and an entire aisle of booths displayed rolls of ribbons, bobbin- and needle-made lace trim, hanks of yarn, kerchiefs and aprons and fancy knitted stockings. Farther on, the goods shifted to pans and pots and crockery, and wooden kitchen tools with fancy carved handles. Here and there were games to play, with little prizes displayed to entice a coin or two.

A sturdy woman old enough to be Harrond's mother waved to them from the end of the aisle, pointing at one of the nicer houses aside the square. Harrond introduced her as Morrin, the headwoman, who would be hosting them during the festival, since Willow Grove was large enough for a tavern, but had no inn. Most travelers from surrounding villages would be camping along the river, but a Bard and his trainee got a roof over their heads and a patch of clean floor to lay their blankets on.

They set their things down, gave their horses over to the headwoman's grandson, and shouldered their instruments. Bruny followed Harrond back outside and across the square to a low platform with a bit of space before it, and soon enough they were playing and singing the song set they'd planned on the way into town, filling the square with music.

Sleeping on Mistress Morrin's floor was more comfortable than camping on the road had been—Bruny didn't miss the mud or bugs or random weather—and the next day all the booths and stalls in the market square were full a short time after the sun had cleared the roofs of the low houses.

Breakfast was a fresh carrot muffin and a little round of white cheese, and Bruny bought one of the raw carrots to nibble on. Willow Grove carrots came in a rainbow of colors, and Bruny tried a purple one, just for curiosity. It tasted much like the orange ones she was used to, may'p a bit sharper in flavor.

She and Bard Harrond strolled about the square while eating. Harrond seemed to know every second or third person they passed, and he greeted everyone cheerfully, introducing Bruny to so many folk that even her Bardic-trained memory was feeling stuffed full by the time they arrived at the performance stage.

They filled the crisp morning air with cheerful music, popular songs everyone could sing along to if they'd a mind. Harrond played his cittern and sang while Bruny played her pipes, backing up the senior Bard the crowd really wanted to hear. It was great fun, and having the attention on Harrond left Bruny feeling relaxed and happy to be playing for folk who were happy to listen.

Their set shifted to dance music during midday, when the folk doing serious business buying and selling let off for a while to eat and drink, and take a bit of joy in the festival. Bruny let out just a touch of her Bardic Gift for that hour, letting her joy at the rollicking songs, and the happiness and peace of a festival day, spread out among the crowd. They wrapped up with a local favorite Harrond had taught her over the past few days, then took their bows and retreated to get their own lunches, surrendering the stage to a trio of local musicians.

Bruny bought a fried river trout on a stick for lunch, and took a careful bite. The vendor hadn't gotten quite all the bones out of it, but the fish was tasty, with crispy skin and some tangy herbs stuffed inside. Another carrot muffin, and she was more than pleased with the food.

One vendor filled her waterskin with fresh carrot juice for far too many coins, but Harrond encouraged her to try it, and she had to admit it was delicious.

"All right, time to build relationships," said Harrond, once they'd finished their food. "Stroll 'round the square, look at things, buy a trinket or two, and talk to people. Everyone who goes away thinking you're a fine young woman is an asset, but you particularly want to get to know the prosperous and influential."

"Because they're the ones who might hire me," said Bruny with a nod. It still felt a bit strange, going about and deliberately sucking up to those folks. Although if it was actually sucking up, then she was doing it wrong.

"But talk to everyone," said Harrond with a nod. "And don't ignore your own generation. You never know who's friends with tomorrow's headman, or who might tell you a story that'd make a good song."

"Aye," said Bruny. "Till later, then."

Bruny strolled about and did her best to make friends. She

asked most of the carrot farmers about their crops, particularly the purple and yellow and red ones. When they heard she'd never seen them before, most were happy to talk about the different varieties and their virtues, and why the challenges of growing them perfectly made it all that difficult to earn a scant handful of coin by the end of the season. And once they were talking, they told her other things—recent gossip, less recent history, other festivals and holidays they celebrated in the area, and more gossip. They asked her about Haven, and the Collegium, and about where she was from, and then about sheep.

By mid-afternoon, Bruny was fairly sure she could grow a fine crop of carrots herself if she ever needed to, had been told six versions of a scandal regarding a man who'd been making his so-called carrot cake for all these years with orange potatoes instead of actual carrots, and had heard gossip about bandits to the south drawing the Heralds and soldiers away from the district.

She was thinking of getting another carrot muffin, and pondering the possibilities of a song about counterfeit carrot cake, when a stout woman some years older than Bruny sidled up to her, a young boy in tow, maybe six or seven years old. The woman looked all about her before saying in a low voice, "You're a Bard, then?"

Bruny nodded and said, "Trainee, that is," and patted her rust-colored sleeve with a friendly grin. "Did you want to hear a particular song?" They were far enough from the performance stage that it wouldn't be rude to sing something for the woman, if she had a request.

The woman blinked a couple of times, then said, "Ah, no, I'm sorry. Could we go speak for a moment?"

That was . . . strange, and Bruny instinctively glanced about, looking for Bard Harrond, who of course was nowhere in sight. "Certainly, if you like." She gestured for the woman to go on.

They left the square and walked a couple streets away to a willow tree beside a brick well. The street was silent save for chittering birds, everyone having gathered at the festival.

The woman, who was dressed in a plain, undyed skirt and

jacket, with a much-laundered apron tied round, slipped under the drooping willow; Bruny followed.

"I work for a woman who needs help," the woman said, her voice still low, despite nobody being about. "There'd usually have been a Herald come through a fortnight or so past, but they're all hunting bandits, or so we hear."

Another glance around at nothing, and she lowered her voice to a bare whisper. "My mistress is a widow, and owns a farm a good walk to the east. It's a fine place, good sandy loam, perfect for the summer topaz carrots. Except it's not quite hers, it's *his*." She raised the hand of the silent child standing by her skirts.

"So her husband left the farm to their son, then?" That made some sense to Bruny, especially with a mother to look after the place while the little lamb grew.

"Not *their* son—*his* son," said the woman. "She was his second wife, and has a little son of her own. She's happy to keep the place for her stepson, mind. She's a good woman and it's only right. Corven here loves his mam—she's the only mother he's ever known, his own having died birthing him—and dotes on Baby Peedy. He's a good-hearted boy, and would do right by his mam and brother, I'm sure."

"I'm sure he would," said Bruny, wondering what the point of all this was.

"It's the mistress's brother," whispered the woman. "Important man. And grasping, never satisfied with what he has, and he has more than most. He owns most of the land aside the road to the north past the river. Even the headwoman steps careful around him."

"All right. It's not uncommon for wealthy folk to not be as kind as they might." Bruny had some experience of *that*, certainly.

"He wants the lad's farm. At least to stay in his own family. He wants it for his nephew." The woman tugged the boy's hand, moving him around in front of her, right in front of Bruny, and put her hands on his shoulders. The boy leaned back against the woman—his nursemaid, may'p? If the family were that prosperous?—and looked down at the packed dirt street between his dusty, cloth shoes.

Bruny said, "His—" and then stopped herself before she could say, "His *blood* nephew, you mean?" because the boy was right there, and too young to hear such things.

"Yes, exactly." The woman gave a quick, jerking nod. "He spoke with the mistress near a month ago, came for a visit, which he rarely does, and they went into the parlor and shut the door. Were in there for a scant hour, then he left without even staying to sup. Very odd. She was agitated for some days, not eating well nor sleeping, and finally told me that he wanted her to help him . . ." She paused and gave a sharp, downward look at the boy. "Help him keep young Corven here *safe*." She scowled at Bruny, making it clear she meant the opposite.

That was . . . that wasn't anything Bruny was trained to deal with. That was a Herald's concern, not a Bard's, much less a trainee's. Except there were no Heralds for some days' ride, and she was wearing a uniform, which like to made her the next best thing in this woman's eyes.

"That do be a problem," she said, "but how could I help?"

"Help take the boy to safety. He has an aunt in Sweetsprings who'll take him in, look after him till he's grown. The mistress has no way to get him there, but Bards travel all about the place, and who would notice one small boy?"

Bruny's brain felt like it was twisting in her skull. She wanted to help, but what would Harrond say? "Could she not talk to the headwoman? Mistress Morrin seems a very sensible woman—"

"No!" hissed the servant, who still hadn't given her name. "Anyone could be in his pocket, anyone could overhear. Mistress is afraid of what he might do if he hears she's crossing him." Another glance at the boy. "He insists on carrying out his own plans for Corrin's safety. He'll not hear any other. She's afraid he'd *punish* her if he hears she's disobeying him."

Bruny heard "kill her" for "punish her," because surely a man so riddled with greed as to think about killing a small boy for wealth would kill his sister, too. He could do away with them both, woman and boy, and raise the baby himself, taking over the farm until his nephew was grown. Unless the baby died as well? Babies were fragile, as well Bruny knew, especially out in the countryside where Gifted Healers were few and far away.

They'd passed through Sweetsprings on the way south, played in the taproom of an inn, then pushed on through, wanting to come to the festival. It'd been four days' ride, but they'd not been hurrying.

She wanted to help, but—

"I'm only a trainee," she said. "I've no say in this sort of thing. We'll explain to Bard Harrond, though, and I'll do my best to persuade him. I'm sure he'll want to help."

The woman frowned at that, but nodded. And off they went to find Harrond.

It'd taken some little time to track down Bard Harrond. They'd retreated to the headwoman's empty house, and the servant woman explained herself once more.

Harrond stared hard at her, then looked at Bruny and raised an eyebrow.

"We can go to Sweetsprings," she said. "Leave tonight, with none to see we've a little with us. We could make the trip in three days if we push the horses just a bit."

"Perhaps." He looked back at the woman. "Just who is this aunt in Sweetsprings? And where does she live, exactly?"

The servant woman huffed, but said, "His Aunt Yavina lives on Potter Street, in a yellow-brick house between the Long Cow tavern and the Kellerist temple. Closer to the temple by a minute's walk or so."

"All right," said Harrond. "And just who are you? And who is your mistress? I notice you've not said."

"I . . ." The woman looked away and scowled. "I'd rather not say. It's not safe for the mistress, who'll be here and easy to find. We just need you to take the lad to his aunt, and all will be well."

Harrond hummed briefly while staring at the servant woman, then nodded. "Very well, we'll take him. Leave him with us, and we'll get him to Aunt Yavina in the next few days."

The woman stared at him, her eyes big and round, then looked down and dipped a low curtsy. "Thank you, sir. My mistress will be very grateful for your help, you and your student both." She glanced at Bruny, then squatted down and turned the little boy to face her. "You behave for the Bards, now. They'll take you to Aunt Yava, and it'll be an adventure."

The boy stared at his feet, then nodded once. He didn't say a word of goodbye, nor protest when the woman turned and bustled out of the house.

"Thank you, sir," said Bruny. She was that surprised it'd taken so little to persuade him, but he was a good man, and like to understand the situation.

"Huh," he said, looking down at the little boy, who was standing before them as if he were like to stay there all his days. Harrond went down on one knee and said, "My name is Harrond, and this is Bruny. You're Corven, yes?"

The little boy nodded.

"Excellent. Are you hungry? We're going to be starting our adventure tonight, and you can't have an adventure if you're empty."

The boy looked up at him, just for a moment, then looked down once more and nodded.

"Bruny, go get him one of those carrot muffins. Corven and I are going to get to know one another. And if you see Morrin while you're about, ask her to come speak with me if she's a moment."

Bruny took a step toward the door, then stopped. "The headwoman? But—"

"I'll make sure none overhear our conversation, and impress upon her the need to keep silent for now. But that servant woman—what's her name, Corven?"

"Vildy," said Corven.

"Thank you, good boy. Vildy reported a crime in the planning, and a serious crime at that. She's free to imagine we'll just drop Corven here off with his aunt and say no more about it to anyone, but that's not how the world works. An aunt a few days' ride away is an obvious place to stash the boy, so what's to stop our evil uncle from searching for him there? That puts Aunt Yava in danger, and we can't leave it at that. To say nothing of the fact that when the boy turns up missing, his stepmother is likely to be in danger anyway, unless she plans to tell her brother he drowned in the river or some such? But that becomes a tangle. Either the stepmother is playing with several snapped strings, or there's something tangled about this situation. Either way, we'll make sure it's untangled before we leave it."

Bruny blinked at him, her brain twisting everything around to look at it from a new angle. She'd never thought that the woman who seemed so worried for her mistress and a little boy might be lying about it all. Or may'p it was the mistress lying to her? Or the mistress was just a fluffhead, and who knew what was going on?

She shook the fluff out of her own head, said, "Carrot muffins, aye," and trotted out the door.

Headwoman Morrin agreed to keep mum about the situation, with the understanding that the Bards would be reporting the . . . whatever it was going on, to a Herald, or at least a magistrate, in Sweetsprings. She saw them off in the quiet of the night, with a sack of cheese buns and carrot bread, plus a couple extra shirts outgrown by her grandchildren for Corven, who'd been left with nothing, and wasn't *that* a bit odd?

Corven rode in front of Bruny, who leaned forward with her cloak covering him on either side, and one arm around his middle to keep the sleepy boy from tumbling off the horse. They traveled as quietly as they could until they were over the bridge, then trotted for a bit in the softer dirt beside the road.

The trotting definitely woke Corven, who was pleased to be on a horse for a while, but soon got tired enough to be cranky and weepy. They slowed to a walk, and kept going till dawn. A nap for Bruny and Corven while Harrond kept watch, some grass, water and rest for the horses, and they went on at midday.

They went as fast as they could take the horses, stopping a few times each day to rest, eat, and let Corven run about a bit.

Little Corven had a bout or two of missing his mam, but

Harrond had a way with him, and the child behaved well enough more often than not.

He was also willing to chatter about anything and everything, once he'd warmed up to his new friends, and while cantering down the road, he told them all about his mam and his brother and the carrot farm. He also told them he knew about the big plot; he'd overheard the talk of it that day, thanks to a pair of open windows, one above the other. He knew his uncle wanted to make him dead like his dad, which was more than a child of six years should ever know. It did explain why he'd been so quiet about being handed off to a couple of strangers, though.

After two and a half days of chatting, singing, and teaching him to tootle on her pipes while they rode, Bruny'd become that fond of the boy by the time they crested a low hill and spotted Sweetsprings.

Harrond knew the town well enough to find Potter Street easily. They passed a tavern with a placard painted with a cow that was indeed longer than any cow Bruny had ever seen, and they started watching the houses.

"Do you remember what your Aunt Yava's house looks like?" she asked.

Corven shook his head. "I never been to her house."

"She came to visit you at the farm, then?" Bruny watched the right side of the street, while Harrond watched the left. She spotted three houses made of yellow bricks, and started looking for a likely person to ask.

"I never seen her," said Corven. "Mam told me about her, but she never visited. Or maybe when I was little?"

Bruny looked down at the boy, then exchanged looks with Harrond.

If Aunt Yavina had never visited in Corven's memory, she wasn't quite doting, then. What if she wasn't willing to take him in?

"I'm sure she'll be delighted to see you," said Harrond. "She'll be surprised to see how big you've got."

Corven nodded firmly. "I'm *lots* bigger than Peedy!"

"That you are." Harrond grinned at him, then turned to call

to a man striding down the street with a basket of bread loaves on his back. "Your pardon, sir, but do you know a woman named Yavina who lives nearby? Yellow-brick house?"

The man called, "Right there," and without slowing down pointed to the second of the houses Bruny'd spotted.

"My thanks," Harrond called after him. He looked over at Bruny and Corven and said, "Well, there we are. Let's see whether Aunt Yava is home."

They tied their horses to a hitch ring set in the wall, and Harrond knocked on the plain oak door. Bruny stood beside him, with Corven in front. He leaned back against her, as he had with Vildy the servant, and Bruny put her hands on his shoulders to give him a comforting squeeze.

It took some moments, but eventually Bruny heard footsteps. A thin woman with brown hair bundled up on her head, wearing a damp apron over her plain blue dress opened the door, then took a step back and stared at Harrond.

"Good morning, ma'am," said Harrond, taking off his hat and making a neat bow. Bruny supposed the sight of a Bard in his scarlets might well be startling to an ordinary person, in a town so far from Haven.

"Yes? What can I help you with, Master Bard?" The woman glanced over at Bruny and Corven, then back at Harrond.

"Might your name be Yavina?"

She frowned at him, then nodded. "I am Yavina."

"And you have a nephew named Corven?"

The woman's eyes opened wide, then she stared down at the boy. "Corven? Dadrig's son?"

Corven looked up at her, then straightened his little shoulders, took a small step away from Bruny, and made a bow. It almost looked like Harrond's. "Hi, Aunt Yava."

Yavina leaned against the doorpost and pressed a hand to her bosom. "Did . . . has something happened? Is Galona well? And Peedy!" The woman looked like she was about to faint.

Harrond held up his hands and hurried to say, "Everyone is well. There's been no accident, nor illness. But there *is* something we need to discuss with you." He paused, then looked down at Corven, then coughed and raised an eyebrow at Bruny.

Bruny nodded and said, "No need to stand about while adults talk of boring things. We'll walk a bit farther up the street and look about—we'll not go farther than the temple."

Aunt Yava frowned, but Harrond said, "Excellent notion. I'm sure we'll not be long," and bustled the woman into her house before she could protest.

"Come then," said Bruny. "Let's go see what there is to see." She took Corven's hand and they strolled up the street.

She bought them a pair of herb rolls, which Corven declared inferior to carrot muffins, but ate anyway. He pointed out the two- and three-level buildings, which he'd never seen before, and goggled at the clothes of the city folk, who only had one row of lacing on their vests, and sometimes wore jackets with no lacing at all, but buttons instead, and wasn't that strange?

It was nearing noon, and a puppet show had set up in a small plaza, a few steps away from a low fountain. Corven gasped in delight and dashed forward to watch the puppets whacking each other with little sticks. Bruny ambled after him, and was just passing the fountain when something caught her eye. She had to look for a moment before recognizing what was odd, but then a cold shock hit her spine.

A man was bent over the side of the fountain, splashing his face with water, looking away from her. An ordinary enough sight, except for the row of brown cord lacing she saw on his vest, from armhole to hip.

Nobody else in town wore that kind of vest. And everyone who did wear that style would be at the Carrot Festival some days' ride away, no?

The man scooped up several long drinks in his hands, then splashed his hands back into the water, scrubbing and washing intently, keeping his head down and his back to Bruny. Then he took another drink.

Bruny strode over to Corven and stood behind him, her hands on his shoulders. He grinned up at her, then laughed at something a puppet-goat said and leaned back against her to watch the show. Bruny ignored it, keeping an eye on the man at the fountain while her thoughts raced.

The puppet show ended with lots of shouting and whacking of sticks, then one of the puppeteers came out to take a bow, announce that they'd be doing a new show in just a few minutes, and work the crowd with his hat, collecting coins. Bruny donated a couple of coins, and got a wink from the fellow performer.

By the time the puppeteer ducked back behind his booth, the man by the fountain was gone. Not knowing where he was made Bruny's gut clench harder.

The new story had just started up, something with a wolf and a ghost (and more whack-sticks), when Harrond came striding up the street, a grim look on his face.

He leaned in so their faces were a bare hand's-breadth apart, and the two of them chorused, *"We need to—"* and then stopped, stared a moment. Then they both said, *"Magistrate—"* and stopped again.

Harrond smirked and Bruny giggled, then he whispered, "She hasn't seen Corven since she went to Willow Grove for her *sister's* wedding."

Bruny blinked. "She be his step-aunt, then. Sister to his step-mum, and to yon murderous not-uncle."

Harrond nodded, scowling.

"I did see a man from Willow Grove, wearing a laced vest." Bruny drew a line with one finger from her armpit to her hip. "By the fountain, taking far too long, trying to hide from me all bent over. I do think it be the uncle, here in Sweet Springs."

Harrond's scowl got deeper, and his hand brushed the hilt of his rapier. For the first time since she'd met him, he looked like someone who could be dangerous if he had a reason. "And the only way he could've beaten us here," he said, "would be if he left ahead of us. Which makes the whole thing a plot."

Bruny nodded. "So. Magistrate."

"Magistrate. After the show." He nodded toward the puppet theater. "He won't try anything here, and we don't want to panic him into doing anything precipitate. We'll let Corven watch the rest of the show, then stroll off with the dispersing crowd."

Bruny bit back a protest, and it wasn't all that long before they were moving across town, following this or that cluster of strangers as they went from street to street.

Then an overturned cart blocked a corner, and Bruny felt a sudden yank, and Corven was gone.

A little boy's terrified scream led her through the crowd, past angry and fallen folk shouting curses and protests, and into a narrow alley. She could hear Harrond behind her, but her focus was forward, where the man in the laced vest was dodging round barrels and crates and piles of rotting rubbish, the crying boy tossed over his shoulder.

Bruny gritted her teeth and went over a crate, splashed through a heap of something disgusting, and hurdled a rolling barrel.

Yon uncle was a landowner, a rich man who had minions to do for him. Bruny was a herder girl who grew up working, and Bardic didn't let any of its trainees grow soft or idle. She ignored the dagger at her belt, not wanting to chance doing any dire hurt to Corven, who was still screaming and reaching out for her with both hands. She'd wrestled plenty of ornery sheep in her day, though, and as soon as she was at the uncle's heels, she tackled him hard, her arms clamped around his thighs.

Uncle yelped, and went down with a splat and a crack. Harrond cursed, and Corven had never stopped screaming.

Bruny grabbed Corven and pulled him away from his flailing uncle, up into her arms. "There, lamb," she murmured. "Be you hurt? Anything aching?"

"My arm!" he sobbed. "And I hit my head!" He threw his arms around her neck and near to strangled her while he wailed.

"What in all the hells were you thinking?" hissed Harrond. He pushed past her and worked at trussing up Uncle, arms secured behind his back with his own belt.

"I were thinking that a bump or even a break could be

healed," Bruny retorted. "But yon rotter meant to kill him if he got away, and *that* no Healer can mend."

Harrond glared at her, then nodded once and said no more.

A pair of guards appeared at the end of the alley and trotted toward them, calling questions and brandishing truncheons. Harrond stood and headed toward them.

He paused beside Bruny and whispered, "Write a song about all this before we get back to Willow Grove. The boy needs a new guardian after this, but whoever that is, he'll be safer if everyone knows *exactly* what happened."

He moved on and called, "Well timed," to the guards. "We have one for the magistrate. And we need a Healer for the boy."

Bruny froze for a moment, then followed behind him, patting Corven on the back. "There, lamb," she said. "You'll feel better in a twitch."

The terror of having to compose a song and be ready to perform it in a handful of days was for later.

And if she kicked the uncle in the head on her way past, well, it were clearly an accident.

Trade is Trade
Fiona Patton

As in most cities, Haven's business districts were usually quiet once darkness fell, with front-facing shops and workshops shuttered and barred and their proprietors tucked in the back or upper rooms with their families. The streets were the domain of the watchmen; their only company lightmen, knocker-uppers, or midwives. The others—vagrants, goods movers, or alley rats—did their best to keep no company with the watch at all.

The Iron Street Watch House, situated in the heart of one such business district, was also usually quiet, but as Constables Jakon and Raik Dann, each with a fist wrapped tight in the collars of two dust-covered boys in torn tavern aprons, pushed through the main doors, a rousing chorus of *"Who broke the bridge in two, was it you, was it YOU?"* broke out.

Bulling through the crowd of russet-clad youths, some clutching gitterns or other instruments, and all the worse for drink, they headed for the duty sergeant's desk, where Night Sergeant Kiel Wright was trying to listen to the complaints of a merchant from Waymeet, come to report an attempted burglary.

"Senior Bardic students on a pub crawl," Kiel explained in answer to the merchant's query, as he waved the two Danns forward. "No one's under arrest, but it's better to keep 'em here than let 'em pass out in some back street."

"We're outta blankets, Sarge," a voice sang out from behind him.

"Go pinch some from Helena. The Awl an' Tongs owes us for at least half this lot," Kiel shouted back as the room erupted in a drunken chorus of *"Who tossed the blanket in, was it him, was it JIM,"* before it stuttered away into giggles. "An' get her to send a basket of fruit buns over around dawn," he added. "A big basket."

The merchant sniffed. "Did a few years in our Town Watch," he noted. "In my day, such as these would have been tossed on the floor to sleep it off, an' none too gently either. When they woke, they'd be fined a penny piece each and tossed out again. There was none of this blankets and breakfast. You'd think this was a coaching house."

"These are Bardic trainees, sir," Kiel explained patiently. "Those that'll grow up to be *Bards* and write songs that'll be sung for a hundred years about people who mistreated them when they were trainees?"

He shook his head at the man's mystified expression, before looking past his shoulder. "Who've we got, constables . . . oh, not again."

Jakon nodded grimly. "Punchin' it up in the middle of the street," he said, shoving his charge forward. "Arek, explain what you were doin' to the nice sergeant will you? It'll save me gettin' interrupted every five words. An' you'll get yer turn, Camrin, so jus' shut it," he snapped as the second boy opened his mouth to protest.

Arek glared up at Kiel. "Weren't doin' nothin," he muttered. "Was just escortin' a couple of patrons out the door when him there starts hollerin' insults at me."

"Weren't neither, you lyin' dung bucket!" Camrin shouted. "I only asked if yer low-quality beer made 'em sick!"

The two youths jerked toward each other, but having anticipated the move, the Danns yanked their captives out of arms' reach.

"Mind yer voices," Raik growled. "This here's a dignified establishment of the law."

Both boys blinked at him as a chorus of *"Who caused the brook to stir, was it her, was it . . ."* continued, and the singer stuttered to a halt with a series of hiccups before the final word *"HER!"* was finished by the crowd.

"Usually."

"He's jus' jealous 'cause the Dog an' Wattle gets to celebrate bein' the oldest pub in Haven next month, an' he's barred," Arek sneered.

"Barred!? Like I'd bother goin' to your rat-trap inn, you puffed up little sack of crap. The Wine Barrel's way older'n you, an' you know it."

"Jus' 'cause some drunken noblemen slept off a boozy night in yer pigeon loft don't make you a pub! C'mon, Sergeant Wright." Arek turned an aggrieved look on Kiel. "We're yer local, back me up."

"I thought the oldest pub in Haven was the Star?" the merchant asked loudly.

An almost dramatic silence fell across the station room as everyone, watchmen and Bardic students alike, turned to stare at him.

He chuckled. "I wish I had that kind of effect on my children."

"The Star?" Kiel sputtered.

"Mm. Small place in Amber Close? Has all those hanging flowers along the window ledges? There's a sign by the door naming every monarch who reigned during their time all the way back to King Valdemar himself. They even have a charter."

"A charter?"

"Mm-hm. Of course, the Crossed Sheaves is my local whenever I'm in town, so I've never patronized the Star to actually see it, but that's what I've heard."

Both Arek and Camrin had gone very still, their expressions changed from outraged injury to outraged cunning in a flash. Kiel exchanged a meaningful glance with Jakon and Raik over their heads.

"That's as may be," he said slowly, "but nothin' to do with right now. There's no room for underweight fish tonight, constables. Toss 'em back, an' have a chat with Graven an' Tatania. They can come in tomorrow an' pay the fines, but impress on them how unhappy the watch would be if something was to come of this. Then take a stroll about, have a chat with a few folk, if you take my meanin'. You can pick up a few stragglers on the way back," he added as the quieter "Bellmen of the Watch House" began around him. "Likely there's still plenty more out there."

"Yes, Sarge."

At the farthest end of Iron Street, two establishments blazed with light despite the late hour: the Dog and Wattle Coaching House and the Wine Barrel Ale and Pie House.

The Danns stopped in the middle of the street, carefully keeping the same distance from each building.

"I did the Dog last week," Raik noted.

Jakon glared down at Arek. "Whose tendin' bar tonight?" he demanded.

"Ma," the boy answered grudgingly as the other boy snickered.

"What's her mood?"

"Last I saw, it were good, but I been gone with you fer the last hour, ain't I, so how should I know?"

"Fine. But I swear, next time we're jus' gonna knock yer heads together an' get on with our rounds." As Raik and Camrin headed one way, he aimed Arek in the other with a brisk shove.

The Dog and Wattle took up most of a square block. It was an old, timber-framed building of three sides, balconies running along both floors of the two outer wings flanking dining and public rooms, a wide alcove leading to stables at the back and a cobbled courtyard in the center. In the past it had held pride of place beside one of the city gates, but as Haven had grown, it had been left stranded. These days it regularly hosted music and plays in its courtyard and was a favorite venue for Bardic students trying out new songs or poetry. And although its most recent publican, Tatania Wattle, did not extend credit, ever, she was known to have a soft spot for musicians, and— very occasionally—a particularly favorable piece would be met with a complimentary, albeit quite small, drink if the piece was sufficiently complimentary to the Dog and Wattle itself.

Tonight, the courtyard was full of clientele, both Bardic and local, and many shouted good-natured greetings to Arek and Jakon as they passed. Although not usually patrons, the Danns' local being farther up the other end of Iron Street, the watch itself was a regular sight with the pub's reputation for sending its more belligerent customers out into the street to settle their disputes, often with a crowd of eager onlookers dogging their heels.

Inside, it was much as expected, warm, noisy, smoky, and smelling of beer and stew. Tending bar was a tall woman who bore a strong resemblance to Arek. She frowned as Jakon deposited the boy in front of her.

"I wondered were you'd got to," she growled. "Off playin' with the catchpoles, were you?"

"Playin' with Camrin Uffler again," Jakon said darkly. "That's a five-penny fine this time, Mistress Wattle."

She stabbed a threatening finger at Arek. "Get yerself out back an' help Blair bring in another barrel. One of us'll be down to the watch house tomorrow, constable." She leaned over the bar as Arek stomped off toward the back of the pub. "You coulda saved us all some trouble by just bringin' him in right off, you know," she admonished quietly.

Jakon raised his hands. "We woulda, 'cept him an' Camrin took their fight up the street and ended up poundin' on each other against Mistress Lassen's shop door. She wanted 'em locked up an' the key thrown away on account of two broken flower tubs."

"The little toe-rags. That's gonna cost me. And them too," she added with a dark gleam in her eye. "They're both sweet on her granddaughter. That's what half of this is about, but she won't let her Daisy step out with either one of 'em now, an' serves 'em right. That oughta teach 'em more manners than a night in the bull's privy anyway. Raik across the street now?"

Jakon nodded.

She smiled thinly. "Good luck to him, then. Graven's in a foul mood tonight. We got the jump on him with the local merchants for next month's celebrations. I've had half the Bardic Collegium in here tonight, busy scribblin' away on songs that laud us. The oldest pub in Haven, that's us, whatever him across the street might think with his fancy new little silver date sign. We were servin' up the best honey-dump an' knock-down in the city before they were a gleam in a huntsman's eye. We're gonna have a right big blow-out with a roast pig in the courtyard an' buntin' all around the balconies. Old Graven's gonna choke himself with envy. Ale and Pie House, my aunt Fanny," she sneered. "Nobody makes pies to our equal, and they know it. You mind the date and put some extra watchman on this end of the street," she added. "We're gonna tear up the night."

Jakon nodded glumly, thought for a moment about leaving the heretical news of the Star to Arek, then sighed.

"There was one other thing." He passed on what had been said at the watch house, keeping a close eye on her face, but her expression did not change.

"What some dark little gem merchant's boozer suddenly claims is nothin' to me an' mine," she declared in a dismissive tone. "It don't change, nothin'. I know what we are. Him over there's been claimin' the same thing for years now, and it's come to just as much: nothin.' Sounds like that merchant of yours was jus' tryin' to stir up trouble. Now, if you don't mind, I've got payin' customers to see to."

Jakon weaved back through the crowd, unsure of why her words just hadn't seemed to ring true to him. Raik had yet to emerge, so he leaned against the Dog and Wattle's gate and pulled out his pipe with a thoughtful frown.

The Wine Barrel Ale and Pie House had stood across the street from its rival for as long as anyone could remember. Not as large or as grand, its original building had been a compact hunting lodge with an adjoining octagonal dovecote for the Lords Orthallen when this area had been mostly woods and fields.

These days it boasted numerous comfortable public rooms and snugs where business and pleasure could be meted out equally to a more conservative clientele. Most of the local merchants held meetings in its private rooms and, as such, its proprietor, Graven Uffler, could usually count on the first and best produce they had to offer. His wife had trained in the palace kitchens, and had brought a new level of sophistication to the food. Like the Dog and Wattle, it claimed to be the oldest pub in the capital. Raik squinted up at the newly painted silver date above the door and did a labored calculation.

"That might just do it," he muttered.

He kept a hand wrapped tightly in Camrin's shirt as he steered him through the smoky main room and down a short hallway to Graven's office. He found the publican bent over his account books, several neat piles of pub tokens at his elbow.

The man gave a pained snort when he saw them. "Fighting with Arek Wattle again?" he asked wearily.

Raik nodded.

"He started it, Da," Camrin protested.

"Possibly. This time. Did they break anything?"

Raik explained about Mistress Lassen's flower tubs, and Graven's face darkened.

"That'll come out of your wages, boy," he said stiffly. "As will the fine. And if you can't pay it, you can spend a few nights enjoying the watch house's hospitality."

"But Da—!"

"No buts!" Graven smacked his hand on the desk, causing his ink pot to teeter precariously. "I'm tired of this. One more squabble with Arek Wattle, and I swear I'll pack you off to your Uncle Jeem's pig farm. Do you understand?"

"Yes, Da."

"Very well." Graven sent his son off with a wave of his hand, then glanced at Raik. "Is that everything, Constable Dann? As you can see, I'm very busy."

Raik chewed on the inside of one cheek for a moment, then sighed much as his brother had. "There was one other thing, yes, sir."

Graven listened politely while Raik repeated the merchant's words, then gave a brief, one-shouldered shrug. "Penn Marble's Star is not unusual in its desire to tie itself to King Valdemar these days, Constable," he sniffed. "Anyone can hire a sign painter. Many taverns and public houses across Haven made similarly unfounded claims. They come and go like the wind, and like the wind, they hardly matter. Trade is all that's important."

"Begging your pardon, sir, but it seems to matter when the Dog and Wattle makes the claim."

A look of impatience crossed Graven's face. "Yes, well, the Dog and Wattle is a loud and vulgar establishment more suitable to the folk of Water Street than of Iron Street. Their proximity is an irritant, nothing more. If Mistress Tatania wants to waste money on roast pigs and the like, she's welcome to it. Now, if you don't mind . . ."

"Yes, sir."

The two brothers met in the middle of the street a few moments later.

"Did yours feel a bit . . . off?" Jakon asked as they carried on their rounds.

"How do you mean, off?"

"Like . . . off, not quite right. Mistress Wattle seemed a bit too . . ." he waved one hand, "*who cares*, for someone happy to carry on a centuries-old grudge against the Wine Barrel. I thought she would have got riled up, but . . . nothin'. It was like she already knew about the Star."

Raik scratched at the line of beard on his right cheek. "That would figure though, wouldn't it? We know about other watch houses. Why wouldn't they know about other pubs?"

"They would, but Mistress Wattle said they suddenly claimed it, an' Graven's date sign's new. Somethin's up."

"You can feel it in your water?"

"Funny, but maybe. We should probably go up there."

Raik stopped walking. "To the Star? What for?"

"To warn 'em that, I dunno, that they know what they're claimin' or somethin'."

"You don't figure Tatania or Graven'd start anything, do you?"

"Not them, but Arek and Camrin are itchin' to do somethin' stupid. You saw how they looked."

"The Star's smack in the middle of Breakneedle Street's patch. We could just let one of their watchmen know."

"We could, but the sarge said to take a stroll, an' that probably means to the Star."

"No, it probably means to the first Breakneedle Street watchman we find."

"'Cept he's gonna be at the party, an' he isn't gonna want anything to sour that."

Raik started walking again. "Fine. It's not like my left boot doesn't already have a hole in it an' it's not like we don't have anything better to do here," he groused as a double group of drunken youths stumbled out of the Dog and Wattle.

"Pat an' Jamie can handle 'em. C'mon."

The Star Tavern was a small, tidy public house on a small, tidy street just off Goldsmith's Row. Its frontage boasted actual glass-paned windows and, as the merchant had mentioned, baskets of hanging flowers that seemed impervious to the lateness of the season. Light shone through the open door, and the sounds of conversation and barking could be heard faintly from within. Not a single pub-crawling Bardic student could be seen.

Jakon paused to peer up at the long list of names painted on a board by the door. "Fixed nice an' tight," he noted.

"What, you figure Arek an' Camrin would try an' steal it?" Raik scoffed.

"Not as such, but . . ."

"It looks brand new. It might not be real anyway."

"How'd you mean?"

"Well, like Graven said, anyone can hire a sign painter, can't they?"

"Sure, but this sign isn't about beer, it's about kings. You can probably get into a pack of trouble makin' up stuff about kings."

"Whatever. Can we just get this over with, please? We're steppin' all over Breakneedle Street for no good reason." Following his brother inside, Raik glared at the list of monarchs as if they were to blame for his discomfort.

Unlike most of the pubs in their own patch, the conversation did not pause when the two constables entered the main room. Usually the sight of a watchman's light blue and gray uniform would be enough to send a few patrons legging it out the back, but here, there was only a few stares and the hushing of various dogs lounging under the heavy goldenoak tables.

Raik scowled as he took note of the rich cut of cloaks and jackets slung over chairs, the gleam of wine glasses, and the sparkle of rings. They were definitely out of their depth here, but before he could mention that to his brother, a heavyset man in a remarkably clean apron looked over from the polished bar.

"Help you?"

Jakon nodded. "Is the publican in?"

"That would be me, Penn Marble. You boys lost?"

"Lost?"

"I hadn't heard that Captain Rilade had hired any new night watchmen for Breakneedle Street lately."

"Oh. No, sir. We're from Iron Street."

"Ah." The publican gave a faint smile. "Yes. Our lieutenant was promoted to your captaincy. This is his local."

Several of the people about the tap room nodded.

Jakon decided to ignore the name-dropping's mild threat. "That's quite a list by your door."

"It is, yes."

"Been there long? Only it seems very bright."

"Paint wears even in the best of weather. We touch it up from time to time."

"We heard that you had an ancient charter, too. Didn't see it."

"That's because it isn't outside, Constable." The publican

nodded toward a document under glass in a heavy wooden frame securely bolted to the wall by the hearth.

As they headed back to the watch house a few moments later, Raik glanced at his brother. "What was that all about? I thought you were gonna warn 'em."

Jakon shrugged. "Did that charter look as new as the list by the door to you?"

"I dunno. It looked official, all ribbons and seals an' fancy words. Why?"

"Seemed new to me. There wasn't any dust on the frame or smudges on the glass."

"So they keep it clean. You need to lie down. I think you've got brain fever."

At shift change, Jakon, with a reluctant Raik in tow, stopped in to see their older brother, Sergeant Hektor Dann.

"So, what do you figure's gonna happen?" Hektor asked with a puzzled expression once Jakon had explained everything to him.

"Somethin'."

"Somethin' like what?"

"I dunno, like maybe the boys'll try an' steal the charter or steal the sign or . . ."

"Arek Wattle an' Camrin Uffler can't agree on the time of day. I can't see them plannin' any kind of foist past their own walls," Hektor retorted. "Besides, throwin' apples at each other or tippin' over piss pots is more their style. They are not thieves."

"Well, maybe Tatania or Graven . . ."

"Are legitimate businesspeople with too much to lose to risk any kind of childish nonsense. It's Breakneedle Street's patch. Let them handle whatever may happen. You did warn 'em, didn't you?"

Both younger brothers squirmed under his gaze. "Er, not as such . . ." Raik began.

"Not as such how?"

"Not as such . . . no."

"Why not?"

"Well, once we got there it kinda felt like tellin' tales on our own. They're Iron Street, you know?"

Hektor rolled his eyes, but nodded. "Yeah, I know. Look, it's nothin', all right? Jus' go home."

The next evening, Kiel pointed them toward two dust-covered boys sitting belligerently on a bench by the duty sergeants' desk. "Breakneedle Street did us a favor an' dropped 'em off for you to take home."

"Why us?" Raik demanded.

"It's your shout. Apparently young Arek here said you were cousins."

"Third cousins."

"Whatever. Sort it out, Constables."

"Weren't you supposed to be on your best behavior?" Jakon demanded as they headed up the street. "Somethin' about a pig farm?"

Arek shrugged. "Da said I weren't to squabble with Camrin, an' we weren't."

"You weren't?"

"Nope," the boy answered promptly to the unusual addition of Camrin's vehement agreement. "This time we were on the same side. An' we only asked to see the charter and that toffee-nosed little muck-sucker told us to sod off."

"Who?"

"Sy Marble, Penn's youngest."

"You started a brawl in the Star?"

"Course not." Arek looked affronted. "We were outside by then. An' besides, he started it. We were headin' off when he got pushy with Cam. Couldn't have that, could we?"

"You've gotten pushy with Cam since you were littles."

"That's different. That's Iron Street business, innit?"

"S'right," Camrin added.

"I think I liked it better when you two didn't get on," Raik noted. "Did you at least win?"

The boys shared a grin, then shrugged.

"We woulda, but their watch showed up," Camrin admitted. "They're a lot faster'n you lot."

"Watch yer mouth."

"What'd you want to see the charter for?" Jakon asked.

"Just wonderin' . . ." Camrin trailed off.

". . . if it could be pulled off the wall? That's theft, you know, you daft piglets."

"Hey, I never said nothin' about thievin' it! We just wanted a look at it 'cause maybe it were a fake or someone else's like."

"Someone else's?"

"They coulda thieved it from us maybe."

"Or us," Arek added.

"Years ago."

"So long ago that no one remembers where it came from."

"Really? How many holes can I poke through that?" Raik demanded.

"Why couldn't it've been?"

"Because they're a tavern in a gem merchant's close," Jakon snapped. "They don't need to go around thievin' stuff from Iron Street."

"They do if there's gonna be an actual plaque put up an' all," Arek retorted.

"What?"

Both Danns exchanged a look as Camrin elbowed Arek in the ribs.

"Shut it, gob-skull," he hissed. "That's s'pposed to be a secret."

Raik glared at them. "Spill," he ordered.

Arek sighed. "Word came 'round that the palace was gonna set a plaque on the oldest pub in the city on account of it being some special year for King Valdemar or somethin'. Ma's known about it for a month now."

"It's not a competition, neither," Camrin added. "Some council of historians or scholars are in charge of it."

"No one we know's ever had a plaque, not about anything," Arek finished. "It'd be a real feather in the cup of a pub with a plaque."

"Cap."

"Ma said cup since we're a pub."

Jakon shook his head. "So why go to all this trouble with parties an' new paint? They aren't going to pub crawl to every boozer in the city to ask 'em how old they are, you know?"

"They might," Raik replied. "We would."

"They'll likely jus' figure it out in some old archive or another," Jakon concluded, ignoring him.

"Sure, but Ma says there'd probably be all kinds of mix-ups after all this time," Arek retorted. "So they're gonna have to pound some pavement, an' we gotta be ready. An' nobody's gonna out-ready us. We're the oldest. It's our plaque."

Camrin clenched his fists as Jakon glanced at his brother. "You get the feelin' this is just the beginning? There're a lot of pubs in Haven that might throw down like the Dog and the Barrel over this. Folks can get touchy about their locals."

"Never mind Haven, an' never mind might," Raik answered grimly. "There's lots of pubs on Iron Street that will definitely throw down over this."

They paused in the street between the two establishments.

"Right," Jakon glared at the boys. "Sod off home, the pair of you."

They stared at him. "Wait, you're not comin' in?" Arek asked.

"No, like you said, it's Iron Street business, an' you might of just helped us with our inquiries, so we'll keep it between us. Jus' this once!" he added as they began to whoop. "But you get caught off your own patch again an' some uncle's pig farm's gonna be the least of your problems. Got it?"

"Got it."

"Beat it."

That night saw the watch called to disturbances all along the street with patrons as well as servers fighting over claims to being the oldest pub in Haven.

"That wasn't the half of it," Kiel said, waving a fistful of reports when they brought in their third set of combatants. "It's started up all across the city. There hasn't been this many punch-ups since the statue of that Bard Dion fella got erected in the wrong park. Before your time," he added as they looked puzzled. "I just hope that council of yours hurries up, or there's gonna be riots."

It was the same for the next three nights. Finally, when a seventy-three-year-old patron of the Awl and Tongs got arrested for throwing a chair at a seventy-six-year-old patron of the Iron Lily, Captain Torell stepped in. The next day he and a contingent of fellow watch captains went to the palace to ask, very politely, that the council move its collective arse and pick a pub, any pub.

Two weeks later, celebrations at the Dog and Wattle were in full swing, spilling out from the courtyard into the street, when Jakon and Raik made their rounds. Even the Wine Barrel had added some outdoor seating, where its more sedentary patrons could watch the festivities over a pint and a pie.

Graven just shrugged at their expressions. "Trade is trade," he said simply before heading back inside. "Oh," he added over his shoulder. "If you see that treasonous son of mine anywhere near that place, you tell him to get his tail back home before I apprentice him to a boar hunter in Forst Reach."

"We will."

Camrin was, in fact, standing in the street with Arek Wattle, Daisy Lassen, and several others, pretending to ignore a bowls game going on between two rival branches of the Cooper's Guild.

Jakon caught his eye. "Not plannin' to go and see the plaque on the Five Penny Tavern, then?"

Both boys shrugged. "We saw it," Arek said dismissively.

"And?"

"And, it's just a little blue circle between two upper windows. No biggie."

"Who's gonna see it?" Camrin added. "Who goes up Five Penny Street, anyway?"

"Just the patrons of about a dozen pubs," Raik answered.

Both boys shrugged again. "Who looks up?"

"Fair point."

"So you don't care about the Five Penny, but you did care about the Star," Jakon pressed.

"Not care, exactly," Arek answered.

"Then what exactly?"

"That was just scopin' out the competition."

"Together?"

"Sure. Nothin' wrong with that, Ma does it all the time. She an' his Da are always going off to some pub or another. That's how we got our cook. He used to work for the Fox and Dove. 'Sides, it's not like we're gonna knuckle under, are we? Not for some scraggy little plaque. We know we're the oldest pub in Haven; he thinks they are, an' so does he." Arek jerked a thumb at a better-dressed boy standing behind them.

"Father's inside drinking with Uncle Travin," the boy explained once he'd been introduced as Sy Marble. "They'll talk for hours. Boring."

"See," Camrin added. "You can't beat the competition if you don't know what they're up to."

"And cadge a free meal at the same time?" Raik asked, noting the huge chunk of pork in Camrin's hand.

"Sure, why not?" Arek answered for him. "I'll do the same when the Wine Barrel has its anniversary next summer. Only it won't be as big as ours, 'cause they don't have a courtyard," he added diplomatically as Camrin's eyes narrowed. "Trade is trade."

"You mighta followed that line of thinkin' before we had to drag you halfway up Iron Street night after night," Jakon groused.

"Yeah, well, there's pride, too, isn't there? Sometime's you gotta stand up for your own, you know?"

Jakon glared at him, then shrugged. "Yeah. I guess we do."

"You goin' in? We got a special on, a half for half."

"We're on duty."

"We got meat pies," Camrin interjected. "Three for a five

penny. What?" He added as Arek snorted. "Like you said, trade is trade."

"No. Thank you," Jakon said sternly. He poked a finger at them. "Just you all behave yourselves. I don't wanna get called back here tonight. Got it?"

He stomped off before they could answer.

As Raik turned to follow his more demonstrative brother, he cocked his head toward the Dog and Wattle as a sudden chorus of *"Who drank it dry, was it I, it was I!"* filtered through the gate.

By the Ticking of My Thumbs

Rosemary Edghill

Dwellingwell Town was located on a spur off the Southern Trade Road a short distance from Haven. Its farms produced fruits, vegetables, and livestock in abundance; its bakers produced delicious breads; and its clockmaker's creations were marvels of artifice. On market days, people came from farms and towns far beyond Dwellingwell to buy or trade for what they lacked, and if much of what they bought went home to their own kitchens and larders, as much of it—cheese and breads and clocks and wine—was destined for Haven itself.

Verrigan was proud that he could say the clocks he'd made graced many of the finer homes in Haven and even (so he had been told) some of the lecture halls in the Collegium itself. Verrigan was a man of middle years, which left him confident that his greatest triumphs were yet to come. His greatest dream was to someday have the Royal Palace commission one of his works. In his spare time, when he wasn't making or mending timepieces, or building Midwinter toys, he worked on the design for what he was certain would be that masterwork. After all, he had decades ahead during which his fame could spread and his eminence become more widely known. Surely it was inevitable that a commission from the palace would come.

And because he was so confident of that, he barely noticed when Milutin Skoros moved into town.

Skoros had come from far away, and he was dark and lean where Verrigan was plump and fair. There might have been—in fact, there probably was—a great deal of speculation about his past and the reasons for his arrival, but Verrigan didn't hear it. He was so busy with his clocks that he sent his housekeeper to do his marketing and didn't attend any of the weddings and festivals held in the town. When Marta tried to talk to him about the stranger—whom she was certain he would like—he brushed her off irritably. How could the foolish woman presume to know his likes and dislikes? As for strangers, they came through the village all the time. What could possibly be special about this one?

A few moonturns later, he found out.

"What use is there for *two* clockmakers in a village like ours?" Verrigan demanded.

Marta twisted her apron nervously. "I'm sure he meant no harm, Master Verrigan. Why, I'm sure young Skoros didn't even know you were here."

If her words were intended to have a soothing effect, they had the opposite result.

"Not know I'm here? Of course he knew I'm here! Clearly that's the whole point of his coming to Dwellingwell in the first place. He wants my secrets."

Marta didn't want to agree or disagree with Verrigan's remarks; she simply wanted to get out of the room without hearing more of them. Over the years, her master's concentration on his craft had refined itself into irritability, and finally become distilled into obsession.

"Well?" he said at last. "Go. There's clearly no help *you* can be. I'll have to fend for myself."

But whatever "fending" Verrigan intended to do was not noticeable, as he did not seem to change his daily routine in any way. Thin sheets of alloy came down the Trade Road from Haven, destined to be sawed and filed by him into complex gears and springs and assembled into clocks. Clocks went back up the Trade Road with merchants for hopeful sale, or even as commissions.

But the ultimate clock—the one in his head, the one in his dreams—remained unbuilt.

Each year, the sennights before Midwinter brought a change in the tenor of Verrigan's days, for that was when he stopped experimenting with clocks and changed to building toys for the upcoming season. Verrigan didn't like children—in fact he *disliked* them; they were noisy and messy and outright destructive—but the coin and trade goods he received for his toys made a welcome addition to what he took in from selling his clocks—and he would do anything for his clocks.

And so he made little wooden frogs that hopped, carousels that spun, Companions that reared up on their hind legs, bouncing boys that sprang out of their boxes when the catch was released, ducks that quacked and paddled, and kittens that pounced. Mere toymakers could create lifeless, immobile trifles—Verrigan's creations *moved*.

But when the trade caravan heading north to Haven stopped in Dwellingwell this year, the wagonmaster did not stop at Verrigan's workshop.

"I already have all the toys I need."

Verrigan had tracked the wagonmaster down at the Dog's Inn. It was on the spur road, a goodly distance out of Dwellingwell. He was cross and out of breath at having to do so, as he had needed to hire a horse to get there, and Verrigan was allergic to horses. He was wriggling in his seat, trying desperately not to scratch, and dreading the ride home. None of this improved his temper in the least.

"How can you say that?" Verrigan demanded. "You haven't bought any of mine!"

"No," said the wagonmaster, "but I bought some just as good and maybe better from Milutin Skoros. It helped that he was showing them off at market. If this weren't Valdemar, I would have sworn some of them were enchanted, the way they move. Here. I'll show you."

He reached into his pocket and pulled out what looked, at first, like a carved and painted wooden ball. He carefully wound the tiny key on its side and set it down on the table between them. First it unfolded itself into an acrobat, then it began doing backflips across the table. The wagonmaster caught it before it leaped off and held it until the spring ran down.

"So you see," he said. "They're quite lovely and clever things. Perhaps the two of you should go into partnership."

"I see," Verrigan said brusquely. "And my clocks?" The Haven-bound caravans usually took at least two or three of his clocks to sell in the city.

There was a long silence. The wagonmaster looked embarrassed.

"I see," Verrigan repeated.

"I'm sorry, but—"

"There's no need to explain," Verrigan said through gritted teeth. He got to his feet. "If you'll excuse me, it's a long ride back to Dwellingwell. I'd like to be there before dark."

The thought of the things he had made that would now linger unsold on his workshop shelves kept Verrigan warm with fury for the entire ride back. He returned his horse to the livery stables and trudged toward home, thinking of a warm bath and the hot dinner Marta would have left for him.

Milutin Skoros was waiting on his doorstep.

At first, Verrigan thought he was someone sent by the wagonmaster—not to apologize, of course, for buyers and sellers of goods never did that—but simply to say that he had come to buy after all. Instead, he saw a tall, gangling stranger with unruly black hair, his shoulders hunched as if he was trying to make himself smaller. When he saw Verrigan approaching, he gave a hopeful, apologetic smile.

"I should have come to see you long since, I know. But with one thing and another, and, you know, settling into a new place, well—"

"You're Milutin Skoros," Verrigan said accusingly. "What is it you want with me? Surely you don't think I want to buy a clock."

"Well, that would be foolish, of course," Skoros said. "You make clocks, too, you know."

"So I'd heard," Verrigan said.

"And toys, of course," Skoros added. "I'm sorry I showed off my work in the marketplace. I'm certain that's the only reason why my pieces were bought instead of yours. They saw them first."

"Do you have a *point* in being here?" Verrigan demanded in a stifled, hysterical rage.

"Not really," Skoros said. "Just to say you should really try using a spiral spring instead of a compression spring. It makes a difference." He straightened himself, drew his cloak tight around his body, and walked away.

Who does he think he is? Who does he think he is? "Who do—" Verrigan began, but his voice was as raw and cracked as if he had been shouting all the way home from Dog's Inn, and Skoros was moving rapidly out of earshot anyway.

Still infuriated, Verrigan swept into his home and slammed the door savagely behind him. This impersonator, this *thief*, had come stalking, lurking, entirely to give him *advice*? Ridiculous! Impossible!

Eventually he exhausted himself bouncing around his little house and was able to settle, broodingly, into his bath, where he scrubbed until the last of the rash from having ridden a horse had subsided.

The question is, what are his real *motives?*

And that, Verrigan found he could not imagine.

Verrigan did not attend any of the Midwinter celebrations, nor the Springtide ones that followed a few moonturns later. He sat in his workshop, surrounded by unsold clocks and unfinished toys, and brooded.

Unfortunately, it was impossible to blot Skoros from his mind. Even Marta betrayed him, for one spring day she brought in her market basket some of Skoros's mechanical toys. They were gifts for her grandchildren, she protested as Verrigan confiscated them.

"It is my market basket, and my provender, so logically these abominations are mine as well," was his reply, but he was an angry man, not a cruel one, and he gave her twice as many of his own creations in exchange.

If he had never heard of Skoros, Verrigan could have been a happy man—or if not happy, as happiness was not in his nature, content in his work and his striving toward the impossible ideal he had set for himself. But the more he thought about Skoros, the less work he did, until his days were spent sitting in his unused workshop, staring at nothing.

It was clearly necessary to vanquish his enemy so thoroughly that he ceased to exist. So thoroughly that Milutin Skoros slunk out of town one moonless night after destroying all of his remaining work, and was never seen or heard from again. But at even his most overdramatic, Verrigan was not a violent man. No blood or ruin was involved in these fantasies. He only wished for Skoros to vanish. Like a soap bubble, or autumn leaves, or any other thing transient and unmemorable.

And the only weapon he had to use was his skills.

As the year turned again toward Midsummer, Verrigan got out the rolls of parchment from their cabinet and spread them on his worktable, assessing.

Yes, the basics of the work were sound. The build could be a proof of concept only, for the design was meant to be enormous, a thing to be installed in a tower and visible from the ground.

It was to have three dials: one to show the hours of the day; one to show the passage of the sennights; one to show the change of the moonturns. In addition to this, there would be a ring of figures that progressed around the base of the clock, and others that flanked it and surmounted it, moving in and out of their niches to display themselves as the hours passed.

It would be beautiful. As much a performance as a clock.

But . . .

All of this timekeeping and motion required gears. And

springs. And both must be precisely calibrated . . . once they were made.

Verrigan got his saws and his files and began to work.

It was the closest to joy he had ever come, those many days he spent on work done for no one but himself. For in the end, the work was his shout of defiance into the void: *This is what I am capable of! This!*

The finished mechanism was as long as his torso, but a torso must be clothed, so Verrigan turned to the stores of wood and made his selections. Bright oak and dark kaffiyeh-wood and hard, pale ash. He stacked a whole forest upon his worktable and turned to his parchments once more.

Simple enough to build a plain box, but that was not what his artistry demanded. He temporized, beginning by carving the figures he would need: Heralds and Healers and Bards and nobles to show themselves upon the hour, a whole gathering of Companions to progress around the base of the dials, moving forward with each tick of the larger hand. He carved the prancing creatures with care, enameled them whiter than snow, leafed their hooves with silver foil, and gave them gems of blue glass for their eyes. He attached them to a circular track carved and polished to interlock with the largest of the gears he had made, and set that gear into place among the others. He set the weights that would trigger the escapement and carefully let go.

And the clock didn't work.

The Companion figures were supposed to move in time with each tick of the clock. It should take them a full day to make a circuit, back to where the first of them, the sleeping Companion, knelt in the grass.

Instead, they . . . jolted. Lurched. There was nothing smooth or mannered about their movement. The ring started, stopped, made grating sounds, and did its best to tear the gear from the track as Verrigan watched in horror. The standing figures beside the clock face thrust themselves in and out so sharply that one broke loose and toppled to the top of the workbench.

Finally, the spring ran down and it stopped.

With enormous self-control, Verrigan did not rip his creation to bits. He removed the broken pieces, and undid the gears that were giving him trouble, and set the weights again. On the face of the clock, the minute hand moved as it should. The clock, without the figures, would move as it should—if he did not ask the moonturns and sennights to accompany it.

It was pretty, but it was not what he had envisioned. It was not what he had dreamed of. It was not *art*.

He got to his feet. And then Verrigan stepped away from his workbench, and went from his workshop into his house, and broke things, and wept.

He was not the sort of man who gave up in the face of failure, but now Verrigan was afraid. Afraid he would do some unfathomable thing from which there was no turning back. Break his clocks, break his tools. Instead, he took to his bed and refused to get up at all.

Marta fretted over him, making him bread and broth, and telling him that sitting in the sun would do him good. He ought not to be sick. This was not the season for coughs and colds. It was spring again, and the village was bustling with release from winter's shackles. Herald Anlace would come soon, riding Circuit, to judge disputes and bring news. Perhaps even more news of the clockmaking competition.

And after her visit, the rest of the year will spin out like the springs from one of Skoros's ridiculous toys.

Toys.

Verrigan had forgotten the toys.

He stayed in bed another two days, willing himself to forget. Seeing them wouldn't help anything. Stealing another man's work wouldn't be *fair*, wouldn't help. Verrigan wanted to succeed because he was *best*, not because he was a thief.

He could not talk himself out of looking at the toys.

Finally, he dragged himself out of bed. He was weak and unsteady on his feet, but he forced himself to dress and go to his workshop. It was dusty and cobwebbed because Marta was forbidden to enter it, and it took him all afternoon to find the toys where he had flung them into a corner.

The little tumbler was cracked. It didn't matter. He was going to take all three toys apart anyway.

But first—perhaps to punish himself—Verrigan took his clock key and wound his own clock again. Once more the hands trembled and shuddered, unwilling to keep time. Once more the carven figures bolted and lagged.

Verrigan wished even more than before that he could just lift it into the air and smash it into the ground. But it would be like murdering a child. Or killing a beloved pet. The fault was not in the clock. The fault was in *him*.

He set the clockworks in its cabinet aside and covered it with the dust cloth again. Then he brought his tools close and turned to the toys.

There were three of them: the tumbling figure like the one the wagonmaster had showed him last midwinter. The ball—now cracked—meant to change directions randomly as it rolled. And a little dancer with a skirt in bright colors, held in place with a stand so she could bend and sway and pirouette and bow.

The ball came apart with difficulty, for it, unlike the tumbler and the dancer, was meant to be played with rather than observed. He drew his clock key from among his tools once more and gave the mechanism a couple of turns. He was rewarded with a brassy cascade of fingernail-sized springs from the hollow interior and a long, spiral ribbon of metal that jigged and nodded like the head of a bouncing boy.

He smoothed the ball's weak spring between his fingers, unconsciously straightening it beyond repair. Wind it tight enough and it would provide the force needed to move the gears, granted, but why? The spring was delicate, vulnerable to breakage, easily distempered.

Why was Skoros using such flimsy materials?

The ball itself was sound enough—leather over wood. The tumbler was painted paper over wood. But at the heart of the toys . . . trash.

The bouncing boys Verrigan had made all used a simple

compression spring. All his toys did. Why waste something more delicate on a toy a child was bound to break?

He took the ball completely apart, but there was no second spring, or any other form of interior works. He stretched the spring between his fingers. He regretted breaking the ball now. He ought to have seen how it worked.

He carefully wound the tumbler, letting it parade across his table half a dozen times before he took it apart. This time he was more careful, and captured the spiral spring still wound.

He could guess at what it was doing. What he couldn't guess was how.

He wound up the little dancer and gazed at her morosely as she twirled. There was no point in taking her apart until he was sure of what he was looking for.

Or why he was looking for it.

He held the spring he'd taken from the tumbler between his fingers, frowning. After a long time, he uncovered his clock-work again. The spring was too small, but he fitted it into place anyway.

The track of dancing Companions moved—smoothly—for just a moment, then stopped. The spring had expanded to its furthest stretch, and all its power was spent.

Verrigan wound the little dancer and watched her morosely. He did it over and over again, as if he expected that gazing at her would tell him something, though it didn't.

He didn't try to take her apart.

Every summer, Herald Anlace and her Companion Turrikane stopped at Dwellingwell on their Circuit. The Herald and her Companion were there to hear complaints and settle disputes, but most of all she was there to offer help and to bring news.

Everyone in the village and most of the farmers from around it gathered in the village square when the Herald came. The youngest children were kept out from under Turrikane's legs with some difficulty, those who would approach him at all.

"Is Master Verrigan here?" Herald Anlace asked. "Today I have news for him in particular."

Townsfolk flurried like chickens at the promise of excitement. Hilda scurried off to drag Verrigan out of his workroom.

Skoros was already among the crowd.

Verrigan blinked owlishly at the bright sunlight. He knew, of course, that Herald Anlace was here. And that her Companion was named Turrikane and that they were on Circuit and tomorrow they would leave Dwellingwell and ride on, since nothing exciting (or disastrous) ever happened in Dwellingwell. He knew all these things since he'd been a resident of Dwellingwell Town for his whole life.

"Herald Anlace, I am told you have news for me . . . in particular?" Verrigan said. No matter his inclinations or his temper, Verrigan could not find it in his heart to be rude to a Herald. At least not to one who had done nothing to annoy him.

"To you and to all who make and build clocks. There is to be a clock added to the belltower in Haven," Anlace said simply, smiling up at him. When she was not on Turrikane's back, she was a handspan shorter than Verrigan, and Verrigan was not a tall man. "The King is asking for designs and models to be submitted from every clockmaker in Valdemar. They are to be judged two years from now, to give even the most outlying craftsmen time to participate."

Verrigan nodded, to show he understood. In reality, designs would not be coming from much further away from Haven (in any direction) than this, since clocks—and the materials to make them—were luxury items. Verrigan had ordered the painted faces for his masterwork from Haven itself. He could make cogs and springs, and carve cases and figures, but he lacked the skill to master some of the more esoteric elements of his craft.

"So we shall have *two* clockmakers with work to send to Haven," the mayor said happily. "Who will surely present the King with two very different designs."

Everyone around Anlace cheered. Verrigan hung his head, hoping he looked modest instead of defeated.

When he looked up, he was staring into Skoros's eyes. Skoros didn't look pleased. The man looked as if he was on the edge of panic.

Anlace went on her way, and the summer went on, and Verrigan was no closer to a solution. The thing he'd hoped for and wanted and halfway expected all his life was so close he could reach out and touch it, and Verrigan couldn't close his fingers around it, and knew he never would be able to.

He embraced—he truly understood—*failure*.

He sanded the compression spring off his drawings. The depiction looked improbably unfinished without that vital missing element, but there was nothing to put in its place.

His inability to solve the problem was like something large and indigestible, only in his thoughts and not his stomach. There was something he wanted desperately, and he wasn't an unreasonable man, but he still couldn't understand why he couldn't *have* it. He even returned to his workshop and carefully took apart the little dancer. He held the spring carefully, and put her back together, and she still worked.

But the spring wouldn't power his clock. It was too small. He gazed morosely into the innards of his clock, and got some spring steel out of storage, and made a much larger spring. Then he brooded furiously over it until he could manage to make the spring move the hands and the dials and the weights that wound the clock.

It worked. Mostly.

And it *still* wasn't enough.

Because it wouldn't move the figures. It wouldn't move the bottom spring. And even if it did, the model wouldn't scale to something the size to fit into a clock tower. Make it larger, and it wouldn't lift and lower the weights and turn the gears and wind the springs and make everything live and breathe and *sing*.

He bet Skoros was having no trouble at all.

Summer turned to autumn.

It was the time of year to begin making toys, but this year Verrigan had no heart for it. The villagers would probably prefer

Skoros's toys anyway. So would the traders. And next year, when it was time to at least begin to think about going to the capital and submitting his work to the contest, there would be no point in doing so, because it wasn't finished.

It would never be finished.

Skoros's would be finished. He was sure of that. Skoros's design, which would move fluidly and charm the King and be selected to be made larger and installed in the tower and forever after people would say: *Oh, look, there is Milutin Skoros's wonderful clock. No one, alive or dead, has ever been so skilled at clockmaking!*

Verrigan found the thought so unbearable it choked him.

He couldn't eat. He couldn't sleep. All he could think about was the clock Skoros must be making. He had to see it.

He had to *destroy* it.

Smash it to pieces, burn the drawings, and Skoros wouldn't be able to submit it to the contest. Verrigan would add coil springs and leaf springs to his plans; he was sure that would fool the judges long enough for him to come up with an actual solution. And the scale model he'd built would work—more or less—with the springs he'd already made. He'd proved that.

By now Verrigan wasn't thinking very clearly at all.

It was cold and dark. Late autumn. Harvest-tide past, frost on the fields and bare-leafed trees. Tonight, the moon had passed mid-heaven long ago, and the sight of its passage made Verrigan think of a clock dial that measured the passage of the moon.

Now. He must do it now. He'd spent moonturns wrestling with the ethics of breaking into Skoros's workshop and stealing all his tools, his plans, and possibly his clock as well. He'd been ashamed that he could even imagine it. But everything had finally come down to harsh and unyielding choice between two things: steal Skoros's work and pass it off as his own, or have nothing to show to the King's Ministers.

(In reality, secretly, he wanted to be stopped, but Verrigan refused to let himself know that. He was a man who did not take well to the idea of risks, and he didn't like surprises either.)

He reached the door of Skoros's home. It was the same design as his own: two doors side by side, one leading into a small cottage, the other into the workroom.

Let it be locked, he prayed silently. *Oh, Powers, let it be locked.* He put his hand on the workroom door. As he did, Skoros opened it, a small lamp in one hand.

"Come in," he said. "I expected you sennights ago."

Verrigan wanted to turn and run, but Skoros already had him by the shoulder and was pulling him inside. The lamps were lit. There was not enough light to work by, but more than enough by which to see. The room was barren in comparison to Verrigan's workplace.

"Why have you come?" Skoros said. It was not quite an accusation.

"I came to see—" *to steal* "—the clock you're working on for the contest."

"Well then, come, my friend. Look your fill. Your only trouble will be that there's nothing to see. No drawings. No models. No proof of concept. Because *I can't make clocks.*"

"Nonsense!" Verrigan snapped. "Everyone knows you're the best clockmaker in the village. The wagonmaster of the trade caravan agrees. I think everyone in the village must have one of your clocks by now. And your toys are beautiful. Don't lie to me!" All the pent-up frustration and anguish of moonturns tumbled forth in a rush. The combination of discovery and confession made him feel light-headed.

Skoros blinked at him in surprise. "People buy my clocks because they're cheap. I buy wheels and cogs and gears from the city because they're cheap, too. I *assemble* clocks. I don't make them."

The words only increased Verrigan's sense of unreality. He stared at Skoros. Skoros smiled unhappily.

"Yes, you look at me like that and think me mad, I know. But everywhere I go I hear that your clocks are beautiful, but cost more than people can afford. Mine they can afford, because they are assembled from a host of spare parts, and I buy those cheaply. Shall I show you? Sit."

Numbly, Verrigan did as he was bid. Skoros reached beneath his worktable and set something on the table.

It was a clock.

It was very small, with a single simple dial. Skoros wound it and it began to tick, the longest hand moving around the dial smoothly. The case was made of plain, polished oak.

"I make the cases, nothing else. The cogs, wheels, and springs I buy. I paint the numbers on the dials and sometimes a little design. But I do not think the King will want this in his high tower, do you? Oh, and I should mention: they're very fragile and need to be repaired every year or two."

"But—but—but—*why*? Oh, I don't mean why do you make such abysmally awful clocks, because I'm sure everyone is entitled to do just as he pleases, but why hide it from me? Why pretend you are going to submit one to the contest when you have no chance of winning? Why—?"

Skoros sighed just a little. "All these questions, and they exist entirely in your own mind. Marta told me you were mad, but until now I only thought you wanted to murder me."

"*Murder* you? Only—what has Marta to do with clocks? She's my housekeeper."

"Marta is my mother. That's why I came back here."

Verrigan had never thought of Marta as having children, though if she had grandchildren, children must have entered the picture at some point. Still, he found it deeply unfair that all this time she had been working for his greatest enemy and never said a word about it.

"Since you make clocks as poorly as you make explanations, I have no reason to murder you at all!" Verrigan snapped.

"I am grateful to hear it. I never said—to you or anyone else—that I meant to enter this contest. And I have hidden nothing from you. It is you who have hidden in your burrow like a mole. What threat can I be to you?"

Verrigan mumbled something inaudible even to himself. "I

should go," he said, louder. "Since you don't have a clock." *And
since I'm not going to kill you.*

"And what about *your* clock? Why did you come here in the
first place?" Skoros asked with dismaying insight.

The question gave Verrigan fresh energy. "There is no clock!
There will *never* be a clock! I didn't come here to murder you—
I came here to steal your clock, and there's nothing worth steal-
ing! There! Happy now?"

"Haldis Verrigan," Skoros asked gently, "why is there no
clock?"

It was as much an accusation as a question, and Verrigan
heard it as such. In the midst of rising to his feet, he sank back
heavily to the bench again. "It's too complicated," he said
at last.

"The explanation or the clock?" Skoros asked.

"Either. Both. I can't get the escapement to do what I want.
With a leaf and coil spring I can make the main dial on the
model work, but I already know it won't scale up, so why bother
to submit it?"

"There is more than one dial?"

It was as if the simple question had opened some floodgate
of words. Verrigan had never talked to anyone about his clocks,
and no one had asked before. He talked until his voice was
hoarse, his hands waving in the air as if he would pluck images
from it for Skoros to see.

At last he stopped, slumping forward on the bench.

"I would like to see it," Skoros said softly.

The sky was cloudless, and the sun was summer bright. The bell
of the great clock tower of Haven rang noon. The figures on
either side of the main dial came out from behind their carven
doors and looked down at the people standing below. The nobles brandished their swords; the Heralds waved blue bridles
with silver bells; the Harpers held up a variety of instruments;
and the Healers carried bags with the tools of their trade. The
Companions at the bottom of the clock face moved forward,

heads turning from side to side, as if they were looking down at the people looking up. The three hands of the clock face made their incremental advances. The four dials showed the time, the season, the phase of the moon, and the day.

And if the figure of the Herald bore a particular resemblance to someone, spectators were too far away to see.

It was ten years since Herald Anlace had come bringing news of the King's contest to Dwellingwell Town. It was nine years since Skoros and Verrigan had come to Haven. It was eight years since their joint submission had been chosen to become the clock in the tower. And it was one year since the finished clock had been laboriously installed in its proper place.

They never tired of looking at it. Marta joked that the two of them spent as much time in the square as in their workshop. Verrigan said this was a patent falsehood, as the clock could not be observed to any advantage in the dark.

"It's just as well you agreed to use my design," Verrigan said.

"It's just as well you agreed to use my mechanism," Skoros answered, gazing up at the clock. "That way, we each get what we want. I have built a clock, and your name will be known forever."

"*We* have built a clock, and *our* names will be known forever," Verrigan corrected.

"And all it took was ending a feud that never was," said Skoros.

Harmony
Anthea Sharp

The end of the school year at the Collegium was both exhilarating and exhausting. Bard Shandara Tem pushed the papers on her desk aside and glanced out her office window at the furled buds of the rosebushes. Just as the flowers were burstingly eager to bloom, so were the students impatient to finish their studies and graduate or begin their summer breaks.

"Almost done?" her partner, Healer Tarek Strand, asked, looking up from the comfy chair he was ensconced in, book in hand. "It's lunchtime."

"Just finishing up the ensemble sectionals schedule." She sighed. "This contest the Bardic Circle just announced has everyone distracted."

He closed his book. "You have to admit, the prize of a position at the palace is a sweet one. Everyone knows old Master Guillard is stepping down soon."

She nodded. "I just wish the Circle had waited. I respect them, of course, but this is *not* the year to run such a high-stakes contest." Not when two of the most Gifted senior trainees at the college seemed determined to polarize the entire school.

As if to prove her point, a roar of applause came from the square outside.

"Sounds like they're at it again," Tarek said, rising.

"Unfortunately." She stretched and stood, too, then gave him a quick hug. "If we're lucky, we can beat the crowd to the dining hall."

2025

As they left her office, another spate of cheering filtered in through the propped-open door leading to the commons.

"Won't the Bardic Circle intervene?" Tarek asked.

She shook her head. "They think it's better to have the trainees work out the range of their Gifts at the Collegium, instead of wreaking havoc once they graduate."

"So they get to wreak havoc here instead?" He gave her a wry look.

"Apparently." They stepped outside, and she paused to survey the square.

Two crowds had formed between the three-story buildings that enclosed the green spaces and cobbled main plaza of the Collegium. Both groups wore a mix of trainee colors—rust, gray, blue, and pale green, with here and there the brighter silks of full Bards and Healers. There was even a spot or two of white, indicating the presence of Heralds. Shandara hoped they were there to observe and help keep the peace.

Despite their similarities, there was one main difference between the groups. Those at the south end of the plaza wore a gold ribbon tied around their left arms, while those in the north sported silver.

"Sunny and Midnight, showing their colors," Tarek murmured.

She nodded distractedly, her empathy humming at the swirling energy in the square.

To the south, Trainee Sunin Javer's exuberant tenor was bolstered by his masterful gittern playing. He'd climbed up on the wide rim of one of the fountains, and Shandara could see his red-gold curls shining as he strutted back and forth, casting his Bardic spell as far as he could fling it. His listeners clapped along, and now and then cheers would erupt, followed by laughter. His nickname of "Sunny" was well earned.

In contrast, to the north, Lady Midaren Stearn presided over a crowd that seemed hypnotized by her dusky alto and the shimmering chords of her harp. The listeners swayed back and forth. Shandara could feel them breathing together, inhaling and exhaling in time to Midaren's sinuous chanting.

Even though the use of titles was discouraged, Midaren made no secret of her noble origins. She demurely called herself a trainee, but her followers insisted on styling her "Lady Midnight."

"At this rate, everyone will be late for lunch," Tarek said as they crossed the square, skirting the edges of the listening crowds.

Shandara shook her head. "No—they won't let their followers go hungry."

Even as she spoke, Sunin played a final set of chords. He bowed flamboyantly, grinning at his audience as they cheered and whistled in appreciation. Then, to Shandara's surprise, he hopped down from the fountain and strode directly toward her and Tarek, his followers parting to give him clear passage.

"Bard Shandara!" he called with a cheery wave.

She could feel his Gift still hovering about him, and kept up her guard against his Bard-enhanced charm.

"Trainee Javer." She nodded cordially to him. "Your listeners seem well entertained."

"Sunny's the best!" a nearby fan called, and those around them cheered in response.

"Healer Strand, hello to you, too." Sunin grinned at Tarek. "Glad to see you both looking so well."

Shandara raised her brows. "Is there something you need?"

"I've been talking with Master Alvee," Sunin said, falling into step as they continued toward the dining hall. "And he mentioned you'll be assigning the solo piece for the competition."

She almost missed a step, and only Tarek's hand at her elbow saved her a stumble. "I am?"

The trainee gave her a conspiratorial wink, his blue eyes twinkling. "My teacher said a member of the Bardic Circle will be speaking to you this afternoon. And I know you're an amazing harp player, but I was hoping you'd take pity on a lowly gittern player when choosing the piece."

"I . . ." She tamped down her surge of annoyance. Master Alvee shouldn't be divulging the particulars of the contest or the Circle's plans to a mere trainee. It seemed even Sunin's instructor had fallen under the young man's spell.

"Oh, Sunshine, trying to curry favor again?" The husky alto voice came from behind them, sounding both dismissive and amused.

Sunin turned with a frown. "Look at you, Darkness, creeping up behind us like a thief. Trying to eavesdrop?"

Trainee Midaren gave him a look, one corner of her mouth curling in disdain. "I don't need to sneak about. And I certainly know when to keep my nose out of the Circle's business." She glanced at Shandara. "Good afternoon, Bard Shandara. Don't let him bother you. He's annoying enough for both of us."

Shandara blinked. The tendrils of suggestion cast by the trainee were so subtle as to be almost unnoticeable.

"Stop it, both of you," she said sharply. "Bardic magic should never be used for personal gain. You know that. Now, I trust you to leave me and Healer Strand in peace so we can enjoy our lunch."

She looped her arm through Tarek's and continued to the dining hall, leaving the two trainees glaring at one another.

"Their Gifts are very strong, aren't they?" Tarek asked quietly once they'd gotten their food and seated themselves in the private partitioned area where the instructors and masters often ate.

"Yes." She frowned, shredding a piece of roll between her fingers. "I don't like how well they can continue to project their Gifts after they're done performing."

"Can't most Bards?"

"Well, yes. But usually not until they're closer to master status. Those two have power, but no sense of responsibility." She sighed. "I wish they were in different years. Or even generations. Two such strong influencers at the same time is only creating problems."

"Indeed." An older man dressed in scarlet paused beside their table. "May I join you?"

"Please, Master Tangeli." She smiled at her old teacher while Tarek nodded a greeting to him and slid over to make room.

"Thank you." He took a seat on the bench beside Tarek. "I couldn't help but notice you were discussing our problem children."

She nodded. Both trainees would be insulted to be referred to as children, but there was no question they were acting childishly. "What can we do? It seems the entire Collegium is splitting into factions. My advanced ensemble is definitely showing cracks."

At rehearsal the day before, there'd been a spat between a flute player and the tambor player seated in front of him. The tambor player had insisted the flute was playing too shrilly, and asked Shandara to shift the seating arrangements. Several other musicians in the ensemble had spoken up in defense of the first student, while others staunchly defended the tambor player.

"The ensemble is arranged to give concertgoers the best listening experience," she'd said in exasperation. "We're all in service to the music here, and don't forget it."

It had taken a while for the grumbling to die down. And it hadn't escaped her notice that the supporters of the silver-banded flute player all sported Lady Midnight's colors, while the tambor player and crew wore Sunny's gold ribbons.

"The two trainees are indeed becoming a problem," Master Tangeli said, setting his mug down with a thunk. "Which is why the Bardic Circle would like your help, Shandara."

Tarek sent her a significant look. Trainee Sunin had been right.

"What can I do?" she asked warily.

Master Tangeli steepled his fingers. "This upcoming competition has a few challenges. Two in particular. Our brightest candidates are also our most difficult. And you've always worked well with students who have problematic Gifts."

"Yes—but neither of the trainees in question are struggling," she protested. "I'm good with late emergence or misunderstood talents. But that's not the case here."

Tarek tipped his head. "Seems to me a too-strong Gift is still a problem. Maybe in the opposite direction, but that doesn't make it any less of an issue."

"Still, I don't see how I can help."

"You have a talent for improvisation, and finding unique solutions, Shandara." Her old teacher smiled warmly at her. "We were hoping you could help find an appropriate solo piece for the competition."

She frowned. "I'm not nearly as familiar with the repertoire as the members of the Circle. I mean, I am on the harp, but certainly not gittern."

Tarek shot her a sympathetic look, and she felt his foot brush hers under the table in a gesture of support.

"The thing is . . ." Master Tangeli glanced around the area, then leaned forward, his voice lowering. "Not every member of the Circle is, shall we say, impartial on the matter. You are the best choice in this. Just make sure the piece is purely instrumental. We don't need either of those young siren's voices muddying things up."

It was obvious what the master was leaving unsaid. Sunny and Lady Midnight were both trying to sway the Bardic Circle. And their voices were too potent.

She sighed. "I'll do the best I can," she said, her thoughts whirling.

Master Tangeli nodded, his eyes bright under his gray brows. "I expect nothing less."

Master Tangeli has set me a hopeless task, Shandara thought as she shuffled through yet another pile of sheet music in the Bardic Library. The smell of old paper filled the air, along with plenty of dust motes floating in errant sunbeams, as she discarded solo after solo. The days were passing, and she still hadn't been able to find a suitable piece that wouldn't favor one instrument or the other.

Music that was challenging on the gittern was easy on the harp, and vice versa. Her only hope was to find something composed for a different instrument, which would be equally uncomfortable to play on both harp and gittern.

Accordingly, she'd dug into the flute repertoire, where the keys were challenging for a stringed instrument to play, even though the melodies might seem simple. She'd found a few possibilities scored for ensemble accompaniment, but none of them were quite right.

Until she lifted a sheaf of music entitled "Canonic Concerto," and the light dawned.

This. This was the answer. She slumped back in relief, tears of gratitude pricking her eyes, especially when she discovered that the orchestral score was nicely straightforward; a fitting accompaniment to the flashier solo part. She thumbed through it twice, just to make sure, then grinned and hugged the music to her chest.

She'd need to retitle it, to make sure the trainees got no hint of what was in store. But oh, what an excellent solution this was.

Humming the opening bars, she left the library, the precious sheet music tucked under her arm and a spring in her step.

The soloists wouldn't be very happy when it came time to perform, but her job wasn't to coddle them. Her job was to help the Collegium train the very best Bards possible; to ensure that when a student left Bardic they had, in addition to their musical skills, the maturity and insight needed to help them navigate the broader world.

She could hardly wait for the competition to arrive.

The nearer the day drew, the more evident the cracks were between factions in the Collegium. All the instructors were on edge, though both Sunny and Lady Midnight were clearly reveling in the attention.

It wasn't uncommon for an appreciative audience to amplify a player's Bardic Gift, but the level of adulation showered on the two students simply made everything worse. The Collegium was split into three groups: those who adored Sunny, those who worshipped Lady Midnight, and those who despised both equally and wished the whole thing was over.

Rehearsals in the advanced ensemble were a microcosm of the divisions splintering the school. Their practice space was small, but the players still found ways to move away from one another when seated next to an "enemy." With every rehearsal, the music sounded worse as the ensemble stopped listening to each other and instead focused on getting in the other faction's way.

It was no way to run a group, much less a Collegium.

"Stop!" Shandara said sharply, cutting the music short and shooting a pointed look at the ensemble members seated before her. "Half of you are rushing, the other half dragging. Please recall that *I* am setting the tempo here."

"I'm on tempo," young Edwold piped up, and she sent him a quelling, though amused, look. The boy was firmly in the despise-them-both camp, and she appreciated his candor.

"Jaya, you're leading the gittern section," she said. "Stop leaning into the beat."

The girl wrinkled her nose. "Sunny says the tempo needs to be sprightly, so his abilities can be showcased."

"It's way too fast," one of the boys playing a hand drum argued. "Slow and sweet is the way, according to Lady Midnight."

Voices rose as each side tried to convince Shandara that they were in the right. She needed to conduct faster. No, slower.

Edwold folded his arms and scowled, refusing to take part. "This is ridiculous," he said loudly. "We're supposed to work *together*. Otherwise, the music is broken."

Precisely.

Shandara held up her hands for silence. When the squabbling musicians finally quieted, she folded her arms. "I've decided."

Jaya looked smugly at the drum boy, clearly thinking the argument had gone in favor of Sunny.

"It's time to rehearse with a soloist," Shandara continued. "We'll play at whatever tempo they prefer."

"But . . ." Jaya blinked at her. "Sunny is too busy to come rehearse."

"Lady Midnight can't, either," the drummer said, sounding disgruntled. "She's such an accomplished musician, she doesn't need to work with the ensemble."

"So I've heard," Shandara said dryly.

She'd already approached both soloists to see when they could come in for rehearsals, and each one had brushed her off. Trainee Midaren had made it clear that working with lesser musicians was beneath her, and Trainee Sunin flat-out told her it would be a waste of his time.

"I know you mean well, Bard Shandara," he'd said earnestly. "But nobody will be listening to the ensemble anyway. I mean, I'm sure you'll do a good job getting them ready, but they're just a backdrop."

She'd blinked at him. Did he really have such a high opinion of himself? It seemed the reinforcement of his followers had blown his ego entirely out of proportion. When she'd gone to his instructor, Master Alvee, the Bard had only given her a sour look.

"Sunin's too busy," he'd said. "Really, Bard Shandara, just do your job with the ensemble and don't worry about my student. I've no doubt he will rise to the occasion."

Master Tangeli had been more apologetic, but equally clear that Trainee Midaren would not be joining them at rehearsals. "If you can get Trainee Sunin to come, then maybe Midaren will follow," he said. "But you can't force her to rehearse with the ensemble."

"Maybe make it a requirement of the competition?" Shandara suggested, without much hope.

Her old teacher gave her a look that was equal parts frustration and amusement. "Be honest, Shandara. Do you really want to work with either of them in rehearsals?"

Well, not really. And the less the two soloists heard of the accompaniment, the less prepared they'd be when the truth was revealed. Grudgingly, she let it go.

"Who else is entering the competition?" she asked.

She'd heard snippets of the melody coming from the practice rooms, once on flute, and another time the gentle plucking of a harp.

"My student Andelle is working on the solo," Master Tangeli said. "She's planning to enter in order to gain more performance experience."

Shandara nodded. That would be the harpist she'd heard. "Anyone else? We need one more."

"I believe Trainee Johen is working on the solo as well." Master Tangeli waggled his brows. "He's an amiable fellow. If you need someone to rehearse with, I'd definitely recommend him."

"I'll pick both," she said. "The ensemble needs the experience of rehearsing with different soloists, and it's good practice for Trainees Andelle and Johen too."

As it turned out, both students were happy to attend a few rehearsals with the ensemble. Unlike two others she could name, they weren't puffed up with their own self-importance. Indeed, Andelle could have shown a bit more confidence as she tentatively agreed, but Johen had grinned when she'd asked him.

"Need a training horse, do you?" he'd asked. "I'll be happy to serve."

"It's not like that," she'd said. Well, not entirely.

"Oh, I'm under no illusions," he'd said, clearly unbothered by the fact. "We all know I'm third in line here, as far as winning the competition. But I'll be glad to come play. Could use the extra practice myself, honestly. And it's always a good idea to know what the accompaniment is doing. We'll be playing the music together, after all."

Too bad Johen isn't the flashy Bard his main competitors are, she thought as she penciled him into the rehearsal schedule. Though he might lag in showy technique, he far outstripped the others when it came to maturity.

As Shandara had hoped, having an actual soloist to play with settled the orchestra down. They were, after all, excellent musicians when they weren't distracted by petty squabbles.

She was glad to hear Johen's playing develop as they worked through some of the more nuanced sections. There were some players who found strength in ensemble work, letting it free their musicality, and the flute player seemed to be one of them.

Trainee Andelle, however, was clearly intimidated by the role of soloist. Her playing was hesitant, and she tended to pause whenever she made a mistake instead of continuing on with the flow of music.

"Sunny doesn't have anything to worry about, does he?" Jaya whispered loudly to her stand partner.

"Concentrate on the music, please." Shandara gave the young woman a look. Still, it was clear Andelle wasn't ready to play the solo alone. "Trainee," she said, turning to the miserable-looking harpist, "what do you think about rehearsing in tandem with Johen, to get a feel for how the solo part works with accompaniment?"

"Yes, please," she said fervently.

"We'll do that tomorrow, then." Shandara smiled inwardly. She knew Johen would help steady Andelle, grounding her in the music.

As an added bonus, having the two trainees used to playing together would help when Master Tangeli sprung the surprise on everyone at the performance.

Finally, the day of the competition dawned. It felt like the entire Collegium was holding its breath. A brawl broke out at lunch. Two Heralds separated the fighters, and the participants were sternly commanded to remain in their rooms until the next day. There was much gnashing of teeth at this punishment, as it meant they'd miss the performance, but no further fights occurred.

"I can't believe I'm this nervous," Shandara confided to Tarek that evening as she got ready for the performance. "Honestly, the last time I had stage fright was at the Midwinter Recital all those years ago."

"And that turned out just fine." He smiled at her from where he leaned against the doorjamb.

"Though unexpectedly." She let out a rueful chuckle. "I suppose this performance will turn into something equally surprising."

To her extreme gratitude, no word had gotten out about the nature of the concerto. Although there had been a dicey moment during rehearsal that afternoon, when Andelle had fallen behind Johen. Shandara had quickly cut the ensemble off, but not before she saw Edwold sit upright in surprise. After a moment, he gave her a conspiratorial wink. The rascal had figured it out, but she trusted him to say nothing. He was a fan of pranks, after all.

"You look beautiful," Tarek said, stepping forward with an appreciative smile. "Try not to outshine the soloists."

"Ha." She leaned over and gave him a quick kiss. "You're biased. Everyone will be in their best silks, and I have no doubt both Sunny and Lady Midnight will be elaborately dressed."

He shook his head. "I think everyone is tired of those two. Even their followers."

"I hope so. This rivalry has been exhausting."

"Do you think it will continue after tonight?"

She frowned in thought, then let out a sigh. "Unfortunately, yes. Those two will be at odds forever. Music can't solve everything, but I hope they'll walk away wiser from the experience, and that the tension will subside until graduation."

"When they'll become someone else's problem."

"Provided they graduate," she said sourly. They should, of course—unless their behavior during the competition made it necessary to hold them back. She shuddered at the thought.

"Ready, milady?" Tarek offered his arm, along with a gentlemanly bow.

"As ready as I can be." She tucked her long braid behind her shoulder, slipped her elbow through his, and went to face the musical dragons.

Tarek gave Shandara a quick squeeze for luck, then left her at the stage door of Bardic's main recital hall. Backstage, there was a jittery air of excitement. The advanced ensemble was ready to take the stage, though they stood in groupings split along party lines.

In one corner, Trainee Andelle bent over her music, doing some last-second practicing. Trainee Johen stood, arms crossed, beside Edwold. Shandara was glad to see the older student had taken the troublemaker under his wing. The last thing they needed was some kind of disruption during the competition.

"Where are the other soloists?" she asked the trainee.

Johen shrugged, but Edwold rolled his eyes. "Lady Midnight poked her head in a few minutes ago, so she's around. Just didn't want to mingle with us commoners. I haven't seen the other one."

On the heels of his words, the door opened, and Trainee Sunin strode in, holding his gittern.

To no one's surprise, he sported gold accents everywhere— from the shimmering embroidery on the cuffs and neckline of his rust-colored tunic to a thick gold chain around his neck and a gold stud in one ear. Shandara half-expected him to be wearing gilded boots, but thankfully he'd retained a shred of good taste. The supple leather was dyed a pale orange, though the buttons running up the outside of each boot were, of course, bright gold.

Trainee Midaren followed, her multilayered skirts swishing with each step. Though the top fabric of her gown was the customary rust of a Bardic trainee, her underdress was black silk shot through with silver-thread embroidery. Her hair was artfully braided and coiled, and rubies sparkled from the silver comb she'd used to fix her coiffure.

With a silent sigh, Shandara went to the wings to survey the assembled audience. The seats were filling rapidly. It was going to be standing room only at the back and sides of the hall.

"Ready?" she asked, turning to look at her ensemble. They nodded, and she flashed a quick smile of encouragement. "Remember, we're making music *together*. No matter what happens out there tonight, keep in mind that the end result is bigger than our individual parts."

Lady Midnight sniffed in disapproval. Clearly, she thought her own talent should eclipse the whole.

Ignoring the girl, Shandara gestured for the orchestra members to go onstage. They'd tune up, she'd take the stage, and then Master Bard Tangeli would step up and make his introductory remarks.

And unveil their surprise.

She couldn't help smiling at the prospect.

A few minutes later, the ensemble and Shandara were in place. Master Tangeli rose from the front row, where the entire Bardic Circle was seated in a blaze of Scarlets, and mounted the stage.

"Welcome, everyone," he said, his trained voice carrying to the back of the hall. "The winner of tonight's competition will be offered a place at the palace, under the guidance of Bard Guillard—a highly sought-after position, as I'm sure you're all aware. The Bardic Circle's choice of winner is final. I'm sure I need not remind you of that fact. Complaints will not be entertained."

There were a few murmurs of discontent, but they quickly faded under the master's stern gaze.

"Good." He turned, sweeping a hand over the ensemble and toward the wings. "All the musicians, ensemble and soloists alike, have worked diligently over the past few weeks to prepare the concerto—a piece chosen by Bard Shandara Tem for two purposes. Firstly, it's a relatively obscure composition. No one had the undue advantage of knowing the music beforehand."

A ripple of approval moved through the crowd, and Shandara bit her lip. This next part wasn't going to be nearly so universally accepted.

"Secondly . . ." Master Tangeli paused dramatically. "Well, I'll let the music speak for itself. Without further ado, please welcome our first two soloists to the stage. Trainee Sunin and Trainee Midaren, please come out."

The audience broke into confused whispering, and Shandara saw Sunny and Lady Midnight exchange a shocked look backstage. Probably the first time the two had acknowledged one another's existence in weeks.

Master Tangeli cleared his throat in expectation, and the two trainees emerged, carrying their instruments. Sunny's customary smile was gone, and Lady Midnight's eyes were dark with anger.

"What is this?" she demanded. "I'm not going to play in unison with *him*."

"You won't be." The master bard gave her a mild look. "This is a canonic concerto. Which, if you recall your lessons—"

"Means it's like a round, where one of us goes first, and the other follows." Sunny shook his head. "I should've seen it. This is a cruel trick to play, sir."

There was quiet chorus of agreement in the audience, but Master Tangeli held up his hand. "Not at all. If you cannot make music together, then I fear neither of you are eligible to graduate from the Bardic Collegium, let alone take up a position in the palace."

Lady Midnight's glare was scorching, and Sunny looked like he wanted to argue loudly, but both knew better than to incur the wrath of the Bardic Circle.

"I'll go first, then," Lady Midnight said. "To show how it's done."

"Fine." Sunny's voice was hard. "I'll go second. But I'm not taking my musical cues from *her*."

Shandara's brows went up. She'd thought both musicians would fight over who started, even though playing second was a more strategic choice. Master Tangeli even had a coin in his pocket to help settle the question.

As they'd been speaking, a stagehand brought out a second stool and music stand. She placed them next to the first set, angled so they'd be in front of the ensemble, but still in Shandara's line of vision.

"I expect you'll take your musical cues from the director," Master Tangeli said, nodding at Shandara. "At your convenience, Bard Tem."

He returned to his seat and an uncomfortable quiet descended. With a toss of her head, Lady Midnight took the outside stool and set her harp gently on its pedestal feet. Mouth scrunched in irritation, Sunny seated himself as well, making a show of scooting a few inches away.

"Trainee Sunin," Shandara said to him, "the count is eight measures after Trainee Midaren begins. I'll signal you."

"I won't miss my entrance."

He probably wouldn't; there was no disputing his musicality. But she'd cue him, all the same.

"Ready, Trainee Midaren?"

The harpist nodded once, her eyes fixed on the music.

Very well. Shandara turned to the ensemble and lifted her hands, quietly counting them in. Despite their internal tensions, the group came in perfectly on the downbeat. They played the short melodic introduction, and then Midaren plucked the first notes of the solo.

She was trying to drag the tempo, Shandara noted, but *she* was the one in charge. When the drummer started to lag, she sent him a sharp look, and he shifted back on beat. Sunny's entrance was flawless, a bright flurry that echoed and harmonized with Lady Midnight's part.

No surprise, he attempted to push the music faster. Again, Shandara kept the tempo steady, this time sending a warning glance at Jaya in the gittern section.

It wasn't utter cacophony, but the piece definitely stuttered. The duet parts seesawed between dreamily hypnotic and jauntily upbeat as the soloists wrestled, each one trying to assert their musical dominance. Shandara set her jaw and kept conducting. In the tambor section, she could see Edwold's grimace.

Slowly, almost imperceptibly, the piece smoothed. A whole section went by where dark was tangled with bright, Lady Midnight's fluid playing a backdrop of dusk for the spangles of notes sparking off Sunny's gittern. As if realizing they'd been working together, the soloists frayed again. Sunny hammered the notes out, a ferocious frown on his face. Lady Midnight's brows were drawn together as she accented things oddly, trying to throw him off as he followed in her wake.

Master Tangeli coughed loudly in the audience—an unsubtle reminder that they were supposed to be working together. Grudgingly, the soloists adapted to each other once more.

This time, when the piece settled, the whole audience sighed in relief. More than relief. Shandara felt a tinge of awe at how the simple concerto was suddenly transformed, from melody to a great weaving of mystery. The harp and gittern were no longer two separate instruments, but one—a multilayered mix of shadow and sunbeam, silver and gold.

The ensemble melded together, too, and that particular stillness that only manifested in the presence of wonder enveloped the hall. The melody twined and untwined, the tension of subtle disharmony building in the music, as it was meant to, then dissolving, resolving. No animosity, no ego. Simply the notes, reminding each listener of their own particular sorrows and joys. Of the inevitability of loss, and the reminder that hope always remains.

The last note rang out into a perfect silence. The soloists remained frozen at their instruments, consummate performers that they were.

After a heartbeat, the audience erupted into thunderous applause. Lady Midnight rose, Sunny at her heels. They bowed in unison, and Shandara heard Sunny say to his nemesis, "That wasn't so bad."

Lady Midnight's mouth curled in disdain. "I still despise you."

They rose, smiles in place, and Shandara gestured the ensemble to stand and take their bow.

"Good job," she said. "All of you."

Master Tangeli strode onstage, preventing the soloists from taking a third bow, and the audience quieted.

"The competition isn't finished yet," he reminded everyone. "Trainees Andelle and Johen will be playing next. But before they do, I want to acknowledge two things."

He turned and looked at the soloists. Both of them had an eager light in their eyes, as though they expected he'd come up to personally name them the winner.

"Firstly, I think we can all agree that there were moments of true brilliance in that performance." The audience applauded, with a few cheers sprinkled in. Master Tangeli held up a finger. "Secondly, that brilliance *only* happened when you set aside your differences and worked together to create something bigger than either of you. Bring your strengths, yes, but put them in service to the whole. Without the ability to do so, there is *no* music. There is only noise and striving. And who wants to live in a world like that?"

The crowd murmured in agreement. Sunny looked a little abashed, and Lady Midnight's haughty expression was tinged with embarrassment.

"This is why we are here," the master continued, turning back to the listeners. "To truly understand that we are all in this together. Every bit, no matter how small, is an important part of the whole. We must all strive to live up to the name of Bard, and Healer, and Herald. Don't you agree?"

The audience clapped and shouted their appreciation as Master Tangeli motioned Sunny and Lady Midnight off the stage, then beckoned the two other trainees to take their place.

The second performance lacked both the awkwardness and the breathtaking luminosity of the first. Johen did an impressive job of bolstering Andelle when she faltered, and the ensemble enfolded both of them. The soloists rose to the occasion, especially Trainee Johen, and did justice to the piece, channeling the purity of the music instead of trying to impose their wills upon it.

It was a true demonstration of what Master Tangeli had just been saying.

When the competition ended, the Master Bard announced that the Bardic Circle would deliberate and choose the winner on the morrow. Amid whispers of speculation, the Scarlet-clad Circle rose and filed out of the hall. The camaraderie between the ensemble faded as they packed their instruments away and split back into their factions.

Shandara had heard that both Lady Midnight and Sunny had planned parties in celebration of their victories. *They'd best do their reveling while they can,* she thought, *for clearly there can only be one winner.* And she had a strong suspicion the Bardic Circle had one more surprise in store.

The next morning, the winner of the competition was posted outside the dining hall. Word spread like wildfire through the Collegium.

To the consternation and disappointment of both Sunny and Lady Midnight's followers, neither of them had won. Instead, the Bardic Circle had chosen Trainee Johen for the position in the palace.

When Edwold breathlessly brought the news to Shandara's door, she'd nodded in satisfaction. "An excellent choice. Thank you for telling me."

"I'm off to tell Lyssa, next," the boy said, eyes bright. "We were hoping neither of those puffed-up pieces won." He dashed back down the hall.

Smiling, she closed the door and turned to where Tarek sat on the edge of her bed, pulling on his boots.

"That ended well," he remarked.

"Indeed. Johen is an excellent choice for the palace. I can only hope our star trainees learned their lesson."

Whether Sunny and Lady Midnight would change remained to be seen. But even if they didn't, they'd graduate from the Collegium in a handful of weeks and go their separate ways. Hopefully in opposite directions, to the farthest corners of Valdemar.

"If they didn't, it's not your fault." Tarek grinned at her. "Once again, Bard Shandara saves the day."

"Oh, you." She sat beside him, giving him a quick kiss. "Next time, it'll be your turn."

"No more saving trainees from themselves, for either of us. I'd rather settle in for a quiet summer." He slid his arm around her shoulders, and she leaned into his embrace with a small sigh.

"So would I, love. So would I."

Playing Peacemaker
Once More
Dee Shull

In the late morning shade beneath an oak tree that had stood in the Healer's Collegium for at least a century, Serril exhaled slowly. The day was already warm, the late summer air pressing down on the city, and anyone with sense was either deep in the coolest parts of the palace or the Collegia buildings or hiding in the shade. At least a dozen others were spread out throughout the grove, but Serril had claimed his spot just as the sun began to peek over the horizon.

Jayin arched an eyebrow at her mentor. "I'm out here studying—the least you could do is help me prepare for Healer Neena's exam." She rattled a sheaf of notes in Serril's direction.

The Healer rolled off his back with a quizzical look at the young woman. "I thought exams were long over?" He shifted a bit to sit cross-legged across from Jayin, and smiled a bit lopsidedly. "Or is this one of those things where Neena thinks you didn't meet her rather exacting standards?"

"No, not any of that. She wants me to skip her class next semester, or that's what she said." Jayin raked her fingers through her short hair. "What I wouldn't give for a breeze."

After a moment's thought, Serril nodded. "Brone's helping her with that class in the fall. Technically, you shouldn't know this, so be discreet." He tapped his chin with a finger. "And Brone, well, he's not the most reasonable Healer around."

"Water is wet and Heralds stand out in a crowd, you'll be telling me next," Jayin huffed.

Startled, Serril laughed. "Indeed. Even if nobody else is in earshot, I'm not willing to say some of the things I could. But what's the exam on, specifically? I know you passed the basic anatomy classes with flying colors."

Jayin was about to answer when a harried looking man in Healer Green scurried up to them, clutching worriedly at his hands when he wasn't using them to tug on his thin, blond hair. "Oh, my, there you are, Serril, there you are!"

Serril waved and answered, "Marten? It's been years! What brings you to the oak grove in search of me?"

Marten glanced at Jayin, who waved to him, then back to Serril. "I need your help. Desperately. Now, if you can, but today if not."

A knot began to twist somewhere in his midsection, and Serril pushed himself to his feet. "The family you're assigned to—the Valerins, was it? Have they come down with something?"

Pacing back and forth, Marten occasionally glanced to the south. "Not unless you count the escalation of their feud. I told them I'd get someone I trusted to help them out. There's been trouble recently, and the heat's made them all angrier than hornets 'round a downed nest."

"Stop. Marten, you're barely making sense." But Serril had a sinking suspicion what Marten was leading up to: playing peacemaker between two groups who'd gotten riled up over something.

The Healer's next words confirmed it. "You were always so good at getting two sides to calm down, Serril! The Valerins have finally come to blows with the Barretts. Simeon, the youngest son, has a broken arm, and his father Elias was muttering about hiring some folk to go over to the Barretts and deliver a thumping."

The world went hazy for a moment, then Serril felt Jayin's hand on his back. The Mindhealing had been going well, but he knew there were still snares from his childhood and time as a student. For all that Jayin was his trainee, she was also a reminder that he wasn't as alone as he had been, even a year ago.

"Marten," Serril said after a few moments of watching the man pace, "I can't promise anything. Bright Havens, I can't even promise they'll listen to me. And why hasn't the watch been called, or even a Herald?"

"They don't like people knowing their business. Elias heard enough of my stories about you that he said he'd give you a chance." Marten looked to the south again before turning an imploring gaze on Serril. "He said he'd wait, but only until after sunset. I don't *think* he'll find people immediately? But I don't want to chance it."

Before Serril could respond, Jayin piped up. "Begging your pardon, Healer Serril, but this would be an excellent opportunity for me to get some field experience, wouldn't you say?"

Before Marten could object, Serril answered as calmly as he could with his blood whooshing through his head. "My trainee, Jayin Avelard. She's Gifted, and while I won't ask her to do any Healing, she deserves to get a bit of insight on what it is to serve as a Healer."

Marten nodded so hard Serril worried he might wrench his neck. "Yes, yes, it'll be fine, anyone you'd take as a trainee I'm sure would be acceptable to Elias. But we should hurry back to the wagon. I'm sure Devin—he's the second youngest—isn't happy about waiting."

On the ride along the South Trade Road to the Valerin estate, Marten told Serril and Jayin a bit more about the families. The Valerins had been nobles several generations back, but fell on hard times during Roald's reign. They'd gone into trading, and succeeded thanks to their connections. Then along came the Barretts, commoners who'd built their trading business up in the same span of years. According to Elias, the Barretts had snatched a profitable trading contract out from under his family. While the Valerins finally showed their skill in the end, the two families had been competing with each other ever since.

"But it's never come to blows until now, at least that's what Elias said," Marten miserably finished. "It's all been quiet competition for contracts, one family sneaking business away from the other."

The wagon creaked as it rolled along the road, hardly anyone else out in the midday sun. Serril was grateful for the arch of cloth over the wagon bed, shielding them from the worst of the sun. He sighed and rubbed his temples. "What changed?"

From the front, Devin answered. "Barretts got a contract that'll keep them afloat for several months, but we're the better choice because we have better connections downriver." The young man looked to be a few years older than Jayin, and his red hair was tied back in a simple club. "Plus, that Lorn Barrett decided to lord it over Simeon, telling him they'd be eating cream and we'd be left with soured curds."

Jayin rolled her eyes in a way that Serril knew all too well; without witnesses, she'd have compared these families to nine-year-olds taunting each other. Instead, she said, "But your family still has other contracts, right?"

"That contract meant both profit and proving ourselves for even better ones. Now?" Devin spat off to the side, and the placid mule pulling the wagon flicked an ear in response. "We'll have to work twice as hard for a chance like that, even though we know better than the Barretts how to work with the nobles."

Serril resisted the urge to roll his eyes.

The Valerin estate, about a candlemark and a half south of Haven, stood in testament to the family's history. The elaborate main house stood flanked by more utilitarian outbuildings, gardens that had once been decorative now grew food, and an ornamental gate proclaimed to the world that this was the home of the Valerin Trading Concern.

Marten practically scurried toward the front door, waving for Serril and Jayin to follow him. "Elias will be inside, I'm sure, and I healed Simeon before I went to find you, but I don't know if he'll listen to me or start trying to use that arm again, and maybe he'll listen to you."

"Breathe, Marten. I'm sure a few moments won't hurt." Serril stepped in front of his old classmate, and waited until the other Healer had settled again. "Why are you so nervous?"

With a gusty sigh, Marten looked up at Serril. "I tried for so long to do things the way you would. Keep the peace. Heal the Valerins when they got sick. Not rock the boat." He sighed again. "The feud wasn't going away, but both families had kept it to harsh words for several years, and before that it wasn't even that bad, just the occasional cold but polite exchange when they met."

"What changed?" Jayin asked as she looked around. They were alone, or alone enough; Devin had taken the wagon around to one of the outbuildings, and several people were busy loading it with wooden crates lashed together with sturdy rope.

"I wasn't there for it," Martin started miserably, "but a month or two back, Devin and Mattias Barrett got into a bad argument. Devin's a bit of a hothead, but swears he was minding his own business and it was Mattias who started things."

Serril nodded. "And the summer's been hot, which I'm sure hasn't helped. Let's go in. I'm sure the head of the Valerins is waiting on us." He shook his head, then glanced briefly at Jayin. "Mind yourself, here."

She nodded. "I will."

Elias gave both Serril and Jayin mistrustful looks, but settled down after Serril promised the man he wouldn't go to the watch or the Heralds.

"The Barretts have been a thorn in our side since my grandfather's time," he said in a deep, rumbling voice, "stealing our best contracts and trading on the fact that they've always been working folk, unlike our family. But we stayed competitive, kept our family and business going, even through the Tedrel Wars. But this time they've gone too far!" He thumped his fist on his desk, causing the ink bottle to jump a bit. "Lorn Barrett started a fight at one of the waystations, broke my youngest son's arm. We've kept things civil between our two families for decades now, but this is the last straw!"

Serril waited a moment, and asked in as calm a voice as he could manage, "Surely this kind of trouble between your families would be best resolved with a Herald's help?"

From further back in the room, a man called out, "It hasn't, because they're stubborn fools who think they're right, and believe the Heralds would just rule against them."

Elias turned in his chair and growled, "Wilton, you've no right to say that."

"Why, because I'm your younger brother who went away and made a life for himself in Hartsbridge?" The owner of the voice stepped up to Elias's side, clearly his brother even though Wilton's hair was thick while Elias's red mane had receded from his forehead. "Greetings, Healers. And yes, I know you're a trainee," he said with a bit of a smile at Jayin, "but clearly you're not here because you were bored."

"Wilton, why are *you* here? Shouldn't you be out in Haven, looking for something more productive to do?"

"I've found a place I can rent for when my daughter gets here. We're finally free of my wife, thanks to the Avelards—"

Jayin gasped. "The Avelards?"

"I take it you've heard of them?" Wilton bemusedly asked.

Serril started laughing. "It's a small, small world, Wilton Valerin, and maybe you and Jayin should go talk to each other, since she's an Avelard herself."

The two of them headed off to a nearby sitting room, while Serril gave Elias a thoughtful look. "What would you have me do? I'm not a Herald, and the Barretts will take me for one of your partisans if I advocate for you."

The head of the Valerin family glared at Serril, who simply blinked at him. Finally, he grumbled, "Marten—"

"Healer Marten," Serril interjected with a bit of frost to his voice.

"Ah, right, Healer Marten said you were good at making peace between feuding folk. We can't afford for things to get worse with the Barretts right now. It's been almost two years since the end of the war with Hardorn, and we're only mostly recovered." Elias grimaced. "And I wouldn't tell you these things, except Healer Marten swears up and down you can be trusted."

Serril took a deep breath, and said, "I'd like to talk briefly with Healer Marten about this. I'm sure my trainee will be fine here, and it sounds like there's a story behind your brother coming here." He stood, and bowed formally to Elias, who nodded brusquely and left Serril alone with his classmate.

Serril frowned at Marten. "I'd ask what you were thinking, but it's clear that man thinks I can work a miracle. Which means you've been telling more stories about me than I'm comfortable with."

Marten hunched his shoulders. "I'm sorry, Serril. I was trying to make a point with him, get him to see that maybe it'd be easier if he put down the grudge he's been carrying for years now." The other Healer added, "I should've known Elias would take the wrong parts to heart. He only really hears what he wants to from me."

"You know, when Ostel became dean, I thought I wouldn't have to try to make peace any more. I could just settle back in the Collegium, train Jayin, teach a class or two if needed." Serril shook his head. "And instead, I'm here, pulled in because we knew each other back in the day."

"I said I'm sorry, Serril."

"It's all right. Just keep an eye on Jayin. I'll ask the way to the Barretts' house, see if I can talk with them and find out their side of things."

Serril got directions to the Barretts' estate. It took him less than a quarter of a mark to walk there, and all the while, he wondered how best to broach the subject of the feud with that family. At least with the Valerins, he'd had an introduction in the form of Marten. With the other family, he'd likely need to do some fast talking to get them to even listen to him, much less accept his help.

Or at least, that had been the plan, until he spied a child near a signpost next to a turning off the South Trade Road. The sign proudly proclaimed the Barrett Trading Concern could be found up the road, and the child bounced up and down excitedly as he waved Serril over.

"Got here quick, Healer!" The boy grinned briefly, then his face scrunched as though he'd bitten into something bitter.

"Lorn's in a bad way, seeing as how that Valerin broke his arm, an' it's not like we ever needed a Healer before."

Wary of this particular stroke of luck, Serril responded, "Let's see what I can do, then? I'm Healer Serril, and you are?"

"Teva Barrett!" the boy proclaimed proudly. "Let's go. It's not far, and I'm sure my Da'll have somethin' for you to drink since you walked all the way here."

The house wasn't far from the road, and looked more like someone had transplanted a warehouse from the docks than a place of residence. But Teva escorted him around to the back, where a crowd of people were standing around and muttering darkly, blocking the path to a more normal but cramped-seeming house huddled against the back of the larger building.

"Oy! Healer's here, get Da!" Teva called, and the crowd dispersed, some heading into the house and others around to the front. A few moments later, a burly man with thinning black hair stomped out of the front door of the house, glared at Serril, then waved him inside without even a word of greeting. Teva made to go inside as well, but the man pointed him back out to the road.

As Serril went in, he took careful note of his surroundings. There weren't many people standing around, while the ones going through were clearly angry, and probably spoiling for a fight. He felt his breath hitch a bit, but reminded himself that they'd wanted a Healer, so he should be safe—as long as he minded how he dealt with the head of the family and the young man with the broken arm.

In a sitting room away from the main area, the burly man stopped next to a couch where a young man sat, carefully cradling his left arm. "Healer, my son, Lorn."

Lorn grimaced, and said, "Sorry. Da's not a talkative man." He gasped, and Serril immediately went to the couch to examine his patient. After a few minutes of checking him over, Serril looked to the older man, and said, "If your son hasn't had any willow-bark tea, I'd suggest it now. A Healing won't completely take away the pain."

The man frowned, nodded, and moved off, leaving Serril

alone in the room with the young man. "Tell me exactly how this occurred. Bone healing needs all my focus, and I'd like to know the details so I know what I'll need to do."

Lorn paled but nodded. "I was at one of the waystations south of here, minding my own business." He inhaled sharply as Serril prodded gently along his left arm. "Simeon Valerin started giving me grief about the most recent contract we'd signed. Apparently he thought the Valerins should have gotten it."

"And then?"

The boy looked away, a frown on his face. "He kept after me, even though I stayed quiet. He pushed me, which led to a scuffle. Which led to him breaking my arm." He paused, then added, "I must have hit the ground wrong."

"Looks like it to me," Serril said neutrally as he extended his Gift into Lorn's arm. The break wasn't what he expected from years of dealing with broken arms. This was more like something a person might get after falling further—or harder—than being knocked to the ground. He shook his head, and said, "You get the tea in you first. It'll take a bit to work, but hopefully by that point your arm will be on the mend and you'll be sleeping it off. No physical labor after the healing, today or tomorrow. Light exercise for three days after that. Healer's orders."

Lorn exhaled and nodded slowly. "Da, his name's Cal, he'll be back shortly with the tea, I expect. Or he'll have one of my sisters bring it."

"One of your sisters indeed," a grumpy voice said from the doorway. It belonged to a young woman a bit older than Lorn, her black hair in a neat braid down her front, carrying a tray holding a sturdy, steaming mug. "I'm Brida, and Da's busy sorting out the workers and the rest of the family. He's probably telling them we can't afford a fight with the Valerins."

"A pleasure, Brida Barrett. I'm Healer Serril, and I presume that's the willow-bark tea?"

"Oh, it is, double strength." She bobbed a head at her brother as she set the tray down on a table next to him. "And chamomile to calm him down, with some honey so he doesn't spit it all out."

"A good mix. You've studied, I take it?"

"Books only, sadly. Da doesn't want me going off to Haven, says my brains'll serve better here for the family." Serril heard bitter undertones in her matter-of-fact statement.

"Well, Lorn, drink up, thank your sister, and if you've no objections, she can stay and watch. Healing with a Gift isn't fancy, but I can at least share what I'm doing." He kept a smile off his face as Brida curtsied to him with a grateful look, and then settled to Lorn's left for the Healing. "So, first of all, you'll want to have the patient brace themselves . . ."

When Serril finally headed back to the Valerin estate, he wanted nothing more than to be done for the day. Brida had fed him before he left, Cal thanked him, and the rest of the Barrett family seemed to have calmed down at least somewhat. Or at least the muttering didn't involve tearing off down the road to break some heads.

But there was something off about the story both boys were telling, and it wasn't just how they'd broken each other's arms. The break could have happened the way Lorn had told it, but it was odd that *both* of them had suffered broken arms. And Serril only had Marten's description to go on, though he resolved to ask if Simeon would consent to an exam. And maybe tell his story about the incident as well.

He'd gotten as far as the front porch when Jayin popped out with an intent expression on her face. "Wilton's offered to treat the four of us to dinner in Haven," she started, and Serril immediately understood.

"That's quite generous of him, and of course we ought not to say no to hospitality. Besides, it'll give me a chance to find out what the Avelards were up to back in—where was it again?"

"Hartsbridge," Jayin answered, a twinkle in her eye. "Wilton's got all sorts of stories to share."

At that moment, Elias stepped out and squinted at Serril in the late afternoon sun. "So?"

Sighing, Serril replied, "One of the young men of the family needed Healing. When I left, the Barretts didn't seem inclined to come after you, but Cal didn't exactly talk much to me. I think you're probably safe from trouble, but I can come back tomorrow and see whether I can smooth things out a bit more between your families."

Elias sagged a bit. "I'd appreciate that greatly. I won't lie, I didn't think much of Marten's stories about you, but you seem a level-headed sort. Maybe we can get ourselves back to just being business rivals." He shook his head as he went back inside, and Jayin raised an eyebrow at her mentor.

"Dinner sounds like a fine time for stories," he said, then winked at her.

The Tipsy Griffon was only half full that night, and Wilton commandeered a table in the corner for himself, Serril, Jayin, and Marten. The other Healer looked to be a bit more nervous than usual, while Wilton had a determined look on his face.

"Marten? Tell me about the break in Simeon's arm," Serril asked once they'd settled. "And don't leave any detail out. There's something odd here."

The man clutched his ale like a lifeline. "Simeon said Lorn started needling him about the contract and kept after Simeon even though he tried to stay out of it. They started scuffling, Lorn pushed him, and he said he must have hit the ground wrong." Marten paused as Serril held up a finger. "What is it?"

"Lorn's arm was broken too, and almost word for word, that story matches his, except for the person who started the fight. But tell me about the break."

Marten frowned. Slowly, he said, "It wasn't like a break you'd get from hitting the ground, not unless you were shoved by a much larger person, or slipped and your elbow hit the ground wrong." He shrank a bit, and looked to Jayin. "She asked to look, and I figured you wouldn't say no?"

Serril chuckled. "Field experience can substitute for hours of class time. Jayin?"

She grinned. "So Hesby was trying out a routine on a tight-rope, and he slipped and fell. It was my first time in Healing trance, scared the family half to death, but the break looked a lot like Simeon's, like he fell from maybe ten feet up, maybe more."

"That . . . is something you've never mentioned before," Serril said with some concern. "Clearly you're here, clearly you didn't burn yourself out, but."

Jayin nodded. "There was a reason I was so quick to suggest going with you. I was laid out for almost a week after that." She tapped the table thoughtfully, then continued, "Simeon was a bit woozy from the willow-bark tea, but there was something about how he told the story. I don't think it was just him being muzzy from the healing."

One of the servers brought a platter of food, and for a while the only sounds around the table were the four of them eating. Serril ate more slowly than the others, but once Jayin was done he asked, "What did you notice about his story?"

"It sounded rehearsed," Jayin answered almost instantly, "like he'd been practicing it in his head. But there were things that didn't make sense. Like, why were the two of them at the waystation to begin with? It's a fair distance south of both their estates, according to Wilton."

He nodded. "At best, it's a bit of shelter for people and horses and mules, kind of a smallish barn more than anything else. No reason to go there unless you're on your way to something else."

Serril frowned. "Or you're doing something you don't want anyone else to know about. Considering the families, that could be anything from an arranged fight to an arranged tryst."

Blinking, Jayin said, "Tryst?" nearly at the same moment that Wilton echoed her and Marten huddled closer around his third ale. "Surely there'd—oh, right, sporting around with someone who *isn't* one of your enemies probably would have been fine in the Valerins' eyes."

"I suppose it's possible," Wilton agreed, "but I've been away for long enough I've no idea if Simeon tends that way. Elias cares more if you've got a good head on your shoulders than who you're attracted to." He paused, and glanced at Marten, who'd shrunk down far enough that he risked slipping under the table. "You've been there a long time. Surely you know something. Your body language practically screams it."

Marten blushed redder than Serril had ever seen, and said in a low voice, "Simeon asked about hygiene, cleanliness, and a few other things that suggested he had his eyes on someone who wasn't a girl. I made sure his father wasn't listening, gave him the standard lecture *we* got at the Collegium, and got him a few supplies." He looked up with a sickly smile. "He didn't tell me who, of course, and I didn't ask. And he hasn't been the first to ask those kinds of questions. I've been there nearly twenty years. It would have been a surprise if nobody asked."

"And, of course, they wouldn't want to say anything," Serril said, tapping his finger on the table. "Wilton? Do you know what the original grudge was that blossomed into the current feud?"

After several moments of muttering under his breath, Wilton finally shook his head. "No more than the usual tales told around the hearth in winter I'm sure Devin repeated to you on the ride from Haven. Not like it matters for the current mess." He snorted. "I certainly hadn't wanted to get pulled back into the trouble between my family and the Barretts. It's why I moved in the first place."

Following a moment of quiet, he continued, "And I'd wanted to build a business of my own now that I'm back. Too many people around here know of the Valerin and Barrett troubles, and *they* use it as leverage against both families. In a generation or two, they'll have dug themselves a hole they'll never get out of."

Marten stared morosely at his ale, then said, "If we could get the two to confess, or at least own up to the fact that they weren't fighting, maybe things would settle down a bit more?"

"Healer Marten," Jayin said with a slow grin, "I think I have a plan."

* * *

The next morning, Serril and Jayin met Wilton at the south gate, then they walked south along the road, discussing Jayin's plan. Marten had gone back to the Valerin estate after dinner, saying it could raise suspicion if he wasn't available. The summer sun gave everything a tint of gold as it rose, the early morning air slowly warming as the trio walked.

Wilton and Jayin split off when the Valerin estate came into view, and Serril walked on to the Barret place, keeping his fingers crossed that his trainee's idea would resolve the current troubles between the two families. He'd need to have a talk with Marten at some point in the near future, too. His classmate had started out with good intentions, but hadn't considered that Serril might not want to play peacemaker. He'd set boundaries with Ostel after the man had been made dean, and it seemed like he'd need to set boundaries with Marten, and anyone else he'd trained with.

The Barretts' yard was busy with people loading and unloading wagons, with Cal Barrett standing off to one side. He'd nod and point, people would move, but the only time he spoke was to give more specific directions to one of the workers, who then trotted into the warehouse.

He looked at Serril curiously, and gestured for the Healer to come over. "Here again?"

"Bad news, I'm afraid. I don't know how, but the watch heard about the fight between Simeon Valerin and Lorn. They're sending someone along later this morning to investigate what happened." Serril knew the watch was too busy for a couple of broken arms, but he also knew both families had been trying to avoid the attention of the watch for however long they'd been fighting.

"So?" Cal's eyebrows drew together, and he looked like he'd eaten sour fruit.

"Well, it's up to you, but if you and the Valerins got together, met with the person from the watch of your own accord, and assured whoever they sent that you'd all learned your lesson, there probably wouldn't be any real consequences."

Brida had come up while Serril was talking. With exasperation clear on her face, she said, "Da, do as the good Healer says. He's got more sense than any of us, and I'm sure he knows how the watch handles things. Better we get this cleared up now, right?"

The man smiled at his daughter. "Smart. I'll gather the family. You get Lorn." He strode off, and Brida gave Serril a considering look.

"I get the feeling you're up to something, but I'm tired of all the trouble my family gets into. I hope you can fix this." She curtsied to Serril and headed toward the back of the house.

In short order, Cal had assembled several people who could be spared, including Brida, and given instructions for the people who were staying behind. Meanwhile, Lorn had come out to stand near Serril with a sick expression on his face.

"The watch?" he asked quietly while his father made final arrangements.

"I know you didn't break your arm in a fight, Lorn. You'll want to come clean about whatever it was so the watch won't drag you and Simeon off for fighting." Serril watched the young man pale with a bit of satisfaction.

About a candlemark later, the Valerins and Barretts stood in a clear spot off the South Trade Road, keeping to their respective families, and occasionally glaring at each other. Thankfully nobody had started anything, though Serril wondered how long that would last.

Jayin bounced up, and whispered, "Simeon went all green when I told him I knew about his arm. Now we just need to wait for Wilton to get Elias going."

Before Serril could respond, Elias grabbed Simeon by his unbroken arm and dragged him toward the cluster of Barretts. The older man looked grim, while the other simply looked scared. Conversation died down around the two families, both turning in the late morning warmth toward each other, tensing for what might happen next. With the exception of a distant wagon rolling toward Haven, the area was silent.

With a frown, Elias jabbed a finger at Cal Barrett. "You get your boy Lorn out here so he can apologize to Simeon. If we hadn't had a Healer, my boy would be laid up for weeks. We get this out of the way, then when the watch shows, we can tell them it was all a big misunderstanding."

Nobody said anything for a moment. The wagon sounds had faded into the distance.

"Simeon should apologize. He started it, Lorn said." Cal stepped forward, just out of reach of Elias's pointing finger. He drew himself up, and continued, "Healer Serril fixed up my son's arm, otherwise he'd not be able to work." Lorn, behind Cal, shrank in on himself.

Angry muttering started up in both families, the two groups standing apart from each other but squaring up as if preparing for a fight. Serril watched with growing concern, but the threat of the watch's appearance was apparently enough for the moment to keep the families from doing anything more than muttering.

With a decisive movement, Lorn stepped out from behind his father, walked over to Simeon, and took his hand. "All of you, stop it!" he yelled. "We've been seeing each other for six months now, since well before Devin and Mattias had their little spat. We knew you'd all be unreasonable, so of course we hid it from you!" People's jaws dropped in shock. "And we broke our arms because we were fooling around in the loft above the waystation, I rolled a bit too far, Simeon tried to save me, and we both went over the edge. We didn't think you'd be fine with the two of us, so we lied about what happened." By this point, the two young men had pulled each other into the middle between the groups, Simeon curling an arm around Lorn.

Serril managed to keep from snickering at the poleaxed looks on the faces of the various family members, though he noted Brida was nodding and smiling.

"Well," he interjected, "it seems now is as good a time as any to tell you there is no watch coming." Before their astonishment could shift to something less pleasant, he continued, "Marten asked me to settle things between you all, and though I wasn't expecting a love story, I'm fairly sure you'll agree that it's a good reason to put down at least some of your feud."

Silence fell across the group, until Cal extended a hand to Elias. "Can't say I'm happy, but I won't fight you anymore."

Elias stared at the hand for a long moment, then shook it briefly. "We'd better figure out how we're gonna make this work. How about dinner tonight, my home? We can start there."

Cal nodded, and the two men turned to face their sons, both of whom paled but stood their ground. Elias added, "You two have a lot to make up for. But I'm happy for you." Cal nodded again, and with that the two families started to move toward each other with more uncertainty and fading anger.

Marten bustled over, followed by Wilton, and then Brida. Jayin looked like a cat who'd devoured all the cream, Marten looked hopeful instead of nervous, and Wilton and Brida looked relieved.

"Wilton, stop by the Collegium when you can so we can talk more, and Brida, see if you can't get your father to unbend enough to get you some training. But for now, Jayin and I need to head back. She's got an exam, and I'm putting away my peacemaker's cloak for good."

Serril exhaled slowly, and looked at Marten. "And you? Keep these hotheads in line yourself next time." Without waiting for an answer, he turned northward, toward the Collegium and a life hopefully less filled with conflict.

Pairmates
Ron Collins

Nwah laid her head between her forepaws, enjoying the heat of the fire radiating through Winnie's mudbrick hearth. The scents of apple and spice came along with the stewpot full of rabbit and broth simmering over the crackling flames. Supper would be soon, though that fare was not on her list of favorites.

She was the kind of tired that only comes from covering pain. Sore from the travels that had brought her and Maakdal here to Winnie's place in Oris, which was small, but warm and comfortable, along with Maizy—the stable hand who had saved Nwah's life only a few spare days earlier—and Prim, her sister. Nwah's hip throbbed in the fire's heat. The muscles of her legs felt dead from use. The pad in her right front foot had picked up a thorn the day before, and still hurt when she walked. On top of everything, she was still recovering from her torturous inquiry at the hands of Maizy's baron, though only Maakdal was aware of just how tenuous her health was.

The pack leader, who was outside now, patrolling the woodlands to ensure it was safe, had doted on her the whole way here.

Perhaps she was over-sensitive now, but she felt a deeper concern lying under his rough exterior. His attentions had made her equal parts angry and grateful. She could no longer deny her attraction to him, but despite his dedication to her, Maakdal seemed often distant, as if once he'd revealed too much of himself, he'd push himself away to stand apart from her in the way a pack leader should be properly apart from all in his care.

She couldn't blame him, though. Nwah was a broken kyree. Her life was a mess, really.

She'd come to Maakdal's woods fleeing *from* Haven rather than running *toward* something else. Even if she had been healthy, she didn't know what to do. In the quiet night times she'd spend alone, these thoughts churning through her mind brought a deep sense of embarrassment with them.

The pain in her hip made her think of Kade, too.

She missed her lifebonded friend, who was still in Haven, studying to become a full Healer at the Collegium. After their years together, it was hard to think of him as a young man Heralded to Leena, his Companion. Life was different now, though the memory of him plying his Gift was enough to make her forget the dull ache in her hip for a moment. Everything about the life she'd known while growing up with him had become upended now. Where once Kade had been the only thing in Nwah's world, events had made things complicated. Elspeth and Darkwing had touched her life. Her own Gift had changed her. And finally, Maakdal, the pack, and Winnie were here. Maizy and Prim, too.

Sometimes, she missed the times when life was simpler.

"I'm so glad you came here," Winnie said to Maizy as she gave the pot a stir. She stood straight and arched her back, pressing her palms down over her simple skirts. "I don't think I realized how lonely I'd become."

"Lonely?" Maizy replied. "There's been nothing but a stream of visitors all afternoon."

"There is a difference between visitors and patients," Winnie said. Her smile was as weary as it was winsome.

"You get along well enough, it seems."

Maizy was impressed with Winnie. Maizy had followed her movements from the moment they'd arrived, and had taken in her words as Winnie worked with townspeople who had visited her. She seemed to understand the power of the small apothecary Winnie had created here, and saw—like Nwah saw—that the young woman's pragmatic sense of energy made her seem bigger than life.

People liked her. She had her own way.

The sheriff's daughter had grown greatly since the day Nwah and Kade had first met her. When Winnie talked, Maizy absorbed the ideas that lay inside her thoughts as if they were water and she was a root plant.

For her part, Winnie had also already taken a liking to both Maizy, dark-haired and strong in the way a life in the stables built, and Prim, fine-haired and blonder, who seemed more comfortable in a kitchen. It hadn't taken Nwah's Gift to see Winnie was excited to hear of Maizy's interest in healing crafts, and she would have had to be blind to miss how Winnie's attentions picked up when Nwah described how Maizy's natural compassion had shone through as she doctored Nwah during her time under the guard of Maizy's past baron.

"We'll eat in a moment," Winnie said, moving to pull down sets of bowls from the cupboard in the corner.

A heavy pounding at the door startled her, though, and Nwah braced herself as a pounding continued.

"Medicine girl!" a gruff voice came through the slats. "Medicine girl! Come quick."

Winnie put the bowls down and, grabbing up her skirts, stepped rapidly to the door.

"I'm coming," she said, opening it to find the full, night-darkened profile of a bullish, muscular man filling the doorway, the light of Winnie's fireplace highlighting his forehead and cheekbones over a dark, unruly beard.

"Jebidiah Kard," Winnie said. "What is the matter?"

As her eyes adjusted, Nwah could see his horse and cart bathed in the early moonlight behind the man.

"My boys," Kard blurted, pointing, his face flushed from a hurried ride. "They ate a bad stew," he said. "Now they got the evils."

Winnie was already on her way to the cart. Three shapes were laid out and covered in blankets. They were definitely sick. One of the boys groaned.

Grabbing her skirts, Winnie took one leap to arrive on the cart with the boys. She covered her nose and mouth with a hem,

then bent to look at them. Maizy and Prim were right behind her.

"Can you fix 'em?" Mr. Kard said fervently, his gaze dark
and worried in the moonlight. "I don't trust the fools in Oris,
but you're different. You made Charlotte well again, and now
she's strong as ever."

"Give me a moment," Winnie said, pressing the back of her
free hand over one of the boy's foreheads and then running it
down to his belly. He was maybe twelve, wearing a tattered
overshirt and a pair of work-stained pants that showed dirty
knees through torn holes. When she put pressure on the stomach, the boy moaned. She bent to examine his eyes, which despite the lighting, seemed obviously bloodshot.

"There's more at home," Kard said. "I couldn't get more
than the boys on the wagon."

Winnie frowned, but said nothing further to him.

She turned to Maizy first. "Let's get these boys into the
house. Then take the wagon with Mr. Kard and gather the rest
of the ill." Then she turned to Prim. "Take the stew off the fire
and begin boiling fresh water from the well. I'll give you other
ingredients as we go." To Nwah, she said, "Go to town. Get my
father."

"I want to stay here and see to my boys," the large man said,
standing with enough sudden confrontation against Winnie
that Nwah began to bring her Gift forward in preparation of
the need to defend her.

As the magic kicked up inside, she enjoyed the sensation of
life that wafted around her.

The heat of tiny rodent heartbeats came to her firm and
clear. The power of an owl hiding in the strongest limbs of a
nearby tree gave her comfort. She could not ignore the strength
of Maakdal in the distance, too, sensing something amiss and
moving rapidly toward the clearing and Winnie's home.

Winnie didn't back down, though, and she didn't need Nwah's
help. From her place on the platform, she stood taller than the
man. "You can't help me, Jebidiah Kard. You know that now,
don't you? So take your pride and stick it somewhere it's not in

the way. Help me get your boys into the house now, then go get your womenfolk, or else I'll stop working until you do."

Mr. Kard pursed his lips hard enough the prickly part of his beard pushed forward.

Winnie took a challenging step back from the boy.

The casual way she'd used the man's name said she'd had dealings with the Kards before. Winnie had power here. She had position and seemed happy to use it. So Nwah was unsurprised when the man capitulated and began moving toward the front of the wagon.

"Come on," Maizy said, already pulling at the blanket wrapped around the closest patient.

It took only moments to clear the three.

Shortly thereafter, Prim had water boiling, Maizy had climbed into the Kards' wagon, Jebidiah Kard beside her, and Nwah was running to the main streets of Oris to fetch Winnie's father.

"You're sayin' it wasn't bad stew?" Jebidiah Kard said, his face suddenly dark and his fists clenched. "You're sayin' the Tuckers tried to kill us all?"

He was standing in the open clearing outside Winnie's doorway. The nighttime was giving way to the light growing on the horizon, and the fresh scents of dawn in the woods mixed with the smell of thin woodsmoke from the smoldering fireplace in Winnie's home.

It is a solid place, Nwah thought. Built of stone and mudbrick with help from her father, the firm-minded sheriff who stood now beside her, and even more help from the friends firm-minded sheriffs have the wherewithal to muster.

Prim, who had spent all night proving a capacity for brewing the concoctions of nettle and briar that had halted the Kard family's shared sickness, was still inside, doting on the boys as they took in bits of bread and stew from Winnie's pot, and helping the girls as they finished their own recuperations. Maizy sat on the edge of the porch, obviously worn from a night of aiding Winnie at every step.

Nwah had enjoyed watching the pair work through the night together, Winnie in full concentration, Maizy following with warm rags and humming in the wonderful way she had as she administered medicines under Winnie's watchful gaze. Nwah had been right about them. They were much alike. Both comforting with their soft touches and close attentions.

"No, Jebidiah," Winnie replied, wiping her hands on a dry rag. "I'm saying they've been poisoned in some manner. I have no idea what happened beyond that."

Nwah, who was lying on the planks of Winnie's porch, crinkled her nose. The foul smell coming from the sick Kards had long ago confirmed Winnie's diagnosis to her. The odor was finally fading, though. Despite her weariness, she was enjoying the dew-fresh aromas of peat and wildflowers that came with the new dawn.

"What are you gonna do about it, Sheriff?" Kard said, snarling. "You know I'm right. It had to be 'em. I want Loella Tucker's head on a pike, and I want it on that pike now."

"You've got to calm down, Jeb," the sheriff said. "Nobody knows anything yet, and people in town are getting tired of you and the Tuckers mixing things up for no good reason."

"They tried to kill my entire *family*!"

"I've got nothing to prove that."

"You know better, Sheriff," Jebidiah Kard said. The vein in his neck pulsed and the form of his meaty chest growing firm under a stained work tunic served as a threat. "I pay my burden to this hoax of a town like everyone else. I demand justice, and I'll have it one way or the other."

"What I know better about," the sheriff said, pointedly focusing on the man as he put his hand on the pommel of his dagger, "is that this thing you have with the Tuckers is threatening to bleed over into the town, and I'm not having it anymore. Right now I figure whatever poisoning happened here was because of something you did to yourself."

"You sayin' the Kards can't cook a meal?"

"Take it as you will. Maybe I ought to haul both you and the Tuckers all in now, anyway. The town could use a break from you both, and whether it's stealing livestock, burning crops, or ambushing each other, I'm certain one of you's done something worth jailing."

"Not our fault the Tucker kid served the wrong side," a young voice accompanied fresh bootsteps from the doorway. It was one of the Kard boys. He leaned against the door jamb and wiped a long sleeve across his cheek.

"Keep your nose outta this, Paulie," Jebidiah Kard said. "Go on in and stay sittin' down."

"I can say my piece, too, Pa. Everyone knows none of this'd be happenin' if the Tucks' kid hadn't gone turncoat, or at least if they'd had the guts to discipline their own like we do. You can't fight against the old ways and expect to live, right, Pa?"

:What does he mean?: Nwah asked Winnie.

:The Tuckers and the Kards are old families here outside Oris. Both openly support the resistance that still try to follow Ancar's old ways. But years ago one of the Tuckers turned, and the Kards killed him. The families have been warring ever since.:

Nwah twitched a whisker. It was turning out that Ancar's followers seemed to still be more of a problem than anyone was letting on.

:I thought I recognized him,: Maizy added. Nwah turned to her. *:Jebidiah Kard has visited the baron while I lived there. I saw him arriving a few times.:*

"I need you to calm your boy, Jeb," Winnie's father said. "Or I will definitely be shackling you for your own good."

"You're just one man out here, Sheriff. I don't think you'll be able to manage that on your own, now, will you?"

Hearing "on your own, now," Nwah suddenly sat up.

Maakdal.

Where was he?

Last she'd known, he was out in the woods. But he hadn't come in. Now she perked her ears, straining. Her nostrils expanded. The fur at her neck prickled.

Nothing.

Concentrating, she pulled her focus together as Darkwind

had taught her so diligently. A ley line fell a distance away, but close enough she could taste the coppery spice of its energy as she pulled from it. She let her thoughts coalesce, bringing up the emotions she felt when seeing Maakdal, recalling his scent and remembering the power of his will as her presence scoured the woodlands around Winnie's abode.

Panic clotted her throat as she came up empty.

:*Maakdal,*: she said to both Winnie and Maizy. :*He's gone.*:

"What?" Maizy said.

"Where is he?" Winnie added.

Not able to follow their Mindspeech, Winnie's father looked confused, and Jebidiah Kard seemed put off.

But Nwah ignored them to throw more of herself into her magic, pressing harder to extend her reach like Darkwind had taught her, adding control to the magic that came from her, feeling its power scrub through her body and raise the hair along her back and flanks. She called to hawks wheeling through the air, and jays slicing between the trees.

:*Scout,*: she called. :*Search.*:

Finally. There it was. The essence of Maakdal in the far reaches of her magic.

The coarse feeling of wood grew under her feet. The smell of cold iron bars surrounded her. She rode along as one of the hawks swooped low, and Nwah sensed tendrils of magic wafting from the lock holding the door to the cage clasped shut. Her heart fell off a cliff.

Maakdal was locked in. She felt it all as truly as if she were there with him.

She felt something else, too.

This was her fault.

Maakdal had agreed to escort Maizy and her sister to Oris as a boon for their aid in saving Nwah from the baron's ministrations. Now the pack leader was being held against his will. His anger at captivity was a wall of fire inside her. She sensed bruises on his shoulders and head where he'd fought against the bonds throbbed in her mind. Maakdal would not be an easy prisoner. She hoped he wasn't so hard to manage that his captors turned to even more brutal ways to keep him subdued.

Agitated and heart pounding, she rose to all fours and gave a chuff.

:Did you find him?: Maizy said.

:He is captured.:

:Where?: Winnie asked.

:That direction.: Nwah turned her snout to point eastward. *:Near a low barn of some type. Along a line of huts and buildings painted sparingly. I see pigs and chickens. Loose ploughshares lean against a wall.:*

Winnie looked at her father, eyes narrowed. "The Tuckers have taken Nwah's pairmate hostage."

"Why?" the sheriff said.

She shook her head. "They must think we're working with the Kards."

Nwah stood boldly as emotions ran through her. Normally she would have taken offense to being misnamed as Maakdal's pairmate. Or at least felt some kind of discomfort. But suddenly it felt right. Indignation rose inside her. Then anger. Feeling the intense strength of his personality, Nwah cleared her mind. To be associated with him was a compliment she wasn't sure she deserved, but standing in fresh scent of the morning, she decided she was finally going to live up to it.

Just as suddenly, the only thing that mattered was getting the pack leader out of his prison.

Nwah reached out to her hawk spies as she leaped off the porch and dashed eastward toward the woods. *:I'm coming,:* she said to the hawk. *:Guide me.:*

"Wait!" Maizy called as she raced behind Nwah. "I'm coming with you!"

:You stay,: Nwah admonished. *:I need to move fast.:*

"You need help," Maizy gasped as she ran. "And this is my fault! I'll keep up."

That was good enough for Nwah.

The others seemed frozen in time, but while Nwah picked

her way quickly through the woods, Maizy tramped along behind her.

Nwah let the hawk's sight guide her. If the avian's direction was correct, they were something less than a league away.

Time enough for plans to come together. But as her dander rose, Nwah decided that if no plan came to her, she would simply attack the first captor she found.

:Take it easy, Nwah!: Maizy said, panting with a burst of speed that helped her catch up. In tandem, they jumped over a dead tree that had been felled in a recent storm. *:The first rule of dealing with an emergency is that you don't make anything worse. Do you understand? Don't do anything you'll regret!:*

:I won't regret ripping the throat out of whoever's locked Maakdal away!:

:And he will never forgive you if you get killed doing it.:

The comment brought Nwah up short. Maizy was right.

Standing in the silence of the moment, the tendrils of her spellwork brought her the presence of life around the woodlands. Skittish deer and ravenous racoons. Squirrels and birds of a hundred types. The trees breathing and growing in the clean air. The dampness of peat underfoot and moss on the tree bark. Far away, a mother bear and her cubs lumbered through a path. The world was talking to her. Calming her.

She breathed in the energy and let her heart rate settle.

In the stillness, Darkwind's voice came to her.

:Control yourself or you cannot control your magic,: he would repeat, almost as a mantra.

A glance at Maizy, who was standing before her with her own chest heaving, brought Nwah back to the moment.

Life is complex, she thought.

That was what Darkwind had really been trying to teach her all along as they traveled together from Haven to the wild forests near the Hardorn borderlines where Maakdal and the pack lived. It's what he *had* taught her, really. He had cloaked the lessons in control, compassion, and a sense of the natural energy of the world around her. But his common message was one of observation and balance. She was just now realizing the entirety of it.

"*Take your time,*" he would say. "*Forced magic is bad magic.*"

It felt good to see it on her own. Or at least almost on her own.

:*Thank you,*: she said to Maizy. :*You are a good person.*:

Maizy stroked Nwah's forehead. "It's all right. I know you love him."

Nwah chuffed at that, but didn't argue because Maizy was right, and it felt dishonest to even pretend to disagree.

:*So what do you say we go get him?*:

:*All right,*: Nwah said. :*Let's go.*:

Nwah's initial read had been right. The lock to Maakdal's cage was magicked, though not with a form of spellwork she recognized.

The Tuckers' land was mostly wood, with a patch of field wheat on one side and another of beans opposite, both grown halfway to harvest. Nwah and Maizy slowly crept through a wooded area, then took positions hidden by an untended clot of thatch. It butted up against the water well the family had dug a distance away from both a sturdily built but weatherworn barn and a much more properly maintained living compound comprised of a main manor, a guest building, and what smelled like a slaughterhouse—all encircled by a slatted fence.

Maakdal was in a cage pushed up against the wall of the barn, small enough that he could not stand or pace.

They were closer to the cage than they were to the gaping barn opening, and a distance away from the manor. As they settled, Nwah saw her pack leader's ear and nose twitch in a way that told her Maakdal had smelled their arrival.

:*Maakdal,*: Nwah said calmly. :*Are you all right?*:

He turned toward her. His jawline was matted with blood.

:*Nwah. You need to leave. Now.*:

:*You can stop talking that way, because I'm not leaving without you.*:

:You don't understand. They know of your ties to Valdemar. They know you escaped from the baron's control. They captured me as they returned from raiding their enemy because they recognized you, and knew it would draw you here.:

:What?:

The door to the slaughterhouse opened. Two men and a woman emerged to step toward the barn and Maakdal's cage. The woman's posture, force of stride, and cut of clothes said she was most definitely in charge. Her riding breeches were fresh. Her tunic was green, embroidered, and sharply creased at the shoulders. One of the men held what appeared to be a bone of some sort before him.

A ripple emanating from the bone—which she recognized now came from a pig—pushed through Nwah's magic. It was a talisman, she thought, remembering more of Darkwind's teachings. The rib was a store of magic. The wielder was focusing intently on it, keeping the lock on Maakdal's cage closed through its power.

:Run, Nwah. They're coming for you,: Maakdal said.

"I recognize her, too," Maizy whispered, pointing at the woman.

:I don't understand,: Nwah replied.

Maizy switched to Mindspeech. *:That woman came to the barony several times. Like Jeb Kard.:* A dark cloud crossed her expression, then a bolt of enlightenment. *:They were part of the conspiracy! That makes sense, doesn't it? Both the Tuckers and Kards? Winnie said they sided with Ancar's people during the struggles. I've seen them going in to speak with Baron Haffti. When they aren't trying to kill each other, the Kards and the Tuckers are both working against Valdemar and the new leadership of Hardorn. They knew you were there. They knew . . . :*

Nwah saw it now, too. And when the woman spoke—*Loella Tucker,* Nwah thought, recalling the name Jebidiah Kard had used—everything else clicked into place.

"Shut the kyree down!" the woman called, the tone of her voice coming back to Nwah as if from a dream. "If we can get

her back to Baron Haffti, I'm sure there will be quite the re-
ward for us."

The hackles on the back of her neck rose. She had heard the
voice before. Loella Kard had been in the room while under the
baron's interrogation. She had put Nwah into some kind of
trance before asking questions and prodding into the workings
of Haven and all of Valdemar.

Nwah wasn't in a trance now, though.

Instead, she was in control of herself, and better, she was
balanced and in tune with the rest of the world around her.
Recalling the low tones of Darkwind's voice from the recesses
of her training made her comfortable, and that comfort helped
her call to the woodlands around her.

:*Fly,*: she sang. :*Swoop low. Break them down!*:

From the canopy above flew a white owl to fall upon Loella
Kard herself, wingspan wide and massive as it beat the air and
clawed at her face and shoulders. From the heights above dived
the pair of hawks, their talons ripping the pig's rib from the
would-be sorcerer's grasp. Flying low, a brace of jays attacked
the two men, pecking hard at their skulls as they ducked and
then fell.

When they were finished, Nwah pounced, snarling and
spitting as she leaped hard onto Loella Kard. Pushing her down
as the owl flew off, pinning her to the ground as her curved
canines dripped saliva from barely a breath above.

:*Move and you lose your face,*: Nwah said.

"Don't think she won't do it," Maizy said to the two men,
who were still fighting off the jay's bombing runs while seeming
to contemplate an attempt to save their matron. The warning
seemed to answer their questions, and they sat back again, still
defending against the jays.

Maizy strode to stand behind Nwah, then bent and reached
keys from Loella Kard's belt. With the lock no longer held by
magic, a metallic scratching came, and she opened the cage and
let Maakdal free.

The pack leader stepped from the cage, then stretched.

Standing free, he was a sight Nwah would not soon forget.

:What are we going to do with them?: Maakdal said. But even before the words were out, a clattering came from the pathway that led to the manor.

It was Jebidiah Kard's horses and wagon, guided by Winnie's father. Behind him came three more such wagons, each driven by an officer in Oris's guard. They pulled to a stop, and the sheriff hopped down with a heavy thud.

Only then did Nwah let the head of the Tucker family free.

"Loella Tucker," the sheriff said as his officers collected all three, and as others went to scour the manor for the rest of the clan. "You and your family are under arrest for the attempted poisoning of the entire Kard family."

"You don't know half of it," Maizy said with a wickedly devious grin.

"What do you mean?"

"Well, let's start here . . ."

Several minutes later, when Maizy finished laying out the entire conspiracy, the sheriff of Oris had to agree. He hadn't known half of it. But now that he did, he was pretty sure the trials would be swift.

Maizy and Prim stayed with Winnie, of course.

As Nwah had suspected from the beginning, it was clear Maizy and Winnie were going to be friends for life. And, who knew, maybe more. They certainly enjoyed each other's company, and Winnie had already realized she needed help to serve the people of Oris. Her business boomed even more when word got around she'd brought the entire Kard clan back from being poisoned. That Maizy was so adroit at understanding the concepts of healing and so comfortable with animals was even that much better.

Prim, of course, had proven to be an amazing alchemist. She loved playing in the fields, too, finding this root and that flower to mix together and use in inventive ways Winnie often found useful. In their extra time, the sisters enjoyed traveling into town to visit the marketplaces, the sweet shops, and the seamstresses, giggling to each other and sometimes speaking of their mother.

"Wouldn't she love this?" one would say.

"Try that on?" the other would respond, drawing a matching giggle or some form of exasperated raspberry in return.

Being able to go to town might never grow old. There was much for the girls to do here, and Nwah was more certain than ever that they would both soon make their marks in the world.

Nwah and Maakdal stayed with the trio for several days while Maizy plied her attentions to Nwah's aches and pains. But both kyree knew they couldn't stay in Oris forever.

The pack needed its leader.

And as she healed, Nwah, too, knew she didn't belong in the city any more than she did in Haven. There was more to her restlessness, though, as she knew there was more to Maakdal's than any simple need to return to his packmates.

:It is time,: she said one day.

It was that time of the evening when the sun had not quite finished setting, when the far side of the sky was transitioning to dark, and the insects were beginning to sing in heavy rhythm. They had taken a stroll through the woods, racing together at moments, yipping and growling with their straining. Nwah felt good. She felt the power of Maakdal beside her, but felt restraint there, too. A barrier of sorts that had seemed distant many days ago, but seemed to grow stronger as her own vitality returned.

They had come to the edge of a creek to lie down and rest. The stream burbled over rocks below.

:I am glad to hear it,: Maakdal replied in relief. *:I'm not sure I can stay still another day.:*

:I agree,: Nwah said. *:It is time to return to the pack. But that is not what I meant, and I think in your heart you know it, even if your thoughts are clouded.:*

Maakdal stood cautiously still.

Nwah took control. *:You feel it, too. The things between us,:* she said. *:I know you do. We've felt it for some time, but never truly spoken of it.:*

In a moment that broke her heart, Maakdal turned away at first, then when he looked upon her, the strength and passion in his gaze set her soul on fire.

But still, he hesitated before speaking. *:I wish I could be worthy of you,:* he said. *:But I have no gift. I am nothing but a kyree.:*

:You are wrong, Maakdal. You have the greatest gift of all.:

The pack leader seemed stymied.

:You are yourself, my pack leader. Always. And the kyree you are is more than worthy enough for me, or any other kyree who has ever been born. It has taken me a very long time to see this, but it is true. I have been searching for an understanding of who I am for my whole life. I've been split from my den mates. Left for dead, and wanted to die. I have been lifebonded twice, and that is something special to happen even once. I have been trained in my Gift, and that too is something beyond my ability to explain. Life is hard, though. Nothing is simple. But neither my lifebonds nor my Gift have ever been who I am. I know that now. For the first time, I know who I am and why I am here. And the strength of your example is the greatest reason for that understanding.:

:But your Gift—:

:Does not make me a good kyree. Nor does the lack of one make you anything less than you are.:

Maakdal was silent for long enough that the hiss of the creek seemed to rise into the empty spaces around them. *:I understand,:* he finally replied.

:Do you?:

His gaze caught hers, and they stayed that way for an amount of time that might have been only a few seconds, or might have been several lifetimes. He rose then. Took two tentative steps to stand boldly before her. The fur on his muscular chest seemed to grow firm, and the scruff of his neck fluffed.

She rose, too, facing him.

His musk was overwhelming. He leaned down so close that his breathing seemed to warm her.

:Nwah of the Pelagirs,: he said. *:Would you have me as your pairmate?:*

Nwah's heart pounded. She ran her snout alongside Maakdal's strong jawline, tasting his closeness.

:I will,: she said, then looked at him. *:And you, Maakdal? Would you—:*

:Forever,: the pack leader said before she could finish. *:I would have you as my pairmate forever.:*

Battle of the Bands
Dayle A. Dermatis

The rundown shed that was their practice space smelled faintly of goat, and Eldriss had no doubt it always would.

The weathered gray boards gapped, letting in streams of sunlight. In the summer, hot air filled the space, and in the winter, the gaps let in the cold air, which meant they had to keep retuning their instruments and warming them up with a small fire. Musical instruments hated temperature and moisture change more than people did.

Despite all that, the old shed was far away from the house, so they didn't bother anyone when they practiced, and Eldriss was grateful to have it. They all were.

He took a sip of sweet, watered-down wine and bent his head back to his beloved fiddle, drawing a hunk of beeswax along her strings so she would sing with the passion of a lover.

Even his dear wife, Shalna, called the instrument his mistress. She said it with fond laughter and a twinkle in her brown eyes. She might not have understood, but she respected his passion for music. That she loved to dance figured in to that.

One by one, the rest of the troupe arrived for practice: Davon, with his deer-hide drums; Kyrissa, with her shawm; Lon, with his recorder.

Lon looked grim.

"There's a musical contest to be held in Haven," he said. "Best troupe plays before the Queen. A Herald came and posted a notice at the town hall."

Before they could reply, Lon added, "Apparently someone removed the notice—I only heard about it now. The competition is in three weeks."

Eldriss gasped, sucking in the faint stench of goat shit. "I assume by *someone*, you mean . . . ?"

Lon nodded. "Who else?"

"No matter," Eldriss said. "We know now. We'll compete, of course!" he added, looking at the others.

Davon, who hadn't yet unpacked his drums from their cowhide cases, ran a hand down his face and rubbed his close-cropped beard. "We are, aye. But . . ." He hesitated. Eldriss knew what he was going to say, even before the words came out.

Eldriss and the others looked at him, and if the rest didn't have a sinking feeling in their stomachs, he certainly did.

He knew what was coming, and he didn't blame Davon at all.

"You know I can't go with you," Davon said, a catch in his voice. "Wytha . . . she's so close to birth."

"We know," Eldriss said, shaking his head. "We all knew you'd have to take time, and this competition isn't more important than Wytha and your child."

"It's more than that," Davon said. He sighed. "Once the baby's born, well . . . I love playing with all of you, but I've been realizing I have to focus my time elsewhere . . ."

"We understand," Kyrissa said. "Did any of us not expect this?"

They all shook their heads.

"We all support you and Wytha," Eldriss said, his heart both heavy and light. "We'll play at the babe's first birthday, and all the others, won't we?"

There was much hugging, but with Davon leaving, there wasn't much sense in practicing.

Participating in the competition felt like a distant dream.

Eldriss knew three things for certain:

He knew Davon would be hard to replace.

He knew who had taken down the notice.

And he knew they had to participate in—and win—the competition.

Finding a drummer as good as Davon in this short amount of time was impossible. Eldriss and the others knew every musician in Traynemarch Reach and in the neighboring towns.

The best they could hope for was someone from a troupe that wasn't competing, or someone who was good enough to keep time with the music.

It turned out, however, that there was in fact a third option.

Shalna's best friend's cousin, Orla, was visiting from the south.

And Orla, amazingly, was a drummer.

Eldriss refused to let himself hope. No, that was a lie. He allowed himself a glimmer. Maybe a tiny bit more.

They had to win the competition. Maybe Orla was the key?

They had her to the former goat shed for an audition.

She was tall, with long strawberry-gold hair that fell past her shoulders in a riot of frizzled curls. Beneath her dark blue eyes, her nose was long and thin, her cheekbones pronounced, her jaw sharp.

Not someone who would be described as beautiful, but arresting, interesting.

Her breathy voice, calm and quiet, held a hint of an accent. Almost girlish. She carried a round leather case. But it was curiously flat, not like a normal drum.

What she pulled out was a flat drum stretched across a wooden frame with a crisscross of round dowels beneath it so she could hold it with one hand. Eldriss cocked his head, unsure how her fingers could create a big enough sound.

But then she produced a wooden stick about eight inches long, one end wrapped in cream leather, the other in thick brown fabric.

Her smile was small, but there was a twinkle in her eye as she spun the stick between her fingers. Then she rapped it against the drum.

The speed at which she played made Eldriss's jaw drop. Each end of the stick gave a slightly different tone, richer or brighter, and where each end hit on the drum gave a different pitch. The stick was a blur in her hands.

"Think that'll be enough for you, then?" she asked, that twinkle still in her eye.

For a moment, nobody could answer. Then Eldriss said, "I think we can work with this, don't you, lads?"

Their faces answered his question. Including Kyrissa, who was quite fine with being called a lad.

They did a couple of traditional tunes, then ran through several of their songs, starting with the easiest, which Orla mastered without effort. As the songs got more complex, she stumbled one or two times at the beginning, but picked them up quickly and mastered them by the end, adding flourishes that Davon had never—that none of them ever—thought of including.

The contest rules said each group had to perform one traditional song and one original song. Eldriss figured a more interesting song, played well, would give them a better chance.

At their next practice, they started the discussion of what songs they would play.

Eldriss knew it wouldn't be easy. They all had their favorites.

"What about 'The Ballad of Jacosta and Sims'?" Orla suggested.

"It's a duet," Kyrissa said. "And I'm no singer. All we've got is Lon."

"I can sing," Orla said. She looked at Lon.

He nodded. "Let's try it."

The band had to balance Lon's recorder with his singing, which sometimes meant choosing one or the other on certain songs. He had a strong tenor, though, and easily slipped into the part of Sims.

Jacosta's verse was next.

Eldriss assumed from her speaking voice that her singing voice would be high and thin, with a pleasant lilt that would go well with many of the traditional songs. But what came out of her mouth was so unexpected, they all sucked in a surprised breath, took a step back.

Rich and clear, almost magical in its depth. Eldriss felt the hair at the nape of his neck prickle.

The chorus was both parts intertwined, rising and falling

and dancing with each other. Orla's and Lon's voices fit together well, although it would take some practice for them to find the correct balance of volume as well as a bit of timing.

"I think we have our traditional song?" he asked when they finished.

The rest of the band gave their enthusiastic agreement.

"Good, then," he said. "Now for the original song . . ."

The debate began anew.

Haven was a two-day journey from Traynemarch Reach, but that was on horseback. With a wagon and team, it was likely to be closer to three, and they had to arrive at least one day early.

Thankfully, someone loaned them a wagon and horses. Eldriss worked as scribe and records-keeper for the mayor, who kindly gave him the time to go. A winning troupe would bring honor to Traynemarch Reach, and possibly more business, if people came to the local taverns to hear the band. The others' employers did the same.

They took turns, two up front driving, two resting in the back with the carefully padded instruments and the rest of their belongings. The weather was in their favor. In late spring, there could be anything from sun to rain, to cold or hot days.

They met other traveling troupes as they grew closer to Haven.

Eldriss didn't see the one he was expecting.

Perhaps they'd arrived earlier.

At any rate, he knew they'd be there.

Haven was a far sight different from Traynemarch Reach. Eldriss had been there several times, and every time, including this one, it had taken him time to get over feeling overwhelmed by the sounds, sights, and smells.

Inside the gates, the road was crowded with carts and wagons drawn by horses or oxen, people on horseback and people on foot, even a small herd of sheep driven along by a shepherd and pair of border collies. The various animals were the source of most of the smells thus far.

A pair of Heralds went by on their snow-white Companions, bridle bells jingling. Orla stared. "They come every year, but I'm still in awe of them," she confessed. "Those beautiful, beautiful horses."

One of the Companions snorted, as if he or she had understood Orla and took umbrage at being called a mere horse.

They wended their way to the arts district, and found the theater where the competition would take place.

Eldriss examined the schedule. Tomorrow was the day for original songs, and the day after that for traditional. They were scheduled to perform in the late afternoon each day. Late enough to get nervous, but early enough that they could relax afterward.

They were then directed to the hostel where they'd be staying at a reduced price for musicians. As they gathered their instruments and belongings to take inside, Eldriss finally felt the first nervous stirrings in his stomach.

So many bands. So much talent.

He just had to believe in himself, and in his friends.

Troupes were expected to arrive no later than eleven o'clock the first morning, with the first performance starting at noon sharp. After they were noted as present, Eldriss and the group went outside to the park behind the theater where everyone would wait until they were called in to take their place in the queue.

The day was sunny and warm, but shade from the building and trees made the space pleasant, and flowerbeds perfumed the air.

Musicians tuned their instruments, playing a few notes here and there, the different chords causing a pleasant dissonance. In various corners, the first vocalists warmed up, singing scales or other practice tunes.

Eldriss and the others found a corner of the park and settled down to wait until it was closer to their turn.

"Er," Orla said, "there's someone over there staring at you. Do you know him?"

Eldriss, Kyrissa, and Lon all turned to look. Lon winced, and Kyrissa sucked in a lungful of air.

Eldriss ignored the pang in his heart. "Yes, we know each other."

When he didn't continue, Orla said, "There's got to be more to it than that. He's looking at you as if he wants to murder you in your sleep." She cocked her head, then amended, "No, I think he'd rather you were awake for it."

Eldriss tilted his head back and blew out a long breath.

"He's my brother."

He explained.

They'd grown up in a musical household. Their father sang, his rich tenor known throughout Traynemarch Reach. Their mother could play almost any instrument.

Brower had taken to the recorder at an early age. Eldriss, a year younger, had tried several instruments before finding the fiddle. And loving it.

As they grew, Eldriss and Brower found others to play with, forming and reforming different groups along the way.

People said they had some sort of special connection, the way the recorder and the fiddle wove melodies together, one taking over, then the other. The songs they wrote together were magical, or at least Eldriss thought so.

"So what happened?" Orla asked in her soft voice.

"We met Shalna," he said simply.

It was more complicated than that, of course. They'd known her since they were children, and they'd been the best of friends. She'd loved to dance to their music, and although she wasn't a musician herself, her suggestions often made their music better.

Brower had been sweet on her. Eldriss, a year behind, took longer to recognize the woman she was becoming.

He never thought he was pursuing her, or even that there was a contest. But when their connection became more obvious, when their love bloomed, Brower had seen things differently.

Brower thought Eldriss had stolen her away from him. No

matter how much Shalna swore she'd seen Brower only as a friend, cared for him as a friend.

The troupe they had together crumbled under the weight of their dispute. They each gone on to create separate bands.

Competing groups. Rivals.

Brower's recorder, which wove depths like the river along the town, became a favorite for more somber events, such as funerals. Birthdays and other celebrations tended to fall to Eldriss and his bright, sprightly fiddle. Weddings were split between them, depending on the tone the bride and groom wanted. Taverns, inn, alehouses, and the like fell the same way; some wanted music for dancing, others wanted music in the background to complement the food and drink.

Eldriss knew Brower, or someone in his group, had removed the announcement of the competition in Haven from the town hall in Traynemarch Reach. It was far from the first subtle sabotage Eldriss's group had experienced.

Planned engagements were canceled because "someone" had advised the venue—someone not in the group—that they'd be unable to perform. (Ironically, Brower's band was conveniently available to step in.) Clothing disappeared, fiddle strings and reeds were found cut or otherwise damaged. Eldriss couldn't be sure that the time they all fell ill before a wedding was because their food had been tampered with, but . . .

The instruments were never touched. Even Brower respected their sanctity.

Eldriss couldn't claim to be innocent, as occasionally he or one of the others would retaliate in kind. But his heart was never really into it.

Still, he had to defend himself and his friends sometimes, didn't he?

Which was why this competition was so important.

Once and for all, he wanted to prove that he—and his band— were the superior musicians.

To Eldriss's dismay, Brower's troupe was scheduled to perform immediately before them. He wondered if the order had been chosen by town name; he hadn't been paying attention until now.

In the dimly lit backstage, the two groups kept to their own corners as the two previous bands played, and two new bands entered in the wings. Eldriss ignored Brower while at the same time being painfully aware of him.

He hated their estrangement, their rivalry. But he wouldn't be the first to speak. How could he? He wasn't the one holding the grudge.

Things might have gone more smoothly if Brower had fallen in love with someone else, and married. But he had done neither, and Eldriss had no idea if there was anyone in his brother's life.

They waited at the side of the stage while Brower's troupe performed. The knots in Eldriss's stomach were making their own knots. He was nervous for himself and his band members, and he'd also not heard Brower play in several years.

Brower and his group were good. Very good.

Was his troupe better? Maybe they weren't . . .

No. He couldn't think that way. He couldn't question his own talent, nor could he question Kyrissa's, or Lon's, or Orla's.

They were good, very good, too. It was the judges' job to decide who was better, and he had to go on stage believing in his heart that they were.

Their original song was a merry jig, with some intricate fingerwork by Eldriss and fast movement by Lon on the recorder, with Kyrissa's shawm a lower undercurrent, and Orla's complex drumming making what could have been a simple song for dancing sound layered and sophisticated.

They played without a hitch, without a slip or mistake. They played with heart and joy; it was a song that never failed to lift Eldriss's spirits, at least.

Seeing the judges' feet tapping didn't hurt.

Afterward, exhausted, they returned their instruments to the hostel and went out for a meal and a drink or two. The tavern, the Unstrung Harp, was filled with musicians, both locals as well as competitors. Here, nobody seemed to care about the competition. Everyone was in good spirits, chattering about their own performances and the others.

People slapped their backs and told Eldriss and the others how good they'd been. More than one drummer dragged Orla into conversation about her unusual instrument.

The Harp wasn't the only tavern in the arts district, of course, and although Eldriss found himself looking, he didn't see Brower again that day.

He wasn't sure how he felt about that.

The next morning, the groups from all across the country gathered again in the park behind the theater to await their turn to play a traditional song.

"I don't see your brother," Orla said.

Eldriss had already noticed. What, he wondered, was wrong?

He wasn't sure whether he cared more because it meant their own victory would have less meaning (for him, at least), or because he was concerned.

So he couldn't quite identify the emotion he felt when Brower rushed in just before eleven o'clock and spoke with the coordinator checking in the bands. There was some back-and-forth, and Brower left, only to return a few minutes later with the rest of his band.

No . . . not all of them. Aslom, their drummer, was missing.

Probably just running late, Eldriss decided. Apparently having the majority of the group there was enough to be counted as present.

Then he realized he was spending too much time and thought on something that didn't affect him and wasn't his business, and he turned his attention back to his own troupe.

They were still energized from the previous day's performance, but one piece never meant the next would elicit a similar reaction or even go as smoothly.

As their time grew nearer, Eldriss made minute changes to the tuning of his fiddle, and Orla quietly tapped her stick against her drum. Kyrissa put a reed in her shawm, took it out, selected another one. Only Lon seemed calm, but that was his way before a performance, and didn't mean he had different feelings churning inside. Heavy-lidded, he lounged in the grass as if he were seconds from succumbing to a nap.

Brower's name was called, and he and his group, minus Aslom, went inside. Shortly thereafter, the most recent band to play came out, and Eldriss's troupe were next to enter the backstage area.

As they did, Eldriss walked headfirst into someone. He began an apology, then realized who it was.

Brower.

Each brother took a step back.

Brower moved to walk around Eldriss, but Eldriss, following an impulse that surprised even him, grabbed Brower's arm. "What's wrong?"

Brower scowled, but couldn't seem to hold the expression. His shoulders slumped. "Aslom had too much to drink last night and fell. We hoped he'd recover enough to perform, but he's been at the healer's all day, so his arm is probably broken. At any rate, if we miss our turn, we're out of the competition."

"That's terrible news," Eldriss said. "I'm so sorry."

"Are you?" Brower shot back.

"Yes," Eldriss said, and he meant it. "You should have the opportunity to compete, fair as fair goes."

Orla tugged on Eldriss's arm, then leaned in to speak quietly in his ear.

He blinked at her, surprised at her request—and also impressed. "Of course."

Orla turned to Brower. "I'd be happy to stand in for Aslom."

"Oh, right," Brower's singer sneered. "Just to mess things up for us."

Orla blinked, the hurt clear on her face. "Why would I do something like that? We're all here for the same thing: the music. I can't promise to be perfect, because I haven't practiced whatever you're going to play, but I can promise you I'll do my best. I'm Orla, by the way. Gineva's cousin, if you know her."

Brower glanced at the other members, who shrugged. "Do you know 'The Gryphon's Lament'?"

"I do," Orla said.

Brower turned to his people, and Eldriss and Orla stepped back to let them discuss the offer in private. When Brower turned back, his singer still had a pinched look, but the other three looked relieved.

"We'd be grateful for your assistance," Brower said.

Both bands entered the back of the theater. The organizer promptly beckoned to Eldriss. Eldriss and Brower quickly explained the arrangement to her, and she nodded. "Very well, if you're ready?" she said to Brower.

"We are," he said.

Eldriss and the others watched from the wings. Brower's recorder gave the melancholy song a richness that raised it to bittersweet. Orla's drumming was flawless, although simpler than what she'd shown in rehearsals—for obvious reason. She hadn't played with Brower's group before, nor had she practiced the song with Eldriss's.

She came off stage, then reentered with Eldriss's troupe.

Once again, Eldriss's nervousness melted away once he was on stage. This was where he was the happiest, and he had faith in his—and his bandmates'—abilities.

When they finished and left, however, Brower and his group were gone, without so much as a thanks to Orla for her assistance.

Eldriss was livid. Not only had Orla done Brower and his troupe a huge favor, allowing them to remain in the competition, but it had been the first time he and Brower had spoken in several years. He'd hoped that they'd made the first step toward a reconciliation, or at least the early beginnings of a détente.

To walk away without a word was a slap in the face to both him and Orla.

Orla seemed to shake it off, but he hadn't known her long enough to know how well she could hide her emotions. When he expressed his own feelings, she simply put a gentle hand on his forearm and quietly said a few calming words.

She reminded him of Shalna in that way. Slow to anger, not

easy to ruffle. Annoyances slid off her. Of course, there was a point where Shalna could be pushed too far—and then everyone had to watch out.

That evening at the Unstrung Harp, the mood was both more relaxed (the competition was over!) and yet more tense in a different way than the night before. Tonight, musicians were fretting about how well they had done—or not, reliving every flaw, including ones that were probably only in their heads.

The drinks flowed more freely, since there was nothing left than the next morning's gathering to learn which troupe had won the competition. Impromptu bands were formed and re-formed as different singers and musicians got on the tavern's low stage.

Some in the audience danced: to remember the excitement of the competition or to forget their real or imagined mistakes.

Eldriss nursed an excellent spiced rum, not sure if he wanted to drink very much tonight. He hadn't brought his fiddle with him, which was fine because he didn't feel much like performing, either.

He found himself wondering if winning the competition would feel the same as he initially thought, now that he'd encountered Brower. In truth, he wanted their differences to be put aside. He'd never wanted this estrangement. But, he supposed, he'd gotten caught up in it, fighting back when he felt the need to protect himself and his friends.

When Orla had asked if she could also drum for Brower, he'd agreed without hesitation—and, if he was going to be completely honest with himself, he was ashamed he hadn't thought of it himself.

But his brother's actions after that . . . Eldriss shook his head, took another small sip of the delicious rum he couldn't appreciate. Maybe he should stop hoping.

Truth was, he was looking forward to going home to Shalna almost more than he was looking forward to learning the results of the competition.

The latest random group of musicians left the stage, reducing the volume in the tavern to loud conversation.

His own table, however, suddenly went quiet. He looked around.

Brower stood there, holding his recorder in one hand, the expression on his face one Eldriss couldn't decipher. "I'd like to . . . talk, if you're willing."

"Of course," Eldriss said, although his churning emotions were less assured than his voice.

As one, Lon, Kyrissa, and Orla stood up and headed to the bar.

Brower took one of the vacated seats.

"I'm sorry," he said finally, his voice so low Eldriss had to lean in to hear him. His fingers moved on his recorder as if he were playing a song, even though the instrument wasn't near his face. It gave him something else to look at.

"I wasn't fair to you—or to Shalna," he continued. "It hurt too much to accept she didn't love me, so it was easier to blame you for stealing her. And then it was easier to be angry."

Brower finally looked up. "Then I saw you, and I realized I wasn't angry, not anymore. I'd just held on to it because it had become normal. I'm sorry," he repeated. "I'd like—if you're willing—to be in each other's lives again."

Eldriss felt an unfamiliar pain in his chest, as if his heart were cracking open. "I'd like that, too."

They stared at one another. Eldriss couldn't figure out where to start a conversation after several years.

"What are you drinking?" Brower asked with a small jerk of his chin at Eldriss's horn mug.

"Spiced rum." He slid it across the table.

Brower tasted it, approved, and waved to flag down a server.

Moments later, they were talking about the thing that had always connected them: music.

The next afternoon, all the bands gathered in the theater. The stage jutted out onto the floor, where people—such as the musicians who'd competed—stood to watch performances. Except for behind the stage, the rest of the theater was curved tiers of boxes around the floor for several stories.

Five names were called, along with their groups, Eldriss and Brower among them.

"Top five," Eldriss said confidently.

But when they were taken behind the stage, the other three groups were separated from Eldriss's and Brower's.

The stage organizer met them, wringing her hands.

"I'm so, so sorry," she said. "It's all my fault. When I allowed you—" she looked at Orla, "—to play with the other band, I hadn't realized that wasn't all right. And then we found out that you also weren't a permanent member of your original band, which was also against the rules."

Eldriss struggled to speak, despite his mouth having gone dry. "What does that mean? Are we . . . disqualified?"

"I'm afraid so," the organizer said. Then she brightened. "But the Queen wishes to speak to you."

"The Queen?" Orla squeaked.

But then they were being hustled away by a Herald, up to the Queen's Box on the top level, directly across from the stage.

Queen Selenay sat in a high-backed wooden chair with a comfortable red cushion and gold-painted details on the back and arms.

They all bowed and curtsied, more or less appropriately. Eldriss's knees quivered, and he imagined everyone else was similarly affected.

"Oh, please, sit," the Queen said.

There weren't enough chairs, so some did as requested, and the others stood behind them.

"I'm terribly sorry to hear you've been disqualified," the Queen said. "From what I've been told, you both were top contenders."

Eldriss bit back a groan. He wasn't sure how close they'd gotten before victory was snatched away.

"However," she went on, "sometimes there are more important things than winning. You've impressed me with your willingness to take on a last-minute member, in both cases. To help a fellow competitor shows integrity and kindness."

She lifted a hand, and a lady-in-waiting emerged from the

shadows in the back of the box, handing the Queen a number of woven gray and rust cords. A silver medallion dangled from each cord.

"Please accept these as tokens of my respect not only for your musical skills, but for your understanding that when we make music together, we make Valdemar a better place for everyone."

After the concert by the winning troupe—who were, Eldriss admitted, very good indeed—they packed up their carts and began the trek back to Traynemarch Reach.

This time the two bands traveled in a convoy. Occasionally some switched carts, now that the rift was mending. Even Brower's singer was no longer scowling.

It didn't escape Eldriss's notice that Orla and Brower frequently found themselves next to each other, their heads close as they talked.

He had a feeling Orla might not be traveling back south any time soon.

Already, he was looking forward to performing at their joining ceremony.

In fact, a song for them was already blooming in his head—and heart.

Tangles
Diana L. Paxson

Deira staggered as a gust of wind tried to loft the wicker basket out of her arms. She had stopped trying to secure her headscarf five paces past her door. The only way to keep the honey-colored strands out of her eyes was to turn her face to the wind.

This year, winter was at feud with spring. Each sign of the new season had been countered by a sudden frost or a wintry blast. Last night, that wind had whistled and wuthered around the Collegium tower, spinning clouds into the white wisps the Bards called "Companion's tail." This morning, it whipped out the banners that flew from the palace towers. From the window of Andry's rooms, she'd seen branches strewn across the Companions' Field.

In a week, he would be riding Circuit with Herald Arlend, beginning his intern year.

Last night, they had slept in Andry's rooms at the Collegium, he on his side, she on hers, as if the pain of the approaching separation could be eased by practicing it now. It was that year of actually *doing the work* that completed the transformation and made the commitment to being a Herald of Valdemar real. When Deira remembered how their journey to his old home on the southern border had deepened Andry's relationship to *her*, she believed it. Having spent most of this year assisting at the City Court, he was eager to get on the road.

They had married just after he got his Whites last autumn. She was not supposed to know how long the Collegium had argued about whether their relationship would prevent him from making a full commitment to the job. They should be cherishing each moment they had together, but her emotions were as tangled as the branches that littered the road.

Was she trying to armor herself against the pain of his absence by being cold to him now?

The gusts lessened as she passed through the gate and started down the road. The wind had had its way with the estates of the highest, or the richest, of Valdemar's highborn families. Drifts of fallen branches lay tangled against their stone walls. By the time Deira reached the commercial section, she only faced a brisk breeze, but here too, she could see damage—the alleys were littered with wisps of thatching, scattered roof tiles, and even laundry that had been left on the line.

She turned a corner, and the half-timbered façade of Baldon's Import Emporium rose before her, its suspended sign jerking fitfully in the wind. Madame Baldon had worked hard to make this the place where a lady with social ambitions would go for a hostess gift, unusual trim for a new gown, or just the right ornament for her entry hall. Deira retied her scarf. She was not going to pass for one of the highborn ladies Madame Baldon fawned on, but her reflection in a windowpane told her she looked sufficiently respectable to enter the store.

The door stuck as she pushed, then gave way suddenly, slamming shut behind her as she stumbled inside.

"Well, that was a warm welcome!" Deira looked over her shoulder to make sure her cloak had not gotten caught in the door. It was new, woven in a subtle mingling of blues that harmonized with the gear worn by Andry's Companion. *Even if I have no other function,* she had thought as she worked on it, *I can create a pleasing backdrop.*

But she had learned not to say so aloud. The thought brought a memory of the derisive snort Lochren met her periodic expressions of self-doubt with. She could not Mindspeak with her husband's Companion, but he had a talent for making himself understood, and during their journey to Andry's old home the previous summer, the three of them had developed a surprisingly effective link.

The showroom was crowded with shelves bright with fancy goods from all over Valdemar and beyond. Flowers crafted from silk or paper trailed from wicker baskets hanging from the ceiling. From somewhere in the direction of the warehouse behind it, Deira could hear men's voices raised in ire.

Madame Baldon, stout, corseted, and perpetually in motion, hurried forward. "Mistress Westerbridge!" she exclaimed. "But I must call you Mistress Denorsdale now, and congratulate you on your marriage! Are you hurt? Is your cloak torn? That devil wind! It's got everything and everyone in a pother. Sit, catch your breath! Let me ring for the girl to bring tea!"

Deira blinked, a little surprised at the intensity of the welcome. But there were no other customers present, and she, while not a big spender herself, had the ear of highborns who would pay a great deal to acquire just the right accessory to go with one of Deira's custom-woven rugs or tapestries.

From her precisely curled red hair to her pointed ankle boots, Madame Lioneta Baldon worked hard to present herself as a woman of breeding, anxious to share beautiful things, but she had a reputation for sharp practice, backed by her four sturdy sons, no doubt the source of the uproar echoing from the rear. Once there must have been a *Master* Baldon, but he had died some years before. Deira suspected his absence made it easier for the lady to uphold her pretensions. Certainly, the shop had become more successful after he expired.

Madame Baldon was already jerking the bell-pull.

"No need to fuss! No harm was done—" Deira folded her cloak and laid it over the back of a chair. "But if you will sit down and join me, a cup of tea would be welcome!"

From beyond the curtained doorway, a clink of crockery accented the reverberations of masculine wrath. Deira might not need the tea, but from what she could hear, her hostess could use a restorative cup right now. "Have I come at a bad time?"

"'Tis always a good time when *you* visit us here—" Madame Baldon replied, yanking at the bell once more. "Feel free to look around." She bustled back toward the door. "I must go see what my louts of sons are complaining about today!" As a door was opened a burst of yelling echoed from beyond. It turned to a faint rumble as it closed once more.

Deira began to wander along the shelves that lined the walls. There was always something new to see. Just now, part of the back wall was occupied by a cabinet as tall as she was and as wide as it was tall, richly carved and dark with age. Brass fittings and pulls ornamented the drawers. To call it furniture was an insult—it was an invitation to imagine distant places and ancient mysteries. She pulled a few random drawers open as she moved along. Most were empty of anything but dust, but even that smelled faintly of flowers that never grew in Valdemar.

The carving on the framework drawers invited her fingers to trace their intricacies: exotic flowers, leaves, and beasts half-seen, half-sensed within. They all seemed to be looking toward the right. The wood was strange to her—Andry might know what it was. The surface could use some oil, but clearly it had once been well cared for. The fronts of the drawers were incised with lines. Her fingertips tingled as she traced them, but she could not tell if they were an abstract design, or an inscription in an alphabet she did not know.

Deira pulled open another drawer, drawing in a breath of ancient incense like a ghostly memory. *Another empty,* she thought, but then her fingers brushed what felt like a knotted cord. She pulled again. In the light that filtered down from the high window she glimpsed a tangle of knotwork, perhaps a belt or a sash. At one end the strands were interlaced and tucked neatly under, but at the other the pattern had become a knot from which protruded a few fibers, stretched and torn. In a lifetime of handwork, Deira had had to disentangle more than a few such snarls. Automatically her fingers began to probe and pull.

A girl in an embroidered linen apron shouldered through the door, carrying a steaming teapot. Behind her came Madame Baldon with a second tray holding two cups, sugar, and cream. As the tray was set on a small marquetry table, Deira slipped the tangle into her belt purse and sat back down.

She took a deep, appreciative breath as the other woman

poured golden tea into cups nearly translucent, the porcelain was so fine. A scent of herbs from some land that had never heard of snow was beginning to permeate the air. The china, edged with an interlace of golden leaves, was of the sort that would be labeled "second-best" in a highborn household, but still a compliment.

"'Tis been a time since we have seen you—" said her hostess. "Have you been well? And your husband? I understand he is a full Herald now . . ."

That explains the hospitality, thought Deira as she murmured polite assurances. It was not her income, but her connection to the Heralds on the hill that was winning her this consideration. She sipped her tea. She could feel the heat through her fingertips. They continued to tingle after she set the cup down.

"This would soothe a kyree . . ." The flavors were subtle, teasing the tastebuds with hints of fruit and flowers. "Should we share some with your boys?" she added as a louder shout penetrated the door.

Madame Baldon sighed. "Only if I put it in a mug and call it beer . . ."

"That would not be worthy of a fine blend," Deira replied.

"Forty years I have worked to build a reputation for good taste and good manners, and those young louts think only of breaking heads." Madame Baldon sighed again.

"But what is the trouble?"

"'Tis those Macraines, always the Macraines." The woman shook her head. "Anatol sends his bully boys to threaten me, and of course my lads want to respond. I've kept them out of the army so far, but when foes show up on your own doorstep it's hard for a young man to wait for the watch to come."

"On your doorstep?" Deira replied. Better not to mention Master Macraine's emporium was the next stop on her list. The two merchants carried similar stock and had been competitors for generations, but this year their rivalry seemed to have reached a new high.

"Foul words chalked on the pavement, and filth scattered in

front of the door!" Madame Baldon's face was growing more flushed than could be blamed on the tea.

Deira looked around for a change of subject. "That cabinet's new—wherever did you find it?"

"Loot—" Madame Baldon shook off her irritation with a sigh. "Or so I assume. It appeared in the Eastgate market with a low price and no history. Our soldiers are forbidden to scavenge houses they find abandoned, but it's a sore temptation."

"I can understand carrying off an ornament or a bit of jewelry, but a piece of furniture this size?" Deira exclaimed.

The older woman shrugged. "I'd guess some enterprising wagon driver found it when he was about to return to headquarters for supplies. 'Tis fine work, but the design seems unbalanced, and there are few manors, even on the Hill, where it would fit in well.

"Anatol Macraine wants it," she went on. "They've been at us to sell it to them since we got it in. If he'd asked nicely, I might have agreed. But it's not going to the Macraines!" Madame Baldon shook her head. "My boys would feel dishonored, and just now, I'd sooner chop the thing up for kindling than let them take it away! But that's no concern of yours!" Her cup clinked as she set it down. "What can I do for you today?"

"I am making a tapestry for Lady Auster, and she insists that the background must match the drapes in her sitting room. It would make more sense to get new ones to match the tapestry, but the highborn have their ways. I need thread or dye stuff in that deep rusty red they are so fond of in the Shin'a'in lands." It was, in fact, almost the current shade of Madame Baldon's hair.

"With so many men and wagons serving the army, trade is as unpredictable as last night's wind," came the reply. "We've not seen a caravan from that direction since just past harvest. Tell your client to get new curtains." Madame snorted. "That can be her contribution to the war!"

By the time Deira left Madame Baldon's shop, it was nearly noon, and the wind had faded to a fitful breeze. The streets were full of people picking up debris.

She found a food cart selling pocket pies and sat down on the rim of a public fountain to eat. The central pedestal from which the water poured boasted an image of King Valdemar, his strong features worn with age. His contributions to the kingdom were symbolized by the clear water that welled in a smooth sheet from the bowl he held, free to all. She cupped some in her hand and drank, then brushed crumbs off her skirt and took up her basket.

The Macraine warehouse stood on the bank where the Terilee widened and slowed as it ran out into the plain. Master Macraine sold rare woods for building and traded in unusual fabrics, furniture, and ornaments for the garden and the home. If Deira could not find dye to match Lady Auster's curtains, he might have yardage to match the yarn she already had.

The wind had been busy here as well. Boats were tethered to the short dock, and ducks quacked among the reeds. Axes thunked as workmen hacked at a tree that had been blown against the warehouse wall. Other men, lean and watchful, lounged against the walls, cudgels dangling casually at their sides.

The front of the building served as a showroom, its contents displayed more for ease of access than style. A bell tinkled as she entered, but no one seemed to be around. Deira took another step in and stopped short. A large and highly ornamented cabinet dominated the room—a very familiar cabinet, except that where the designs on Madame Baldon's cabinet faced to the right, those on the one before her at faced left.

No wonder Master Macraine wants the one she has, thought Deira. *It's the mate to his. How long, I wonder, before someone tells her? They'll be throwing more than turds at each other then!*

She should not have been surprised. Macraine's agents were always on the lookout for antiques from the manors of highborns whom poverty kept in the country, and handicrafts that might attract the fickle favor of those who could afford to live in town. The cabinets were clearly very old, and in a style she had never seen. Singly, they were impressive. Placed together in the right setting, they would be stunning.

Deira did not even try to resist the temptation to brush her fingers along the swirling patterns of the cabinet's drawers, and then to close on a brass knob and pull. An aroma of spice and flowers diffused through the air. She took a careful breath, recognizing the scent from the cabinet at Madame Baldon's. She closed the first drawer, felt her hand drawn to another, and pulled. Here, the perfume was even stronger. She reached inside.

"Mistress Denorsdale! I see you appreciate our new prize!"

Deira jumped, her fingers closing on—something—and swept it into her pouch as she turned, bracing herself to meet Master Macraine's sometimes awkward gallantry. He was tall, angular, with the air of some stilted water bird that paces beside a stream. He had never married, and was more used to dealing with the workmen that remodeled fine houses than with the highborn ladies who hired them.

Another step brought him to her side, but rather than seizing her hand, he greeted her with an awkward bow. A boy came behind him, carrying a tray with two silver goblets and a bottle of wine.

He has heard about my marriage . . . Deira thought, nodding a polite reply. *But is this respect due to* my *change in status, or Andry's?* How long did it take a newly minted Herald to realize how he was perceived? When she told Andry about this encounter, what would he say?

"Did you find it in the market at the Eastern Gate?" she asked.

"Now how should you guess that?" The affable smile grew chill. "We did, and we found its mate as well. But we had only the one wagon, and those bastard Baldons came after us, and bargained up the price, though the dealer said it was already bespoke, and carried it off before we could return."

Deira took a sip of wine. "It does look a little unbalanced," she observed. "Does Madame Baldon know that hers is one of a pair?"

"I think not," his rather high voice thinned, "and don't you be the one to let Lioneta know, or she'll refuse to sell just to spite me!"

"From all I've heard, either one of you would refuse to let

the sun shine if you knew it would warm the other. Sell the cabinets together and split the price, and I'd guess you'll both gain more."

Macraine shook his head. "I'll not give that woman the satisfaction!"

Deira sighed. "Well, 'tis not like either of you to pass up a profit, but even in the Pelagirs, pigs don't fly. I suppose you two have been fighting each other too long." She set down her goblet. "Some wood-rose dye is what I came for. Would you happen to have any on hand?"

The packet of red powder Deira left the warehouse with should have given her a sense of triumph, but she was surprised to be coming away with mingled sadness and frustration at the impasse between the Baldons and the Macraines. Why should she care whether either one made a profit? Or was she bothered by the cabinets? They had clearly been designed to frame a hearth or a doorway. They were old, and must have spent decades paired, and it troubled her sense of order to see them in hostile hands.

And if you are troubling yourself over the feelings of furniture, she told herself as she started back up the hill, *you are paying entirely too much attention to your artistic sensibilities, my girl!*

Andry came through the door to his rooms on a gust of wind that sent smoke from the small hearth swirling around the room. The great winds had ceased, thank the Powers, and everything that could be blown down was already on the ground, but the airs were still unstable.

Deira went to him, kissing the chill from his cheeks, and using her fingers to untangle his dark hair. How much gray would the year away on Circuit add to the strands already sprinkled there? How much flesh would be worn from the lean body she held in her arms?

"There's tea on the hearth," she said as she let him go. He

picked up the bag he had brought up from the kitchens and began to unload the waxed cloth packets it contained. When Deira was working late at her loom in the workshop in Haven, Andry ate in Heralds' Hall, but these last weeks the staff of the kitchen, who had been among the most enthusiastic supporters of their romance, had prepared dinners that could be warmed up in his rooms. Her clients would have to wait for their orders. She could spend her nights weaving in her workshop when Andry was sharing a waystation with Herald Arlend somewhere near the border with Hardorn.

Deira had already laid a cloth across the table. In the silver vase the Healer trainees had given them at their wedding stood a sprig of budding Astera's tears brought down by the wind. She watched him as he ate the stew, careful of each spoonful as a man who has labored to bring food from the earth has learned to be. By now she had heard enough tales to know Heralds were not always received with enthusiasm, and accidents could happen on the road. Andry's ability to survive on short rations might serve him well.

"On my way home from shopping I stopped by the Companions' stable to see Lochren," she said. "He kept nibbling at my cloak. Does he want it for a blanket, or has he developed a taste for wool?"

Andry raised an eyebrow. His expression went inward, and after a moment he smiled. "Lochren says you have great insight as well as great skill, and that such a blanket would make him the envy of the stable. Also, that your association with him has clearly developed your abilities, and you should be tested for the Gift of Empathy."

Deira snorted. "Right after we test *him* for modesty." Shaking her head, she picked up her belt pouch and took out the packet of dye she had got at Macraine's. Encountering the tangles of cord beneath it, she drew out those as well.

"What have you got there?"

"I don't quite know." She turned to him. "It was the oddest thing—I visited Madame Baldon, and then Master Macraine.

Each of them has acquired one of what appears to be a pair of mysterious cabinets. I was . . . looking into the drawers . . . and in each I found one of these—" She held them out for him to see.

"Macraine and Baldon? Are they still at each other's throats? It seemed as if one of their people was in the Haven City Court for one thing or another almost every week when I was training there."

"I am afraid the feud is getting hotter now," she said wryly, and he sighed.

Deira picked up one of the tangles and attempted to pull it flat. It was a stiff and contorted mass of knotted string about two feet long. The other was much the same. She could not yet tell how much of the confusion was caused by the way the cords had been crushed, and which twists might form part of a design. Both had broken fibers at one end and at the other a neatly finished border with a bit of fringe.

"The cabinets match—why not their contents? Could they both be parts of a single thing?" Andry asked, seeing her frown.

Time had dulled the color, but the surface of the twined cords had a muted gleam. What was it made of? Deira poked the end of one cord into the flame and jumped as it sparked and charred. The wisp of smoke carried the odor of a rain-soaked cloak hung too close to the fire to dry—wool, then, but from what creature it came she could not say. She felt a rush of excitement. Anyone who ever had to process a fleece knew how wool fibers yearned to link together. If the band of knotted cords was made from some kind of wool, it might be possible to rejoin the severed ends as she did when a thread broke on the loom.

Deira rubbed her fingertips against the tablecloth to ease their tingling. Why would anyone make an adornment from something so irritating? Even nettle fibers could be tamed. Or perhaps it was not the fiber—she frowned at the design— perhaps it was magic.

The cords were stiff with age and compression, but with a pin and a fingernail Deira teased apart the fibers and, working her way from the center outward, began to join the severed ends and twist them together, encouraging the tiny hooks along the shaft of each hair to catch and bind.

From somewhere down in the city, a temple bell began to ring. Deira felt Andry's hand on her shoulder and looked up to meet his apologetic smile. "I have to get some sleep."

Appalled, she stared up at him. How could she have allowed herself to be distracted? In three nights, he would be leaving!

She started to rise but he pushed her back into the chair. "Finish it. Heralds are like artists—when a pattern is broken, we have this compulsion to make it whole. Come to bed when the work is done."

Deira nodded, her throat too tight for words. She knew he loved her, but there were so many times when she had felt unworthy to be his partner, especially now, when every day advanced his transformation into one of those legendary beings who were the bulwark of Valdemar. To know that he considered her calling equally valuable shook her soul.

She listened until the creak of the mattress told her he had lain down, and began again. The remaining joins went quickly now. Linked, they made the pieces into a band like the one a priest used to bind a newlywed couple's hands. It was stiff and contorted, but she had a solution for that as well.

She filled a bowl with water and coiled the lengths of knotwork inside. As the cords relaxed, the water was tinged by a dark stain. Was that old blood or the dust of ages? She stirred the tangle gently to ease it away. The cords absorbed the moisture quickly, and when she laid the length back on the table, all the contortions had eased. She bent, skillful fingers releasing, stretching, flattening the fibers against the tablecloth. In . . . and out . . . in . . . and out . . . and around they twined . . . and the pattern implicit in the twists and turns of cord began to come clear.

Another candlemark had passed by the time she pressed down the last bit of fringe. The other end was already beginning to dry. She laid the rest across some upturned baskets to let the air reach it. The lamp flame rippled suddenly, and she turned to see Andry standing in the bedroom doorway. He saw

the band of knotwork lying on the table, smiled, and held out
his hand.

In the sheltering darkness of their bed, his hands moved upon
her body with the same sure touch she had used to restore the
cincture, unknotting muscles, releasing taut nerves. As the
bells confirmed another candlemark, the pattern was completed, and two became one.

Secure in Andry's arms, Deira dreamed. People in brightly
colored garments were feasting, chattering in a language she
did not know. Her gaze fixed first on two cabinets that framed
a dais where a couple sat beneath an embroidered canopy. *It is
a wedding,* she thought, watching as a priest bound the wedding
band around their wrists and blessed it with a shimmer of
power, but even as she recognized what was happening, the vision changed.

Flame erupted from the canopy, sparked from the blades of
swinging swords. Women screamed. Men in black surged
around the table, seized the bride. A sword slashed across the
husband's breast, splattering her gown with crimson as it severed the band by which they had been bound.

The noise grew louder. Deira lurched awake, gasping, and
realized someone was knocking at their door.

"Sir, sir, please wake up, you're needed in the town!" It was
a boy's voice, shrill with urgency.

Andry was already fighting free of the blankets. He reached
for his breeches as Deira pulled on a shift and headed for the
door. She pulled it open and reached to catch the boy before he
fell into the room.

"What is it, lad—" Andry stopped as he recognized one of
the pages who ran errands for the Collegium.

"Herald Elcarth says there's a riot at the Eastern Gate and
you have to come." The answer came out in a single breath, and
the boy stood panting.

"That's what the watch is for! Why in Sethor's hell do they
need *me*?"

Deira handed him his shirt and be pulled it on.

"It's the Baldons and the Macraines," gasped the boy. "Herald Elcarth says you judged them at the City Court, and will know what to do."

"Pitch them all into the Terilee . . ." muttered Andry, and sighed. "But I suppose I have to go." For a few moments his gaze went inward, then fixed on Deira, his brows lifting in surprise. "Lochren says you know these people, and you should come too."

Deira nodded. "I told him I visited them both this afternoon."

"Well, get some warm clothes on, woman. They're putting on his gear. In a few minutes he'll be at the door. Go on—go on—" He waved the boy away. "Tell them we're coming down!"

Why did this have to happen now? thought Deira as she stuffed the skirts of the shift into a divided skirt. *In another three days Andry would have been gone!* She pulled a padded coat over it, tied on a scarf. No need to impress Madame Baldon with her elegance now.

As she turned, her hip knocked against the table. She put out hand to steady it and dislodged the wedding band. Fingers tingling, she grabbed to keep it from falling, thrust it into her coat pocket, then followed the glimmer of Andry's white uniform down the stairs.

Later, what Deira remembered of that ride was a confusion of movement through the windy darkness, the warmth of Andry's back as she clung to him and the way the cantle of Lochren's saddle dug into her belly at the jolts even the Companion's smooth gait could not avoid.

She could see a red glow against the curdled clouds above the eastern side of Haven where Macraine's warehouse stood near the river, alone in its yard. Someone must have told the Baldons the other cabinet was there. Deira shuddered to think of what would have happened if the Macraines had attacked Baldon's building in the crowded center of town.

As they neared, the ring of Lochren's hooves was lost in the clash of angry voices, the angry hiss as water spat at the vicious crackle of the fire. They rounded a corner to find a scene vividly illuminated by the flames that spouted from one corner of the warehouse and gleamed from wet pools on the cobbled road.

Deira hoped the pools were water. Everyone she could see was upright and active. Madame Baldon's sons were shouting. One gripped a bleeding shoulder. A second was being relieved of a cudgel by a City Guard. The other two stood by their mother, who was enveloped in a cloak with a fur collar, her hair, flaming in the firelight, curling wildly from its pins. Another contingent from the watch had corralled Macraine's batch of toughs by the stables. Macraine's piercing protests cut through the noise of the fire.

There was a momentary hush as Lochren halted. Andry swung a leg over the Companion's neck and slid to the ground. He lifted Deira into the seat from the back housing of the saddle where she had been riding pillion.

"Stay here—"

At least, thought Deira as she settled into the padding, *I have a good view.*

Andry strode to the center of the yard. "Isn't the carnage in the south enough for you?" As he looked around him, the clamor began to still. "Is it not enough that the Tedrels pillage and burn? Is the blood of your neighbors the only thing that can quench the fires of your rage?" He shook his head. "Master Macraine—Madame Baldon—since midwinter you've been in court three times because your men were brawling. But apparently it was not enough to simply disturb the peace. Does your quarrel require you to burn the entire town?"

"A torch fell on the fallen branches!" cried the youngest Baldon boy.

"We didn't mean to—" echoed his brother.

Master Macraine pushed forward, his men, fists raised. "They are lying, cheating bastards, like all their line!"

"And your word is so good, Anatol?" exclaimed Madame Baldon. "What about your promises to me?"

"You get 'im, Red-top!" a woman cried. More comments followed. A flicker of excitement ran through the crowd. The wind was picking up, reawakening the fire. Faces flickered into vision, avid or afraid.

"Lioneta, you bitch! It was you—" He broke off as a brick arced past his ear.

"Shut your mouths, you dock-rats!" bellowed the watch captain, "Or we'll take the lot of you in!"

Deira tensed as Lochren moved restively beneath her. She could feel the conflict within him. Andry had clearly commended him to protect her, but would the watch be able to protect the Herald if the crowd went wild? When she shut her eyes against the smoke, what she saw was an after-image from her dream.

"Be still!" Andry's command rang through the air. In that moment of inaction, Deira got a foot into the stirrup, swung her other leg over, and stepped down. Her pocket caught on the stirrup. When she wrenched herself free, the band of cording fell like a handful of nettles into her hand.

"Anatol! Lioneta!" she shouted into the silence. "What binds you?"

"They forced me to marry Baldon!" The woman shook off her son's hand and started forward.

Macraine was already moving. "I hired the carriage to flee, but you never came!"

"Let all broken bonds be mended!" Deira cried. As they met, she flung the twitching length of cording toward their reaching hands.

Had those hands been poised to clout or to clasp? The corded band opened out as it flew forward, then wound itself around their wrists. Breast to breast, they glared into each others' eyes.

"Sorcery!" cried one of the Baldon sons. As they stepped forward, Macraine's men moved like a distorted reflection to bar their way.

"Lochren!" cried Deira. "Get between them, or it will start all over again!"

The Companion was already in motion—a glowing white shape from which people recoiled as if he were twice his size.

She had seen how a Companion could hide in plain sight. Apparently, they could magnify their presence as well.

Both sets of combatants reeled back, attention shifting to *her*. Andry was shoving through the mob, his face as pale as his uniform.

"Get that thing off 'im!" cried one of the Macraines.

Lochren whirled, forehooves skimming a radius precisely calculated to repel the combatants while Deira darted to his side. He swiveled, putting himself between her and the crowd as she side-stepped toward the two she had bound.

"Tell them to stop!" Her voice startled them back into awareness of their surroundings.

"Take it off!" snapped Madame Baldon.

"Leave it on—" Master Macraine growled. "I wanted to marry you then, and though I am not so good a bargain as I was, I would marry you now . . ."

She blinked, and the glare began to soften. Her gaze moved appraisingly from him to the yard and the warehouse behind it, then back again.

"In some ways, I think we are both better bargains than we were . . ." she replied. "I am a better match for you now!"

"Mother! You *can't* mean to marry him! It's that woman! You are under a spell!" The oldest Baldon son pointed at Deira. Andry grabbed his arm as Master Macraine lifted his free hand to wave back his own men.

"These woven cords are meant to *confirm* a binding—" said Deira. "No marriage is valid if it is compelled." She reached for an end and loosened the cord.

Andry, having handed the Baldon son over to two of the City Guards, took the band from her hands and held it high.

"This band was severed by hatred, and healed by love and skill. It would appear that once there was love between you, but for half a lifetime you have wasted your energy in hate. Your feelings are your own affair, but you *will* make peace if you want to continue to do business in this town!"

So much for romance! thought Deira, stifling a snort as she saw their faces change. The crowd, sensing the show was over, began to disperse. Encouraged by some of the guard, the Mac-raine men were filing back into the warehouse. Others escorted the Baldons through the gate. But Anatol still stood in the doorway, and as she followed her offspring out to the road, Lioneta looked back at him.

"Do you think they will marry?" Deira asked as Lochren carried them back up the hill. The wind was blowing once more, but from a different direction, untangling the tumbled clouds, carrying even the memory of smoke away. She had spent the first part of their ride telling him about her dream.

"I'm not sure if they'll end up with a marriage or a merger," Andry replied. "That piece of cording carried a powerful magic."

Lochren snorted agreement, and Deira reached back to give him a pat. *I will miss you, too . . .*

"I am glad the fire didn't reach the warehouse," she said then. "I think those two pieces of furniture wanted to be reunited as badly as the halves of the wedding cord."

As they approached the gate to the Collegium, the night guard emerged. Andry shifted his weight back and Lochren slowed. "As when I must be away, I will long to be reunited to you." His voice was rough with emotion.

She tightened her grip around him and whispered, "We are connected by a deeper magic."

Payment in Kind
Stephanie Shaver

Wham!

The doors to the Copper Spindle banged open and a Herald tumbled out. Fast on his heels came a woman in Bardic Scarlet, her hands curled into fists.

"Lelia!" he said, pleading.

"Just get out!" The words reverberated, buoyed by over a decade of Bardic training, as well as a touch of her Gift. Heads turned.

She stormed back inside, leaving him standing in the road.

Several onlookers—some the weavers who primarily occupied the village of Brightneedle, some garbed in a red and gold livery—watched as the Herald dusted himself off.

A guard approached cautiously, concerned. "Everything all right, Herald Lyle?"

"Fine," Lyle replied, his eyes a little glassy. "My sister . . ."

He smiled bitterly.

"We're having a bit of a disagreement."

When they'd ridden into Brightneedle a few days prior, it had been to much acclaim by the local weavers and shepherds. Taken individually, a Master Bard or a Herald would already have been warmly welcomed. *Together* felt like a gift from the gods.

So, upon arriving, the twins had done what they did best. For Lelia, that meant exchanging lodging for performances at the Copper Spindle, the biggest inn in town, and making sure everyone saw her tuning her gittern in the public room.

And for Lyle: getting embroiled in local politics.

Lord Jannus Alsop marched him down to the river and let him inside a two-story warehouse with a water wheel attached to it. Accompanying Alsop were two heavyset men in red and gold—the Alsop colors—and a slender man named Galton, Alsop's steward.

Once inside, his lordship gestured to an enormous contraption of wood and steel and said, "As you can see, Herald, *someone* broke my janni."

Lyle looked it up and down. The "janni"—like so many other artifices—might as well have been magic to him. It towered three men tall and spanned half the room. If Alsop were to be believed, this one spun cloth in a quarter of the time of a weaver, using the power of the river outside.

Or it would, if someone hadn't taken a hammer to the frame.

Lyle touched the splintered wood, briefly wishing for a Gift like his old mentor's, Wil, which would allow him to reach back through the threads of time and *See* who had done this damage. But he had only a bit of Farsight and enough Fetching to rattle a ring of keys. Nothing useful in this situation.

"Do you have any enemies, Lord Alsop?" he asked.

Alsop straightened. "The weavers, obviously," he said. "They see me as a *threat*. All I want to do is speed up their work, and they sit and moan that I'm taking away their *livelihood*."

"Well, are you?" Lyle asked, from where he crouched at the base of the massive artifice.

Alsop seemed to waver. "Certainly *not*."

Lyle stood up, dusting his hands off on his trews. "I'll start a formal inquiry."

"Will you be using Truth Spell?"

Lyle *hated* that question when it was asked with such undiluted eagerness. He could cast only the most basic version of a Truth Spell, which somehow always disappointed the likes of Lord Alsop.

"If it warrants it," he said, then grinned. "Sometimes people just cave and throw themselves at my feet when they come up against my natural good charm and sparkling Whites, milord."

In his head, Lyle's Companion Rivan snorted.

Alsop didn't cozy to his humor—or didn't care. "These weavers are miscreants, Herald," he said. "Backwards and ignorant. They have no *clue* how expensive my janni is, how much she cost to build, and I *will* extract full payment once you suss out which one of them did this."

"And if they can't pay?"

"Send them to the Border, for all I care. In chains."

Alsop and his entourage quit the meeting, leaving Lyle with the broken machine, the dust, and the quiet rush of the river outside.

:Well!: Rivan said. *:He seems like he's fun at soirées.:*

:Someone did *smash his . . . :* Lyle looked up at the thing Alsop had called a "janni." *: . . . thing.:*

:Think it works as fast as he says it does?:

:Someone thinks it can.: He walked around it. Strands of thread hung off the frame like spidersilk. Metal cogs gleamed in the late afternoon light, the spokes and teeth shiny with grease. But also—

He leaned over and peered into the workings. Some of the staining on the wood seemed irregular. Dark.

Blood?

Why would the thing have *blood* on it?

Did it happen during the act of vandalism? While it ran? He tried to imagine it in motion. The gears spinning. The rise and fall of the wooden frame. It seemed dangerous.

"Oi oi," Lyle muttered as he walked out of the dusty warehouse, then paused again. There were a *lot* of footprints in the dust. Mostly adult-sized, but some—smallish. Children?

Something? Anything?

He went back to the Copper Spindle to find a packed common room. Someone handed him a mug of ale as he enjoyed his sister's performance. Judging by the levels of raucousness, she was nearing the end of her set.

Finish on a high point. She always closed with "Faithful and Fancy." The simple chorus let the audience join in, even if they didn't start off knowing the words. They did by the time it ended.

"Thank you all!" she said. "I need to rest! It's been a long ride!" And then she ducked through the crowd and up the stairs.

Lyle started to push his way through the sea of bodies. At that moment—wading through a throng of people in Alsop's red and gold and locals in their own well-tailored garments—he started to notice the ugly mutterings and jostling.

Tough crowd, he thought, as a burly youth in a journeyman weaver's smock bumped into one of Alsop's servants with unwarranted roughness. The servant spun around, and with no hesitation spat in the weaver's face.

The weaver exploded. He grabbed the servant by his red and gold shirt and flung him across the room. After that, all hell broke loose.

Lyle dodged fists and elbows—luckily, no weapons—as he split brawlers apart, tossing them out the door or into corners. His Whites did as much heavy lifting as his arms—the moment the brawlers registered that they were being bounced by a *Herald*, they recoiled and slunk off. At least *some* sanity reigned.

Guardsmen in blue appeared, doing much the same as Lyle, to limited effect. One of them, a tower of a man with a voice deep and loud enough to crack a glacier, bellowed, *"Knock it off!"*

The fighting ceased immediately. A single bottle fell and shattered in the ensuing silence, and someone whimpered in pain.

"The lot of you," the guard went on, still yelling. "Go home! We had a nice night, and you ruined it!"

One by one they all limped off, bloodied and bruised. A couple bodies curled up on the ground, moaning. They looked like they'd been stomped.

"Get a Healer," the guard said to one of the other Blues, then turned to Lyle. "I suppose we'd have met eventually. I'm Sergeant Marik."

"Lyle." They shook hands. "Normal night?"

Marik grunted. "At least no broken windows this time."

"Do you have things under control, Sergeant?"

"'S'all good," he said. "Usually they keep it to one place."

"Cheap bastards," the innkeep said, coming out and wrinkling his nose at the mess.

"Hey, now," said one of the guards.

"Not you, Jorry," the innkeep said. "I mean Alsop's people. None of 'em buy anything but the watered-down beer, but they all act like little lordlings, and then they do—*this*." He eyed Lyle. "I ain't one to jaw, but people talk when they're drinkin', and I heard Alsop ain't paid 'em in naught but promises for a fortnight."

Lyle and Marik exchanged a look.

"Might explain why they were desperate for a good song," Marik said.

"Might explain why they're desperate," Lyle said.

And if so, things may be more dangerous here than the Heraldic Circle thought.

Lelia staggered through the door and crumpled onto her bed. Several minutes later, she forced herself to pour a cup of water, draining it dry.

Her world narrowed down to the water cup as she poured and drank another. When she got to her third, she heard a knock on her door.

"Enter."

Lyle peeked in, his dark hair falling over his eyes.

She squinted at him. "Are you all right?"

"You didn't hear the brawl?"

She shook her head.

"Well, I survived," he said, wryly. Then, with more seriousness, "You look—"

"I'm fine," she lied. "It's been a while since I performed like that." *That* part, at least, was true. Lelia had been confined to Haven for over a year. She hadn't done a *real* performance in a *long* while, and though she'd practiced before they'd left on this trip, nothing replaced the raw energy of a crowd. "What did you learn?"

"Cyril's information wasn't wrong. There *is* an artifice that spins cloth," he said, pulling up a stool and sitting down. "Someone took a hammer to it. And the locals are definitely on edge."

She drank slowly. "And it was Alsop who requested an inquiry, right?"

He nodded. "He did. Looks like things have turned nasty since the initial request. I'll start asking questions tomorrow. Maybe just having me around will pour oil on the waters. Anyway, I'm off to the Waystation." She took another slow sip of water, and a faint crease appeared between his brows. "Are you *sure* you're all right?"

"Lyle." She tamped down on the annoyance in her voice.

"You look . . . *tired*."

"Okay, first—*rude*. Second, I'm *fine*. Go to your Waystation. We'll regroup in the morning."

He kissed her forehead. "See you then."

The door shut, and she listened for the sound of bell-like hooves receding in the distance.

Certain he'd departed, she reached into her saddlebags and took out a velvet pouch. Her hands shook a little as she crushed herbs into her cup and poured water over. It would steep overnight and hopefully in the morning keep her from collapsing in a heap of pain.

Then Lelia shuttered her lantern and went to bed.

Lelia scarcely paid attention as Lyle and Guild Mistress Murreil discussed the business at hand. She leaned against a wall and prayed the thumping in her head would someday cease.

She'd woken up, chugged the sludge in her cup, and crawled back in bed until her body had more or less cooperated. A *lot* of her mornings started this way: glass of sludge, followed by bartering with the pitiful bag of meat and bones she called a "physical form" these days. She'd been fine on the ride to Brightneedle, but it seemed the moment they'd gotten somewhere her body deemed "safe" it had planted the war flag. Her fingertips constantly felt like someone was sticking her with multiple tiny, hot needles, and she'd lost all feeling in her toes.

"Alsop's just a low-life lordling," the Guild Mistress said. "He came to town last year, built his warehouse and artifice, and then expected *us* to work it for less than apprentice wages." Her eyes flashed. "For cloth I wouldn't dress a poxy chicken in."

They'd met her in her upstairs office at the guild hall. An impressive building on the river, it housed the large, multiple-person looms that wouldn't fit in a croft. Below her, Lelia could hear weavers working at tapestries and massive rugs, singing work songs. The kind of songs she knew—as a Master Bard—but rarely sang.

"So he hired those men instead," Lyle said.

Murreil shook her head. "He brought in children. Tedrel orphans."

Lyle furrowed his brow. "He got . . . children . . . to work that thing?"

She nodded.

"What do the *adults* do?"

"Guards and builders, mostly. And get in fights with my people, who don't much like the idea of someone spinning shit cloth and pretending it's worth the price of gold-threaded samite."

Lelia closed her eyes, listening to the song below. She recognized it. She realized suddenly she recognized *all* the songs they sang. A note of disquiet ran through her.

Later, at a quiet table back at the Spindle, Lelia ordered drinks and said, "We have a *very* big problem. While you were talking to her, I was listening to the weavers in the guild hall. They were singing 'Nelly Fain.'"

Lyle shook his head. "I need more context."

"It's a little ditty about a weaver—Nelly Fain—who works under a cruel master. He beats her, sells her works without sharing the profits—and then she acquires a hammer and bashes his skull in."

He grimaced, sipping his ale. "Maybe it's just a coincidence."

"It is *not* a common song, Lyle."

"Maybe here it is?"

"Lyle."

"Okay." He held his hands up. "We clearly need to act quickly. Alsop's predilection for employing children is what disturbs *me*."

"Why? Cheap labor. Sounds like Alsop." She sniffed her mug of tea.

"You haven't seen the contraption." His gaze got distant. "A child . . . inquisitive, impulsive, near that thing when it's in motion . . ." He shuddered.

She took a sip of her tea. "So where *are* they—"

The tea went down the wrong pipe. In a normal body, this wouldn't have been a problem. But *she* found herself seized by a coughing fit so violent she slammed the mug down and yanked a handkerchief out of her coat, putting it to her mouth.

It eventually passed, but Lyle had a look of worry on his face. "Are you all right?"

"Fine," Lelia gasped, clearing her lungs. She knew without looking that there would be blood on the kerchief.

"'Lia."

"I'm *fine*." She stood up. "Good night."

Oh, how much longer are you going to be able to convince him, Lelia? she thought. *You could be the greatest Bard in the world, but you know your twin will always see through it in the end.*

An unexpected visitor found Lelia at the Spindle the next day: Alsop's steward, Galton.

"Milady Bard," he said, bowing to her. "My lord would like to retain your services."

"Oh?" she said.

"Milord hasn't had *proper* entertainment in ages. He would be honored if you would come out to his estate. *With* compensation."

This is actually—useful, she thought. "I'd love to! Let me get my things."

Rivan had settled himself in the Spindle's stables while his Chosen puttered around town; she approached him while her palfrey was saddled.

"I'm going to Alsop's estates," she said. "I should be back tonight."

He nodded his understanding.

Alsop lived in an estate outside town. The ride there did not take long, and as they curved down the final stretch of road, Lelia caught a whiff on the breeze: strong and musky, with a hint of urine. In the distance, she heard what sounded like a hundred dogs barking.

Because it *was* a hundred dogs. Easily. A whole pen of brown, white, and black hound dogs with a large kennel house attached. They bayed excitedly as she and Galton passed.

As Lelia watched, a woman in green emerged from the kennel house. The dogs jumped all over her as she wrestled her way through them and out the gate.

Inside the manor, Lelia paid attention to the furnishings and decorations and found them . . . wanting. At first glance they might pass muster, but a closer look revealed sun-faded curtains and tapestries, worn rugs, furnishings with dings and scrapes that hadn't been properly repaired, and all of it of a fashion that hadn't been in style since Sendar's reign, possibly before.

"What charming furnishings," she said to Galton as he took her to a salon off the entrance.

"Alsop family heirlooms," Galton said, too curtly, and left her to check her tuning.

Several people filtered in, including Alsop. The woman in green arrived, and Lelia overheard her say in halting Valdemaran, "Pup. Sick."

"You're the Healer," Alsop said coolly. "Heal it."

The woman frowned. "Sick. Cough." She added in a southern dialect, "I need to go to town for herbs."

"You know I don't speak your language," Alsop snapped.

"Well, *I* do," Lelia said. "She needs to go to town for herbs."

Heads turned. Lelia continued, in the woman's language, "Are you Alsop's Healer? You can Heal animals, too? What a blessing."

"I haven't spoken freely to someone else in months," she said.

"Hemmi tends to the kennels," Alsop said. "A condition of me leasing the estate. She's also why you're here. She begged me to bring you when she learned a Bard was in town. She is parched for music."

Lelia smiled and said, "Well, let's see what we can do about that."

Her small concerts were not the same as the ones she did in bigger venues like an inn. She kept the tunes personal, less rowdy, though never dour. Everyone enjoyed a Bard—even Alsop lightened up as she played—and Hemmi glowed like the sun.

"Milady?" she said at one point. "Do you know 'The Bird, the Bear, and the Bee'?"

Hemmi's face lit up as Lelia strummed the first notes. She slipped a few chords, but part of being a Bard of her caliber meant making the mistake *part* of the performance. Everyone clapped—not polite claps, but enthusiastic, cheerful claps—and Hemmi quite abruptly burst into tears.

Alsop turned, annoyed. "Get ahold of yourself."

The Healer stumbled out of the room, sobbing.

"Is something amiss?" Lelia asked.

"Homesick," Alsop said. "Thank you, Bard. It's been lovely." He gestured to his steward. "Galton will see you out."

As the steward walked her to the door, Lelia could feel the familiar ache soaring up her fingers and arms. She rubbed her wrists and flexed her fingers, but it all hurt.

Even so, no amount of pain made her forget the obvious question every Bard must ask, "So, about payment—"

"Milord does not have funds on him now," Galton said, a little too quickly, with the same curtness he had used earlier. "I will see that you're paid later this week."

Unh-huh. She'd been in this business too long. She *knew*

that tone. "Well, see that he does. I'd hate to have to get the Bardic Circle involved."

His eyes flickered. "Of course not, milady."

Hemmi appeared, seemingly out of nowhere, startling her and Galton. "Milady Bard!" she said, speaking rapid-fire in her language. "I could not let you go without thanking you for your performance!"

Lelia grinned. "You're welcome!"

She towered over Lelia, and it occurred to the Bard just how *muscular* the woman was. But she probably had to be, to work with all those dogs. She seemed to take note of how Lelia flexed and rubbed her wrists and fingers.

Before Lelia could stop her, the Healer had seized her hands in hers. A flood of Healing poured through her.

Oh, you're supposed to ask! Lelia thought. *Is this an Out-Kingdom thing? Do they not teach ethics to OutKingdom Healers?*

Hemmi stiffened, her eyes widening. Galton watched, one eyebrow lifted, his mouth set in a harsh, clinical line.

"Milady?" Hemmi whispered. "Milady, you are . . ."

Lelia smiled, a little sheepish. "You can let go now," she said. "There's nothing else you can do. Others have tried. It's just stalling the inevitable, now."

Hemmi's hands dropped to her sides. Tears glimmered in her eyes.

"Why are you *here*, milady? You should be—elsewhere. Resting."

Lelia considered the question. How much truth to give her? She decided on a little. "I wanted to spend time with my brother. He's a Herald—do you know what that is?" Hemmi shook her head. "Heralds do the Queen's work, but they're *very* busy." She half-smiled. "I had an opportunity to come with him, to help make peace here in Brightneedle. I don't have many opportunities to do good deeds, and I wanted to be there when he did what he does. But you're a Healer. I assume you know what it's like to do good, yes?"

Hemmi looked down at Lelia's hands. "Yes."

Lelia looked back at Galton, who seemed increasingly agitated that they spoke in a language he didn't know. She switched back to Valdemaran. "I look forward to that payment, sir."

"Of course," Galton said, with a smile like his face was made of slightly warmed wax.

She rode back alone in the late afternoon sunlight, quick at first to avoid the musky odor of the kennels, and then slow—enjoying the coolness on her face, and the joy of simply being.

Lyle found his twin back in her rooms, retired early and with no plans to perform that night. She ordered up some food for him, and they exchanged the day's information as he ate.

"No sign of the children," she said. "Also, he doesn't own his estate. He's leasing a hunting lodge under condition of taking care of the owner's dogs. The whole place looks like he's on his last penny."

Lyle nodded. "That tracks. He hasn't paid wages in a fortnight. He's insinuated to all his men the weavers are to blame—that they sabotaged his artifice, and if they hadn't, they'd all be rich as lords now. It's part of what's got everyone riled up."

"Gods." She gnawed her lower lip. "I think he poured all of his money into this damned contraption of his, and it's cost him *everything.* Lyle, *what if he broke it himself?*"

The Herald furrowed his brow. "Then why so insistent on Truth Spell?"

"I don't know!" She waved her arms around. "Maybe *he* has a twin brother and he'll have him testify in his stead! Then he circumvents the Truth Spell and—"

"'Lia, that's *crazy.*"

"But it would *work.*"

Lyle opened his mouth, then shrugged, conceding the point. "I feel like you have invested *considerable* mental effort into working this out."

"You would be amazed at the number of story-songs I have half-composed on the road that you will *never* hear."

He chuckled. "Well, I guess I'm left with little choice."

"Going to Truth Spell the whole damned town?"

He nearly choked on the last of his ale. "You've mistaken me for a Herald of greater talent. We can start with Murreil and Alsop—"

"Or his twin," she muttered.

"Jannus," he said firmly, "and go from there. If we do it publicly, it *should* quell the impending riot."

"Fine, fine." She wiggled her brows. "Let's get to quelling."

Lyle chose the town green, the only reasonable neutral ground he could think of. Marik offered to round everyone up.

"But, Herald," he said, "I got my opinions."

"Let's hear 'em."

Marik shrugged. "Just feels like Alsop's trying to set Murreil and the weavers up somehow."

"It does work in Alsop's favor if Murreil isn't around."

"Sure does." Marik kicked a rock. "Anyway, we'll see what tomorrow reveals."

Buoyed on a wave of cautious optimism, he headed to the Copper Spindle for breakfast. He expected to find Lelia there, but instead found the innkeep talking to a tall, red-headed woman in a green cloak.

The innkeep pointed to him, saying, "He's who you want."

She looked him up and down, and said, "Bard-brother?"

"Yes?" Lyle replied.

She shoved a pouch in his hands. "For sister," she said, firmly.

"Okay. Thank you?"

"Not you. Sister. Herbs. For sick. *Not. You.*" She poked him in the chest. "Make *you* sick. But not her. Understand?"

He frowned, shaking his head. "No."

She looked frustrated, then said something in a language he didn't know.

:Rivan, can you help?: All Companions had the Gift of Tongues.

He could sense his Companion "listening in," and then . . .

:*This is awkward.*:
:*What?*:
:*The herbs are to help Lelia. She says that Lelia is—*:

Rivan said words, but even as they ran through Lyle's head, it somehow didn't register. The shape of it felt all *wrong*. The idea that *that* might be happening to his sister just didn't make sense. That she wouldn't have *told* him—his twin—felt like a figures equation that didn't add up.

But other things did. The shadows under her eyes. How *thin* she looked. The coughing fit.

You seem . . . tired.

"Thank you," he said at last to Hemmi. "I'll go talk to her."

She breathed a sigh of relief before leaving. "Must go."

Lyle sat down, breakfast forgotten.

Lelia eventually crawled out of bed, got bathed and dressed, and made her way downstairs for a bowl of stew.

The moment she saw Lyle's face—a mixture of hurt and sorrow all wrapped up in one confused welter—she knew.

"Hellfires," she said.

"When were you going to tell me?" he asked.

"I wasn't," she said tersely, as she crossed over to the hearth and scooped herself a bowl from the blackened pot.

"*Why?*"

"Who told *you*?" She glared over her shoulder at him.

A shadow chased over his face, and then he tossed a pouch on the table. "Hemmi brought this today. To *help* you."

Lelia stared dumbly at the pouch. "Godsdamned OutKingdom Healers."

"Lelia, you can't be mad at her. She *thought I knew* because by all rights you *shouldn't be here*."

"Where should I be, then?!" she yelled, slamming her hands down on the table so hard her bowl danced, slopping stew everywhere. "Rotting in a bed? Waiting to die? I spend most of my days fighting my own body, Lyle. Why wouldn't I want one last chance to be with my twin?"

They glared at each other.

His voice had gone low and soft when next he spoke. "I wouldn't have brought you—"

"That's the *point*!" she yelled at him. "Are you even listening?"

"You need to go. For your own health. I'm just thinking about you."

"No, *you* need to go. I can't *talk* to you right now," she said, half-growling.

"Lelia—"

"Get! Out!"

She backed up the words with her Gift, an emotional shove that caught him totally by surprise—and sent him stumbling back, out the door of the Copper Spindle, and into the street.

"Just get out!" she yelled after him, so furious she could feel her eyes tearing up—and her head thundering.

Dammit, I've worked myself up.

Inside, she snatched up the pouch before retreating to her room, and the promise of cool darkness there.

Lyle struggled through a restless night, finally asking his Companion the question he didn't want the answer to.

"Am I wrong?"

Rivan took a long time to answer, then finally said, *:I think . . . you have just learned a very difficult thing, and that your sister kept something from you . . . but also, I think it* was *her secret to keep, and* her *privacy that was violated. She has a right to feel a little hurt and betrayed.:*

"So what you're saying is you want to stay out of it."

:Gods, yes.:

At the appointed time, Lyle went to the town green, dressed in his smartest Whites. Guards milled about warily. Murreil arrived in her black and gray, flanked by several equally well-dressed weavers. And Alsop with his bodyguards and steward. Hemmi, notably, was absent.

Time to start, he thought.

"After investigating the issue of the destruction of Lord Alsop's janni, I've decided to question some of you under Truth Spell," he said. "Guild Mistress Murreil, please step forward."

Lyle briefly shut his eyes as she approached, entering the light trance needed to enact the spell. A blue glow appeared around Murreil as he focused on her. "Are you in any way responsible for the destruction of Lord Alsop's property, either by your own hand or direct order?" he asked.

"No," she said. The glow remained steadfast and cheery.

"Do you know who is?"

"No."

Lyle transferred the spell to Alsop. "Lord Alsop—"

He stopped, remembering his sister.

"Your name *is* Jannus Alsop, yes?"

"Yes."

Lelia's going to be so disappointed. "Are *you* in any way responsible for the destruction of your own property, either by your own hand or direct order?"

"No!" Alsop said, indignant as ever.

The glow never wavered.

"What of the children?"

Alsop looked confused. "The children . . . ?" He looked over at Murreil. "Did you pester *him* about them, too?"

"It's a fair question," she said. "We've *all* wondered where they've gone, Alsop."

"'The children, what of the children?'" Alsop said in a nasal whine. "She hounds me on it constantly, like I'm some two-bit villain in a play. I gave them food and shelter, and a future beyond the Temple!"

Lyle saw again in his mind the blood on the artifice, the tiny footprints in the dust. "So where are they now, milord?"

Alsop's eyes shifted. "Back at the Temple," he said. "After my janni got brutalized by *someone*—" His glare swept the crowd "—I had no more use for them."

The glow remained. But something about his answer . . .

It seems like he's phrasing that response rather carefully.

:It's because he is,: Rivan said. *:And we have proof.:*

Lyle did his best to keep his face still, despite aching to raise a brow.

:We?:

Lelia hadn't moved much since yesterday, other than to find food, avoid Lyle, and turn herself into a human tea bag. She hated that she couldn't even have a good *cry* anymore without feeling like she'd been trampled by a herd of dyheli. The silent war within her body went on, and her usual course of herbs and soaking in hot water hadn't helped. She felt desperate.

After a while, she remembered Hemmi's bag. She reached over to the pouch and pried it open.

She found herbs—they smelled close to the ones she already had, with a few key differences—and a note, written in carefully formed Valdemaran characters.

She squinted at it in the dim light of her room.

"Check the kennels."

"Oh," she said. *"Oh."*

Pushing through the pain, she threw on clothes and scrambled out of bed and down the stairs.

Once again, she found Rivan in the Spindle's stables, waiting out the trial. "I need to find Alsop's Healer. I think she's at his estate. Can you help? It's about the investigation."

Lelia *knew* Companions were fast. She'd never been on one at full gallop. It felt like a blink of an eye, and they were at the estate.

The rank odor of the kennels made even Rivan pull up short. He shook his head and snorted, as if to say, *Really? Here?* Lelia insisted.

He got her close, and she slid off, walking up to the enclosure that separated the dogs from the rest of the world. The hounds bayed and bounced—eager for food and soft pets.

"Hemmi!" she yelled, putting the force of her Gift behind the shout.

The Healer emerged from the kennel house, blinking in the sunlight. The dogs immediately swerved and ran for her. She pushed through them and came to Lelia.

Lelia took her hands. "Hemmi, what's in the kennels?"

She cast her eyes down. "You found my note. I nearly didn't . . . but you seem like a good person. And I cannot do this anymore."

"What's 'this,' Hemmi?"

Hemmi's face crumpled. When she told Lelia, it felt like a chill wind had sucked all the color out of the air.

Lelia contemplated it a long time, then turned to Rivan. "You're the Companion," she said. "Can you get us both to the town green in time?"

He nodded. Hemmi cocked her head at him.

"Are you talking to a horse?" she said. "And did he—answer?"

"Yes. And that's because he's not a horse. But you are from OutKingdom and don't know that. Alsop *couldn't* have a Valdemaran Healer on staff. She'd have had him locked up so fast his head would have spun."

"I don't understand."

"No, you don't, and that's the point. I'll explain on the ride." Lelia grinned. "C'mon, Hemmi. Let's go do something good."

"Milord Herald," Murreil said, "who will you be questioning next?"

Lyle's gaze stayed fixed on Alsop, whose smug expression had begun to fade.

"What?" the lordling asked.

"Did you say you sent *all* the children back to the Temple?" Lyle asked. "I need you to be *specific*."

Alsop went pale. "I . . . I don't see what this has to do with who broke my janni!"

Just then he heard the sound of bells—Rivan's hooves. With Lelia on his back—and Hemmi.

:Lelia says to move the Truth Spell to Hemmi,: Rivan said, as the Healer slid off to stand, head high, back straight. Alsop glared at her, his jaw grinding.

Lyle moved the cloud.

Lelia cleared her throat, and then said, "I'm going to question Hemmi, Lord Alsop's Healer."

"Now, hold on—" Alsop said.

"The Healer will speak!" Lyle said.

Alsop shut up.

In Valdemaran, Lelia said, "I am explaining Truth Spell to her," followed by words in Hemmi's language. The Healer nodded.

"Now I am asking if she broke the janni."

Hemmi responded. The blue cloud never wavered.

Lelia took a deep breath. "Hemmi says yes."

"What?" Alsop says. "What—no. No, it was the weavers!"

Murreil snorted. "I told you it wasn't."

"It has to be!" He looked from Hemmi to the Herald to the gathered masses, incredulous. "It *has to be*!"

Lelia felt strangely calm, despite the thunder in her head. Sitting astride a Companion and being able to look out over the crowd helped.

"Tell him," Hemmi said with quiet determination, as Lelia translated. "Tell him I could not keep seeing children come to me with mangled hands." The crowd grew hushed. "I thought by Healing them I could make it good, but I see now. I am complicit."

The Healer wept, twisting her hands as if wringing a cloth out. Murreil's eyes burned with hatred in Alsop's direction. For his part, the lordling merely looked confused, as if someone had yanked the rug out from under him and left him spinning in space.

"I did not know the laws or ways here," Hemmi said. "In hindsight, this is *why* he hired me."

Alsop said, "We can stop talking to her now."

"We could do that," Lelia said. "Milord, would you like to answer what's in the kennels?"

Alsop turned the color of chalk.

"No? I'll ask Hemmi, then, since she practically lives there."

Hemmi cleared her throat and said a word. Lelia repeated it back.

"Children."

An uproar went up. Alsop looked around, frantically, shouting, "*Come* now. She *Healed* them. They're *fine*. Better than when they scraped by in the Temple! A few—minor, I assure you, *minor!*—injuries for larger progress, and if I get enough time, *no one* gets hurt."

His bodyguards stepped away, shaking their heads. One yanked his tabard off, muttering, "Not worth it."

"The janni is *important*!" Alsop yelled. "I just need time to adjust it and figure out where it went wrong. You don't understand!"

"Oh, I think we do," Lyle said. "Congratulations, you got your Truth Spell."

He nodded to Marik, who stepped forward with a grim smile. "You're under arrest, milord."

The Brightneedle weavers made a bonfire of the janni and Alsop's livery, but the twins didn't join them around it, retiring instead to the Spindle's hearth and a warm mug of Hemmi's tonic for Lelia.

The estates had been turned into a makeshift orphanage while they sorted out what to do with the children. Lyle's suspicion had proved out: *some* of the children *had* gone back to the Temple. But fully half had been retained, kept in horrible conditions in the kennels. Most had to have their hair completely cut off, it had become so matted and infested with fleas and ticks.

Lyle intended to follow up with the Temple who had exchanged the children with Alsop, though Lelia didn't expect much to come of it. On paper, his offer had no doubt sounded decent—a career with room and boarding. He'd left out the details about the hand-crushing machine and the *conditions* of their housing.

Alsop was in the business of taking advantage of others, Lelia thought. *The Temple is just another link in that chain.*

Hemmi volunteered to take the children back to Haven, where she would also accept judgment from the Healing Circle. "My ignorance of the customs here has scarred them for life," she said. "I may spend my own life atoning."

Lyle came to sit beside his sister. They still hadn't spoken since that day, not really, and she dreaded every conversation between them. It felt like someone had wrapped a chain around her chest, and she hated it.

"So," he said, sipping the ale the innkeep had handed him.

"I'm dying," she said.

"And the Healers . . ."

"Can only slow it, not stop it."

"When did you plan on telling me?"

She shrugged. "How good are you at talking to ghosts?"

"Wretched. 'Lia—"

"This is why I didn't tell you. Do you feel it? You've changed. You're treating me *differently*. I didn't want that. I wanted to pretend it was all still *normal*. I didn't want this." She scratched an inn cat behind the ears. "Why can't we just go back to how things were?"

He put his arm around her shoulders, pressing his forehead to hers.

"Nothing has ever been normal with us, you know that," he said. "You're right, it *is* different. We can't change that. But I'll adjust because I love you, and I want to be here for you, like I always have."

Tears slid silently down her cheeks, and she resented every one. "I'm so mad at my body, Lyle," she said. "It's not fair. We should have longer."

He kissed her forehead.

"So, when are you going to tell our parents?" he asked.

"I will haunt you," she hissed.

They arranged for separate transport of the children and prisoner, and next day left Brightneedle together.

A candlemark down the road, Lelia suddenly swore, slapping her hands together.

"What?" Lyle asked.

"Alsop never paid for that performance."

Lyle snorted.

"He owed me! You can't pay for ale with kindness, Lyle!" she said.

"Not true. *I* didn't pay for a single ale in Brightneedle."

She smirked. "That's because *I* did."

"What?" He recoiled. *"Why?"*

She shrugged. "I wanted to do something nice for you."

"You didn't *have* to. Most people buy Heralds drinks!"

"True. But just because you're a Herald doesn't mean that innkeep didn't deserve to be paid for his work."

He mulled this for a bit. "Well, *now* I feel guilty for every time someone's bought me an ale."

"Don't. Doing something nice for you meant doing something nice for *him*, too. And worthy causes rarely pay well."

"There's no poetry in your honesty today," he said. "But to be fair, I wouldn't be happier doing anything else with my life."

"Well, dear brother, that is why you got Chosen and I—"

"Yes?" he asked, archly.

She smirked. "Get *paid*."

"Except in Alsop's case."

"Well, just this once," she said, "I'll take his arrest as payment in kind."

A Determined Will
Paige L. Christie

Teig had been preparing for her final tests to move on into Palace Guard training when the sad letter arrived.

Old Belton. She'd always called him that, but she'd never thought of him as old enough to die. So when she opened the letter from Sweet Springs, and read the words that meant she'd never again be able to have dinner with him, or ask his advice, or be chastened with subtle amusement for something foolish she'd done, Teig just sat on the edge of her bed and stared at the message. Sat and stared until the evening meal had come and gone, and Delvin came looking for her. Only then did she cry. And cry and cry.

And she cried again now, standing in the doorway of Belton's tiny house above town, unable to imagine that the stale silence greeting her was permanent. And it was hers—the silence, the house, everything within. She pulled the letter from the pocket of her blue jacket and read again the words that declared it so.

When we went through his lock box, we found the deed to the house. It had your name on it, as well as his. We checked with the land office. He changed it three years ago. It's yours, Teig. We've sent a copy of his will. He left you everything. No one ever doubted what you meant to him, and this is no surprise. Come home when you can so we can hug you.

She read it twice, still unwilling to believe it—mostly because doing so would mean Belton was truly gone. But he was, and standing here proved it.

She gazed across the room toward the painting of the Collegium that hung over the mantel, and at the smaller portraits that topped it. One was of Belton as a young man, dressed in the Guard Blue. The other was of her, in her first training uniform. He'd been so pleased when she sent that to him . . .

She moved through the tiny house, fingertips touching furniture, trying not to sneeze at the thin layer of dust. He'd been gone long enough that everything was covered by it. Everything but the patch of floor leading to the tall bookshelf beside the fireplace. She stared at the footprints, half-again the length of her own, and then followed them to the shelf.

Long afternoons she had spent in this house, before she was accepted to the Collegium, and she knew every book and keepsake on the shelf. They had all been moved, touched, and examined. The streaks in the dust showed that. But only one was missing: the worn, brown journal that contained Belton's personal thoughts. Not a diary, as such. He was never regular in recording his musings, but important things, events, secrets, those went into it. Everything special he had learned at the Collegium. He'd promised to show her those parts the next time she came home. She'd wanted to compare how things were done in his day to what she was learning. But that wasn't possible now.

Who could have taken it? Any number of people. But why? That was more important.

She frowned through her tears. Mero, maybe? Or someone else from town? Someone discreet enough to want to keep his secrets, even now that he was gone. Especially now.

With another glance around the room, Teig wiped at her eyes. She'd come here before stopping in town proper with the intention of spending the night, spending some time with her memories of her friend before seeing anyone else, but now something pulled tight knots across her shoulders and she gave a small shiver.

Tonight was best spent at the inn, with those she loved who were still among the living.

By the time Teig got to town, her emotions were mostly under control. She took her horse to the stable, tossed her pack over her shoulder, and headed for the inn.

Mero looked up when Teig came through the door, and for a heartbeat the innkeeper's expression held the carefully pleasant welcome that marked her profession, then recognition flashed into her eyes and her face split into a smile edged with just a hint of sadness. *I'm glad to see you* it said, *but I am sorry for what brought you back here.* And something else as well, something uneasy and tinged the slightest bit with anger.

She came around the registration table and crossed the entryway to wrap Teig in a warm embrace, but the words she whispered were not of comfort or greeting, but rather a warning. "We've got trouble, dear heart, enough to interrupt all our sadness."

A start went through Teig, even as she returned the hug. After what she'd seen at Belton's house, this was not good news at all. She pulled back and looked at the woman who'd raised her. What she saw in Mero's face pulled Teig's spine a little tighter, snapped her guard-trained mind to alertness. Nothing outside the inn had spoken to a threat to Sweet Springs as a whole, so whatever was wrong, the issue was immediate and probably more personal. "Danger? Are you all right? Is Wilhem?" She had to make sure of that before she concluded for certain this had anything to do with Belton.

Mero nodded crisply and shifted her hands to squeeze Teig's upper arms. "Yes, we're both fine. But a . . . complication . . . has arisen for you."

"Complication?" Teig asked, as though repeating the word would somehow bring her understanding without the need for explanation. What more complication could there be in her life at the moment than the loss of her friend and first mentor?

"Yes, indeed," Mero said. She turned a little and slid an arm around Teig's shoulders, hugging her close to the side. "Come. Wilhem and I will get you fed, and I'll explain."

At that, Teig relaxed a little and leaned into the older woman. As long as Wilhem was still willing to feed everyone, things couldn't be as bad as all that.

They walked through the familiar space, the scent of waxed floors and warm ale and stews comfortingly embedded in the dark wood. A few patrons occupied tables, laughing and talking with a lightheartedness Teig wished she too could feel. She shook off the thought and slipped into the kitchen with Mero.

At the stove, Wilhem looked over his shoulder. His face lit up, but the same touch of discomfort Mero had shown hung in his expression. He put down his spoon and turned to fully face them as Teig moved away from Mero and stepped forward to hug him. He grasped her tighter than she could ever recall him doing.

Her unease increased. After years of chiding and gentle correction brought on by the troubles her imagination and bluntness brought to most situations, this gentle concern was unnerving.

Teig stepped back, kept her hands on Wilhem's shoulders. She took a deep breath, glanced at Mero, and told them what she'd found at the house up in the hills.

Her news offered no relief to the tension, though they seemed unsurprised, as though she was bringing them more confirmation of what they already knew. Their faces grew more somber, tightened around the eyes.

"Right," she said. "Serve up some plates of whatever is smelling so delicious in here and tell me what's going on."

Wilhem sighed. "He arrived two days ago, with Belton's death notice in one hand and a contract from a Haven solicitor in the other. Said his name is Larud, and that he's Belton's grandson. Said by all rights, what Belton had should belong to him."

"Wait," Teig said, waving her fork before her, the chopped meat on her plate forgotten. "Belton had children? *Grand*children?"

In all the years she'd known the old man, he had never mentioned family beyond an older sister, dead several years past, and his own parents. No wife or children, no nieces or nephews, no cousins thrice removed, or any other relations.

"Not that anyone in Sweet Springs knew of." Mero shrugged.

"But he spent those years in Haven when he was training . . . and something could have . . . happened . . . there."

The hesitation in Wilhem's voice brought a smile to Teig's lips, but before she could respond, Mero said, "Oh, stop, Wil. You're no purer than I. Men and women can have lovers, and a 'happening' is more likely than a secret marriage."

Teig stifled a laugh at Wilhem's slight blush. As awkward moments went, it was a small one, but it helped lighten the shock tickling the back of her skull.

"Woman, I know what *happens* to make such things, well, *happen*, but if Belton had an inkling he was a father, much less a grandfather, he'd have said something."

"He would, at that," Mero agreed. She looked at Teig. "And that's why we're not sure what to make of his claim, Teig. The only papers Belton left with the clerk here say you get everything there is to get. This Larud's papers say otherwise, but where did they come from? Some office in Haven with a bunch of fancy legal writers. How are any of us here to know what's real and what's made up for greed?"

Teig shook her head, paused, then shook it again. "What exactly do these papers say? Does anyone know?"

"Oh, yes." Mero pushed her chair back and got to her feet. "This Larud left us a set. Copies. Said he knew you'd be coming here." She headed for the small office tucked behind the kitchen.

"It's a complicated contract." Wilhem's voice was sorrowful.

Teig speared a portion of the food on her plate and forked it into her mouth, thinking as she chewed. "You keep saying 'contract.' Not 'will.' Why?"

"Well, that's a good question," Wilhem mused. "I guess because that's what it reads like. More than a list of what and who gets. Reads like a sales document."

"Like a deed? Or a bill of purchase?"

"More the latter. Like the purchase of a whole business and all the accounts and files associated with one. Like if someone took over here, and got all the files and contacts and such."

How did that make any sense? The copy of the document she had received was simple, but three pages with a list of what Belton owned and that it all went to her, one page taken up by his signature and that of witnesses, and the seal stamp of the town clerk.

She pulled them out and handed them to Wilhem. "Not like these?"

He shook his head. "No. Those are what we all write up here in Sweet Springs. That's the way it's done here. Orn and Blanch often witness things, in fact, because they're always in town and easy to find."

That made sense. Almost no one was easier to seek out than the blacksmith and his wife. And their shop and home were just steps from the town offices.

Mero reappeared, crossing the room with determined strides, her skirts swishing. She set a sheaf of papers beside Teig's plate and dropped back into the chair. "Maybe you can make sense of it."

Teig pushed her plate aside and pulled the papers in front of her. The language was bold and flowery, with lots of 'wherebys' and 'therefores' and 'in the matter ofs.' In no way did it resemble what she had received. But which was more usual? She didn't have the experience to know. And what was usual for Sweet Springs might be very different from what was usual in the capital. How to know? And how to know which was more valid?

"Where can I find this Larud?"

Wilhem answered. "He went to the town office this morning. You can't miss him. He's wearing purple. *All* purple."

Teig tipped her head. "Purple? No one wears only purple."

"You would think not," Mero agreed, and smiled the first smile Teig had seen from the other woman this day.

"All right," she said, returning the grin as she imagined just how bold Larud must be. That almost felt like a clue of some sort, but to what she wasn't certain. A ripple of anger went through her, but she was no longer the furtive child she had been, and she contained the emotion.

Instead, she sorted the papers into a neat pile, picked them up, and stood. "I'll be back."

It should have been the easiest thing in the world, to find someone dressed completely in purple, and it was. She was only halfway down the street toward the town office when she spotted the man she was looking for.

The people of Sweet Springs had their own love for bright colors, but in specific places and specific amounts. In no way did they dress with the flamboyance of the man walking toward her. His shirt and pants were not only bold purple, they billowed, the fabric light and flowing. His boots and belt were a half shade darker than the fabric, and polished to a reflective sheen, as was the satchel slung over his shoulder. And the hat. The hat was something from a child's fantasy. Something, in fact, that she might have dreamed up in her youth, with a triple-wide brim and a height that from the mean-minded would demand mockery. Something about the whole outfit was so ridiculous as to almost be familiar. She was almost surprised to see, as she drew closer, that his beard wasn't dyed to match.

In fact, his beard was hardly a beard at all. It was scraggly and slightly desperate and—he was barely her own age! The realization stumbled the angry determination filling her. What in the world was going on?

Stepping in front of him, she held up a hand both to greet and to stop him. "Hello. I'm—"

"Teig. Yes, who else would you be?" His gaze, as dismissive as his words, swept her up and down. His accent was pure Haven. "My rival. I hope you don't plan to fight my claim."

The disconnect between his appearance and the arrogance of his tone and words started a headache behind her eyes. Her training kicked in. And suddenly the situation, in her mind, went from a problem to be solved to something more worrisome. Whatever this was, it went beyond an inheritance claim, because that could have been filed without any pageantry.

"Oh, I do plan to," she said. "And I plan to find out who you really are." Why she added the last bit, she wasn't certain, except that this strange man-boy had been expecting her, and why would that be the case?

Mero had said Larud knew she would be coming. And it certainly seemed that he had. How?

"I wish you wouldn't. It's so little to fight over."

"Enough that you're here to do so."

"Yes, well, you've got your whole life taken care of, what with your soon to be living in the palace and all. I don't figure you need any of this."

"And you do?" She stared at him, trying to see through the barrage of his clothing to find any resemblance to Belton. Was it true there was none that she could see, or was she just so distracted by his outfit she could barely see anything else? No. She was trained now to notice details in a way that went beyond her own imaginings, and this person bore no resemblance to the man she had known. Not even to the portrait of Belton as a young man that sat on the mantel of the house in the hills.

"Who are you, really?" she asked.

"I'm Belton Narr's grandson. He met my mother in the pleasure district when he was a student at the Collegium."

Teig folded her arms, aware that a couple small knots of people had gathered at the edges of the street to watch the encounter. "And it took your mother forty years to speak of who your father was?"

Larud rolled his eyes. "I've known since I was a boy."

A boy? Wasn't he still a boy, in the ways she was a girl? Just far enough from the edge of maturity that the youthful titles still applied . . . "And you've just been waiting for him to die so you could come here and claim everything he owned? You never bothered to write him a letter? Never tried to travel here to meet him?"

"Who says I didn't?" Larud's voice pitched itself a fraction higher than his previous words. "You lumpy donkey lizard! How dare you?"

Donkey lizard? Teig pulled a breath into her lungs and let it out slowly. "I say so," she said. "Because he would have told me." She lifted the bundle of papers. "And these are nothing like the documents marked by the clerk of this town. Nothing like the ones *witnessed* by people who knew Belton for years!"

"Well, weasel kicker, you'll just have to see what that very clerk has to say about my claim!" Larud said, straightened himself, and walked around her in the direction of the Inn.

Teig pivoted to watch him go, her brow furrowed, more puzzled than she could ever remember being. Larud had been to see the clerk already. Could it be that his claim somehow *was* legitimate? Legitimate enough that he felt comfortable insulting her in the most childish way? There was only one way to know. She started again toward the town office, her thoughts still tripping as though she could answer the looming questions with pure force of will.

From Haven, Mero had said . . . *Hmmm* . . . Why would a mysterious heir know anything about Teig at all? How would he even know she existed? Who was he?

An unknown child of an unknown lover who managed to learn enough about his parentage to take advance action to achieve an inheritance? Someone who had seen Belton's death notice and decided to forge documents on the fly? Someone who knew enough about *her* past to factor her into his plot to gain . . . what? All Belton's 'riches'? A small house in a small town where he might be resented for seeming to take an inheritance from one of its own? If the claim wasn't real, what was the point of any of this? Teig's mind skipped through possibilities, each more strange and unlikely than the last.

Or were they? It wasn't as though she was the quietest mouse ever to roam the streets of Haven and the halls of the Collegium. Especially since she kept finding herself involved in strange occurrences, from assassination attempts to the mysterious relocation of farm animals. And she'd made no secret that

Belton's support and encouragement were a large part of the reason she was in Haven at all.

She considered Larud's clothing again, and something tingled in her head. What if she had spoken so often and so fondly of Belton that she had unwittingly made the old man the target of some scheme? What if her hard-won good luck had looked to another like somehow-unearned success? Could it be that her praise of the old guard made it seem like he had more, was more financially and politically important, than anyone in Sweet Springs was ever likely to be?

She forced herself back into the moment as she yanked open the town office door. Inside, she followed signs to the clerk's office. When she stepped in, the man behind the desk, Clerk Dard, looked up from the paperwork scattered across the surface, saw her, and heaved a sigh.

"Teig. Have a seat. We have quite the mess before us."

"So I'm not the only one he's insulting. And you're telling me this is *real*? More real than the one you helped Belton himself write up? The one you sealed right here in this office?"

"No. I'm telling you that the documents he brought me are complicated enough to mean sorting all this out will not be an easy process. I can't imagine a sudden claim like his standing up to judgment. But by the time we get it sorted, you may wish you'd just handed everything over to the fellow."

"That's not what Belton would want me to do. He'd want what's right."

"And if this Larud really is his grandson?"

Teig sat back and folded her arms across her chest, her certainty that that was *not* the case warring with her ingrained sense of fairness. "Well, then, if he can really prove it, I'll happily share. But Belton left me all of it, as far as you know. And I think that means he'd at least want me to have *something*. Maybe his weapons. Or some books. But I'm positive that I'll not surrender everything in sight."

Dard nodded his graying head and tugged at his chin whiskers. "Given what he had to say about you the day he created that will, I can't help but agree. I've an appointment with Larud in the morning. Ten o'clock. Come back then. I'm going to re-search all I can about inheritance law in the meantime. Now if only a Herald would wander through, we could sort this with so much less suffering."

Teig laughed. "We can hope," she agreed.

Dinner at the inn was beyond awkward, with Larud across the room slurping stew with a gusto unwarranted by anyone, and Teig's banked anger gnawing at her belly until she couldn't eat at all. How could he sit here in Belton's hometown, among his friends, in sight of her, and just . . . eat? Finally, she got up and crossed the room to join him at his table.

The dining hall fell silent.

He met her gaze. "Well. You're like a lighthouse in the desert—trying to shine bright, but useless."

The childish insult bounced off Teig's senses with an almost audible ping, and suddenly her anger fled. How was this her rival for Belton's estate?

She snorted and choked back a laugh. "Are you supposed to be Lord Umplick Highball? That's that all you can think to say to me?"

"I just thought you'd be more entertaining. Instead, you mope with your friends and run to the clerk to save you. You're more disappointing than an unsalted pretzel."

"Un . . . salted *pretzel*?" And suddenly Teig knew exactly what was going on. She'd only heard that phrase in one place—the theater district of Haven. And only near one group of actors—the ones housed right around the corner from her favorite sweetshop.

The outfit Larud was wearing . . . Was it someone's idea of what country finery looked like? Something from ignorant ru-mor and old stories or . . . *the exaggerated costumes of street plays*? By all that breathed, it could *not* be that simple. "You're one of the Vandi!"

The boy flushed and sat up straighter and glanced around as though looking for prying eyes and ears. "The . . . what?"

"Oh, don't pretend! This is a test, isn't it? Like the one I have to take to get into the next level of training. *You* have to prove you can convince people—out in the real world—that you're a character you're not! In order to become a mainstage player and get out of the corner theaters. Right? Delvin told me about this."

"What are you on about? You—you gray sprinkle on a rainbow cupcake!" He reached down to the chair beside him and grabbed his hat. With a huff, he pulled it onto his head, rose, and, chin lifted, strode from the room.

Behind him, Teig doubled over with laughter.

She arrived at Dard's office well before the appointed time, with her copies of Belton's will under one arm, and a book on the theater culture of Haven under the other. Thank goodness Sweet Springs had an excellent library, and that Mero's friendship with the librarian had granted late-night access.

Teig and the clerk spent the time before Larud's arrival double-checking law books against all sets of documents and Teig's tome.

When Larud arrived, ten o'clock on the dot, he wore a blue outfit so bright it rivaled the sky on the brightest spring day. How much money had he spent on these getups? Especially the brightly dyed leathers? Or were they all stage props? No way to tell, and it was unlikely he would share.

"Does it count," she asked before he could even take a seat in the chair beside her in front of the desk, "if we tell your mentors that you fooled us enough to make us angry, and that you worried us enough to cost us sleep?"

"You are as sharp as wet bread," Larud replied, settling into the chair without looking at her. Instead, he met Dard's gaze expectantly. "Everything is in order, I assume?" A single bead of sweat crept out of Larud's hairline and wandered down his temple.

Teig smiled and let Dard pass on the bad news. "It is," he agreed. "Guard Teig will inherit."

The flush started at the very edges of Larud's face and swept inward like a backward-blooming flower. "I have—"

"You *have*," Dard interrupted, "a finely crafted legal forgery with a Vandi watermark on the lower left corner of the last page. See?" He shoved the paper across the desk and set a magnifying glass atop it. "Feel free to examine it yourself. It's an ancient mark, used for centuries, according to this book." He tapped the library volume Teig had brought on the desk beside him. "It's used to disclose the identity of the Vandi ordering up the prank in order to prove it was a joke all along and to defuse any legal repercussions."

Beside her, Larud's sweat droplet grew and expanded into a full soaking of his face and neck. As he spluttered, she got to her feet and went to open the office door. Outside, the local lawkeeper waited, ready to take the young man into custody to be held until a Herald passed through to render judgment.

Dard interrupted Larud's bubbling excuses. "Had you not shown up this morning, this could have been written of as a cultural coming-of-age trick. But you decided to press the rightful heir, and for that there are consequences." The clerk lifted his chin toward the door.

Larud turned in his seat and looked back at Teig and the serious-faced man beside her. "What gave me away?"

Besides everything? Teig thought but didn't say. Instead, she told him, "You took Belton's diary. And one thing I know he wrote down was everything about his time in Haven. And if he'd had a lover, he would have noted it there. You had to see if he'd written anything to counter your story. And he must have, or you would not have taken the book."

"My mother—"

"Whoever she is, please don't call her a night-time lady available for one-time adventures. One thing Belton was not was foolish enough to endanger his livelihood among the guard by taking to bed women he would need to pay." While not looked down upon, such activities were not encouraged. And Belton had always been one for the rules.

Though she would not have thought it possible, Larud flushed deeper.

"Where is the diary?"

Larud hung his head, blue hat flopping a little. "In my room at the inn."

Teig let out a breath. He hadn't destroyed it. If, in the end, he was too young to understand how obviously fake his persona had been, and too foolish not to keep his testing from drifting into greed, at least he had not been destructive in *that* way. He had held onto it.

And Belton had held onto belief in *her* and given her a future, not just at the Collegium or the palace, but one to some-day come home to as well, if she wished.

And she had, for too many days, held onto the worst of her grief.

She stepped aside and watched Larud taken into custody and led from the room. Then she smiled through sudden tears at Dard. "I'll come back tomorrow to finish what needs doing."

At his nod, Teig turned and left.

There were explanations to be given to Wilhem and Mero, letters to write to Haven, a diary to be retrieved, and, most importantly of all, a night to be spent in a house above town, communing with the memory of her friend.

The Ballad of Northfrost
Phaedra Weldon

Using his good arm, Herald Reyes dragged his battered body over the debris-strewn ground. Each shallow breath reminded him of the enemy's blade still lodged in his back. His searching fingers encountered scattered rock and grit in the pitch-black dark. When his knuckles scraped against a solid piece of rock, or his nails bent backward as he overreached the distance, he bore the pain and pulled his body forward the precious inch . . . because it was another inch away from where his attackers had left him.

He couldn't remain here in the dark. Viessa was in danger. He could not, would not fail to get himself out of this situation and protect her. He'd tried repeatedly to speak to Eshenesra, but there was only silence. He couldn't remember a time when his Companion had not answered. Was his call too weak to her? Was she too far away to hear him?

His left arm had been wrenched from its socket in the vicious fight. He had no memory of how many had attacked him, only that he'd been overwhelmed and knocked unconscious. Only the dull, throbbing ache in his head, the pain in his useless leg and arm, and the knife in his back told him how it had ended.

The one thing he clung to was the familiar male voice he'd heard when his torch was knocked from his hand.

"You shouldn't have come back." A voice from his youth, when he'd been a kitchen rat in a hold, an orphan, being fed bread and scraps to do the odd jobs no one else wanted to do. That voice had pursued him through the hold, intent on beating him. He'd only caught Reyes once, and that was a lesson fully learned by the younger boy.

He was named Brash Embers, who lived in the nearby village, and wasn't even a part of the hold that took care of Reyes.

Sharp, unyielding pain brought him back to his present situation. His breathing came heavy again as he tried again to push himself into a sitting position . . .

And failed.

He called out for help. For someone . . . to save Viessa. Someone to protect her. Reyes had tried to protect her since their first assignment together. Something she had resented.

Their small arguments had become loud, inescapable fights now.

No, no, no. Not the time to think about these things. He reached out again, though with less speed than before. Something rough and brittle met his fingers. He was sure he felt ash and charred wooden fragments—the remains of a long-dead campfire.

Which meant this was a place of rest. Or a meeting. A possibility he was closer to a way out than he thought. He needed light. Anything to define his position. Movement disoriented him—he wasn't even sure he was moving in a straight line.

He proceeded another inch or so before pain shot from his back to his shoulder. He cried out, his voice echoing against the darkness. The constant, searing pain reminded him again, as it always had, of the dangers of being a Herald.

Heralds never lived to a ripe old age. The brutal winnowing that thinned the ranks of Heralds frightened him.

He'd wanted Viessa to stay in Haven.

But she had misunderstood his concern, and again, they fought.

They always . . . fought.

Once more he attempted to reach out to Eshenesra, his Companion, and again, was met with a deafening silence. For the first time in a decade, he felt the cold loneliness of his forsaken childhood grip him, as tangible as his mother's voice echoing hauntingly in his mind.

"Get up and keep moving. I didn't raise my son to lay idle in the dirt."

Ever since waking in this tomb, that familiar rasp had tormented him, goading him onward as it had in the long years after she abandoned him to the howling wilderness in their flight from Karse.

"Hush . . ." he managed in a pained whisper as weariness threatened to drag his eyelids down once more. "You're naught but a fever dream . . ."

"I am the dream that keeps you living, my son. Yours alone to heed or ignore. Do not sleep! Do not succumb!"

But her voice went unheeded as delirium's claws pulled Reyes back into its feverish embrace, where visions of flame, the sounds of screams, and the beauty of a singular, kind woman in Whites danced in his memories.

Two days earlier

"I figured I'd have this meeting with you in private," Master Farthen said from his seat across the table from Reyes. It was midday, and the sun was just passing over the trees outside the Herald's Office window.

Farthen picked up a piece of paper and placed it on the desk in front of Reyes. With apprehension, he picked it up and scanned it, and then placed it back down, his index finger pushing it forward. "This is her decision?"

"She insists she can no longer work with you. And to be honest, many here would like a respite from your incessant bickering. She's firm in her decision." He held out his hand. "And I support her."

"I didn't realize my company was so . . . foul."

"It's not that, Reyes. It's the same as I've always said. No one knows you. You've never really cultivated any friendships, and you've managed to alienate the one Herald willing to work with you."

Reyes pushed his chair back and stood. He wore his usual Whites, and his gray hair was pulled back in a leather tie, with several errant strands brushing over his face. He clasped his hands behind him as he strolled to the sitting area by the bay window.

:My love . . . : He felt and heard the sympathy and adoration in her voice.

He sent loving thoughts to Eshenesra. *:Not . . . now, my dearest.:*

"There is," Farthen began, "a problem, though—something that's come up."

Reyes half-turned back to him. "This has something to do with the Bard found in the next town?"

Farthen chuckled as he stood and joined Reyes. "Nothing escapes you, as usual. And yes. Our information gatherers have worked quickly, since the boy's parents are demanding justice. We retraced his activities, and found he came from Whisper-winds."

Reyes looked at Farthen. "Where?"

"You would remember it as Northfrost Hold. They commence a celebration of sorts in two days—a sort of self-aggrandizing festival to show how they mitigated their own problems after the fire that took Northfrost, and have now established a town."

Reyes looked away, then turned his head to the window. Yes, he knew Northfrost Hold. It had been his home for six years—before the night of the fire, before the night of betrayal. He had known safety as well as danger there. He'd also learned many trades, as well as developed his culinary skills.

"Are the Ashcrofts still in charge?" he said, still looking out the window. He saw a bird, a gray one, with white accents on its wings.

"Yes. I thought you'd remember them. The town's two families, the Ashcrofts and the Embers, are the ones sponsoring this event."

"And our injured Bard?" Reyes held up his hand and concentrated as a bird the same size and shape appeared. A few more thoughts and it was an exact copy of the bird outside. It moved, hopped around on his hand, flicked its wings, but it made no sound. Illusions did not have a physical foothold in the world with all the five senses. To master that would indeed make one powerful. His could only be seen, not smelled, or heard, or felt.

"That is beautiful."

Reyes dismissed it. It disappeared in a puff of smoke. Another illusion. "The Bard was hired by Ashcroft to sing?"

"We've not heard from him directly, as he is still unconscious, and will be for some time. His parents said he was asked to write a song to commemorate the wedding."

Reyes tilted his head. "Wedding? I thought they were self-aggrandizing their cleverness?"

"There was a wedding the night of the fire. Yes, I was just as surprised. I only heard about the fire and the looting. The number of deaths in that conflagration was astounding. Almost everyone in that hold died."

Reyes heard the shouting in his memories, smelled the smoke, watched the ash fall like snow. "There was also a Bard who disappeared from there. That night."

"Ah, yes. Bard Cyrene. She was called there due to a death in her family. She never returned."

"You want me to find out what happened to both of them?"

"No, just the young man, Jenson Wilkes. Bard Cyrene's disappearance is more than ten years old. There would be very few clues left, and I don't want to prolong the two of you working together."

"Working . . . together?"

"Viessa has already left."

Reyes blinked. "You just explained, in great detail, that she doesn't want to work with me. Northfrost is a very dangerous assignment, sir."

"It's called Whisperwinds now. As for Viessa, she is a Herald, same as you. Riding Circuit is also dangerous—"

"Not like this, sir. Northfrost—I mean, Whisperwinds—isn't like other places. The guard doesn't operate there. They have their own rules."

"Reyes—"

"They're a fringe town, on the border. My experience has

taught me caution. She's not been on Circuit long enough." He hoped that excuse would placate Farthen.

"I understand your concern, but she wants to help people, and she loves her work, just as you do. You both have different ends to the means, and regardless of your little feud, you both have a successful completion record. Accompanying you is the last thing she is requested before I separate the two of you."

"Did she take a copy of knowns?"

"Yes. And I have a copy for you as well. Look . . ." Farthen put a hand on Reyes's shoulder. "You two are the best at finding resolutions to disagreements. I've read reports where I never believed there was a solution, but the two of you found one.

"But in the six months you've worked together, you've never been able to solve your own issues. So, this once, put this conflict between the two of you away and find out what happened to Jenson Wilkes. When you return, I can put you back on Circuit if you'd like."

The side of Reyes's mouth twitched, but he did not smile. "Of course."

Back to traveling.

Alone.

His coughing woke him. Reyes was lying on his front, his right arm asleep. He felt a little stronger, so he tried again to push himself up on his left knee. His right arm shook as he slowly rose. He gritted his teeth, grunted, and finally pushed himself onto his backside—and stayed there. He was sitting up on his own!

"That's it. You can do it."

Just . . . shut up. You're not real.

But he could see her. As real to him as was the darkness itself. She was squatted down next to him, like she had when he was small.

Reyes reached out with his right hand as dizziness took him. He didn't expect to find anything there, but his hand was stopped by something. He heard a crack, and something fell.

He quickly moved his hand away and kept reaching out until

he felt stone. Once the dizziness passed, he reached that same hand around his back and felt on the ground . . .

His fingers mingled with wet, moist dirt.

He brought it to his nose and smelled copper.

He was bleeding again . . . had probably been bleeding while he was out cold.

Taking in as deep a breath as his bruised ribs would allow, he felt along the floor near the wall until his hand found a long piece of wood. It was small at one end and then swelled larger and larger until the end was . . .

Sticky.

Pitch.

He pulled his hand back and grabbed the thinner end. He hoped this was his torch, the one they'd knocked from his hand. If that was so . . . then he was in the same place he'd been attacked and hadn't been moved. If the pitch was still there, it meant the torch hadn't burned down—right? Or did that mean it had?

His thoughts were too confusing. Too . . . mismanaged.

Ignoring his rising panic, Reyes set the stick down and started searching the pockets of his Whites. He'd meant to change out of them, but he'd also been afraid to return to his rooms before descending into the tunnels beneath what he had known as Northfrost.

In one of the pockets he found his flint and steel, and then had to figure out how to use them with only one hand. Thinking of no other way, Reyes reached over and took his left hand. He bit his lower lip as he screamed at the pain of bringing his left hand to his left inner thigh.

After he braced himself against the wall, he felt around for the stick and put the sticky end toward him and held the smaller end with his left knee. He'd long since closed both his eyes so he could concentrate on feel instead of straining to see. Luckily, the illusion of his mother remained silent.

Breathing even heavier than before, he braced one of the rocks with his left hand and struck it with a flint in his right hand. He had to open his eyes to see. Again he struck it and saw a brief spark, but with each strike it wrenched his left arm. Tears rolled down his cheeks, the only reaction he had left to the pain.

Abruptly the torch caught and flared, and Reyes had to scramble to get out of its way so that it wouldn't set his thighs on fire. But when he moved, he fell backward into the wall and felt the knife jolt and push deeper in.

He screamed.

Before leaving for Whisperwinds, Reyes returned to his rooms and started searching through his things. He hadn't accumulated much in the past ten years since coming to Haven. Most were books, writings, a few musical instruments he wanted to learn, as well as notebooks. He loved empty notebooks he could fill with his musings on negotiations, jot down facts in about rivalries. And learn.

Always learning.

Now that he was returning to a place he'd called home for nearly six years, he thought of a single piece of paper. It had neat, script writing on it, the lyrics of a song, written in verse form, with no music written to it.

A piece of paper important enough for him to save for ten years, integral to a place in his past. He found it tucked inside the notebook he'd used with the other Illusionist, and the missing blue stones.

He pulled it out and was re-memorizing the lines when Eshenesra told him she was ready. And so was he.

The festival was in full swing when Reyes arrived the next morning. Colorful streamers hung from every pole, stalls with games and food lined the main square, street performers abounded, with a singer at every corner, and in the center of the town square was a dais with nothing on top of it.

Most towns, hamlets, or even villages, placed historic figures in the town's center. Perhaps placing something in the center was part of the festivities?

Reyes was stopped by a few people and asked why a Herald was here.

"Just here to enjoy the festivities," he'd said with a forced smile.

"Ah, then welcome to Whisperwinds. Wondering what the dais is for?"

"Yes."

"That has been the topic of many arguments. Some believe it should be the town's founders, Ashcroft and Embers. Others believe it should be a visage of Cyrene."

That was not a name he'd expected to hear. "That's the Bard who disappeared the night of the fire."

"And the wedding," the passerby said. "Eyewitnesses all said she was key in guiding many of the inhabitants of Northfrost out of the hold. They removed the last of the walls just a year ago—except for that patch near the back where the hold and village once met." She smiled. "Cyrene was a sweet lass. Too bad the Heralds never bothered to find out what happened to her."

Reyes decided to take no offense. "Do *you* know what happened to her?"

"A broken heart, dear. She loved Seth Ashcroft—and he loved her. But she would never bend to his father's will. Not like her sister would."

Seth . . . and Annyth. He'd forgotten their names. He'd never met them, only knew of them because of the gossip of the kitchen staff.

Reyes pulled out his small leather book and scribbled down the conversation and names. He'd forgotten about Seth and Annyth because he'd only heard the gossip about Seth and Cyrene. It was rumored they would marry, until she learned she possessed the Bardic Gift, and was sent to Haven.

Reyes eyed the dais. It was in the shape of a pentagon. Five sides. More than six feet in height. But what had been there when this had been the courtyard of the hold? Six years was a long time, and he'd spent very little time exposed in the middle.

"You have questions?"

"No . . . I'm—" He straightened and looked at the speaker.

It'd been a long time, but he recognized the man's face. His hair was fully white now, as was his beard. He wore a dark set of clothing for such a joyous festivity, and his rotund middle protruded like a cap mushroom with legs for stems.

He stepped forward and offered his hand. "Lionel Ashcroft. I'm the town's mayor."

Reyes took his hand and gave a firm handshake. "Herald Reyes."

"And what brings a Herald to Whisperwinds?"

He tucked his notebook into his tunic. "To enjoy the festival. And to locate a Bard who was commissioned here."

"A Bard?" Ashcroft rubbed at his chin. "I don't recall commissioning one. Name?"

"Jenson Wilkes. The request letter was sent to Haven and received. Wilkes was dispatched, but we've heard nothing from him. So I was sent to check in on him."

"I see. Well, I can reassure you we hired our Bard only today."

"Today?"

"Yes . . . oh, and here she is. Please, come meet Miss Viessa."

The two of them stared at one another as Viessa appeared. She looked the part of a Bard, complete with a lute. Reyes hadn't realized she sang.

He cleared his throat and offered her his hand. "Nice to meet you. My name is Reyes."

"Viessa. So, what brings a Herald to the festivities?"

Ashcroft laughed. "I already asked him that. He's looking for a Bard we hired, which would be you. Now . . . I think Jules is waiting for you at the apothecary."

Viessa glared at Reyes and left.

"So you see, I'm unsure who sent that letter. But if there is anything at all I can help you with, please don't hesitate to call on me, or Sheriff Embers."

"*Sheriff* Embers?" Reyes's attention snapped back to Ashcroft. He remembered Phillip Embers. He wasn't a very pleasant sort. Used to rule the village like a military regiment, echoing his time in the guard before he was dismissed.

"He's over there. Watching you."

He looked in the direction Ashcroft pointed. The man stared, but didn't move. Reyes remembered the man had a son. A bully, and someone who hated Reyes.

Brash Embers.

"Head over to the tavern if you haven't found a place to stay. You might get lucky," the mayor said, and then disappeared in the crowd.

Reyes looked back at Sheriff Embers. *Maybe this isn't such a good idea.*

The tavernkeeper gave the same answer as the mayor. They had hired no Bard until recently, and did he need a room? Luckily, one had just come available if he wanted it—at twice the usual rate.

Reyes took it. She guided him there, took his coin, and left.

There was no evidence the room had been occupied by Jenson Wilkes. It was only a hunch—that a room this large was available on a festival day. It would make sense if the previous occupant had disappeared.

Setting his bag aside, Reyes set to examining the room and came to two conclusions. Either Jenson had never set foot here, or someone had thoroughly cleaned it after he was taken and beaten. There were no obvious clues, so it was time to look for the less obvious. He'd learned on his travels that most fireplaces had little hiding holes behind bricks or stones, and this one was no exception.

He found a loose brick with a key behind it, and quickly put it in his pocket. After replacing the brick, he checked the door and locked it before heading downstairs.

Reyes took a seat at a table in the main room and ate a hot meal as he made notes.

One, Ashcroft insists there was no Bard hired, and yet I have seen the letter requesting one.

Two, I also don't remember the dais in the middle of the town square. So much has been done to the interior of the hold, I don't recognize it anymore. The only thing I do recognize is Ashcroft and Embers, and they're watching me. But are they watching me because I'm in Whites and that makes them nervous? Or because they recognize me?

Someone pulled a chair out next to him and sat down. It was Viessa. She looked frustrated and pointed at him. "Why are you in your Whites?" she hissed.

"Because I'm a Herald."

"I'm in disguise."

"I can see that."

"Why aren't you?"

"What?"

"In disguise?"

"Because I see no reason to be. Why hide who I am?"

"A Bard was attacked and left for dead."

"Yes. Really, Viessa, I fail to see the point of this—"

"Stop it!" She banged the table.

Those seated nearby looked at them, then looked away.

Reyes sat back.

Viessa leaned forward. "Stop doing *that*. Can't you please, just for once, talk to me and not argue?"

"I'm not arguing. You asked why I'm in my Whites. I answered, and then you started your usual stream of nonsensical—"

Viessa reached up and pushed her finger against his lips. Reyes was so stunned at the contact, he stopped talking. He wasn't sure what else to do. But whatever it was she intended to say was interrupted, by an all-too-familiar voice.

"I know you."

Viessa lowered her fingers and Reyes looked to his left, up at the man standing between the two of them. He was older now, and still unattractive, with his oily mustache and stringy hair. He wore dark clothing, just like Reyes had seen his father wearing.

"I'm afraid your knowing me is impossible," Reyes answered.

"Ain't many with gray hair and green eyes. You're that Karse brat, used to scurry around the cellars. Look at you now—think you're important in those white clothes, don't you?"

"You have mistaken me for someone else," Reyes closed his notebook and stood. Before, he had been shorter than this man. Now he towered over him.

"No, I haven't. You shouldn't have come back here, *Reyes*."

Reyes moved his chair and left the tavern. He barely noticed the light rain that fell as he hurried to a nearby building's shadow and stood in it to watch the tavern. He waited for the ghost of his past to leave, step outside, look both ways, and then stroll away from where Reyes stood.

Something touched his arm. He stopped himself from yelling when he saw Viessa. She grabbed his arm and pulled him away from the tavern view. "Who was that? He really did recognize you—he even knew your name."

"Viessa, I introduced myself to the mayor as Herald Reyes. I'm sure they spoke."

"That's not what I mean, and you know it. Do you have some kind of connection to this place? Did you know the Bard who was attacked?" She narrowed her eyes. "Because I know your expressions, Reyes. You did recognize him. And he makes you nervous. Now talk to me."

He grabbed her upper arms and tried to keep the desperation out of his voice. "Leave. *Now*. Tonight. Get back to Haven. Don't try to write that man a song. The Ashcroft family—"

She pulled back and looked at him. "Reyes . . . what aren't you telling me? Damn . . . this is exactly why I can't work with you. You never tell me *anything* and now, once again, you want me to leave. Why won't you ever let me help you?"

"Because I don't want you to get hurt."

Viessa pulled out of his hands. "I think it's just you, wanting to achieve something here. You know this place, and someone recognized you. Whatever it is—let me help you."

"You can't, Viessa. These people are bad. Very bad."

"Are they trying to *do* something bad?"

"No . . . they already did it. They're just covering it up."

He looked past her to the center of town, to the dais. He looked at the cloudy sky as the sun set, and the buildings, and suddenly he knew what the dais *had* been. What lay beneath it.

"It's . . . covering it up . . ." he said softly.

:Are you okay?:

:I . . . just remembered something.:

"Reyes . . . what's covering what up? Will you please tell me what's going on?" Viessa had her hands at her sides, balled into fists.

He pulled the notebook from his tunic and handed it to her. "If you're not going to leave, then take these. I have to check something out."

"Wait . . . I'm going with you."

"No." He put his hand on her shoulder. "This is something I have to do alone. You're safer up here. Go somewhere and read my notes. There was a wedding the same night as the massacre. A wedding between the Ashcrofts and the Embers. In the village. Ravensbergs owned the hold, and they were attacked that night, during the wedding. Anyone left in the hold was murdered. Only a few survived."

"Reyes . . . ?"

"I was one of them. Listen to me. It's all there, in my notes. It was about a merging of family assets, between a village and a hold. And a girl who stood in the way, who came back because her father died, and her uncle wanted control to make the deal with Ashcroft."

Her eyes searched his face. "You mean . . . Cyrene? She was from here?"

"Yes. She was a Ravensberg. Please, Viessa. These men are ruthless, and they have no regard for anyone but themselves. I escaped that night because Cyrene was there, guiding us out. I owe her to look for—"

"Look for what?"

He put his hand to her cheek as the left side of his mouth lifted. "Justice."

He called to Eshenesra in the dark. They had to go to the back side of the town, where the hold's wall still stood.

There, hidden by brush and clever stonework, was the entrance to the cistern . . . where the attackers had entered the hold that night and killed everyone. He felt there was something important there . . . something long buried. Once he was inside, his torch lit, he told Eshenesra to keep an eye on Viessa and her Companion, Miela.

And he was pretty sure Jenson Wilkes had left the key in the fireplace so it wouldn't be found. It could be he had been beaten because he'd taken it, and they never found it. But what was the key for? Reyes didn't know yet. But Jenson had left a clue, and Reyes intended on finding the answer.

When Reyes came to again, there was light in the room. It flickered. Shadows danced against the wall, on the ceiling above him. He could see the walls, and the low ceiling. He was close to a small fire pit where a fire burned. The torch had rolled into it and ignited the wood that was left. He moved, and yelled when his back bristled with agony.

Reyes pushed and pulled himself, cursed and yelled and made promises to the heavens as he slowly stood, his right hand against the wall. He stood on his left leg and balanced enough to grab the torch and hold it high.

That's when he saw what he'd touched before. What had broken under his weight.

The remains of Bard Cyrene Ravensberg.

She'd died sitting against the wall. He recognized her scarlet tunic. Recognized her long, dark braids. Remembered her sweet face that night, as she guided him, and so many others, down the cistern in the center of the city, into the very entrance and exit the attackers had used.

While they were busy hunting down people, she was leading them to freedom. He remembered her kind words to him. Reyes also remembered she was worried about anyone left behind or lost in the tunnels. *Even though everyone begged her to come with us through the underground water reserve, she insisted she had to help everyone.*

She had given Reyes a small, folded sheet of paper. She told him his illusions were good, and that he should go to Haven. Run as fast as he could to escape the lies, to find who he was, and to live free as he wanted.

So many memories came back to him. So many little things he'd forgotten. Cyrene had kissed his sixteen-year-old forehead, and he was scared for his life, but even more for hers.

Reyes closed his eyes and made Cyrene from memory as the voices came back that night, as the community came together to help one another. And when he sank all of those emotions into the thought, he opened his eyes and she stood in front of him. Not complete, but enough of herself that she smiled.

That's when he heard the music. And voices. There was a performance.

He was close to the surface!

A wave of exhaustion robbed Reyes of his strength and he leaned against the wall, his action brushing the knife. He moaned, and had to stop himself from reaching around and pulling the blade out. He couldn't see it—he could only feel it. But he had been taught by his mother to never remove a knife. To wait until it could be treated, and the blood stanched immediately after its removal.

Music changed, and a voice reached him in the tunnels beneath the city. A woman's voice, haunting and clear.

"In the hall of feasts, where banners fly
A young groom pledged, 'neath the azure sky
With vows of love, he took her hand,
Amid cheers and laughter, across the land."

Reyes didn't recognize the voice, but he heard the words, the words from the paper he'd kept in his notebook. The paper given to him by Cyrene. The cheers and clapping vanished.

Cyrene's form offered her hand to him, and though he knew it was simply his fevered mind, he nodded to his useless arm as it hung from his shoulder. She looked sad and came even closer to place her hand on his unmoving one. He listened to the song as he used the wall to balance. He had no choice but to try his weight on his left leg. The pain nearly took him out again when he did, but he felt . . . or he believed he felt a slight pressure on his hand.

Reyes looked at Cyrene and she nodded to an open door he hadn't seen before. He glanced back at her remains. He suspected she'd been killed to prevent her from interfering with the wedding. Reyes had run from the fire and been found by Eshenesra that night and never looked back at the hold, and had only heard weeks later that Cyrene had gone missing.

He took his time as he hobbled against the wall, the torch even with his shoulder because he didn't have the strength to raise it any higher.

"As vows were spoke 'fore altar's light,
A dreadful cry rang into the night!
From deep within the earth they poured,
With steel and flame, a savage horde."

Reyes turned into the hall with Cyrene's illusion and she patiently, lovingly, guided him forward into a greater darkness. There he heard the song clearer now. It spoke of the attack. Mercenaries hired by trusted leaders had come up through the cistern and into the heart of the Hold.

"Their bloodied swords and sharpened spears
Brought death and ruin, countless tears.
No soul was spared on that dark day,
As ash and embers led the way."

Reyes half smiled as he heard that last lyric. Ash and embers. Ashcroft and Embers . . . *Oh, Cyrene, you knew this?*

"Don't slow down, son," his mother said as she appeared in front of him, next to Cyrene. Now there were two influences in his life, one who birthed him, and one who he knew so briefly, but saved his life in that instant. *"Keep walking. You're doing so good, my wonderful boy. You are going to need to go up. Reserve your strength."*

He remembered the stairs. Reyes stumbled before the first step and looked up into a faint outline.

The door . . . the door at the base of the dais was there.

*"So Northfrost Hold was razed to dust,
Its people slain, a betrayal of trust.
Upon that land so bright and green
No life again shall e'er be seen."*

Cyrene took the first step. His mother ran up ahead. He leaned to his right, his shoulder against the wall. Reyes lifted his good leg as fast as possible and placed it on the step. His vision blurred at the exertion, so he counted to five before he pushed up on that leg and balanced his bad leg on the step. He pushed up again on the bad leg to get the good leg on the next step, and on, and on, and on.

:Reyes? REYES!:

He nearly passed out at that moment. To hear Eshenesra again . . . to feel her love for him surround him.

:My love . . . am I dreaming?:

:Where are you?:

:The dais . . . in the middle of town. Please . . . I need you.:

:You're in such pain! Who did this? I couldn't find you! Tell me!:

:I need . . . your strength . . . :

He started focusing on Cyrene, who had now become Viessa. The dark, short hair, dressed in her Herald Whites, and her patient look—whenever she deigned to give it to him.

Reyes looked into her eyes. Just a few more steps and he would be at the door—

But when he arrived and heard the next lines, he didn't know how to open the door. He was nearly on his knees, breathing heavy, his left eye no longer opening at all. He held the torch down low and saw a diamond-shaped plaque, and in that, a keyhole.

But where was this key?

:What's wrong? I can see the dais . . . Viessa's singing.:

:That's Viessa? Can you tell her to keep singing?:

:I will.:

Reyes wanted to cry—he was sure he did—as he remembered the key he'd found in the fireplace and slipped into his pocket. He weakly tossed the torch on the steps before using his numb fingers to dig into his pocket. He was tumbling into fatigue, wanting nothing more than to close his eyes and let go.

"Don't you dare give up on me," Viessa said. The pretend Viessa. The one who didn't want to leave him.

He found the key and, with shaking fingers, moved it to the lock.

"Till sun did rise with Ash and Ember
I task those souls, in honor, we remember."

Reyes slipped the key in—not without great difficulty—and turned it as he heard voices start several beats after the song ended.

"Wait . . . is that the truth?"

"Is that how they got in? They used the statue?"

"That horse! That's one of those Herald horses!"

"Is it the missing Herald's horse?"

"It used to be a cistern, with an entrance and exit near the village! I remember that now!"

"What . . . who wrote this song? How . . ."

"Did anyone else hear Ash and Ember in that song?"

"I used to live here. I was there that night. They were just there as we were all outside watching the wedding from the wall of the hold."

The darkened panel on the dais clicked, and everyone became silent. Reyes pushed the door out and winced at the light of the torches around the statue. He looked at the people staring at him as he stumbled. He was sure he was a terrifying sight in his filthy Whites.

"It's a Herald!"

"Someone grab him!"

"Get out of the way . . . the horse is coming!"

"The missing Herald!"

"REYES!"

The last scream was close to him and made him jump. Someone grabbed him around the neck, and he went down as his legs collapsed.

:My love, grab my flank.:

"There's a knife in his back!"

"Someone get the healer!"

"Here!"

Reyes was losing his battle with consciousness. He couldn't climb on top of Eshenesra. He was spent. He saw Cyrene standing behind the real Viessa, who bent over him. Cyrene mouthed, *"Thank you,"* before she vanished.

His mother blew him a kiss.

And then there was Viessa, her cold hand on his cheek. "He's so hot . . . he's feverish . . ."

"There's . . . a body . . . down there . . ." Reyes said.

More voices, and he was aware others were taking torches off their poles and heading down the stairs. He was lifted and carried to someplace warm and placed on a table on his stomach. He felt Eshenesra's kisses on his head. Was she with him?

Someone noticed his arm was out of its socket. Reyes cried when someone moved it.

"Reyes, I'm here," Viessa said so close to his ear. "I'm right here."

He started to tell her he was sorry—until someone popped his arm back into place, and Herald Reyes knew nothing for a very, *very* long time.

Two months later

The sun was up, and he was in his usual perch in the garden. Farthen had come back, along with several other teachers. They were correcting the records of Northfrost Hold and the Whisperwinds settlement. Reyes agreed to give them a history as long as they kept his name out of it.

All that talking with them had tired him out. He'd only been awake and active for two weeks. He'd been in a coma for a lot longer than that. The knife wound required a lot of attention, and he had to be still. His leg had been broken, and his walk down that corridor and up those stairs had damaged it further. His arm was still sore when he moved it the wrong way.

Reyes would be off his leg for another three weeks, and it would take longer than that for him to stand for more than five minutes and not fall over.

He felt useless.

"You look better."

Reyes jumped as he turned to see Viessa approaching. This was the first time he'd seen her since waking up. And he felt . . . excited, and fearful. He knew she was here to let him know she was moving on.

"I—" He swallowed as she pulled a chair up beside him. She reached out and moved a strand of his hair from his face. Reyes knitted his brow. "It's good to see you. I really don't know how I looked before—"

"Bad. When you didn't come back, the only thing I could think to do was sing that song. The one you'd stuffed into your notebook."

"You did the right thing, Viessa."

She put her hand on his chair. "It took about a month to calm everyone down. Lionel is no longer the mayor, and Phillip Ember is missing. Lionel will stand trial for Cyrene's murder, plus the murders of all the victims of the hold fire and attack, as well as attempted murder against Jenson Wilkes and you. It seems Brash Embers and several of his lackeys were the ones who took Wilkes from his room and beat him, then left him for dead. Brash was the one who followed you into those tunnels, and then stabbed you."

Reyes winced. "Yes . . . that much I remember well."

She smiled at him. "Justice is coming slowly, but it's coming. Good job."

"I didn't do anything . . . except nearly get killed."

"Reyes . . ." She licked her lips. "I'm sorry. Initially, I thought you didn't talk to me about solutions or mysteries because you didn't want me to be involved, or worse, you believed or thought me an incompetent Herald. But after reading your notebook, as well as speaking to those who do know you, I realized you shut out the ones you don't want hurt."

He chewed on his lower lip. Confused. "I'm not—"

"Reyes, did it ever occur to you that you don't share with me because subconsciously you're always comparing the fate of the ones who protected you with that of anyone you protect?"

Reyes didn't know what to say. He felt as if he'd just been handed a great answer, but he didn't understand the question. "Viessa, I . . . might have done that. Still do. My mother protected me, and she died. Cyrene protected me and disappeared. I supposed I knew all along she'd died. And if I have done that to you, I'm not sure I can stop doing it."

She put her hand on his. "Which is why I'm going to start gently reminding you. And if that doesn't work, I'll possibly throw things at you."

Reyes opened his mouth to respond, then closed it. He leaned his head forward and did speak. "Reminding me? I thought . . ." He stared at her. "I thought you wanted to be away from me."

"I did, until you handed me that precious book of yours. You have never let me see any of your notebooks. I read it front to back. Everything we've done, you figured it out like chess moves—except this one. The Whisperwinds case had you running around."

Reyes nodded. Then, "You're not leaving?"

"No." She squeezed his hand and pressed her fingers into his. "I'm not. I'm staying right by your side. Wait . . . Reyes, are you okay? Do I need to get someone?"

He'd held his emotions in check for as long as he could. But too much had happened, too many memories, old ghosts . . . The healers all said he needed to talk about what happened, about what he saw, what he felt, and how he could walk in pitch black, on a broken leg, carrying a torch, and survive.

The raw emotion . . . the realization there could have been another skeleton sitting there next to Cyrene. Forever abandoned. Forgotten.

Viessa was up and leaning over him, her arms around him. Reyes sat forward, as others in the garden came over and hugged him. He let decades of fear go, and when he was done . . . he was exhausted.

Viessa had a napkin and tried to help him wipe his face. But he was smiling at her.

"I heard every Herald in Collegium has come to see you. If for no other reason than to say hello. It's a community, Reyes. Might be a good idea to enjoy it."

"But why? What did I do?"

"You survived, Reyes. Another testament to the shear stubbornness of Heralds. So many of us don't live to tell the tale. So we celebrate the successes. Another mystery solved, and a heroic Bard vindicated. The criminals were punished."

Reyes squeezed her hand. "I think . . . I need to sleep again."

She moved out of the chair to kneel in front of him, locking her eyes with his. "Then let your partner help you back to your room and make sure you're tucked in properly. You can't do this alone, Reyes. It takes a family, friendships, and community to stay alive in this life. As Heralds, we take risks. We put our lives on the line. And we sacrifice for one another." She moved more hair from his face. "We'll still argue . . . but it won't be as bad."

"Thank you, Herald Viessa," he said as he smiled at her.

"Thank you, Herald Reyes."

Uncivil Blood
Mercedes Lackey

Herald Savil pounded on the door to her nephew Vanyel's room in the Herald's Wing of the Palace. She knew he was in there; he'd been back from his latest Circuit for a full day. She also knew what he was doing; he was brooding and working himself into a major case of depression, because it was only a week to Sovvan, and that was what he did every year at Sovvan, unless someone hauled him out of his state by the ears.

Which nobody did, because although he was young, he already had a reputation for being a powerful Herald-Mage, and nobody wanted to be on the receiving end of an emotional outburst from someone who could face down an ice-drake. And in fact, the hall was so quiet and so empty the wing might have been deserted. People were *literally* tiptoeing around him.

Except for Savil, who had limited patience for wallowing in despair, and none whatsoever for wallowing in despair when there was work to be done. This was a personal fault on her part, and she knew it, but right now that fault was useful. If his friends couldn't coax him out, then by all the gods, she'd bully him out.

:I know you're in there, Van,: she Mindspoke. No point in shaming him by yelling through the door. *:Get your soggy ass out of bed and open this door. The King has a job for us and the time-candle is burning.:*

There was silence for a moment. Then, because Vanyel was finally a grown adult and not a sullen lad inclined to reply "Go away! Leave me alone!" anymore, she heard the lock being thrown and the door opened for her.

Vanyel's room, as she expected, was *completely* in the dark, even though it was barely sunset. The curtains had been thrown shut, and a blanket hung over the window for good measure. The gloom of his room reflected the gloom of his soul, but she not-quite-pushed her way in anyway and shut the door.

"What is it?" Vanyel asked thickly. From the sound of his voice she didn't have to see him to know what state he was in. Eyes red, nose red, hair a mess, probably disheveled as well. *Probably still in his nightclothes. And he probably hasn't eaten since he got back from his last Circuit.*

:He hasn't,: her Companion Kellan confirmed. *:And it was just broth and a little bread. He started grieving early this year, probably because he got back early from Circuit.:*

:Well, he can finish early. We have work to do.:

"Get dressed in something other than your uniform, the flashier the better," Savil ordered. "Then get packed and pack up your gittern, your harp, and more fancy clothing. You have a quarter-candlemark to meet me at the stable. We have a job to do, and we're the only ones that can do it. King's orders, and King's orders are we're to leave quietly."

With that, Savil turned on her heel and headed for the stable, where Kellan and her packs waited already. Also a supply of meat and fruit hand-pies to eat on the road during the first part of the journey, because when he finally shook off his wallowing in grief, her nephew would be ravenous, and nothing satisfied like a good beef hand-pie.

Fortunately, it was supper-time, and pretty much everyone was packed into either the Collegium dining-hall or the Great Hall of the Palace. That was a good thing, because the King had said specifically he didn't want *anyone* but the Circle knowing he was sending Heralds out on this mission.

Still, a little stealth wouldn't hurt, and Savil cast the lesser spell of invisibility as she left the Herald's Wing. It wouldn't actually make her invisible, but it would make the eyes of anyone who wasn't looking specifically for her slide right past her. With that to help, she made it down to the Companion's Stable without anyone intercepting her.

Kellan waited in her loose-box, already geared up in her best formal barding with everything but the bridle bells, full packs on each hip. But with time of the essence, Savil passed her and opened Yfandes's loose box. To save time and explanation, rather than tacking Vanyel's Companion up the way her own was, in her own set of formal Companion gear, Savil went hunting for ordinary tack. After looking in the tack room for something that would fit, she found down an old, worn, plain saddle and blanket. She heaved the saddle over her shoulder, took a common hackamore with reins from the wall, and tacked the mare up in that instead. There was something very tactile and comforting about the smell of well-cared-for leather, and she rather wished there was time for Van to do this himself . . . but there wasn't.

:I've told her all about it,: Kellan said, as Yfandes stood statue-still for Savil's ministrations. *:She's agreed to wait for you to tell Van.:*

:Excellent. He might argue with Yfandes, he won't argue with me.: She tightened the old saddle down comfortably, made sure the chest and rump-bands were secure but not so tight as to be uncomfortable, and as Yfandes dropped her head, pulled a hackamore and reins over her ears and fastened the chin-strap.

:Oh, she says he will, *but not in your hearing.:*

Savil snorted. While she was, of course, entirely in sympathy with her nephew's continuing grief and prolonged mourning for the loss of the literal love-of-his-life, this business of making an annual Wallowing In Sorrow Ceremony out of it wasn't doing him any good. Plus, with everyone feeling as if they had to tip-toe around him in the week before and after Sovvan, he affected the productivity of the Heralds around him as well as effectively taking himself off the roster for half a moon.

:Your lack of Empathy is showing,: observed Kellan, making a play on the word and the literal Gift.

:I find your lack of faith disturbing.:

Kellan snorted. Savil could hear her all the way across the stable.

About the time Savil and Yfandes left the latter's box stall,

Vanyel showed up laden with packs and instruments. He looked better than Savil had expected; his eyes and nose were still red, but he'd made an effort to wash up and tidy his hair back into a tail, and he'd at least taken care with his clothing. Even if it was black. Where he'd gotten the outfit, she had no idea—black boots, black breeches tight enough to show the muscles of his legs, black tunic of twilled raime, black linen shirt, and a black woolen cloak. She *hoped* it was something he'd had made up to go skulking in, because at least that would mean he hadn't bought it on impulse to go with his depression.

"I hope this was what you wanted, Savil," he said, with a nod down at his clothing. "I just assumed you meant I wasn't to dress in Bardic red, and that you meant 'prosperous musician' and not 'impoverished musician.'"

"There's a difference?" she quipped. "But yes. They don't have Bards where we're going, and—well, I'll explain when we're on the way out of Haven."

He nodded, and fastened his baggage up behind Yfandes's saddle, then swung up into place while Savil mounted Kellan.

By now it was twilight, the air scented with fallen leaves and woodsmoke, and as was usual this time of year, people who weren't Vanyel were warming up to the Festivities at Sovvan. Courtiers and Trainees alike were gathering around carefully created bonfires in the Palace gardens to roast nuts and apples, drink cider, and listen to Bardic students practice their art. There would be lots of singed fingers for the Healers tonight— somehow everyone seemed to forget how hot those apples and nuts got. Savil felt a twinge of momentary regret that she was going to miss out—but even if their efforts on the King's be- half came to nothing, it was worth it to get Vanyel out of his slough.

:Mindspeech will be easier, I think,: she said as they headed down the Hill toward the road out of Haven going east. The lights of the city spread out before them as they left the Palace and rode down through the manors of the highborn and pros- perous. *:I'd rather no one had even a chance of overhearing me. As you can see, we're headed east.:*

:Why east? Isn't that part of the Border quiet?: Well, that had gotten his attention. He actually sounded interested.

:It is, and it's not trouble. At least, not for us. Prince Herrend, of a little independent principality called—:

:Perlona, I remember it,: he interrupted. *:Known for wine, glassmaking, and as a trade hub.:*

:—sent an envoy to the King. He's got a situation with two feuding families that is about to tear the place apart and nothing he has done has solved the problem. There's a lot of internal politics we don't need to get into, plus the fact that he's heavily related to both families, that's keeping him from acting effectively. Hardorn has been putting a bit of pressure on him to join them as well, since their border is inching up to his. He's afraid if things get out of hand, they'll just ooze their way in and take over under the guise of "helping him keep the peace," but do nothing that actually fixes things and just leave everyone angrier than before, mostly at him. So, the short form is Herrend told the King that since the Heralds have a reputation for solving the insolvable, if we can fix it, he'll join us instead.:

Vanyel mused over all of that for a moment as they wound their way through the streets of Haven, where the taverns were all brightly lit as people indulged in this year's hard cider. Sounds of laughter and snatches of song came from doors left open, since the weather was still good.

:That would be a good situation for us, I can see that. Do you have any further details?:

Savil shook her head. *:Nobody remembers how the feud started. Neither family is backing down. Servants and members of the families are picking fights in the street, people not in the families are taking sides, the fights are getting worse, weapons have been drawn, and the Prince is afraid one of those fights is going to end in a fatality, and then there's going to be no stopping wholesale rioting. And if that happens, Hardorn absolutely will swoop in with a 'this is endangering our mercantile interests, and if you won't fix it we will' attitude. I'm going to openly be the Valdemar representative with the Prince's Court, which will hopefully make that less likely. I want you to pick a family* *and ingratiate yourself as a Court entertainer. Use magic and Mindspeech as you need to. Slap an illusion on Yfandes to turn her something other than white. Other than that, I don't have a plan, because the situation is volatile enough that any plan we make is likely to fall apart within moments of our getting there.:*

He mulled that over as they reached the outermost wall of Haven. *:All right then,:* he replied. *:We ride tonight until we can't stay in the saddle anymore, stop to rest, and start again as early in the morning as possible. I can handle it if you can. And we hope things don't get worse before we get there.:*

Heh. Think you have to cosset me? Think again, youngling. But Savil could almost *feel* Vanyel's mind engaging with the problem, working out a potential persona, deciding what magic he was likely to need to use, and trying to figure out the best angles to approach with as little information as they had.

And she smiled to herself in the darkness. The first part of her personal mission had been accomplished. He wasn't sunk in bleak despair anymore.

:Yfandes says she can make it all the way to Perlona with brief stops for water and food, and Van can sleep in the saddle if you can.:

Savil snorted, though not loud enough to be heard over the cantering Companions' hoofbeats. *:Did you tell her I was doing that when she was still suckling at her mother's teat?:*

:Of course I did,: Kellan replied with amusement. *:I mean, what does she think we are, Trainees? I also told her I could probably outpace her all the way to the Border. We do know a trick or two, now, don't we?:*

Savil grinned in the darkness, as the houses gave way to open fields. *:Old age and treachery will overcome youth and enthusiasm every time, won't it, my love?:*

:You're damn right.:

They stopped just outside of the capital of Perlona to change clothing, although "capital" was something of a misnomer, since there really was only one city in the principality.

An inn with a bath-house made a good spot for that; they

separated before going in, Vanyel going in first. He bathed and dressed quickly and, while waiting for his aunt at a table in the inn, staved off hunger with some of the local wine and bread and cheese. He'd changed to another all-black outfit, since black was almost as expensive to maintain as white and had the advantage of not showing smudges or sweat-stains. Or blood, though he hoped that wasn't going to be an issue. This one, however, had striking accents of red; piping on the linen shirt, tunic, and down the outer seams of the breeches, and red knotwork down the tunic front. Back in the stable, Yfandes now sported a shining black coat to match. Prosperous musician? Everything he sported now practically screamed the part.

Savil finally appeared in her formal Whites, but didn't acknowledge him openly. In Mindspeech, however, she let him know her approval. *:Do you want to wait here until I have more details for you?:*

:That's probably for the best. And I'm starving. I can't imagine why you aren't.:

:I am, but I fully expect the Prince will feed me. Start making your reputation and see what the local gossip is.: She said, as she paid the innkeeper and headed out the door.

:Now who's telling whom how to do their job?: he retorted, and leaned back, making sure his harp and gittern cases were well in sight. Sure enough, after a flurry of customers had finished engaging the innkeeper's attention, the man sought him out.

"Musician, my lord?" he asked in the local tongue, which was a sort of polyglot of Valdemaran and Hardornen, and one Van was familiar with. "Come here for the celebration?"

"Minstrel, indeed," Van said, with just a *touch* of flamboyance. "I am Jackomo, Prince of Minstrels and Minstrel of Princes. I am sure you have heard of me."

"Of course I have," the innkeeper lied, since Van had made the name up on the spot. "And I am *certain* that if Prince Herrend has no immediate need of your music, Sieur Mayard will, what with the celebration and all."

"You keep speaking of a celebration—and just who is Sieur

Mayard?" Van replied with a lifted brow. "My services are . . . expansive. And expensive." He brushed at the twilled silk of his tunic with a little flourish. This was turning out to be interesting. He wondered if this "Sieur Mayard" was the head of one of those two feuding families they were here to reconcile.

"Sieur Mayard is one of our first families. Closely related to the Prince himself," the innkeeper told him. "And in two days, his daughter and heir comes of age. There will be a great fete held so he can introduce her to the largest possible number of suitors."

"Trot her out and show her paces, hmm?" Vanyel replied with a raised eyebrow, drawing a laugh from a few customers nearby. "That sounds festive." *And potentially embarrassing and awkward for the girl. Or maybe she'll enjoy it; I'm not sure what sort of girl she is. She might like the attention.*

The innkeeper nodded. "They say the festivities will last the entire day, with a grand fete in the evening. Half of Perlona will be there."

"Only half?" Van raised his eyebrow again.

"Well, *obviously* no one associated with the Corleans will have anything to do with it. Can you imagine if they did?" The innkeeper chuckled, as if he had said something hilarious.

Well, there is my answer. That's our feuding families. And I already seem to have a way in. "I am surprised the Corleans aren't planning to host a counter-fete. It seems the obvious thing to do," Vanyel replied, examining his fingernails, then buffing them on his tunic.

"So obvious that Lady Mayard secured *all* the best provisions before Sieur Mayard announced it." The innkeeper laughed. "There's not a Gestard ham or fatted goose to be had. Even all the eggs to make custard tarts are spoken for! Good thing I have my own hens!"

"Well then, my mind is made up. I shall definitely have to use this opportunity to show all of Perlona what the Prince of Minstrels can do." Van let his hand stray toward the gittern, which would be the easiest to tune. "Would you care for a sample to entertain your guests, in return for more of this excellent wine?"

The innkeeper was very pleased to accept that bargain, and Van regaled the customers with a good candlemark-long concert, embellished with just a touch of his Bardic Gift. By the time he was done, he not only had that wine, he had dinner, breakfast, stabling for Yfandes, and a free room to himself for the night, in exchange for a longer stint after the dinner hour.

That should give him the privacy to confer with his aunt via Mindspeech and a chance to learn more about this fete and the Mayards and Corleans, who were almost certainly the feuding families they had heard about.

Bridle bells attached and ringing merrily, Savil and Kellan trotted up to the Prince's palace looking as smart and cool as if they had just left their home half a candlemark ago. It was pretty obvious which building in the city was the Prince's palace, since it stood three stories above everything else.

From the street, it was clear that the origin of this palace, as was often the case, was a defensive keep, the sort everyone in the town could retreat into if an enemy attacked. Four stories of thick walls with nothing but arrow-slits made for an ominous looking building, but as she crossed the bridge over the dry moat and traveled the long tunnel to the interior, a much more inviting prospect met her eyes, of a handsome three-story building of much more recent construction than the surrounding keep walls. *Probably like some of ours . . . now those walls are used for barracks, storage, and workrooms.* She glanced back over her shoulder. At least the interior walls had windows; the second, third and fourth floors, anyway.

Before she had any more time to admire the architecture, a young-ish man in a green tabard sporting a crossed spear and quarterstaff ran up to her and paused at Kellan's nose. "Be ye the Envoy from Valdemar?" he asked, breathlessly, unconsciously smoothing his tabard.

"I am," she confirmed. "I am Herald-Mage Savil."

"Then I am to take ye to the Prince directly," he said, and putting his hand to his mouth, whistled sharply. Another, younger man, in a brown tunic on which the crossed weapons had been painted rather than stitched, ran up. "Take the Herald's mount to the stables," the first man said. "And have her bags taken to her room. Make sure no one touches the bags but you and she."

"Aye!" the second fellow said.

"A loose box if you have one, if you please," Savil told him, dismounting. "Leave her unbridled and untied. She could use a good grooming, we rode hard and fast to get here, since the Prince's summons came with some urgency."

"Aye, milady, then a grain ration for yon beauty as well," the groom agreed, putting a very gentle hand on the bridle at Kellan's cheek.

:They may not know what a Companion is, but they know how to treat a horse,: Kellan said with approval.

:Just as well that they don't. You'll hear more that way.:

:A very fine point. Off to your Prince, I hope he feeds you as well.:

Hands clasped behind her back, Savil followed her guide—who she assumed to be a "small-h herald"—to the imposing double doors of the actual Palace. She rather regretted all the haste, since the interior was lavishly and tastefully decorated with carvings on all the support beams, and painted walls and ceilings she wished she could get a better look at. It had been constructed in an older style than the Palace at Haven, with no corridors, and one room leading directly into the next.

In the third one they entered, they found three men conferring over some documents, all three richly dressed in a style unfamiliar to her, featuring long, broad-shouldered tunics with lined oversleeves worn over hose. The middle one, dressed in green, had a very simple, plain golden diadem with some sort of pattern embossed or chased into it; she assumed he was the Prince. One of the other two she recognized.

"Ah, see, now, I told your Highness that Valdemar would respond faster than you thought they would," said Ambassador Kirlian of Hardorn, dressed in brown velvet, with a broad smile.

"And a relief it is to me, Ambassador," said the man in the

diadem. "Welcome, Envoy! You have come not a moment too soon."

"Thank you, your Highness." Savil bowed. "I am Herald-Mage Savil, and entirely at your service."

They both took a moment to look each other over, and Savil liked what she saw. Prince Herrend's green tunic of moleskin or velveteen was no more ostentatious than Van's minstrel garb; he wore a single chain of office and no further jewels. Of late middle-age, with a full head of graying hair, he looked like a man who rose early, worked a full day, and enjoyed his work. Mostly. Just now he looked like a man who was seriously worried, and who had been clenching his jaw so much he'd given himself a headache.

As for Kirlian, he looked exactly as he had the last time she saw him. *Old silver fox that he is.* They might have jousted a little in words in the past, but they liked and respected each other.

"Here to snatch victory from my grasp, Kirlian?" she asked with a real smile.

He waved his hand negligently in the air. "By no means. I'm here to wish you the best, and attempt to pick up the pieces if you fail. *Which,* as I have been telling his Highness, I *do not* expect to happen. I knew the King would send one of his best Heralds, and you people do have a knack for solving . . . what I would call interpersonal problems."

The prince took a deep breath, as if Savil's arrival had greatly relieved him, and raised his hand. "This is nothing that cannot be discussed over food and wine, I am certain the Herald must be starving, and Kirlian, we have been analyzing this since long past luncheon. Lancel, send to the kitchen for our supper; we'll take it here. The Court can proceed without us."

"Sire!" said Lancel, with a bow of his own, before speed-walking off.

"Take a chair, Envoy," the Prince invited. "And let me explain what a stew you have walked into."

Savil pulled up a heavy wooden chair, and very quickly learned that the feud was between two leading families of the principality, the Corleans and the Mayards, both of whom were closely related to the Prince and nearly everyone else with money, rank, or both in the area. And that, contrary to what she had been told, the source of the feud *was* known.

"It all began in my grandfather's time," the Prince said as he spread out a map of the principality for her regard. "This manor here—" he tapped the map "—belonged to someone who was an uncle to *both* heads of the families. He died without heirs, and both of them claimed it. My grandfather attempted to calm the situation, but he was dealing with two very stubborn old men, words were exchanged, then insults, then so-called 'family honor' got involved. They've been battling each other over it ever since. My grandfather and my father both tried to get them to some sort of compromise, as have I, but at this point it has become far more of an affair of honor—"

Kirlian snorted, and the prince grimaced.

"—and no one is going to budge. But in my time, the thing has gone from snubs at Court and little skirmishes in which no one comes to more harm than mud-clots thrown at clothing and chamber-pots "accidentally" emptied out of upper windows onto someone's head to actual street brawls. In the last one, swords were drawn and only the intervention of my guards kept blood from being spilled. And if that happens—" He paused, and looked at Savil bleakly. "—there's going to be more than a little blood spilled. Half of my people are going to go to actual battle with the other half, and I don't have enough guardsmen to keep it all contained."

Savil picked up a frog's leg and chewed it thoughtfully. The food here was a bit different from what she was used to, but remarkably good.

:Frog legs? Snails? Eww.:

:Nobody asked you to eat them. Go back to your carrots.:

:They do grow nice carrots.:

"What's changed?" she asked.

"Sieur Mayard's heir and only child comes of age in three days," the Prince said. "That means Fiametta is able to marry, and whoever she marries is likely to bring more weight onto the

Mayard side of the inheritance equation." He held up his hand. "Please don't ask me to explain it, I don't understand half of it myself. Only Lancel can untangle our near-incestuous bloodlines and the lines of inheritance around here. The point is it won't matter *who* Peitro Corlean marries; it won't change the current balance. But depending on who *Fiametta* marries, it will. And *I* can't just make a decree and settle it; by our laws, these things have to be settled in a court of law."

"I'd say that's civilized and refreshing, but it's clearly handicapped you. So why are you saying 'depending on who Fiametta marries'? Isn't that up to her parents?" Savil finished the frog leg and picked up another. She hated to look as if she was stuffing herself regardless of the Prince's clear unhappiness . . . but it had been a long ride, and she actually was quite hungry.

"It would be, but her parents are giving her the opportunity to pick from their approved candidates," the Prince said. "And those do include some men who won't unbalance the situation. They're going to all see her for the first time—and she'll see them—at her birthday fete in three days. It's the custom of our ennobled families to keep their daughters in relative seclusion until they're of age."

"I can think of a few of ours who probably wish we had that custom," Savil said dryly.

:Plot twist. The fair maid is only fourteen. That's 'of age' around here.:

Savil managed not to spit up her wine. Granted, there were plenty of cultures within Valdemar where fourteen was considered old enough to marry . . . but still. Given the likelihood that a good percentage of the "acceptable suitors" were probably in their twenties or even thirties, it felt obscene.

:Cheer up. She could choose someone old enough to be her grandsire, who will drop dead before the consummation.:

:Or during.: She schooled her face. "Kirlian, have you told the Prince anything about my powers?"

"I didn't know it was you who would be coming, so no." He waved a hand. "Reassure him, please."

"I'm a Herald-Mage. I'm an *Archmage*," Savil said. "I'm

pretty sure, unless either of those families has another Archmage in their employ, I can do what your guardsmen can't. I can keep this from turning into a bloodbath if trouble starts just by calling up a thunderstorm or something equally as impressive, and scaring the offenders so badly they'll need to clean their armor out in the millrace."

Kirlian nearly choked, and the Prince *did* choke, forcing both of them to pound on his back. When the poor man got his breath back and took a swallow of wine, he managed, "That's a great relief, but you can't *stay* here. So I still need a solution to the problem. A solution that isn't going to require constant supervision and mending."

"That's the plan," said Savil. "As you point out, I can't stay here. And my King would frown on that notion. So let's see what we can decide for the short term. Let's start with spreading your guardsmen around as eyes on the ground with a way to alert me quickly if trouble starts."

"But how will you get to the trouble quickly from here?" the prince asked. "The city is not small."

"Oh . . ." Savil smiled. "Believe me, that will not be a problem."

By the time he finished his evening performance, Vanyel could probably have had his pick of bedmates. Female, of course, which was to be expected, but almost as many men were not shy about letting him know they wanted to provide a tangible expression of their appreciation. This was surprising—and refreshing—enough that he actually found himself thinking about someone other than Tylendel for the first time in a very long time.

He turned them all down, of course, because while Jackomo could have found himself a permanent home in this inn, Vanyel was here on business. But he did manage to convey enough charm and regret that he didn't evoke any hard feelings, and went to bed in a small, slightly claustrophobic, but comfortable room to contact his aunt via Mindspeech. As narrow as the bed was, it was just as well that he wasn't sharing it with anyone.

He and Savil traded information as their Companions listened silently, which didn't take very long.

:It's mind-numbingly stupid,: he said.

:Feuds usually are. It takes someone willing to step back and be an adult to end them, unless an outside force comes in and does something about it. And it seems the Prince is constrained from doing that.:

:Well, the obvious solution would be to marry Peitro to Fiametta,: Van pointed out.

:The Prince says he can't do that. There's a lot of surprisingly sensible laws constraining what he can and cannot do. We could learn something from these people.:

:Perhaps.: he countered. *:But we don't have people rioting in the streets over someone else's private feud.:*

:Only because we have Heralds and they don't. I assume your next step is going to be to ingratiate or win your way into the Mayard household?:

:I have a better chance there then at the Corleans, what with this fete coming up. Unless the Corleans decide to get the jump on their rivals and hire me before the Mayards can get to me.:

:Either way, it's a good plan. I'd prefer that you try for the Mayards, but if the Corleans get to you first, I'll get myself invited to the fete somehow. We need someone on the spot in case the Corleans decide to make trouble that night.:

That seemed to be the most they could plan for at the moment, and both of them were starting to feel the effects of riding at a nonstop breakneck pace and getting only the uneasy "rest" one gets by napping in the saddle. The Companions could go on tirelessly with short breaks for food and water, but their Heralds were only human. Vanyel had sat down on the (very nice) mattress of the bed to talk to Savil, since there wasn't anywhere else to sit, and when they broke contact he found himself about to fall over sideways. So he didn't bother to fight the need for sleep and his sore muscles anymore. He set his elegant clothing aside, and that was the last thing he remembered until the rising sun hit him in the face from his little slit of a window.

He washed in the provided bowl and pitcher of water, dressed, and ambled downstairs in the appropriate leisurely manner for an entertainer who expects to be up late of nights, only to hear "That's him," from one of the table servers and see a young man in a crimson tabard embroidered with a black and silver bird jump up and march towards him with determination.

:*That would be the Mayard servant that's been waiting for you to come down since almost dawn,:* Yfandes informed him.

:*Why didn't you—never mind. You wanted me to look surprised.:*

"Are you Jackomo?" the young man demanded.

"Prince of Minstrels and Minstrel to Princes. At your service." Van made a very, very, sketchy nod. Because Jackomo had a very high regard for his own importance and wasn't going to actually *bow* to a mere servant.

"My master, Sieur Mayard, commands me to bring you to him," the fellow said, with all the impatience of someone who has been cooling his heels for the better part of two candlemarks.

Van raised an eyebrow. "Since I am not in the service of Sieur Mayard, he can command all he likes. I am having breakfast."

There were a couple of snorts and several chortles. Evidently the fellow had not been making himself particularly welcome, and even those in the Mayard faction obviously found him annoying. Certainly the servers were annoyed. He had probably been sitting at a table, not buying anything, taking up space a paying customer could have been using.

But to smooth things over, Van continued, "When I have eaten, I shall come with you, certainly."

"Master says he's left orders with Cook when you're ready for breakfast, Jackomo," the same server who had identified him called. "I'll just go and fetch your food now."

"My thanks," Van said graciously. He took a seat, and as the Mayard flunky sat opposite him (still not buying anything, not even a drink, trying not to fume), polished off a very fine breakfast. He took his time, because the food really was excellent, and after last night's performance he had a good appetite. Assuming the Mayards did not provide him with food and lodging, he could do worse than this inn. Actually, he *had* done worse than this inn, and often.

When he was finished, and only then, he looked up at the flunky, and stood up. "I am ready, lad," he said. "Lead on."

"Aren't you going to get your instruments?" the servant asked, brow furrowing.

Van looked down his nose at him. "You're here asking for me by name, yes?"

"Yes, but—"

"So your master has already heard of my reputation, yes?"

"Yes, but—"

"And your master does not want me hired by the Corleans, at least not until his fete is over, yes?"

Confusion came over the young man's expression. "How did you—"

Van just gave him a pitying look. "The entire city knows what is going on. Try to keep up." He crossed his arms over his chest. "Now are we going, or do I make arrangements with the inn master for an afternoon performance, and then go have a nap?"

The flunky got up and led the way out of the inn.

As cities went, this was an attractive one, if a little confusing to a newcomer. Van was guided through something that might have been called a warren, if the streets had been little more than alleys. But the streets, while narrow, were clean, all paved with good cobbles, and in very good order. There were fountains, or at least watering-posts for horses and donkeys at many of the crossroads, and now and again things opened up into squares or plazas.

The layout puzzled him for a bit, until he realized what the pattern was. A wheel, where the spokes were the main thoroughfares, there were other major roads connecting the spokes, and lanes and small streets subdividing each of the sections within the larger subdivisions. Presumably the Palace, which he could see when things opened up, was at the hub of the wheel. It was the first time he had ever seen such a municipal layout.

The buildings were absolutely crammed together, with hardly enough room to insert a knife between them. And so far, he hadn't seen a single building that wasn't made of stone. *Interesting.* He took careful note of every turning and all the landmarks. With any luck, not only would he need to find his way back to the inn, but he'd be coming back this way tomorrow night.

At length, the flunky led him into an area where the buildings were replaced by walls, with greenery just visible above them. And finally, through iron gates in one of those walls, and from there into a courtyard with some sculpted bushes and trees, and a U-shaped building around it. The entrance was apparently in the part of the building forming the back of the U, and the flunky hesitated for a moment. It was clear to Van that he was now trying to figure out if he should bring his charge in through the servant's entrance or the main entrance. Van solved his problem for him by heading straight for the main doors, as if this was the sort of thing he did every day.

The flunky scampered after him, but didn't stop him.

The doors stood wide open, and the entrance hall was abuzz with activity. In the center of all of this was a richly dressed woman, expertly directing the movements of servants decking the hall with greenery, flowers, and banners. He waited, the panting flunky standing just behind him, until there was a pause in the work and she caught sight of him. Then he bowed, deeply, and with a flourish.

"Ah!" she said, and fortunately for him, looked pleased. "Master Jackomo, I believe?"

"At your service, my Lady Mayard," he said with another bow. He did not bother with the "Prince of Minstrels and Minstrel to Princes" business; she was busy with the fete preparations, and obviously would not be amused.

"We wish to engage your services for my daughter's coming of age fete. It will be a masque. We would like you to begin at sunset tomorrow night. You will stand just where I am standing and serenade the guests as they arrive, then move to the Great Hall when my majordomo signals to you and continue doing so until the dancing begins. Then you can, as you will, either augment the music for the dancing—we have instrumentalists, but no singers—or sing in the interludes between dancing. The fete will end at two hours past midnight. You will be paid two gold crowns by the majordomo at the conclusion of the fete. And you will *not* accept any offers to perform from the Corleans for two weeks afterward. Is this a satisfactory arrangement?"

Van bowed again, and rose, unable to suppress a smile. "Very, my Lady. It is a pleasure to perform for someone who knows both my worth and her own so exactly."

There was a hint of a twinkle in her eye. "Then be here an hour before sunset tomorrow. I am looking forward to your performance."

"I am very much looking forward to performing for so perceptive an audience." Since that seemed to be a good place to conclude, he bowed deeply again, and took himself off, leaving the flunky behind, who looked stunned, clearly not understanding what had just happened.

:'Fandes, is Savil busy?:

:With her, breakfast is all. Two crowns! Well, she is *paying for you not to work for her rival for two weeks.:*

:Generous of her to think of that. Well, I'll sing for our supper at the inn today and tonight, and the same after the fete. I doubt she'll mind that.:

He was going to wait a little and let his aunt finish her meal before telling her the good news. Well, it might be good.

At least it was going to get him right into the heart of the Mayard entourage for a night. He could learn a lot from just that.

The Prince was, of course, fully occupied when Savil finished her breakfast and consulting with her nephew. While the burden of Vanyel's news was good, when they finished Mindspeaking she was left with an unsettling feeling of urgency. *:I'm no Foreseer,:* she said to Kellen, *:but—:*

:Trust your instincts,: her Companion advised her. *:I'm*

*sensing it, too. And so, I suspect, is the Prince, or he never would
have asked for you to come here.:*

Maybe it was a subtle undercurrent in the city itself. She was
not an Empath, but if a feeling was widespread and strong
enough, sometimes even unGifted people could pick it up. And
a sudden increase in anger and resentment on the part of the
Corleans (due to the Mayard heir coming of age and a potential
marriage wresting that property away from them) could account for that increase.

And that might explain why Van hadn't yet felt it. So far, he'd
only had contact with the Mayards, who were likely to be feeling smug right now . . .

*Oh, now there's a thought. What if the girl's "choice" is no
choice at all? If the suitors they've lined up for her are all old,
unattractive, or absolutely open about just wanting her for what
she's going to inherit? No young girl is going to want any of
those . . . and then they spring a young—or at least not old—
handsome, and kind fellow on her, one who is attentive and
charming? And that is the one with the right degree of claim on
that property.*

*:Then they put pressure on her to pick right now, she caves
into the pressure because she's been raised to be obedient, and
picks the one they forced on her, like a street magician's card-
trick.:* Kellan got it immediately, of course. *:What a dirty piece
of chicanery to pull on a young girl!:*

Oh, Savil could see the other side of it too. In this culture she
was going to have to marry someone, and they couldn't take the
chance it would be someone that would make matters worse.
And they weren't trying to force her into a match that would be
genuinely repugnant. But still . . .

She left notice with the Prince's servants to let her know
when the Prince was free, and to their credit, they came to fetch
her *immediately* when he was, and when they brought her to
him, they ushered her right past about three people who were
already waiting.

She laid out her speculations for him, without specifying
where some of her information came from, because the walls

had ears, and it was a certainty that both families had spies in the Prince's household. Van's presence in the city was akin to a secret weapon in her pocket, and she meant to keep it that way.

"All of that makes sense, and if the Corleans have already thought of it—and I'm sure they have—it accounts for why matters are heating up," he said unhappily. "And there is literally nothing I can do about it."

"Except show up at the fete, congratulate the girl on her coming-of-age, and remind her of all the things she would be losing if she makes a hasty choice," Savil suggested. "Freedom, most especially. *Now* she is free of responsibilities. If she weds, she'll be expected to take command of the household, and that means household accounting, directing the servants, making sure they are doing their duties as she expects them to, and—well, you know better than I what she'd be expected to do. Emphasize the 'responsibilities.' Oh, and remind her that once she is married, there won't be any more courting; she'll have to be respectable. Is there a difference between a matron's dress and that of a girl of courting age?"

"Why yes . . . hair coverings and covered up to the collarbone," the Prince said thoughtfully.

"I'm sure she's enjoying her pretty things now; make sure she understands how much she is giving up." Savil smiled sourly. "And that she not only won't be rid of her mother telling her what to do, she'll gain a mother-in-law also telling her what to do."

"That's a very good point. I'll do that." The Prince did not exactly brighten, but he looked a little less glum.

"In the meantime, I'd like to see the Corleans—without them realizing I'm watching them. Particularly the hot-headed ones. Where am I going to find their household?"

"I'll get you a page, and have him take off his tabard before he goes out with you. No one looks twice at a child." The Prince rang a bell on his desk, and shortly a servant arrived, and was sent off with the order to "find one of the pages that knows his way around the city."

The servant came back with a curly-haired youngling about

ten or twelve with an innocent face Savil thought concealed a head full of mischief. Exactly what she wanted. She waited patiently while the Prince explained what the lad was to do—take Savil to the Corleans' villa, but not too close to it—and without his tabard. The lad pulled the tabard off immediately and handed it to the servant that had brought him.

:Do you want me to come along?:

:I want you listening for gossip. Wherever you think is best. Pull the string on the door of your loose-box and go ghosting through the gardens if you think you can get away with it.: Kellan had some magical tricks of her own up her sleeve—if she'd had a sleeve—including something not unlike an invisibility spell. You'd see her if you were *expecting* to see her, but if you weren't, you'd never notice her. Not a bad trick for a glaringly white horse.

Savil bid the Prince a temporary farewell, and headed for the door with the brown-haired, hazel-eyed lad trotting alongside. "What do they call you?"

She was hoping for a saucy answer, and got one. "Ricarto when I'm at home."

"And when you're not at home?" she asked.

"'You boy,' mostly. And 'Hey you.' Except when I'm with me mates. They call me Banter."

"Because you like to talk?" she asked, with a crooked grin. "Would you rather I called you Ricarto, Ric, or Banter?"

He looked at her sideways, as if an adult had never asked him that question before. Well, probably, they hadn't. "Ric," he said finally, as they exited the building and headed for the gate.

"All right, Ric, tell me what you know about the Corleans."

What Ric turned out to know was quite a lot. Most of it was unsurprising, but some was probably going to be extremely useful, and that was what he knew about Peitro, the heir.

"He's *always* falling in love with girls," Ric told her. "It's a new girl every moon. And most of 'em are people his parents wouldn't let him marry if they were the last unmarried girl in the city. Right now, it's one of his cousins that's *ages* older than him and has about a million suitors, and there's *no way* his parents would let him marry her, because she's as related to the Mayards as she is the Corleans. Last month it was a dairy maid, and he was always hanging around the dairy, snatching spoonfuls of cream and getting in her way, until she gave him a right tongue-lashing. Moon before that it was a girl he just spotted in a window, and he hung around the house until her husband ran him off. And before that I don't remember who it was, but he gets over them in a moon or so."

Savil glanced in astonishment at the lad as they navigated past a carter and a suddenly stubborn donkey. "Where does he get all this free time to chase women? Shouldn't he be with a tutor, or learning how to do what his father does?"

"He's the only child they had that lived this long, so his Papa and Mama let him do what he wants. He said he was done with tutors three years ago when he was fourteen; said he was of age now so he didn't need one, and they just let him run free with his cousins. They're all troublemakers," the child added darkly. "Well, you'll see. I'm taking you to where you can watch them all; there's this square they always hang about in, because there's a wine-seller that lets 'em use the place like their private club, and they're always getting into something."

"Angry with them, or envious?" Savil asked shrewdly.

The lad looked up at her as if, again, he couldn't believe the words coming out of an adult mouth. "Both," he admitted. "*I'd* like to drink wine and eat sausage and cheese and fruit all day, and lark about. But they've messed with so many common folks that it's not fair to bother. They broke all the eggs one poor girl had, and left her crying because she hadn't anything to sell. They bother old ladies going to temple just 'cause they aren't pretty. They scared a bride half to death, thinking they were going to carry her off and ruin her. They pick fights with Mayard servants who don't dare fight back because they're only servants, and no matter what the upshot'd be, it's always bad for the servant who's up against a Sieur's son. It's not fair. And it's not right."

"You're right, it isn't," Savil agreed. "What about Peitro? Is he involved in all this?"

"Well, to be fair . . . he mostly goes along and takes care of what the rest of 'em leave behind. He made 'em put the bride down, and gave her a nice piece of cloth to make a new dress out of. He paid for that girl's eggs. And he apologizes to the old ladies. But only where they can't see him do it, so it's not like he's trying to shame those devils. And we're here. Got any money?"

"A little on me, why?" she asked as they turned a corner to find themselves entering a huge stone square rimmed with stone buildings, with the sun beating directly down on it. There was a fountain splashing merrily in the center, but it didn't seem to cool things very much.

"'Cause the best view is from Auntie Relano's bakeshop, but she won't let you sit there unless you keep buying and eating something." The lad licked his lips, betraying his own interest in using that spot as a lookout.

"That sounds like a fine plan to me," she replied, so with great glee the boy led her straight to the bakeshop, which was on a terrace overlooking the square. They settled down at a wooden table with shockingly heavy bench seats, and Savil made an initial order of tiny sausage rolls and tea. She could tell Ric had been hoping for something sweet, but she wanted to stuff him with things other than sweets before turning him loose on pastries.

"There they are!" the boy said after he'd eaten three fourths of the sausages. He pointed, she squinted, and made out about a dozen young men *much* better dressed than the rest of those in the square, ambling toward a shop with a similar lot of tables and bench seats as the bake shop. It was a good spot, since it was under a canvas sunshade, as this one was.

The proprietor bustled right out to meet them, made a show of dusting off seats with his apron, and bustled back inside once they were all seated. Plates of cheese, baskets of grapes and bottles of wine appeared shortly after this, and the youths helped themselves, languidly. Except for the wine, which they helped themselves to with great enthusiasm.

Savil's fingers moved surreptitiously in a small spell, one that would allow her to hear what was being said over there. Granted, she could have used Mindspeech to eavesdrop, but that was ethically dubious.

It appeared Peitro was coming in for a teasing by some of the others, one wag in particular, about his infatuation with his cousin Marian. The "wit" teased him about visiting a "dream doctor" too often, then made a lot of often derogatory rhyming couplets on the name of "Marian." Peitro finally got angry and was only placated—barely—when the wit offered him a drink and a half-hearted apology.

He was still sulking when the man finally came up with an idea that turned him all smiles again. "The Mayard's fete tonight is a masque," he pointed out. "And they've made it an open invitation to anyone. They're hosting the riff-raff in the square in front of the villa with bread and a wine fountain, but anyone who's dressed well and masked can just stroll into the house itself. And Marian will surely be there. I will bet you that within a candlemark you'll see a dozen girls prettier than she is and *younger* than she is. Peitro, she's practically old enough to be your mother! And if she doesn't give up her flirtations soon and pick a suitor, next year no one will want her, and the only place that will take her will be a cloister! Let's go, and I'll wager you find a new face to fall in love with before the night is up!"

"I'll take that wager," Peitro said instantly.

Savil went on the alert. :*Kellan, is Van busy?*:

:*He's being moved about the house like a fancy piece of statuary by her Ladyship. She's trying to find the best places to show off her prize tonight.*:

:*Tell Yfandes to tell him I need to warn him about something.*: She left it at that, and turned to Ric. "Two cream cakes, and then we go back to the Palace," she told him. She lifted a finger, and one of the servers sped to the table of a reliable spender and took her order. "Both cakes are for you," she told the child before his face could fall. "One to eat and one to take. You've done a smashing job. I'll make sure to let the Prince know."

Ric brightened right up. "You get what you come for, then?"

"Oh yes," she replied, watching the young idlers amuse

themselves by throwing grapes at passers-by. "More than enough."

Van had to think long and hard about warning Sieur Mayard that his fete was going to be invaded by Corlean trouble-makers, but decided against it. First, most, if not all of them, would be finding their courage to invade the enemy stronghold unarmed in the bottom of a bottle, and the Mayards' personal guards had orders to keep anyone visibly drunk out, restricting them to the public square with the commoners. They couldn't do any harm to the celebration out in the square, and a fountain of wine was going to be a lot more attractive than starting a fight. And second, the actual intent was not to disrupt, but to present Peitro with so many enticing options to his current be-loved that he'd fall out of love with her. Starting trouble would get them thrown out before they could achieve that goal.

And the simple fact is that I am so wildly more powerful than the Mayard "wizard"—who is barely up to a few simple illusions—that I can take care of problems long before they be-come problems. Make them so dizzy they just fell down of their own accord, for instance, or trip them up. Intoxicate them. Put them to sleep. The possibilities were endless, and they'd end up dumped in the square without becoming more than a minor nuisance.

So Van stationed himself in the courtyard beside the central planter, with its graceful willow tree and fragrant herbs, and welcomed guests who passed the guards' scrutiny with songs calculated to put everyone in a good mood.

Dusk fell, the servants lit lanterns around the courtyard, and still the Corleans had not appeared. Then came true night, when most of the invited guests and a great many who had not been invited crowded into the villa rather than out in the court-yard, and the time came to move inside and entertain from within. Technically this was a masque, but most people either had something on their faces made of elaborate lace that did little to disguise their identities, or their masks were pushed up on their heads rather than being over their faces.

Van had begun to think the Corlean contingent had decided wine in the square was better than trouble in the villa, and had begun to relax. And it was just about at that point that a half dozen well-dressed, moderately inebriated young rogues, all fully masked, appeared in the gate to the courtyard. It didn't take Mindspeech to figure out who these boys were, but none of them wore anything in the way of weapons, not even an ornamental dagger, and none of them were engaging in the kinds of bullying shenanigans Savil had described to him. It might be too good to be true—but it seemed that they were sticking to the original plan—show Peitro so many beautiful women that he'd lose interest in his love-of-the-moment.

He came into the Great Hall of the villa behind the group— still singing, but projecting good cheer and good humor so strongly that the level of laughter in his wake was considerably higher than it had been before. His efforts had an effect on the Corlean lads too; there was a lot of teasing and pointing and double-entendre comments as some of the younger ladies in the great hall participated in an unmarried-women-only dance— the sort absolutely intended to show off all their beauty, costly gowns, and availability to the single and wealthy men among the onlookers.

Marian was among them (she had been pointed out to Van earlier) and giving her a critical eye, he decided Peitro's cousin was not wrong. She was much older than the others, in her early twenties, and she was by no means the prettiest young lady in the group. Her chief beauty was an astonishing head of hair of true gold that, even braided, reached to her ankles. She'd made the most of it by braiding pearls into it and wearing a cap netted of matching pearls, a clever move that subtly conveyed not only her attractiveness but her wealth.

For a moment, Van toyed with the idea of getting the Prince to throw his weight behind a marriage of Peitro and his infatuation; if she was as related to the Mayards as Savil thought, that might cool the feud.

But all those plans went out the window when the dance ended, and before another could begin, three trumpeters in the minstrel's gallery blew a fanfare, and the crowd melted back against the walls, leaving the center of the room empty. And in floated a veiled apparition dressed in midnight blue velvet, a silver band about her brow, with four girls holding the corners of her gossamer veil. The crowd hushed, the music began, the girls raised the veil, and the maiden danced out from underneath it to meet a line of six men who materialized out of the crowd.

Van instantly knew this must be Fiametta, and the six men were her six would-be suitors.

And instantly he had to commend her father for being a shrewd bastard.

Every one of those men, except one, was old enough to be her father. Two were old enough to be her grandfather. Except for that one, who was handsome, relatively young—late twenties, perhaps—and exquisitely dressed. Her father knew exactly who he wanted for his son-in-law, and he was clever enough to frame things so that his daughter, under the impression she had a choice, was being "forced" to choose as cleverly as a street performer would force a card on an unsuspecting mark.

She had a single white rose tucked into the breast of her gown, and as each of the suitors stepped forward to dance a passage with her, it was obvious to Van that she was intended to present the rose to her chosen suitor at the end of the dance. Her mother and father had probably hammered that home to her. The crowd expected it.

And he couldn't help but cheer a little for her when she ended the dance by curtseying gravely to all of them—and keeping the rose for herself.

:She can't put off making a choice very soon, but her parents aren't going to force the issue tonight.: Yfandes observed. *:And she kept all attention on herself to boot, rather than sacrificing it to a potential husband. It's supposed to be* her *night, and I don't blame her one bit for wanting to keep it that way. If they kept her as cloistered as rumor says, having everyone's eyes on her must be intoxicating.:*

The dance over, a suitor unchosen, Fiametta was immediately drawn into a little circle of what must have been her friends, since they were all about the same age. Van found himself momentarily unoccupied near the back of the room; the musicians in the minstrel gallery had struck up a lively tune, and it was clear people wanted to dance, not listen, even to him.

He glanced about, trying to see if he could catch sight of the Corlean contingent. To his right was Peitro, speaking urgently to Marian, who laughed, and from all Van could tell, treated him kindly, but very much like the puppy he was.

And that was when he heard the first hint of an altercation to his left, where Sieur Mayard was standing, supervising the celebration.

With a face full of wrath, a young man named Lymond, Sieur Mayard's nephew on his wife's side, stormed up to him. "My lord!" the fellow snarled—though he at least had the good sense to keep his voice down. "My lord, there are *Corleans* here!"

Van moved closer and cast a small spell to make people overlook him.

"And what of it?" came the surprisingly calm counter. "We have thrown our doors open to all. They have not caused a problem. There is no harm in them being here. Let them go back to their kennels with the knowledge that Mayard is not only a prouder and wealthier house than theirs, but that we are about to make the marriage that will cement our claim on the Night Rose Manor."

"How can you smile and let their mere *presence* besmirch our honor?" the hothead cried. "Is this not coward—"

He didn't get any farther than that, and Van did *not* anticipate what happened next. In the next breath the hothead found himself slammed into a corner behind some draperies, the older man's forearm against his throat, the other hand clenching a fist full of his tunic.

Well, he's stronger than I thought.

"What! How now, you young cur! How *dare* you upbraid me, tell me what *I* will do in *mine own house*!" Before Lymond could do more than gasp, he found himself flung through a doorway to land sprawling on the floor of what looked like a pantry. "Get out of my sight! And if you *dare* make trouble, there is not one word from your aunt that will save you from my anger!"

This was, fortunately for the fellow's vanishing dignity, out of sight of everyone but the Sieur's bodyguards. The older man turned his back and ostentatiously moved away, leaving Lymond to haul himself to his feet, straighten his clothing, and look around to see who had noticed this altercation.

Van had already cast true invisibility on himself—a hazard, since it meant someone might walk into him, but best not to be in a position where someone that intemperate could take out his anger on a "mere minstrel." As carefully as he could, he slipped away, out of the great hall and into one of the colonnades that lined it and led to an inner courtyard, and from there to the gardens. There were people here, but it was quieter, and the dim light had made it a popular place for flirtations. He dropped the invisibility and had actually put his hands on the strings of his gittern to begin a love song.

And that was when he felt it.

Unlike Savil, he *was* something of an Empath. And no Empath who had once experienced the feeling would ever mistake the rush of tangled euphoria and terror that came when Lifebondeds met for the very first time. It hit him like a slap to the back of the head.

:Is that—: gasped Yfandes, who felt it as well.

:Hush, I'm—: He concentrated, trying to find the source of the feeling.

And then he spotted them, in the shelter of a column, in the shadows. Fiametta Mayard, her cheeks flaming with utter confusion, looking into the masked eyes of Peitro Corlean.

:Savil!: he exclaimed, putting urgency into his Mindvoice. *:Everything just went sideways! Fiametta Mayard is lifebonded to Peitro Corlean!:*

Thank the gods his aunt knew him well enough not to ask stupid, time-wasting questions. *:That explains that sense of urgency we both had,:* she replied with commendable calm. *:Don't let them out of your sight. Tell me if anything happens, no matter how late it is. Tell me if your Foresight shows you anything.*

The Prince and I need to consult. If they split up, tell me. I'll keep track of the boy, you keep track of the girl.:

He leaned his back against the wall, as near to the pair as he dared to go, and began playing an intricate bit of music, all the time straining his ears to hear what they said to each other. It was a lot of nonsense of course; neither of them understood what had just happened, both of them doubted, at least initially, that what the other was saying was genuine. *She* might have been cloistered, but she'd been warned against boys who said things they didn't mean. And *he* could not believe what he was feeling, and was acting just a little drunk with it. Then *he* began saying extravagant nonsense, trying to be poetical, while *she* wanted very badly for it all to be real, but still doubted. But the more they spoke together, the stronger the undeniable pull between them.

And, if it had not been for Fiametta's mother calling her from the other room in a "you had better get over here" tone, they might have gone on gazing into each other's eyes, slowly losing speech in the pull of the lifebond.

But Lady Mayard *did* begin calling—probably to get her daughter back to the dance and out of that colonnade where no one could see her—and once she was gone, Peitro's friends turned up and dragged him away over his protests.

:Savil, his friends are carrying him off. I think they've been getting side-eyed by people who suspect they're Corleans; there was almost an incident with one of the Mayards earlier.:

:I sent Kellan there; she'll pick him up once he leaves the grounds. You stick with the girl.:

That sense of urgency hadn't lifted in the least. If anything, it had gotten stronger and darker. There were far too many ways this could end in tragedy, and preventing that tragedy was going to be like threading a needle atop a galloping horse.

Van moved back into the Great Hall, still playing; the girl stood in the shadows with her mother, head bowed submissively, nodding. But her feelings were powerfully at odds with that outward submission; she was angry, felt put-upon, and rebellious.

Her mother had no notion of any of this, and at length seemed to be satisfied. She turned and gestured in a "come here" fashion, and the favored suitor separated himself from a knot of people watching the dancers and approached them both. He offered the girl his hand; with a tiny curtsey she took it, and he drew her into the dance.

He danced with her for the rest of the night, unless she managed to escape into an all-ladies' dance, or pled that she was tired and needed to sit down, which she did every time the opportunity offered. It was very, very clear he was still trying to get her to give him her rose, and just as clear she had no intention of doing so. Van did the best he could to help her by playing and singing *anything* but love songs when he was at her part of the room. She resisted going into the colonnade with her suitor, resisted being drawn anywhere that they could converse privately.

It must have been exhausting for her.

Van felt a great deal of sympathy for the poor man; he might not have been in love with the girl, but he clearly *liked* her, liked the idea of being married to her, and had all but been handed that position by her father and mother, and she was acting as if the only thing on her mind was another dance, or a chance to admire other ladies' gowns, or how good the refreshments were, and was completely oblivious to all the nice things he was saying to her. And yet, he hadn't lost his temper in the least.

Poor fellow has no idea he's competing with a lifebond.

Finally, the time came for the fete to end. Fiametta's disappointed suitor bade her and her mother and father farewell, showing no sign of his disappointment.

:Peitro has climbed the back wall into the gardens and he's staring at the windows, trying to figure out which one is hers.: That was Yfandes. *:Kellan is sticking close to the wall on the outside, there's no good way in even for one of us.:*

Fiametta stayed at her parents' side until the last of the guests had said their goodbyes and left. Then she curtsied to her parents, kissed their cheeks, and was taken off by an older woman in commoners' clothing, probably her governess or nurse.

Sieur Mayard looked over to where he was still picking out a tender little song and gestured to him to approach. He left off playing, did so, and bowed.

"Well done, Jackomo," the man said warmly. "You have an uncanny ability to play exactly what is needed when it is needed. And I do not believe I have ever heard a better musician. You truly are a Prince of Minstrels." He gestured now to a servant, who brought him a pouch, which he put into Van's hands. "You've earned this. If you are inclined, I shall put in a good word for you with the Prince."

Van bowed again. "That would be deeply appreciated, Sieur Mayard," he said. "Have you any further need of my services?"

"You may seek your well-earned rest, as I shall take mine."

Since that was a clear dismissal, Van bowed again, and left. And as soon as he was out of sight of anyone, he cast an invisibility spell on himself, doubled back through the colonnaded room, and passed out into the gardens through a door he had spied earlier.

It wasn't hard to find Peitro; the lad was almost a torch of fiery emotions. Van slipped in through the garden shadows and set himself up within a couple of horse-lengths of the boy, who was still scanning balconies and windows, hoping to figure out which one was his newly-beloved's.

And then Fiametta appeared on one of the second-floor balconies, clad in her shift, hair unbound and free. She looked up at the moon and sighed. She was, even in Van's eyes, staggeringly beautiful like this. And the boy reacted accordingly.

Peitro could not help himself. He found a way through the foliage until he was right beneath her, and spoke softly into the night. "Why do you sigh, bright spirit?" he called. "Only tell me what grieves you, and I will cross half the world to find the cure!"

She started, and stared down, finally catching sight of his face. "Are you not Peitro, and a Corlean?" she asked, one hand going to her throat. "If my kinsmen find you, they will surely murder you!" Her enormous eyes grew bright with unshed tears, her emotions a maelstrom.

"Let them, as long as your eyes are the last thing my eyes see," he replied.

To her credit, she managed to throttle down the more turbulent of her feelings, and leaned over the balcony rail, desperately trying to figure out if all this was real. "How did you find me?"

"My heart led me, for it is bound to yours, and could not lead me astray!" he declared.

There was quite a bit more of this, as Van stood an unknown guard over both of them, he and Yfandes making sure the usual patrols avoided this spot. That wasn't *too* hard, since the area beneath Fiametta's balcony was overgrown and well off any path, and after all the work of the fete, the guards were disinclined to do anything more than they absolutely had to.

:He's talking his way into her bed, you know,: observed Yfandes dispassionately.

:He was talking his way into her bed from the moment the lifebond took hold,: Van replied. *:And there he goes . . . :*

Because Peitro had managed to find a place where the masonry and a heavy vine allowed him to climb up to the balcony. Once there, it was only a matter of moments before they kissed, and the kissing turned to passionate caresses, and he scooped her up in his arms and carried her inside.

Fortunately for them, Van had already fortified that bedchamber with another spell that made people, even the girl's nurse, disinclined to open the door. With a sigh of his own, because this was going to be a very long night, and he was already using far too much of his own personal power, he slipped his gittern into its case and found a spot where he could get up on the garden wall and hand it down to Yfandes.

She took the strap in her teeth like a dog, and trotted off into the darkness, taking it back to the inn. It was a very good gittern, and he was loath to find himself forced to abandon it.

Then he settled down in a good hiding place from which he

could still see the balcony, and prepared to wait. And try to take tiny, tiny sips of the local ley line to replenish what he was using in the way of magic. He dared not do more. The last thing he needed was to alert any other mages that magic was being worked *here*.

". . . and according to my nephew, he's just talked his way into her bed," Savil informed the Prince, who was in a robe hastily thrown over his bedclothes, and had a cup of some kind of ti-sane in his hand. He'd offered her a cup, which she'd downed without thinking, and now felt as if she wasn't going to sleep for a fortnight.

:We need that stuff in Valdemar,: Kellan observed.

Whatever was in that tea, it had enabled the Prince to go from bleary-eyed stumbling to alert and thinking. "Thank all the gods for your nephew," he finally said. "And now is not the time to upbraid you for bringing a spy along on this mission. In fact, when I have time to think, I'll probably just frown and then agree it was a good idea." He pinched the bridge of his nose, then looked around himself. "What I need now are books," he said. "To the library. I need to consult some law books. There will be a solution to all of this in there, and I just need to find it."

He gathered his robe around himself, downed the last of his tea, and gestured to the page that had helped Savil wake him to follow with a candle. The library was down a floor, and the Prince moved so fast, Savil was afraid he'd trip on his robe and break his neck, and *then* where would they be?

The page managed to get ahead of them by taking the steps two at a time, and swept open the doors, then literally ran around the room, lighting the lanterns that would let them all see.

The Prince went straight to a shelf containing some enor-mous books, all the same size and bound identically in dark brown leather. "L," he muttered. "L, L, L. Thank the gods these things are in alphabetical order. There!"

He pulled one down and took it to a stand right under a

lantern. "We don't see lifebonds often, I *never* have in my lifetime, but I am fairly certain we—yes! Here we go! There are laws about them!" He ran his finger across the page rapidly. "And . . . this is better than we could have hoped! *Neither Prince nor man, mother nor father, priest nor previous arrangement, may stand against a lifebond, for it is the truth, as we have learned to our sorrow, that forbidding the bond will result in the death of both the victims. And such a death must be accounted a murder, though it be by the lifebondeds' own hands.*" He glanced over his shoulder at Savil, who nodded. "*Then let them be wedded, regardless of any other consideration or status, for marriage is better than death.*"

"That's the gods' own truth," she agreed. "So . . . does this mean you have the authority to order their parents that they can be married?"

"More than the authority, I have a mandate," he replied. He turned to the page. "Forten, wake up the household priest." The page nodded and ran off. He turned back to Savil. "The sooner we can get them both here, the better. I think there is more that I can do, I just need to find the precedents in here."

"I rather think that it would be ill-advised for Van to break into the girl's bedroom and carry them both off right now," Savil said dryly. "It would be two against one, and there would certainly be enough screaming and shouting to wake the rest of the household—"

The Prince coughed. "I'm not suggesting that," he said. "But Peitro has to leave before dawn, and if you can somehow intercept him outside the Mayard walls and bring him here and we can explain . . ." He pinched his nose again. "Perhaps if I then order the girl to appear here . . ." He waved his hand vaguely. ". . . to congratulate her on her coming of age? That probably won't raise any suspicions. I'll take the parents aside, the priest can marry the pair while I have them busy, and then I can . . . I need to make some plans. I can't count on either set of parents taking this . . . well . . ."

Savil nodded. "You make plans. Get the priest prepared. Between us, Van and I will manage something."

I hope. Because plans tend to fall apart as soon as they are implemented.

. . . and he has a little bit of every Gift. Farsight. Empathy. Foresight . . .

Half-dozing, Vanyel heard once again the words he had over-heard while in the care of the Hawkbrothers. He never knew when one of those odder Gifts was going to manifest. He had managed to train the most useful ones—Mage-Gift, of course, and Mindspeech, and the Bardic Gift had proved easier than most, but the odd ones . . . well even Heralds and Priests with things like Foresight found them difficult to train. Visions tended to come randomly. *Very randomly,* he thought as he dozed.

Then he woke completely on hearing voices above him. "Oh *why* must it be the lark and not the nightingale!" the girl cried softly. "But if you stay, my father *will* slay you himself."

Peitro straddled the balcony. Van looked up; the sky was lightening, but the boy should be able to get across the garden and over the wall before anyone caught sight of him.

"Remember," he said, leaning over to kiss her. "Make an excuse to go to the temple of Bries, the Lady of the Hearth. Tell your parents you're going to pray about your choice of suitors. I'll meet you there. I *know* I can find a priestess there to marry us. Then *nothing* they can do can tear us apart!"

"I don't care if they cast me out and disinherit me!" she cried. "I'll follow you if we must be beggars!"

"And if my father disinherits me, I'll take the name of Ma-yard! Or no name at all!" He almost fell off the balustrade as he embraced her fiercely. "Not even death will part us!"

The vision came on Vanyel like a lightning strike.

Peitro, on his way to the temple, coming across that hothead friend of his and his cronies taunting a knot of Corleans. A fight breaking out, Peitro trying to stop it. Swords drawn. Peitro's best friend killed as he tries to separate them. Peitro losing his temper, snatching up the sword of his friend, and killing the hothead. Peitro sentenced to death and executed. Fiametta throwing herself from the top of the Mayard manor . . . .

Then the vision let him go, leaving him reeling, his heart racing, and yet with the conviction that *this* was where the urgency had come from. And he knew they had to make exactly the right choices now, at exactly the right moment, or not only would they fail their mission here, but two innocent lives would be snuffed out.

:I told Kellan. Kellan told Savil.: Yfandes, as ever, had known exactly what to do as she shared his vision.

Van struggled to his feet. His heart pounded, and so did his head, but the visions had not quite left him. More fragments swirled around him—he recognized them for what they were, bits of "might be" and "could be" where Fiametta's parents locked her up and she poisoned herself, and Peitro went insane and lay in wait to attack Sieur Mayard and was killed, and the feud erupted into endless blood in the streets.

:Van! You can handle the girl. Get her out and get her to the Prince's palace, Kellan and I will take care of the rest.:

He clung to the bark of the tree next to himself and forced his thoughts to clear. *Get the girl before her parents can lock her up completely. That's the key. I—*

He had barely formed that thought when he heard a ruckus in the room above him.

"But Father!" Fiametta cried, a note of hysteria in her voice.

"I gave you *every* chance last night! I pledged to Esquerry Talient that you would give him your rose!" Sieur Mayard roared. "I thought perhaps it was just maidenly modesty that kept you from making that *obvious* choice, but now you tell me that you 'do not want to marry him.'? Dear *gods,* I should beat you with my own two hands! *Do not want!* You willful, ungrateful brat! The future and honor of House Mayard rests on this, and you tell me *you do not want!* Well, by the gods you shall *learn* to want! You will not leave this room, nor sup on anything but bread and water, until you decide to want!"

"Father! Father, please!"

"Do not speak to me until you say the words, 'Father, I will marry Talient!'" There was the sound of a door slamming, and then hysterical weeping.

Now. NOW! I need to get her out before they think about the balcony!

He cast invisibility on himself again and used Peitro's vine to get up to the balcony and inside. Inside, he felt his personal power beginning to bleed away again. Normally, as an Archmage, he *never* had to use his personal power. This was going to stretch him thinner than a bridal veil.

Fiametta lay sprawled out on the floor, arms stretched towards the closed door to her room, sobbing her heart out. Outside there was more shouting.

Another vision hit him—*himself, on the floor next to her, explaining—Sieur Mayard breaking in on them—*

No time!

He flung a sleeping spell at her, and staggered a little as the cost hit him. The sobs stopped as the spell overcame her. He flung her over his shoulder, let the invisibility spell cover them both, and practically leapt for the balcony.

And not a moment too soon. He was halfway down the vine when he heard the doors above burst open again.

He didn't stop to listen more. There was no way he could get her over the garden wall. Instead, he took the nearest path out through the villa—which, ironically, was the now-open door into the gardens from the courtyard and colonnade room. Shouting from Fiametta's room summoned servants from all over, giving *him* a cleared path to safety.

Yfandes waited in the forecourt, pawing the cobbles impatiently. He threw the sleeping girl over her forequarters, got himself up behind her. He felt his control over his magic slipping, and exhaustion made him drop the illusion just as two servants came out and spotted them.

"Master!" one of them cried. *"Master! The minstrel!"*

Too late. They were already out the gate and on their way to the Prince's palace.

Savil fretted as she sat atop Kellan. The hotheads were already at their usual post, already drinking, and already boasting about how they had invaded the Mayard fete. The noise they

were making drove everyone else to the far side of the plaza.
Savil had gotten to her spot just in time to see Peitro vanish into
the temple, curse him, and she didn't know how long it would
take him to persuade a priestess to perform such a hasty wedding, particularly under the circumstances. He had been sure,
but she wasn't so sanguine.

*:I've got the girl, but I was spotted. I don't think they know
I'm taking her to the Prince, because they only know me as the
Minstrel. But they* might *come to the Prince anyway for help
finding me.:*

*:Let's hope they don't think of that. When did your vision
show the brawling start—:*

A gaggle of men in Maynard livery invaded the plaza. They
were armed, and were probably looking for Van and Fiametta.
And they probably think Van is working for the Corleans . . .

"Hey!" shouted the one in the lead, who was much better
dressed than the others. "You dogs! What have you done with
my cousin!"

And here we go—

"Why would we give a shit about your cousin?" laughed the
best dressed of them. "Why don't you look for her down on
Whore Street? That's probably where she went! After all, your
uncle made it clear last night that Fiametta goes to the highest
bidder!"

The Mayard leader went red in the face. "You keep her name
out of your filthy mouth, you misbegotten bastard! I know you,
you're always sniffing around after your aunt's skirts!"

Swords came out.

Savil almost missed Peitro coming out of the temple—it
wasn't until he began to run towards the two about-to-brawl
parties that she realized he was there.

And she did the only thing she could think to do.

She pulled power out of the nearest ley-line and called lightning down out of the clouds to hit precisely between them.

It was no squib, either; fueled by her panic, it was a massive
bolt that left *her* half blinded and half deafened.

:Hang on!: Kellan shouted, and bolted for the center of the

square. Savil clung to the pommel as she leapt over several prone bodies—

:Oh dear gods, did I—:

:I shielded them. They're all right, just stunned.:

Relief made her want to weep. How bad would *that* have been, to have killed a double handful of the very feuding people she was supposed to settle?

But Kellan was skidding to a halt beside Peitro, who was rubbing at his dazzled eyes and shaking his head. She grabbed his arm. "Up!" she ordered, *"Up!"*

"But—"

"Prince's orders!" she barked, using Command Voice.

It worked. He took her arm and hauled himself up behind her.

And then they were off. *:Van—:*

:We're at the Palace.:

:Then tell the Prince to send his guards down here before these idiots wake up and start fighting again.:

This wasn't over.

But, with a rush of relief, she knew—*knew*—the worst was.

The square in front of the Palace was packed with shouting people who were only kept from turning on each other by the presence of every single one of the Prince's guards, who had trained bows and crossbows on them from the walls, and rimmed the courtyard with shields and pikes. Additional guards kept them separated into the Corlean and Mayard factions, or there might have been war right then and there. The Mayards were screaming for blood, claiming the Corleans had hired Jackomo the Minstrel to abduct Fiametta. The Corleans were howling for blood themselves, claiming the Mayards had hired Savil to kidnap Peitro.

Inside the entrance hall, the "abducted" couple—Fiametta in a borrowed gown much too large for her—gazed blissfully into each other's eyes, oblivious to the turmoil outside, their marriage having happened a mere candlemark ago.

The Prince stood just inside the doors, wearing every particle of his regalia, flanked by Savil and Van, and the Chief Justicier and his personal priest. He shook his head at the noise. "I pray to the gods that what we are about to do ends this strife once and for all."

His priest took that as an actual prayer and nodded. "So let it be," he said, sketching some symbol Van didn't recognize in the air to seal it.

"Open the doors," the Prince ordered.

The noise washed over them like a storm wave.

The Prince nodded to Van and Savil; *now* he could tap into a ley line without betraying that a mage was using it, and he did. With the power flooding into him, he dropped a silencing spell over the entire crowd, as Savil magically magnified the Prince's voice.

"SILENCE!" he roared.

Well, they didn't have any choice but to be silent, as their words were caught in their throats, but it was a nice, theatrical moment that would, hopefully, frighten the breeches off them.

"You! Sieur Mayard. And your lady-wife. Come here!" the Prince ordered, pointing to the steps just below him. "You! Sieur Corlean and your lady-wife! The same!"

Sieur Mayard hesitated, but his wife jabbed him in the ribs with her elbow, and he slowly climbed the steps, a half-step behind the Corleans, who were red-faced with fury. Van freed them from the general spell.

"This—woman—abducted my son!" Sieur Corlean snarled. "You'd better have a damned good—"

Van choked off his words, with a gesture.

Savil looked at him. "Want a taste of lightning?" she asked dryly. He went from red to pale.

"We saw—this man—Fiametta—" Sieur Mayard stammered. "Who *are* these people? Where are our children? What is this about?"

"That is what you are going to find out now," the Prince said, all dignity. "And it's going to put an end to this bitter, deadly feud. Follow me."

The Prince and the entourage all turned and went back up

the steps and through the door, leaving the others no choice but to follow. Literally no choice, although they didn't find that out—Van had every intention of forcing them up the stairs if they didn't move of their own accord.

Once inside, the Prince's group parted so that the first thing the parents saw were their children clinging together.

"Peitro!" cried Lady Corlean.

"Fiametta!" bellowed Sieur Mayard, his face going purple with rage. "What in hell do you think you're—"

Van silenced him as Fiametta shrank away and further into Peitro's arms.

Peitro straightened, and placed himself between her and both sets of parents.

Well, good for him. There's something there besides a pretty face and a penchant for chasing skirts.

"Fiametta and Peitro are lifebonded," the Prince said as the doors closed on the crowd behind them. Van kept the silence spell up anyway. "I trust you know what that is?"

Sieur Corlean cleared his throat and looked carefully at Van and Savil. Evidently the open display of magic had made him warier than his Mayard counterpart. "I thought lifebonds were a myth."

"They most certainly are *not*," the Prince said sternly. He nodded at his priest, who straightened, visibly loaded himself with dignity, and addressed the parents.

"Lifebonds are the gift of the gods," he proclaimed. "Rarely given, true, but very real, and very binding. To attempt to thwart such a gift is a direct offense to the gods themselves."

"It's also an offense to the law of this principality," the Prince said, his tone brooking no argument. "Chief Justicier, please enlighten them."

Looking pleased that he was playing a lead role in this little drama, the Chief Justicier opened the law book and read aloud the passages the Prince had found with great drama and much satisfaction. And seeing the two couples more cowed with every passing moment, Van released them from his spells.

"Now," the Prince said. "I've had them married this very

morning by my own priest, with the Chief Justicier and my Seneschal as witnesses. And don't think this is going to 'wear off' or 'they'll outgrow this' or some other nonsense. Gift of the gods. That's not how this works. Understood?"

They nodded, and looked covertly at each other.

"By my decree, since they are your heirs, and *equally* have claim to Night Rose Manor, they shall have it *now*. Do I make myself clear?"

More nods.

"By my decree, you, Corlean, will immediately bestow on them the acres of fruit orchard abutting the lands of Night Rose, as the bride-price. And you, Mayard, will immediately bestow the acres of vineyard abutting it on the opposite side as the dower. Understood?"

Corlean started to say something—and *his* wife jabbed him in the ribs, so that all that came out was a strangled *"oof."*

"Since neither of these children has any idea how to run a manor, a vineyard, an orchard, or anything else, and since Night Rose Manor isn't fit to live in, they will be living here, in my palace, being educated in exactly that, under my eye." The Prince eyed Mayard. "Under my eye, and the expert tutelage of my Seneschal and my Housekeeper. And as my wedding gift, my people will be rendering the Manor fit to live in again. Then, as an anniversary present, you two will fill the manor, the grounds, and the orchard and vineyard with workers and servants. I will *expect* that you two will be speaking civilly enough at that point that you can work out who will supply what."

This time both sets of parents looked at their children, who could not have been separated with a crowbar. Then they looked at each other for a long moment.

Mayard cleared his throat and spoke first. "I . . . you can count on our obedience, Your Highness," he said, carefully.

"And . . . ours," said Corlean.

"Good. I'm glad it didn't take the deaths of your only children to make you see reason." The Prince tugged at his surcoat. "But be aware that *none* of you are being rewarded! You two—"

He shot the youngsters a stern glare. "—*should* have come straight to me in the first place. And now, you will be undergoing the hardest schooling you have ever undertaken in your lives. I *expect* nothing less than excellence from you, and until you are fit to command the resources of a manor as responsible adults, you *will* remain here, in the schoolroom." His mouth quirked a little. "Even if you have to schedule your lessons around a child."

Both nodded solemnly, all four hands clasped.

:That child is coming sooner rather than later, I venture,: Yfandes commented.

The Prince made a gesture, and from the right-hand stair in the entrance hall came a dignified lady all in black. "This is my Housekeeper. She will show you to your new quarters. You will respect her and obey her as you would me. Her name is Lady Selden, and you will address her as such."

"Yes, Highness," Peitro said meekly as Fiametta sketched a curtsey to Lady Selden.

"Go."

They went.

"Now, both of you go deal with your factions. And send Peitro and Fiametta's belongings here," the Prince ordered the parents. "I do not wish to hear of *any* more incidents. If one of your people so much as throws a custard tart at someone of the other faction, that will be a week in which you will not be permitted to see your children." He looked at the Chief Justicier, who cleared his throat again.

"The law is quite precise," he intoned. "Failure to heed the Prince in these things will be deemed insurrection, and he has the ability to remove properties from you and bestow them on your children, should he choose."

Corlean had finally calmed down. "I believe that will not be necessary." He looked at the Mayards and held out his hand. "Think of the children."

Sieur Mayard took it and shook it. And managed a smile. "And the *grandchildren*!"

Corlean cracked a smile of his own. "I had . . . begun to doubt I would live to see them," he replied, and shook his head. "Be glad you have a daughter."

"Go—school your foolish people," the Prince sighed. "I will send to you when you may come to see your children again. For now, it is best they be left to each other for a fortnight or so. Grandchildren, you know."

They both nodded and started to turn away, but Sieur Mayard turned back. "Highness—" he ventured. "Who *are* these people?"

"Damned miracle workers, is what they are," swore the Prince. "They are Heralds of Valdemar. Get used to seeing them." He cast a glance at Savil and Van with satisfaction. "Or people like them. Their King has invited us to join Valdemar, and I'll be opening negotiations shortly."

Mouths dropped. "I thought they were a myth!" said Sieur Corlean.

"Very real, I assure you," said Vanyel, as he lifted the silence spell from the mob outside, by way of reminding the four that they had business to take care of. "And looking forward to seeing you again under—more pleasant circumstances. Oh, and that reminds me!"

He took the pouch of money that Sieur Mayard had given him last night—

—*was it only last night? Seems like a moon.*

:*Doesn't it, just.*:

And took three steps forward and put it in the man's hand. Mayard looked at him, dumbfounded. "What's this?"

"I've already been paid," said Vanyel. "In peace."

About the Authors

Jeanne Adams writes award-winning romantic suspense, paranormal and urban fantasies, as well as space adventure that's been compared to the works of Robert Heinlein and Jack McDevitt. She's a sought-after speaker, teaching classes on body disposal for writers, worldbuilding and collaboration, plotting for pantzers, and how to write a fight scene that works. Jeanne lives in Washington, D.C., with her husband and two growing sons, as well as three dogs: two Labradors and an Irish water spaniel (don't tell, but she's prone to adopting more dogs when her husband isn't looking). This is her second story to be accepted in a Mercedes Lackey anthology. You can find her books on all major platforms, and connect with her on the web at JeanneAdams.com.

Dylan Birtolo is a writer, game designer, and professional sword-swinger. He's published multiple novels, novellas, and short stories in both established universes and worlds of his own creation. Some of the universes that he's created stories in are *Shadowrun*, *Exalted*, *BattleTech*, *Freeport*, and *Pathfinder*. On the gaming side, he's the lead designer at Lynnvander Studios and has created multiple games, including Pathfinder's *Level 20*, Starfinder's *Pirates of Skydock*, *Evil Dead 2*, and many more to come. He trains with the Seattle Knights, an acting troop that focuses on stage combat, and has performed in live shows, videos, and movies. He's had the honor of jousting, and yes, the armor is real.

Jennifer Brozek is a multi-talented, award-winning author, editor, and media tie-in writer. She is the author of *Never Let Me Sleep* and *The Last Days of Salton Academy*, both of which were nominated for the Bram Stoker Award. Her *BattleTech* tie-in novel, *The Nellus Academy Incident*, won a Scribe Award. Her editing work has earned her nominations for the British Fantasy Award, the Bram Stoker Award, and the Hugo Award. She won the Australian Shadows Award for the *Grants Pass* anthology, co-edited with Amanda Pillar. Jennifer's short-form work has appeared in Apex Publications, Uncanny Magazine, Daily Science Fiction, and in anthologies set in the worlds of *Valdemar*, *Shadowrun*, *V-Wars*, *Masters of Orion*, and *Predator*. Visit Jennifer's worlds at jenniferbrozek.com or her social media accounts on LinkTree: linktr.ee/JenniferBrozek.

Marie Bilodeau is an Ottawa-based author, TTRPG writer, and storyteller. Her speculative fiction has won several awards and has been translated into French (*Les Éditions Alire*) and Chinese (*SF World*). Her short stories have also appeared in various anthologies and magazines like *Analog Science Fiction and Fact* and *Amazing Stories*. She's Chair of Ottawa's speculative fiction literary con, Can*Con, and, in a past life not so long ago, was deputy publisher for the Ed Greenwood Group (TEGG). Marie is also a storyteller and has told stories across Canada in theatres, tea shops, at festivals, and under disco balls. She's won story slams with personal stories, has participated in epic tellings at the National Arts Centre, and has adapted classical material. Follow her adventures in mayhem at mariebilodeau.com.

Paige L. Christie is originally from Maine, and now lives in the North Carolina mountains. While she is best known for her *Legacies of Arnan* fantasy series (#1 *Draigon Weather*), her work can also be found in several anthologies, including *Galactic Stew*, *Witches Warriors & Wise Women*, *Passages (Valdemar #14)*, *Boundaries (Valdemar #15)*, *Shenanigans (Valdemar*

#16), and *Anything with Nothing (Valdemar #17)*. When she isn't writing, Paige runs a nonprofit soup kitchen and food pantry, walks her dog too early in the morning, and is teaching herself to crochet (badly). She is a proud, founding member of the Blazing Lioness Writers. Website: PaigeLChristie.com

Brigid Collins is a fantasy and science fiction writer living in Nevada. Her fantasy series *The Songbird River Chronicles, The Clockwork Kingdom Saga,* and *Winter's Consort*, her fun middle-grade hijinks series *The Sugimori Sisters*, and her dark fairy-tale novella *Thorn and Thimble* are available wherever books are sold. Her short stories have appeared in *Fiction River, Feyland Tales*, and *Pulphouse Magazine*. Sign up for her newsletter at brigidcollinsbooks.com/newsletter-sign-up/ and get a free copy of *Strength & Chaos, Mischief & Poise: Four Cat Tales*, exclusively available to her subscribers.

Ron Collins is a bestselling science fiction and dark fantasy author who writes across the spectrum of speculative fiction. He has published numerous short stories in venues such as *Analog Science Fiction and Fact, Asimov's Science Fiction*, and the *Fiction River* original anthology project. With his daughter, Brigid, he edited the anthology *Face the Strange*. His short fiction has received a Writers of the Future prize, and his short story "The White Game" was nominated for the Short Mystery Fiction Society's 2016 Derringer Award. His latest books are *Home Run Enchanted* and *Curveball Cursed*, a pair of *Fairies and Fastballs* novels, also written with his daughter.

Brenda Cooper writes science fiction, fantasy, and the occasional poem. She also works in technology and writes and talks about the future. She has won multiple regional writing awards and her stories have often appeared in *Year's Best* anthologies. She lives and works in the Pacific Northwest with her wife and multiple border collies, and can sometimes be found biking around Seattle.

Dayle A. Dermatis is the author or coauthor of many novels (including snarky urban fantasy *Ghosted*, spicy rock-and-roll romance *A Little Night Music*, and YA lesbian romance *Beautiful Beast*) and more than a hundred short stories in multiple genres, appearing in such venues as *Fiction River*, *Alfred Hitchcock's Mystery Magazine*, and DAW and Pocket Books. Called the mastermind behind the Uncollected Anthology project, she also edits anthologies, and her own short fiction has been lauded in many year's best anthologies and *Publisher's Weekly* in erotica, mystery, and horror. She lives in a historic English-style cottage with a tangled and fae back garden, in the wild greenscapes of the Pacific Northwest. In her spare time she follows Styx around the country and travels the world, which inspires her writing. She'd love to have you over for a virtual cup of tea or glass of wine at DayleDermatis.com, where you can also sign up for her newsletter and support her on Patreon.

Rosemary Edghill is a *New York Times*–bestselling, multiple-award-winning author. She has worked with authors such as Marion Zimmer Bradley and SF Grand Master Andre Norton—and of course with Mercedes Lackey—as an SF editor for a major New York publisher, as a freelance book designer, and as a professional book reviewer. One of her short stories was nominated for the Rhysling Award, which is given for SF-nal poetry, and she has been a Philip K. Dick Award judge and survived.

English both by name and nationality, **Charlotte E. English** hasn't permitted emigration to the Netherlands to change her essential Britishness (much). She writes (mostly) feel-good fantasy over copious quantities of tea, and rarely misses an opportunity to apologize for something. Ace and autistic, history buff and gamer, baker and voracious reader, she loves few things so much as peace and quiet, long walks, and really good cake. Her whimsical works include the *House of Werth* series, the *Wonder Tales*, and *Modern Magick*.

J. L. Gribble writes speculative fiction and romance, but she's happiest when combining the two and adding a dose of the unexpected or nontraditional. When not writing, Gribble reads an eclectic range of books, adds to her LEGO collection, and plays video games. She lives in Ellicott City, Maryland, with her husband and three vocal Siamese cats. Find her book review blog and info about her publications at jlgribble.com.

Fiona Patton was born in Calgary, Alberta, and now lives in rural Ontario with her wife, Tanya Huff, an assortment of cats, and two wonderful dogs. She has written seven fantasy novels published by DAW Books and close to forty short stories. "Trade Is Trade" is her sixteenth story in the Valdemar anthologies, and the fourteenth to feature the Dann family.

Diana L. Paxson is the author of twenty-nine novels, including the *Westria* series and the *Avalon* prequel novels, nonfiction on goddesses, trancework, and the runes, and over a hundred short stories. Many of her novels have historical settings, a good preparation for writing about Valdemar. She also writes nonfiction on topics from mythology to trancework. Her next book will be *Carrying a Torch for Liberty*, about working with American mythic figures like Lady Liberty to reclaim and re-energize our values. She also engages in occasional craftwork, costuming, and playing the harp. She lives in the multi-generational, multi-talented household called Greyhaven in Berkeley, California.

Angela Penrose lives in Seattle with her husband, seven computers, and about ten thousand books. She writes in several genres, but SFF is her first love. She majored in history at college, but racked up hundreds of units taking whatever looked interesting. This delayed graduation to a ridiculous degree, but (along with obsessive reading) gave her a broad store of weirdly diverse information that comes in wonderfully handy to a writer. Her short stories appear in numerous anthologies, including seven previous Valdemar anthologies.

Kristin Schwengel lives with her husband near Milwaukee, Wisconsin, along with the obligatory writer's cat (named Gandalf, of course), a Darwinian garden in which only the strong survive, and an ever-growing collection of knitting and spinning supplies. Her writing has appeared in several previous Valdemar anthologies, among others. This story was very loosely inspired by Robert Browning's poem "The Soliloquy of the Spanish Cloister" and the idea of a one-sided feud occurring only in one person's head. Working in a John Cougar Mellencamp reference was an added bonus.

Anthea Sharp grew up on fairy tales and computer games, melding the two in her *USA Today* bestselling Feyland series, which has sold over two hundred thousand copies worldwide. In addition to the fae fantasy/cyberpunk mashup of Feyland, she also writes Victorian spacepunk and fantasy romance. Her short fiction has appeared in Fiction River, DAW anthologies, *The Future Chronicles*, and *Beyond The Stars: At Galaxy's Edge*, as well as many other publications. Anthea lives in the Pacific Northwest, where she writes, hangs out in virtual worlds, plays the fiddle with her Celtic band Fiddlehead, and spends time with her small-but-good family. Visit her webstore at fiddleheadpress.com for bonus content, exclusive editions, fancy special editions, and awesome discounts.

Stephanie Shaver lives with her family in Washington state, where she is gainfully employed by Wizards of the Coast, working on *Magic: Arena*. With this story she time traveled back to an adventure with the twins, Leila and Lyle. You can find more about Steph at sdshaver.com, along with random snapshots of life and the food she's made along the way.

Dee Shull has an MA in Communication and, thanks to a shift in circumstances you'd probably see in a story, has been able to use it in their job. In their spare time they read for fun, noodle around with other stories and universes, and very much want to find a stable tabletop roleplaying group. They currently live with their partner near Denver, Colorado, though they've been yearning for the ocean ever since moving out of California.

A lover of local history and fantastical possibilities, **Louisa Swann** spins tales that span multiple genres, including fantasy, science fiction, mystery, and steampunk. Her short stories have appeared in Mercedes Lackey's *Elementary Magic* and *Valdemar* anthologies (which she's thrilled to participate in!); Esther Friesner's *Chicks and Balances*; and several *Fiction River* anthologies, including *No Humans Allowed* and *Reader's Choice*. Her steampunk/weird west series, *The Peculiar Adventures of Miss Abigail Crumb*, is available at your favorite etailer. Keep an eye out for her new fantasy adventure series featuring an ex-soldier betrayed by his king, a child witch tasked with saving the world, and a rabbit-size creature who claims he's a god! Find out more at www.louisaswann.com or friend her on Facebook @SwannWriter.

Elisabeth Waters sold her first short story in 1980 to Marion Zimmer Bradley for *The Keeper's Price*. Her first novel, a fantasy called *Changing Fate*, was awarded the 1989 Gryphon Award. She also edited many of the *Sword & Sorceress* anthologies. Her favorite real place to get away is an Episcopal convent, while her favorite imaginary place is the Temple of Thenoth.

Phaedra Weldon grew up in the thick, hot, atmospheric land of South Georgia. Most nights, especially those in October, were spent on the back of pickup trucks in the center of cornfields, telling ghost stories, or in friends' homes playing RPGs. She got her start writing in shared worlds (*Eureka!*, *Star Trek*, *Battle-Tech*, *Shadowrun*), selling original short stories to DAW anthologies, and sold her first urban fantasy series to traditional publishing. Currently she is working on finishing up series on her backlist, as well as starting a continuation series to *The Eldritch Files*, called *The Amaranthine*.

About the Editor

Mercedes Lackey is a full-time writer and has published numerous novels and works of short fiction, including the bestselling Heralds of Valdemar series. She is also a professional lyricist and a licensed wild bird rehabilitator. She lives in Oklahoma with her husband and collaborator, artist Larry Dixon, and their flock of parrots.